THE MAG FORCE 7

Xris—strategist, leader, human cyborg

Raoul—assassin, chemicals connoisseur, Adonian Loti

The Little One—telepath, empath, assassin, Tongan

Harry Luck—spacecraft pilot, human

Jamil Khizr—former Royal Marine, heavy weapons expert, human

Tycho—marksman, financier, alien commonly known as "chameleon"

Dr. Bill Quong—engineer, mechanic, physician, human

Some of the deadliest people in the universe . . .
loyal to each other, their convictions, and the
almighty dollar—
not necessarily in that order.

THE CLOUDSHIPS OF ORION
by P. K. McAllister

THE KNIGHTS
OF THE
BLACK EARTH

A MAG FORCE 7 NOVEL

MARGARET WEIS
AND DON PERRIN

A ROC BOOK

ROC
Published by the Penguin Group
Penguin Books USA Inc., 375 Hudson Street,
New York, New York 10014, U.S.A.
Penguin Books Ltd, 27 Wrights Lane,
London W8 5TZ, England
Penguin Books Australia Ltd, Ringwood,
Victoria, Australia
Penguin Books Canada Ltd, 10 Alcorn Avenue,
Toronto, Ontario, Canada M4V 3B2
Penguin Books (N.Z.) Ltd, 182–190 Wairau Road,
Auckland 10, New Zealand

Penguin Books Ltd, Registered Offices:
Harmondsworth, Middlesex, England

First published by Roc, an imprint of Dutton Signet, a division of Penguin Books USA
Inc. Previously appeared in a Roc hardcover edition.

First Mass Market Printing, March, 1996
10 9 8 7 6 5 4 3 2 1

This book is lovingly dedicated to:
Bayne and Elizabeth Perrin
and
Donald Bayne Perrin, Sr.

Vengeance is mine; I will repay, saith the Lord.

Romans, Chapter 12, Verse 19

Confront them with annihilation, and they will then survive; plunge them in a deadly situation, and they will then live. When people fall into danger, they are then able to strive for victory.

Sun Tzu, *The Art of War*

THE KNIGHTS
OF THE
BLACK EARTH

CHAPTER

1

Be extremely subtle, even to the point of
formlessness. Be extremely mysterious, even to
the point of soundlessness. Thereby you can
be the director of the opponent's fate.

Sun Tzu, *The Art of War*

Shortly after they landed on Laskar, the four men went out
and bought a car.

They paid cash for it, so Friendly Burl, the friendliest
vehic dealer in Laskar, was not fussy about such details as
Who are you really? and *Where have you come from?* Besides, he thought he already knew the answer. Four gray and
faceless suits; probably on an illicit holiday; an escape from
boss, sig-others, kids.

"You guys planning on being in Laskar long?" asked
Friendly Burl of Burl's Friendly Vehics.

Two of the men carried briefcases; none of them carried
luggage.

"No," said one of the suits, handing over the requisite
number of golden eagles.

The manner and tone in which the man said that single
word sucked the "friendly" out of Burl and caused him to
revise his original estimate. These were not stressed-out
execs. He began immediately and somewhat nervously to
count his money. Finding it correct, he relaxed.

"Salesmen, huh?" Burl ventured. He winked knowingly.
"Or maybe not selling but dealing?"

The men did not answer. They put their briefcases in the
car.

Buying a vehic rather than renting one on Laskar was not

unusual. Like everything and everyone else in the sin-soaked city of Laskar, rental cars tended to lead brief, albeit exciting lives. Consequently, rental dealers demanded a hefty amount of plastic up front. Insurance, they called it.

It cost a bit more to buy a vehic on Laskar, but the purchaser was generally glad to pay extra for the convenience and the peace of mind. Upon leaving the city, the car could always be resold—for scrap metal, if nothing else.

And paying in cash left no trail.

By now, Burl was really curious. He had a lot of friends and some of them in the city would be very interested in knowing if competition was about to move in.

"You fellers ever been to Laskar before?" Burl asked, eyeing the briefcases.

"No," replied the same suit who had paid for the car. He was staring in the direction of the city, squinting against Laskar's garish green sun.

"Then you sure don't wanna lose your way drivin' around town," Burl offered casually. "If you'll tell me where you're going, I can give you directions."

He waited hopefully. No response.

He tried again. "I got a compu-map I can install in half-a-jiffy. No trouble. Just tell me where you're headed and I'll program it—"

"No," said the suit.

The four men climbed into the car—an ordinary, midsize hover, nothing special, nothing fancy—and drove it off the lot. Two rode in the front, two in the back. Friendly Burl saw them off the lot, gave them a friendly wave, then hurried inside to contact a few "friends."

Friendly Burl's was conveniently located near the public spaceport, on the outskirts of the city. Finding the way to the city was easy—the only highway ran past the spaceport.

One man drove. The man seated in the front next to the driver navigated. The two in the back removed needle-guns from their inside suit jacket pockets, kept watch out the windows.

"All going according to plan, Knight Commander." The hover's driver spoke into a small handheld voice-recorder.

The hover reached the entrance to the highway. Here a decision was required. Turn to the left and there, silhouetted against the green sky, were the high-rise whorehouses, the glitzy casinos, the holodomes of planet Laskar's major claim to fame, the city Laskar. Turn to the right and there were cactus and weird rock formations and eventually, a long distance away, the box-shaped barracks, the half-moon hangars, the sand-blasted tarmac of the Royal Naval Base.

Glancing up and down the highway, the driver said, "How far is Snaga Ohme's from here?"

"Straight across country. About fifty kilometers," was the reply.

Those fifty kilometers brought one to the palatial mansion and vast estate of the late Snaga Ohme, former weapons purveyor to the galaxy's rich and warlike. Several years previous, the wealthy Adonian had died, leaving his extensive and complicated financial affairs in complete disorder. To give him credit, Ohme had not expected to be murdered.

Always pleased to be able to help one of its citizens, the military had assisted Ohme's creditors by immediately seizing control of the Adonian's estate, including all weapons, designs for weapons, and prototypes of new weapons that the late Snaga Ohme had invented.

"Is Knight Officer Fuqua still inside the Ohme estate?"

"Yes, sir. But according to his latest report, his unit is due to transfer out anytime now. He'll have to leave with the unit, of course."

The driver nodded. "He has served his purpose. I doubt if we could learn anything more from him. We will proceed to Laskar."

Arriving at the intersection, the hovercar turned left.

Laskar was not a planned community. Its streets had not been laid out according to any grand design. Rather, its buildings had sprung up like fungus, sprouting wherever the spores happened to fall. Buildings rarely faced each other, or fronted a street, but stood sideways to one another, like two hookers working the same block, who pretend to ignore each other yet keep a watchful eye on the competition. Consequently, the streets had been laid out around the buildings, which resulted in a great many serpentine roads, innumerable alleys, dead ends (aptly named), cul-de-sacs, and streets that had started out going somewhere only to end up lost and confused in the center of a very bad nowhere.

The four men were driving to one of the worst nowheres in Laskar.

Which was why there were four of them. And the needle-guns.

The navigator guided them unerringly through the maze of gambling dens, liquor bars, drug-bars, cyber-bars, blood-bars. They drove past the live sex, semi-live sex, semiconscious sex joints. They ignored the hookers of every age, race, sex, gender, and planetary origin. They paid scant attention to the occasional cop-shop—fortified bunkers from which the cops rarely emerged and then only to collect protection money that provided the citizens of Laskar protection against nobody but the cops.

"Travel down Painted Eye half a kilometer, sir. Turn north onto Snake Road. Brownstone walk-up. Number 757. Our man is on the top floor. Apartment 9e."

No unnecessary talk between them. No names. The two men in the back were deferential to the two in the front, especially the driver. The two in back never spoke unless spoken to and then answered respectfully in as concise a manner as possible.

The driver, who was the leader, followed instructions, swerving sharply to avoid hitting a woman with an Adam's apple and a low-cut dress, revealing a hairy chest, who swore at them in a gravelly voice and gave the car a few savage kicks with her high heels as the hover skimmed past.

The driver pulled up in front of 757. He, the man in front, and one of the men in back got out of the car. The leader carried a briefcase. The second man had his hands free. The third man thrust his needle-gun into his suit coat pocket. The fourth man remained seated in the car. His needle-gun had been replaced by a beam rifle assembled from his briefcase. The rifle lay across his knees.

The leader stood on the cracked and litter-strewn sidewalk, gazing intently at the building, studying it carefully. It was nine stories high, made of brick formed from the local stone, which meant that it was sandy-colored and, in the heat of the late afternoon, took on a slightly greenish cast from Laskar's oddly colored sun. (The sun was not green. According to scientists, something in the atmosphere was, which gave the sun its strained-pea tinge. The natives were proud of their green sun, however, and disputed the scientific claim.)

Whether the green was in the sun or the sky, the sickly tint did nothing to improve the building's appearance, but rather gave it an unwholesome look. All the windows on the lower floor were boarded up, with graffiti scrawled across them. Here and there, on upper floors, TO RENT signs had been plastered onto cracked glass—the spots of white looked like an outbreak of the pox.

People on the sidewalk brushed past the men without a glance. The citizens of Laskar had their own problems to pursue, the tourists had their own pleasures, and none of them gave a damn about anyone else. A couple of bored-looking women in see-through plastic skirts sidled over to the driver and, in a few well-chosen words, described a possible evening's entertainment. The leader didn't even bother to answer and, with a shrug, the women sauntered off.

Several of the locals, lounging on the pavement, grinned and laughed, eyed the car with the expert air of those who know the current market value for that particular model, stripped down.

The leader paid no attention to them, either.

"Cover the back exit," he ordered the man with the needle-gun.

"Yes, sir."

The man with the needle-gun took off down a dark and grim-looking alleyway that smelled of body waste and garbage. A hand reached out—palm up—from a bundle of rags and cardboard as the man passed. A voice mumbled something unintelligible.

The man with the gun kept walking.

The beggar threw an empty jump-juice bottle at him. The bottle smashed into the pavement at the man's feet. He crunched calmly over the broken glass, continued into the noisome dark of the alleyway. He might have been less comfortable in his dangerous surroundings had he not been wearing full body armor beneath his nondescript suit.

The two men in front gave the third time to get into position. When a barely heard beep on a commlink informed them that he was ready, the two men mounted splintered and broken stairs—unquestionably the most dangerous obstacle they'd faced yet. Shoving open a rickety door, they walked inside the vestibule.

The leader took another careful look around.

"Security cam?"

"Temporarily out of order, sir," was the answer.

The leader examined the entry door.

"It's locked, sir. Modern system. The owner doesn't want any homesteaders. We could blow it. . . ."

The leader shook his head. He shifted the briefcase to his left hand, reached up, pressed the buzzer for 9e.

No response.

He pressed it again, this time held it longer.

No response.

He glanced at his subordinate.

"Bosk's inside, sir. He never leaves until after dark. But he'll be reluctant to answer the door. He's in debt. Local moneylender."

The leader raised an eyebrow. He pressed the button again, spoke into the intercom. "Bosk. You don't know me. I'm here on business. It could be worth your while to let me inside. I've got an offer to make you."

Still no response.

The leader hit the button again. Leaning down to the intercom, he spoke two words clearly and distinctly. "Negative waves."

He stepped back, waited for as long as it might take a man to get up out of a chair, cross a small room.

There came a click on the lock of the entry door.

The leader and his subordinate entered, shut the door behind them. The leader again took a careful look around.

"You wait down here," he said.

His subordinate took up a position in a shadowy corner beneath the staircase. From here, he could see, but not be readily seen. Outside, the locals approached the car, backed off hurriedly when they saw the beam rifle.

Folding his arms across his chest, the subordinate settled himself to wait.

The leader began to climb nine flights of stairs.

CHAPTER 2

Vengeance, deep-brooding o'er the slain . . .
Sir Walter Scott, *The Lay of the Last Minstrel*

Bosk stood unsteadily by the door, staring at the intercom as if it could answer his questions. He was a little drunk. Bosk was always a little drunk these days. It eased his pain, cut the fear. He was always a little afraid these days, as well.

The intercom had no answers for him. The room seemed to heave a bit, and so Bosk—knowing that it would be a long wait while his guest climbed nine flights of stairs—stumbled back over and plunked himself down in his dilapidated recliner.

Directly across the room from him, the vid was blaring loudly. James M. Warden, personable television personality, was conducting an interview with His Royal Majesty, Dion Starfire.

Bosk gulped a swig of jump-juice from a cracked glass, focused blearily on the screen.

The young king was answering a question about the late Warlord Derek Sagan.

"He was not perfect. No man is perfect," His Majesty was saying gravely. "He made mistakes."

"I beg your pardon, Your Majesty," James M. Warden respectfully contradicted, "but some might consider the word *mistakes* inappropriate for what many consider to be heinous crimes."

"Try *murder*!" Bosk yelled loudly at the screen.

His Majesty was shaking his head, almost as if he'd heard Bosk's comment. "Lord Sagan was a warrior. He acted out of his own warrior code, which, as you know, is a harsh one. But he held to that code with honor. He took part in the revolution because he believed that the government under my late uncle's rule was corrupt and ineffective. That it was about to collapse into anarchy, which would have put all the people in the galaxy in the gravest danger.

"When Lord Sagan discovered that the new government under President Peter Robes was every bit as corrupt as the old, the Warlord concluded that he—one of the few surviving members of the Blood Royal—had the right to try to seize control. Circumstances, the Creator, Fate—call it what you will—intervened. Lord Sagan's ambitious and, some might say, his despotic plans failed."

King Starfire's hand clenched. The famous Starfire blue eyes were lit from within by a radiance that looked well on the vidscreens. The red-golden lion's mane of hair framed a face that was youthful, handsome, earnest, intense. His godlike looks, his vibrant personality—all were rapidly making a reluctant deity of a very mortal young man.

"But I tell you, Mr. Warden, and I tell my people that I would not be here now, I would not be wearing this crown, the galaxy would not be at peace today, if it were not for the sacrifices of Lord Derek Sagan. He attempted to correct the great wrongs he had done and, in so doing, gave his life that others might live. He is one of the greatest men I have ever known. I will always honor his memory."

Bosk tossed the remainder of the jump-juice at the vidscreen. "Here's that for his fuckin' memory." The juice trickled down the screen, soaked into the threadbare carpet which covered the floor of the shabby studio apartment.

A crisp knock sounded on the door.

Lurching to his feet, Bosk went to answer it. On his way, he made a detour to the bottle, poured himself another drink. Reaching the door, he peeped out the one-way peephole, saw a man dressed in a suit, carrying a briefcase. The man didn't look threatening. He didn't look anything. He had one of those faces you meet and five minutes later you can't recall ever having been introduced to him before. Bosk was more interested in the briefcase. It is said that Adonians can smell money.

Bosk's nose twitched. He opened the door.

"Yeah?" he said, looking first at the briefcase, then finally lifting his gaze to meet the stranger's. "What's the deal?"

"I don't believe it would be wise for us to conduct our business in the hallway," the stranger said. He wasn't even breathing hard after the long climb. He smiled in a pleasant and disarming manner. "Your neighbors don't need to know your affairs, do they?"

Bosk followed the stranger's glance, saw Mrs. Kasper standing in her half-open door. He glared at her.

"I heard a knock," she said defensively. "Thought it might be for me." She sniffed. "Another of your 'clients'?"

"Nosy old bitch!" Bosk retorted. He opened his own door wider. "C'mon in, then."

The stranger entered. Bosk shut the door, took a look out the peephole to make sure Mrs. Kasper had gone back into her apartment. She had a bad habit of loitering in the hall, listening outside closed doors.

Sure enough.

Bosk flung the door open, nearly knocking Mrs. Kasper down.

"Care to join us?" He leered.

Disgusted, she flounced back inside her apartment and slammed her door.

Bosk shut his door again, turned around to face his guest. The stranger was tall, well-built, handsome if you went for older guys with hair graying at the temples, which Bosk did not. The clothes were expensive but not ostentatious. Snaga Ohme would have approved the choice of colors: muted blues and grays. The face was a mask. The lines and wrinkles had been trained to betray nothing of the thoughts within. The eyes were one-way mirrors. Bosk looked in, saw himself reflected back.

Having once been close to some of the most powerful people in the galaxy, Bosk recognized and appreciated the quiet air of control and authority this man exuded, like a fine cologne that never overwhelms, never cloys the senses.

"I assume that you are the Adonian known as Bosk?" The stranger was polite.

"I'm an Adonian and my name's Bosk. That answer your questions?"

"Not all of them." The stranger continued to be polite. "Were you once in the employ of the late Snaga Ohme, former weapons dealer?"

Bosk swallowed. "I wasn't in his 'employ,' mister! I was

his goddamn friend! His best friend. He trusted me, more'n anyone. He trusted me. I knew ... all his secrets."

Bosk brushed his hand across his eyes, wiped his nose with his fingers. Adonians are a sensitive race, who have a tendency to get maudlin when they're drunk. "I was his confidant. Me. Not those other fops, those pretty boys—fawning and preening. And the women. They were the worst. But he loved me. He loved me."

Bosk drained the glassful of jump-juice.

The stranger nodded. "Yes, that is consistent with my information. Snaga Ohme told you all his secrets. He even told you about his project code-named Negative Waves."

"Maybe, maybe not." Bosk eyed the stranger warily. "You want a drink?"

"No, thank you. Mind if I sit down?"

"Suit yourself." Bosk wandered back to the bottle.

The stranger walked across the small room. Bosk watched him out of the corner of his eye. The stranger's movements were fluid, controlled. He was in excellent physical condition, with a hard-muscled body, good reflexes.

Pity he's not twenty years younger, Bosk thought.

The stranger pulled up a battered metal fold-out chair— one of the few articles of furniture in the apartment. In front of the chair was a computer. A highly sophisticated and expensive personal computer, it looked considerably out of place in the poverty-stricken surroundings. The stranger seated himself in the chair, regarded the computer with admiration.

"That's a fine setup, Bosk. Probably worth the price of this whole apartment building."

"I'd sell myself first," Bosk said sullenly. He *had* sold himself first, but that was beside the point. He hunched back down in the recliner. "Snaga Ohme gave that computer to me. It's one of the best, the fastest in the whole damn galaxy."

A photograph of Snaga Ohme—bronze, beautiful, as were most Adonians—stood in an honored place beside the crystalline storage lattice.

The stranger nodded, smiled in sympathy, placed the briefcase on his knees, and waited for Bosk to resume talking. But Bosk's attention had been recaptured by the vidscreen. The king was speaking again, this time about the long-expected and widely anticipated birth of the royal heir.

"Fuckin' bastard," muttered Bosk. "I hate the fuckin' bastard. Him and that fuckin' Derek Sagan. Wasn't for that fuckin' Derek Sagan, *he'd* be alive today."

A glance at the photograph of Snaga Ohme clarified the pronoun.

"Tell me about Derek Sagan, Bosk," the stranger suggested.

Bosk tore his gaze from the vid. "Why d'you wanna know about Derek Sagan?"

"Because he was the reason for the Negative Waves project, wasn't he, Bosk?"

Bosk hesitated, regarded the stranger suspiciously. But the Adonian had had far too much to drink to make the mental effort to play games, keep secrets. Besides, what did it matter anyway? Ohme was dead. And when his life had ended, so had Bosk's. He didn't even have revenge to keep him going anymore. So he nodded.

"Yeah. Sagan was. I don't care who knows it. If His Majesty sent you—"

"His Majesty didn't send me, Bosk." The stranger leaned back comfortably in the chair. "His Majesty doesn't give a damn about you, and you know it. Nobody gives a damn, do they, Bosk?"

"You do, apparently," Bosk said with a cunning not even the jump-juice could completely drown.

"I do, Bosk." The stranger opened the briefcase. "I care a lot."

Bosk stared. The briefcase was filled with plastic chips—black plastic chips, stamped in gold, arranged in neat stacks.

Bosk rose slowly to his feet to get a better look, half afraid that the liquor might be playing tricks on his mind. It had been almost four years since the night Snaga Ohme had been murdered. Four years since the night Warlord Derek Sagan had seized control of the dead man's mansion and its wealth. That night, as Sagan's army marched in the front, Bosk had exited the mansion via the secret tunnels in the back.

During these intervening four years, Bosk had never seen *one* black chip stamped in gold, much less . . . how many were in that briefcase? . . . He took a conservative guess on the number of chips in each stack, counted the number of stacks across, counted the number of stacks down, did some muddled multiplication, and drew in a shivering breath.

"Twenty thousand, Bosk," said the stranger. "It's all yours. Today."

Bosk found his chair with the backs of his legs, sat down rather suddenly. Life up till now had been an endless lineup of jump-juice bottles, selling his favors in cheap bars and bathhouses, and dodging the local collection agency.

"I could go back to Adonia," he said, staring at the black chips.

"You could leave tonight, Bosk," said the stranger.

Bosk licked dry lips, took another drink, gulped it the wrong way, coughed. "What do you want?"

"You know," said the stranger. "You tried to sell it a couple of years ago. Bad timing. No market."

"Negative Waves." Bosk's gaze strayed to the computer.

The stranger nodded, closed the lid of the briefcase. The light seemed to go out of the room.

"Tell me about the project, Bosk. Tell me everything you can remember."

"Why do you want to know?"

"Just to make sure we're talking about the same project."

A mental hand was tugging at the coattails of Bosk's brain, trying to get his attention. But the jump-juice and the gold-stamped black chips combined to cause him to shoo it away.

"Yeah, sure," Bosk said. He reached for his glass, discovered it was empty, started to head for the bottle.

He found the stranger holding on to it. Bosk staggered back, blinked. He had no clear recollection of seeing the stranger move, yet the man was standing right in front of him.

"We'll have a drink to celebrate closing the deal," said the stranger, smiling and holding on to the bottle. "Not before." He walked back to his seat by the computer.

Bosk was going to get angry and then decided he wasn't. Shrugging, he went back to his chair. The stranger returned to the folding chair, set the bottle down next to the computer, beside the picture of Snaga Ohme. On his way past, the stranger flicked off the vid. Congenial reporter James M. Warden and His Majesty the King dwindled to insignificant dots, then were gone.

A commentary on life, Bosk thought, staring at the empty screen with watery eyes.

"Where should I begin?"

"The space-rotation bomb," specified the stranger.

Bosk glared, suspicions returned. "You *must* be from the king. No one else knew about that."

"I'm not from the king, Bosk," the stranger said patiently. "Maybe someday I'll tell you where I *am* from. But for now, I'd say you're being paid enough not to be curious. Let me help things along. *We* know about the space-rotation bomb. We know how Warlord Sagan came up with the design for it. How he needed someone to build it. Needed it done quick and quiet, because he was planning to overthrow the galactic government. And so he went to Snaga Ohme."

"The only man in the universe who could have built that damn bomb," Bosk said with moist-eyed pride. He sniffed, wiped his nose with the back of his hand. "Whoever had that bomb coulda overthrown six billion governments." He gazed back into the past, shook his head in admiration. "It was sweet. Best work Ohme ever did. He said so himself. Blow a hole in the fabric of the universe. Destroy all life as we know it."

"That was only theorized."

Bosk waved his hand, irritated at the stranger's slowness of thought. "That's not the point. Blackmail. The threat. Hold it over their heads. Sword of something-er-other—"

"Damocles," said the stranger.

Bosk shrugged, not interested. He coughed, licked his lips, looked longingly at the bottle.

The stranger ignored the look. "Ohme built the bomb according to the Warlord's specifications, using Sagan's financing. But then it occurred to Ohme that, with this bomb in the Warlord's possession, Derek Sagan might get a—shall we say—swelled head?"

"Snaga Ohme was the most powerful man in the galaxy," Bosk averred. "The top weapons dealer and manufacturer alive. No one could touch him. Kings, warlords, governors, congressmen, corporate leaders—they all came running when he so much as twitched his pinkie their direction."

"Ohme feared that the Warlord—if and when he came to power—might put him out of business. So Ohme built the negative wave device to kill Derek Sagan."

Bosk shook his head vehemently. "Not kill him."

"Keep Sagan in line, then."

"If he leaned on us, we could lean back." Bosk was defensive. "We were looking out for our own interests."

"Sagan has the bomb, blackmails the government. Ohme has the negative wave device, blackmails Sagan."

"It was an ingenious idea. You gotta admit that."

"All predicated on the fact that Sagan was specially genetically designed. One of the Blood Royal. The device would kill him and him alone, even in a crowd. Yes, a truly remarkable concept. *If* it worked. . . ."

Bosk snorted. "It worked, all right."

"Ohme tested it?" The stranger appeared surprised, intrigued. "We weren't aware that he'd built a working model."

Bosk opened his mouth, suddenly closed it again. He shrugged, surly now, and deciding to be uncooperative. Who was this bastard? Coming here with all his damn stupid questions. And how the hell did he know so much? What was going on?

Standing up, a bit unsteadily, Bosk stalked over, grabbed the bottle, stalked back, and poured himself a drink. He flopped down in the chair, reached for the remote, turned on the vid. James M. Warden was resurrected. He was still interviewing His Majesty the King. Her Majesty the Queen had joined them.

The mental hand that had been tugging at Bosk's brain gave him a sudden sharp jab that made him flinch, literally. He saw it all now. Everything became suddenly clear, as clear as it could be through a liquor-soaked haze.

You juice-head, he swore at himself. You damn near let him walk off with this for a measly twenty thou. It's worth ten times—hell, make that a hundred times—more!

Bosk stared hard at the vidscreen, his brain flopping around, wondering how best to appear completely unconscious of the fact that he'd scammed the whole scheme and that it was big, really big, and that he was going to make a bloody fortune off it.

I can't let on that I know, though, was his next thought, which of course made him wonder if he'd already given himself away. He slid a glance over to the stranger, slid it back quickly. The stranger was staring at the screen, too, but with the abstracted gaze of one who is using a visual aid to enhance far-removed thoughts.

Bosk breathed easier. Noticing his hand was clenched around the glass so tightly that his knuckles had turned white, he forced himself to relax. He started to take a drink, then thought better of it, then was afraid that not taking a drink might seem suspicious. He brought the glass to his lips, set it down again untasted, and wondered uneasily how to bring the conversation around to where he wanted it.

At that moment, James M. Warden broke for a message from his sponsor.

Bosk cleared his throat. "What I meant to say is that the theory behind the device was sound. Ohme knew it would work. There was no reason to doubt it. It's all in there." Bosk gazed fondly at the computer.

"You ended up with the design," said the stranger.

"I ended up with it," Bosk said softly. "It was my chance, you see. My chance to get even. The night Ohme was murdered, all hell broke loose. Sagan's troops had the goddamn place surrounded. In the confusion, I raided Ohme's own personal computer. I downloaded, then destroyed, all the files on the Negative Waves project. I'm the *only* person alive who's got them."

Bosk added the last with emphasis. He was watching the vidscreen with a smile on his face, felt emboldened enough to repeat himself. "I'm the only one."

The stranger nodded. "Yes, so I understand. You searched for backers to finance the project. But with the government collapsed and the new king taking over, no one was interested in spending a fortune on a weapon with such limited potential."

"Sagan was still alive," Bosk muttered.

"True, Warlord Sagan was still alive and had enemies. But by the time they might have been willing to invest, Derek Sagan had managed to get himself killed. He was the last of the Blood Royal—the only people Ohme's device was designed to destroy. The demand for your product went right down the toilet."

"Not the *last* of the Blood Royal," Bosk said, with a sly glance at the vidscreen. "Sagan wasn't the last. The king. Dion Starfire. *He's* the last."

The stranger was nonplussed. "There could be others."

"Sure, sure." Bosk staggered to his feet. His unsteady hand knocked his glass to the floor. "What do you take me for? A brain-rotted old queen, too juiced to know who I'm climbing in bed with? This is big. Really big. Bigger than twenty thousand fuckin' eagles. I'll go back to Adonia. I'll go back in style. No more hanging around the Laskar bars, letting guys like you in your expensive suits think you're doin' me some big honor by rubbing your ass against mine, then throwin' me out the next morning like I was too filthy to live. You need me, damn it. You need me and I want my share or I'll ... I'll ..."

"You'll what, Bosk?" asked the stranger calmly.

Bosk realized too late that he'd gone too far. Fear knotted his belly, sent the gastric juices surging up, bile-bitter and burning, into his throat. His jaws ached; saliva flooded his mouth. He was afraid he might vomit.

He swallowed several times. Sweat, cold and clammy, chilled on his body, made him shiver.

"I'll find other buyers." He decided to bluff it out.

The stranger considered, said gravely, "Very well, Bosk. We'll meet your price. Just think of this as a down payment." He patted the briefcase.

Bosk didn't like it. The guy had given in far too quickly. Still, the Adonian reflected, I *have* got him by the short hairs.

"You'll need a technical adviser." Bosk slurred his words. The shivering fear caused a tremor in his right leg. He clamped his hand over his leg, to stop the muscle jerking. "There's a lot of data ... I left out ... not in ... the files."

"Bound to be," the stranger agreed. He stood up from the folding chair. Placing the briefcase on the table next to the picture of Snaga Ohme, the stranger smiled, indicated the computer screen. "Bring up the files. I want to see what I'm buying."

Bosk hesitated. "It'll take a while to get the material all in order. Big files, scattered. I'm not all that organized."

"I understand completely. I just want to take a look before I go. Scan it, get a feel for the project. That's all. I think that's only fair, considering my initial investment. Then, when you have the data compiled, I'll be back to pick it up. At that time, I'll bring the rest of your payment. Besides," the stranger added with a slight lift of his shoulders, "I'd like to know the project's really in that computer of yours."

"It's in there," Bosk said, gloating. "And it'll work." He stumbled over to the chair, sat down in front of the computer.

Bosk placed his hands on the input keypads. After a second's wait, the screen began to glow. A red light flashed; the log-on script for Bosk came up on the screen. He had yet to hit any keys. Once the sequence was complete, the menu appeared.

Bosk cast a cunning glance at the stranger. "Why don't you go take a look at the view. Or maybe you should check to make sure no one's stolen your car."

The stranger smiled to indicate he understood completely. Leaving the vicinity of the computer, he strode nonchalantly over to the window and peered out through the grime to the street below.

Once the stranger's back was turned, Bosk accessed a file titled "Classical Literature through the Ages"—guaranteed to be a snorer. Opening that, he selected the choice: "Idylls of the King."

The computer responded by demanding a retina scan.

Bosk moved his face closer to the screen, flinched as the scanning beam swiftly crossed his eyeball ten thousand times.

The word "verified" appeared on the screen, followed by a display that did not appear to be, on first glance, classical literature.

"All right," Bosk said after several minutes had elapsed, silent minutes punctuated by the clicking sounds of the Adonian's fingers on the keyboard and muted voice commands to the computer's audio interpreter.

He gestured at the screen. "There it is. Negative Waves. I've brought up the outline of the initial concept, plus the preliminary diagrams of what the weapon should look like when it's completed. I figure that should be enough to convince you that what I've got is the real thing."

The stranger left the window. Hands clasped behind his back, he strode over to the computer. He bent down to see the screen, leaning over Bosk, who had remained seated. The stranger studied the text intently.

"Scroll on further," he said, making no move to touch the keyboard.

Bosk obediently, and proudly, did so. He, too, was reading the text, written in Snaga Ohme's precise, organized, meticulous style. The concept was sound. It would work. Bosk raised his hand, reverently touched the computer screen.

"Genius," he murmured.

"Indeed," said the stranger, and he sounded impressed.

Bosk heard the stranger straighten. The Adonian turned around, grinning in elation, prepared to name what he considered his absolute minimum price for the files and his knowledge concerning them, and found a handheld lasgun within ten centimeters of the bridge of his nose.

Terror surged. He opened his mouth to beg . . . scream. . . .

With careful precision, the stranger shot Bosk through the center of the forehead. The beam bored a neat bloodless hole through bone and brain. The Adonian slumped, slid out of the chair.

The stranger shoved the body aside, sat down in the chair. "Damn," he muttered softly.

Without Bosk's hands on the keyboard, the screen had gone blank.

The stranger was only momentarily thwarted, however. Though he had not anticipated this problem, he was prepared to deal with it. He spoke calmly into his commlink. "It's finished. Come up."

Bending over the corpse, the stranger slid what appeared to be plastic thimbles over Bosk's fingertips. Then, adjusting his lasgun's intensity, the stranger modified the beam to a cutting tool and proceeded to remove Bosk's right eyeball. This grisly task completed, he placed the freshly severed eyeball in a holder, stood the holder on the table next to the computer. He then removed the fingertip plastics, now bearing the whorls and lines of Bosk's fingerprints. Carefully, the stranger drew them over his own fingers.

Seating himself at the computer, he rested his fingers on the keypad of the blanked computer.

The screen logged in "Bosk." The menu appeared.

Studying the list, the stranger hesitated. There was, no doubt, a trap in here. Even if he happened to guess the right file, bringing it up in the wrong sequence might cause it to self-destruct.

Unable to discover even a hint of a clue, the stranger exited the menu. Bosk had been smart, but he had also been lazy. Hopefully too lazy to make certain all the doors into his files had been shut and locked.

Hands on the keyboard, the stranger typed—in case the computer was attuned to Bosk's voice—the command: "Recall last accessed project." An old trick, but it worked.

A file appeared. Words, arranged in a definite pattern, filled the screen; words in a language long dead and forgotten by all but a few. The stranger was among the few who could read them, but this wasn't what he was after. He tensed. The computer scrolled down to the lines:

> Wearing the white flower of a blameless life,
> Before a thousand peering littlenesses,
> In that fierce light which beats upon a throne,
> And blackens every blot.

Suddenly, "Idylls of the King" disappeared. The screen went blank. This was either what he was searching for or he'd lost it.

The stranger picked up the eyeball, held it to the retina scan. A file came up. He read the header and smiled.

"Negative Waves."

CHAPTER
3

You're not a man, you're a machine.
George Bernard Shaw, *Arms and the Man*

The Wiedermann Detective Agency, with offices in every major city of every major planet in the heart of the galaxy, handled only cases that were far too important, discreet, and delicate for other, less sophisticated (and less expensive) agencies. The Weidermann Agency would not, for example, tail your philandering husband unless he happened to be the prime minister and the ensuing scandal could topple a government.

The agency was expert in corporate intrigue, both detecting it and performing it. They did not handle ordinary or sordid cases. They would negotiate with terrorists and kidnappers for you, but it would cost you plenty. They would not undertake to break your uncle out of prison, or remove him from a penal colony, but they would refer you to people who did that sort of thing. They would not find out who poisoned your sister unless you had proof that the local police were being deliberately obtuse and your credit rating indicated you could pay for a prolonged investigation.

The agency's offices were always located in upscale downtown professional buildings, rubbing shoulders comfortably with law firms that had twenty-seven names on the letterhead, and the offices of doctors whose names were followed by that many initials. The agency's own offices were spacious, elegantly appointed, a soothing gray-blue in color scheme. Corporate headquarters were located on Inner Rankin, the smaller and more exclusive planet of a two-planet system, the larger planet (industrial base) being known as Outer Rankin.

Only the most important clients were ever permitted to enter the agency's corporate headquarters, which was why the receptionist—a live, human receptionist—placed her finger on the security button when the cyborg walked through the main doors.

It was a long walk from the main doors—steelglass, blast-proof—across the polished floor to the receptionist's desk, and so she had time to get a good look at the cyborg. He had obviously made a mistake.

The Wiedermann Agency took on cyborgs as clients, but such cyborgs were sophisticated types. Expensive body jobs. Not even their own mothers could have guessed they were more metal than flesh. Plastiskin and flesh-foam, muscle-gel and quiet-as-a-whisper motors, battery packs and pumps enabled most cyborgs to blend in with ordinary flesh-and-blood beings, the main difference being that cyborgs always tended to look just a bit *too* perfect—as if they'd been tailor-made, not picked up off the rack.

This particular cyborg was, however, what the receptionist would classify (did classify, for security purposes) as "hard labor." Most planets sent their convicted felons to hard-labor camps. Located on frontier planets or moons, these camps were generally mining communities or agricultural collectives. The work was hard, physical, and often dangerous. Those prisoners injured in accidents were provided cybernetic limbs and other body parts made to be strong, efficient, and cheap—not cosmetic.

This cyborg was bald. Acid burn scars mottled the skin on his head. His eyes—one of which was real, both of which were dark and brooding—were set deep beneath an overhanging forehead. His right hand was flesh, his left hand metal.

The security diagnostic that came up on the receptionist's recessed screen disclosed that seventy percent of the cyborg's body was artificial: left side, hand, leg, foot, face, skull, ear, eye. But the receptionist could see this for herself. Unlike any other cyborg she had encountered, this one scorned to hide his replacement parts. In fact, he appeared to flaunt them.

He wore combat fatigues that had been cut off at the hip on the left leg, revealing a broad expanse of gleaming, compartmented, and jointed metal. The left sleeve of his shirt was rolled up over the metal arm, revealing a series of LED lights that flickered occasionally, performing periodic systems checks. His metal hand could apparently be detached from the wrist, to judge by the locking mechanism, and replaced with different hands—or tools.

His age was indeterminate, scar tissue having replaced most of the original flesh of his face. But the right half of his body—the half that was still human—was in excellent physical condition. Arm muscles bulged; chest and thigh muscles were smooth, well defined. He walked with a peculiar gait, as if the two halves of his body weren't quite in sync with one another.

Truly, he was one of the worst cyber-jobs the receptionist had ever seen.

"I would have sued," she muttered to herself, and put on the Wiedermann smile, which would be completely wasted on this man, who had probably come in to use the toilet.

"Good morning, sir," said the receptionist, giving the cyborg the smile but not the Wiedermann warmth that was reserved for paying clients. "How can I help you?" She could hear, as the cyborg approached the desk, the faint hum of his machinery.

"The name's Xris," he said, a mechanical tinge to his voice. "I received a subspace transmission. Told to be here, this building, eleven hundred hours." He glanced around without curiosity, but appeared to note in one swift overview every object in the large room, including—from a momentary pause and stare—the surveillance devices.

The receptionist was confused for a moment, then remembered.

"You're applying for the janitor's job. I'm afraid you've made a mistake. They should have told you to use the rear entrance—"

"Sister." The cyborg placed his flesh hand and his metal hand on either side of her, leaned over her. She was disconcerted to see the artificial eye readjust its focus as his head drew nearer. "I told you. I have an appointment."

"I'll check the files," she said coldly.

"You do that, sister."

"What was the name?"

"Xris. With an X. Pronounced 'Chris,' in case you're interested."

She wasn't. "Surname."

"Xris'll do. There's only one of me."

The receptionist flashed him a look which said the universe could undoubtedly count this as a blessing, then brought up the appointment calendar on a screen beneath the gleaming glass top of her desk. Her fingers flicked over the smooth surface.

The cyborg glanced around the reception area again, noted a security-bot glide out of a recess in the wall. Casually, Xris reached into the pocket of his shirt, drew out a golden and silver cigarette case, adorned with a shield on the top. The receptionist, had she been looking, would have been highly impressed. The shield was the crest of the Starfire family, belonged to the young king. The case was, in fact, a gift from the king. Xris opened the lid and withdrew an ugly, braided, foul-smelling form of tobacco known as a twist. He thrust the twist in his mouth, started to light it with the thumb of the metal hand.

"No smoking." The receptionist indicated a sign to that effect.

Xris shrugged, doused the light. Keeping the twist in his mouth, he began to chew on it. "Got any place I can spit?"

The receptionist glanced up, eyes narrowed in disgust, but she had located his name on the calendar and was therefore obligated to add the Wiedermann warmth to the Wiedermann smile, which had, unfortunately, slipped slightly.

"I'm sorry for the confusion, Mr. . . . Xris. You are to see Mr. Wiedermann."

Xris continued to chew reflectively. "Wiedermann himself, huh? I'm impressed."

"That is Mr. Wiedermann the younger," clarified the receptionist, as if, yes, Xris should be impressed but only moderately. "*Not* Mr. Wiedermann the elder. Please proceed to the eighteenth floor. Someone will meet you there, escort you to Mr. Wiedermann's office. Put this badge on your pocket. Wear it at all times. Please do not take it off. This would activate our alarm system."

Xris accepted the badge, clipped it on the pocket of his fatigues. "About that janitor's job . . ." he began conversationally.

"I'm sorry for the mistake," the receptionist said coldly. The Wiedermann smile could have, by now, been packaged and frozen. "Please go on up. Mr. Wiedermann doesn't like to be kept waiting."

She answered a buzz from the commlink. She didn't like being around cyborgs, even the well-oiled.

The cyborg circled her desk to reach the lifts. The receptionist was talking to a prospective client. A touch of metal on her shoulder made her jump, flinch, so that she accidentally disconnected the call.

"I was about to say, you couldn't afford me," Xris told her. "Sister."

Taking the twist out of his mouth, he tossed the soggy, half-chewed mass in the receptionist's trash disposer, then walked off.

It shouldn't gnaw at him, but it did. Gnawed at the part of him that hadn't been—couldn't be—replaced by machinery. People in general, women in particular—the way they looked at him. Or didn't look at him.

You asked for it, you know.

"Yeah, that's true," Xris agreed with himself. Taking out another twist, he stuck it in his mouth, clamped down on it hard with his teeth.

But he preferred the pity, the disgust to be up front. Better that than later. Behind closed doors.

Not that there ever was a later. A door that ever closed.

It happens to all cyborgs, eventually. Even the "pretty" ones. Sure, when she digs her nails into your fake flesh, it'll bleed fake blood—the miracle of modern technology. But when you hold her close, she'll hear the drone, the whine, the rhythmic clicks. And her flesh, her living flesh, grows cold in your arms, grows cold to your sensor devices. She realizes a machine's making love to her. She thinks: I might as well be screwing a toaster. . . .

The lift had stopped. It had been stopped for some time, apparently, for it kept repeating "Floor eighteen" in a manner that was beginning to sound irritated.

Berating himself—My God! How many years has it been since the operation anyway? Nine? Ten?—Xris strode off the lift. A young man, dressed in a tweed suit, tie, and knife-creased pants, was waiting for him.

"Xris? How do you do? I'm Dave Baldwin." The young man extended a hand, didn't wince at Xris's grip, even gave as good as he got. "Mr. Wiedermann's expecting you."

Turning, Baldwin led Xris down a carpeted hallway, done in muted tones, with muted lighting, polished woods, and the piped-in sounds of a string quartet. Occasionally, passing by an office with its door open, Xris glanced inside to see someone working at a computer or talking on a commlink. In one, he saw several people seated around a large polished wooden table holding cups of coffee and small electronic notepads.

"Where's your shoulder holster?" Xris asked.

The young man smiled faintly. "I left mine in my other suit."

"Sorry. I guess you must hear that all the time."

"It's the detective vids," Baldwin explained. "People believe that stuff. When they see these offices and they find out that we look just as boring as any other office place, they're disappointed. We've had a few even walk out. Mr. Wiedermann—that's the older Mr. Wiedermann—once suggested that we should all dress the part. Wear guns. Smell like bourbon. Go around in our shirtsleeves with slouch hats on. We think he was kidding."

"Was he?"

"You can never tell with old Mr. Wiedermann," Baldwin said carefully. "I know our appearance disillusions people, especially when they find out that most of the trails we follow are paper. The only footprints we trace are electronic. We don't tail beautiful mysterious women in mink stoles. We do file-searches until we find some tiny little discrepancy in her personal finances which proves she's a spy or an embezzler or whatever. We study psychological profiles, sociological patterns."

The young man stopped, eyed Xris quizzically. "But you know all this, don't you, sir? I've read up on your case," he added in explanation. "You used to work for the investigative branch of the old democracy."

"I was a Fed." Xris nodded. "But we wore holsters."

Baldwin shook his head, obviously sympathetic. "Mr. Wiedermann's office is at the end of the corridor."

"The younger," Xris clarified.

"Right. The elder's almost fully retired now. Through this door."

Through a door, into an outer office that appeared to be used as a storage room for boxes of computer paper, stacks of file folders, stacks of plastic disks, old-fashioned reels of

magnetic tape, mags, actual bound books, all thrown together in no particular order.

"Mr. Wiedermann doesn't like secretaries," Baldwin explained in a low tone, pausing in front of the closed door of
the inner office. "He says he's seen too many ruin their
bosses. The staff takes turns running his errands for him.
He's a genius."

"He must be," Xris observed, glancing at the clutter. "Either that or Daddy owns the company."

"He's a genius," Baldwin said quietly. "He doesn't often
see clients. Your case interested him. I must say it was
unique in *my* experience."

He tapped on the door. "Mr. Wiedermann." Opening it a
crack, he peered inside. "Mr. Xris here—by appointment."

"In!" came an irritable-sounding voice.

Baldwin opened the door wider, permitted Xris to enter.
Giving the cyborg a reassuring smile, the young man asked
if he could bring coffee, tea. Bourbon.

Xris shook his head.

"Good luck, sir. Have a seat. Say your name a couple of
times, just to remind him you're here."

Baldwin left, shutting the door behind him.

Xris looked at Mr. Wiedermann, the younger.

A thin man with a pale face and a shock of uncombed
sandy blond hair sat behind what might have been a desk. It
was completely covered over, hidden by various assorted objects, some of which had apparently been elbowed out by
others and were now lying on the floor.

Mr. Wiedermann not acknowledging his presence, Xris
glanced around the room. It had no windows, was lit by a
single lamp on the desk, and by the lambent light shining
from twenty separate computer screens that formed a semi-
circle behind the man's chair. The rest of the room was in
shadow.

Wiedermann sat with his chin in his hands—his hands
bent so that the chin rested on the backs, not the palms—
perusing a document of some sort, studying it with rapt,
single-minded intensity. He breathed through his mouth. A
bow tie—clipped to the open collar—slanted off at an odd
angle.

Xris removed a stack of files from a chair, kicked aside
the clutter surrounding the desk, dragged the chair over, and
placed it on the newly made bare spot on the floor.

Wiedermann never looked up.

Xris had just about figured this seeming abstraction was an affectation and was starting to grow irritated, when the blond-haired man lifted his gaze.

He stared at Xris with watery, very bright green eyes, said, "I've been expecting you."

The glow of the computer screens behind him cast an eerie halolike effect over the man. That and the darkened room made Xris think he'd accidentally broken in on some weird religious service.

Xris opened his mouth to introduce himself, but Wiedermann had shifted his attention to his desk. He made a sudden dive at a pile, snagged and pulled out—from about a quarter of the way down—a thick manila folder. The removal of the folder sent everything that had been stacked on top of it cascading to the floor. Xris leaned down to pick them up.

"Don't touch them," Wiedermann snapped.

He opened the file folder, flipped through the contents quickly. Satisfied, he returned the green-eyed gaze to Xris.

"A gatherer," Wiedermann said.

"I beg your pardon?" Xris blinked.

"I'm a gatherer. As in hunter/gatherer. Racial memory. Our ancestors. Men were hunters, women gatherers. Men went out, hunted food. Women foraged. Men could find game almost anywhere. Women had to remember where the berry patches were located from one year to the next, even after the tribe had moved from one hunting ground to another. Nature gave women the ability to remember the location of various objects that would guide them to the food.

"Take a woman. Show her unrelated objects scattered at random on a desk. Remove her from the room. Thirty minutes later, ask her what object was where and odds are she'll be able to remember. A man, given the same test, won't have a clue. I'm a gatherer, myself. I suppose, over the centuries, some of the gender lines have been obscured."

It occurred to Xris that a lot more than Wiedermann's gender lines had been obscured, but the cyborg kept quiet. Wiedermann did not expect a response, apparently. He was no longer paying attention to his client, had begun flipping through the myriad documents in the file.

Xris shifted restlessly. Tiny beeps from his cybernetic arm and the faint hum of his battery pack blended with the hum of the various computers behind Wiedermann. The detective continued to peruse the file, but Xris had the impression that Wiedermann's thoughts had drifted off somewhere else.

Xris decided it was time those thoughts returned to him.

"Uh, look, Mr. Wiedermann—"

"Ed. Ed Wiedermann. The younger."

"Fine. You sent for me, Ed. I take it that means you've made some progress on my case?"

"Yes. Yes, we have." Wiedermann nodded, continued to study the file. "We've completed it successfully, in fact."

The surge that went through Xris had nothing to do with his batteries. Elation sparked, its jolt nearly stopping his heart with bright, intense pleasure. He spent a moment reveling in the triumph, then said slowly, "You mean you've found him. Rowan."

"Dalin Rowan." Wiedermann savored the name. "We're close. Very close."

Xris shut his eyes. Emotion brought tears, burned behind the lids. His hand—his good hand, resting on his good knee—clenched into a tight fist. Nails dug into his flesh. Good flesh, warm flesh. Blood—warm blood, real blood— throbbed in his temples. A buzzing sounded; his system was warning him that it was having difficulty compensating for this sudden adrenaline rush that was unaccompanied by strenuous physical exertion. He drew in several deep breaths to try to calm himself down.

"Tell me—where is he?"

"I don't think so. I've called a halt to the operation," Wiedermann said offhandedly, frowning at the file in his hands.

"You did what?" Xris couldn't believe he'd heard correctly, thought his auditory system might have shorted out.

"I spoke clearly enough." Wiedermann was testy. The green eyes narrowed. "I've halted the operation. I have a good idea—an excellent idea, in fact—where this case is headed. And I don't like it. We could find ourselves in a great deal of difficulty. Our firm is not, at this point, prepared to accept the risk. I've spoken with my father and he—"

With his good hand, Xris shoved aside an enormous stack of folders, toppling them to the floor. He leaned over the desk, planted the left elbow of the metal arm in the newly cleared space directly under Wiedermann's nose.

"You see this?" Xris wiggled his metal fingers. "Nine years ago, this arm was real. So was my leg, my eye, and all other parts of me. I won't bore you with the details—you've got them on file. I damn near died in that explosion. Dalin Rowan, my friend and partner, saved my life. But I never got a chance to thank him. After the accident, he disappeared.

"I owe him." Xris was forced to pause, readjust himself. He was experiencing momentary breathing difficulty. "I owe him big. I spent a year of my own life searching for Dalin Rowan. No luck. You've spent six years' worth of my money searching for him. You tell me you've found him, but you won't tell me where he is. I think you might want to reconsider. Hand over that file."

"Certainly." Wiedermann was calm, not the least intimidated. "But you wouldn't find it much help. It's not your case. Here, see for yourself."

Xris backed off. He'd played enough ante-up to know when a man was bluffing. "All right, then. Where are my files?"

"In the computer." Wiedermann indicated the screens behind him. "*One* of the computers. You'll never find them, you know. Not if you searched a lifetime. And I didn't say I *wouldn't* tell you. I haven't decided."

"What do you want?" Xris demanded. "More money?"

Wiedermann shook his head. "We operate in this galaxy at His Majesty's pleasure. At any time, the galactic government could revoke our license. If that happened, the total worth of the Crown Jewels couldn't compensate us for our losses. If your case results in legal action against us, I want to be certain we have a chance to win."

"Legal action?" Xris snorted. "What legal action? I'm trying to find my friend—"

"It's up to you," Wiedermann interrupted. "If we decide not to proceed, you won't be charged for our time. We'll refund your retainer. You won't be out anything."

"Only eight years of my life," Xris said through clenched teeth.

"Tell me your story."

"I told you the goddamn story once. Your operative, that is. It's in the blasted files!"

Wiedermann leaned back in his chair. Crossing bony legs over bony knees, he put the tips of his fingers together.

Xris eyed the computer screens. His fingers twitched. He was good with computers, but he wasn't that good. Dalin Rowan—now there had been the computer expert. In all these years, Xris had never run across anyone as good as Dalin.

Slowly, reluctantly, the cyborg sat back down.

Xris paused a moment to get his thoughts in order. It didn't take long. Not a day went by but that he didn't think about it. Wondering, trying to make sense of it.

"It was back during the days of the democracy. I was a Fed, a member of the bureau detailed to handle interplanetary crime. I don't know how much you know about the agency; probably quite a bit."

Wiedermann smiled, nodded. "The bureau hasn't changed all that much under the new regime. Cleaned up some, maybe. But basically the same."

"No reason it should change," Xris said. "They've got good people. We were good, most of us. Dedicated. Loyal. And if there *was* some corruption, hell, that's only to be expected in an organization that big. Of course, I didn't know at the time that the whole damn government was corrupt, from the president on down. Not that it would have made much difference, I guess. I did what I did for the bureau for my own reasons."

"And those were?"

Xris shrugged. Taking out the cigarette case, he held it in his hand, but didn't open it. He tapped it thoughtfully with a good finger.

"It's no big moral thing with me. Right. Wrong. Good. Bad. Ethics vary from planet to planet. On Adonia twenty years ago, it was legal to abandon a child for being ugly. We had a hell of a time with local laws. But that's not important. What got to me, what kept me going, were the people who got fat off other people's misery."

"Yes, go on."

Xris shifted in his chair, attempted to make himself more comfortable. Not an easy task when half his body was metal.

"I don't suppose you'd let me smoke?"

Wiedermann shook his head, patted his chest. "Asthma."

Xris removed a twist from the case, clamped his teeth down on it, chewed it. The bitter juice flooded his mouth, washed out the faint metallic flavor that he always tasted, despite the fact that the doctors told him it was all in his mind. Some days the taste was stronger than others.

"It's what kept me from being on the take, I guess. I had my chances, but I knew where the money came from: babies who were born whacked out from drugs, sixteen-year-old hookers smashed up by their pimps, old people swindled out of their life savings. These people were at the bottom and at the top were guys in the fancy limojets who held handkerchiefs over their delicate noses when they drove through the stinking slums they helped create. Bringing those guys down, making them lie flat on the pavement in the muck and the filth, rubbing those delicate noses in it—that's why I worked for the bureau."

Xris thrust the case back in his shirt pocket. "I had money enough. Everything I needed, everything I wanted. My wife and I—"

Xris stopped abruptly, smiled easily. "But you don't want to hear all that. It was a long time ago, anyway. And it all came down to one job. One simple, routine job. . . ."

CHAPTER
4

To unfailingly take what you attack, attack where there is no defense. For unfailingly secure defense, defend where there is no attack.

Sun Tzu, *The Art of War*

Xris and his longtime friend and partner Mashahiro Ito forced their way through the crowds pouring out of the mass transit station, walked the short distance to the main entrance of FISA headquarters. The season was spring on Janus 2. The gardens decorating the grounds were just beginning to come back to life after their winter's hiatus. Budding trees extended protective limbs over the tentatively blooming flower beds. Ito had once discoursed at great length on the symbology of the protective trees, the helpless flowers. Xris, grinning, had once told Ito what he could do with his symbology.

A large and massive sign read ADMINISTRATIVE GOVERN-MENT FACILITY, JANUS 2. The sign made no mention of the fact that the Federal Intelligence and Security Agency was housed inside the building; it was supposedly top secret. But everyone on the planet knew. Janus 2 was quite proud of it. The building was a regular stop for tour shuttles.

The agents dodged a group of uniformed schoolchildren, who squealed with delight.

"I'll bet he's a Fed!"

"Hey, mister, can we see your gun?"

Xris shook his head, kept walking. A large and ugly electrified fence—a grim contrast to the flower beds—surrounded the building. Xris was always meaning to ask Ito what symbology the fence held.

"Any idea what this meeting is about?"

"Nope," Ito answered, lowered his voice. "But it's bound to be about the Hung. We've been working on this damn case for months now. Word is it's ready to break."

"About time! I hope this isn't another of those goddamn ass-numbing talk sessions. Sit around and yammer at one another for hours and get nothing done."

Ito laughed, but he wasn't very sympathetic. He liked the planning part of any assignment, considered it a "cerebral exercise." Xris considered it bullshit. He liked the action—the forty-four-decawatt lasgun pointing at some punk's skull and the "Freeze, Federal agents! Hands behind your head!" part of the operation.

"Is Rowan coming?"

"I don't know," Xris said shortly. "I haven't seen much of him lately."

Ito cast a sharp glance at his friend. Xris was aware of the scrutiny, did his best to ignore it. Dalin Rowan was the third member of what a few in the agency jokingly called the Trinity. Xris, Ito, and Rowan: Father, Son, and Holy Ghost, so named because Xris was the oldest and the biggest; Ito was short, slender, and the youngest; Rowan was quiet, unassuming, and could walk through a computer without leaving a trace behind. The three had worked together for years now and were one of the top teams in the agency. They were also close friends. Or rather, they used to be.

The two agents entered the first checkpoint—a small access building with two doors. One door provided entrance through the electrified fence, the other door granted access to the facility. Security guards checked ID badges and issued visitor passes to those who were cleared for them.

The senior guard looked up from his newsvid reader and nodded.

"Going to cause any trouble today, Xris? I just need to know, so's I can plan my lunch break around you."

Xris shook his head. "Hell, that was an accident, Henry. I didn't mean to set off the alarms. I forgot I had the damn knife on me."

"Huh-uh." Henry grinned. He'd been an agent once, until he could no longer pass the physical. But that had been at age eighty. He still had a grip like a nullgrav steel vise—as Xris had good reason to know.

"You're in charge of him today, Ito. I'm getting too old for this sort of thing."

"You'll outlive us all, Henry." Ito laughed.

Xris was to remember that remark.

He and Ito entered the main administration headquarters building, encountered another security guard.

Ito pulled his lasgun out of his shoulder holster and placed it on the counter. "Morning, boys." Folding his arms, sighing, he settled back to wait.

Xris laid his regulation lasgun on the counter. He drew forth a small modified derringer from his suit pocket and placed it on the counter. Next came a long, thin blade from the back of his jacket, a needle-gun from a leg holster, and a boot knife.

"Glad you're here to protect us, Father," Ito said.

"And I always will be, my son," Xris returned solemnly, and patted Ito on the head.

They walked without incident through the weapons detectors, headed for the lifts.

"Floor thirty-five," Xris said, and inserted his security card.

The lift whisked them up, stopped. Stepping out, Xris and Ito glanced up at the briefing screen.

"Mission briefing 2122027, 0845hrs, 3506."

"That's us."

The two were early for the briefing, but they weren't alone. Another man sat at a desk in the back, sipping coffee and working on a portable computer. He looked up, smiled, nodded. Xris and Ito nodded back, took their seats at the desks that made this room resemble a classroom.

Xris was back up a moment later, going to get coffee for himself, tea for Ito. He'd just returned to his seat when Ito nudged him. Dalin Rowan had walked in.

"Dalin, how's it going?" Ito asked pleasantly.

"Okay," Rowan replied.

His lips jerked in what was intended for a smile, but didn't quite make it. And nothing sounded less okay than his "Okay."

He took a seat in the center of the room, about four chairs removed from Xris and Ito. The stranger in the back had finished his coffee, continued to work on the computer.

"Been a long time, buddy," Xris said quietly. "I've been worried about you." It was an apology.

Rowan glanced up. He was pale, thin, had obviously lost weight. He attempted the jerky pseudo-smile again.

"Sorry I haven't called, Xris. I . . . I've had a lot on my mind lately." Rowan glanced at the stranger in the back, added, "I'll talk to you after the meeting."

Xris nodded, settled back, relieved. He and Rowan had not parted on the best of terms and he hadn't seen or heard from his friend in a month. All because of that damn bitch. Xris had tried to point out to his friend what everyone else knew but was too polite to mention: The whore was taking Rowan for a ride. A wild and thrill-packed ride, maybe, but a ride nonetheless. An expensive ride.

You goddamn fool! You're thinking with your zipper, not your brains! Xris recalled those words clearly. They were the last words said between them.

Rumor had it now that the slut had left Rowan. When he could no longer pay for the tickets, the amusement park had shut down the rides. Looking at his friend, Xris guessed that this time the rumor was true. He wondered uncomfortably if other rumors were true, as well. That Rowan was in big financial trouble, seriously in debt.

Well, Xris reflected, I'll find out soon enough.

The superintendent entered, accompanied by an older woman wearing a flight suit. Xris and Ito exchanged glances. They'd been right. The super was Jafar el Amadi, top man on the Hung Conspiracy case. So that's what this was all about.

The meeting came to order.

Amadi opened with a frown; but then, he always frowned.

"Agents, this briefing will be kept short. First, I'd like to introduce your controller, Agent Michael Armstrong."

Xris twisted in his desk. The man in the back acknowledged the introduction. Tall, thin, and middle-aged, Armstrong didn't look as if he had the stamina for fieldwork; probably why he was assigned to the more sedentary controller role.

"Next I want to introduce Captain Lisa Bolton, skipper of the *Vigilance,* our new orbital control ship. All right, let's get down to business.

"To sum up: we have reason to believe that the Hung have infiltrated the very top levels of the galactic government. We don't have any hard evidence, but there are several indications, most noteworthy being Senator Gravesborne changing his vote at the last minute on the arms control legislation which went down to defeat last month. Because of this defeat, the Hung were able to start up a munitions plant on TISor 13 and a weapons factory on TISor 8. The syndicate doesn't need these weapons; the Hung are well supplied. Obviously, they're not manufacturing guns for themselves. They're selling them. And now we think we know who's buying—the Corasians."

Xris sat up straight. Even Rowan, who had been staring listlessly at his desk, lifted his head, his attention caught. The Corasians occupied the galaxy next door and wanted to take over the entire neighborhood. Unfortunately, when the Corasians moved in, they had a bad habit of devouring the neighbors. Made entirely of energy, the fiery bloblike entities roamed about searching for food—any living being would do, but Corasians were particularly fond of human flesh.

"This is only a suspicion, mind you. We can't prove anything—yet. That's why you're all here today. As you can imagine," the super continued grimly, "I've got the boss on my back on this one. Chief Superintendent Robison is in my office more than I am lately. President Robes has taken a personal interest in this investigation, ladies and gentlemen, so let's do this one right. I want to retire in four years on schedule. Got it?"

They all nodded. Xris, glancing at Rowan, was pleased to see some color in his friend's wan face. Work—the best remedy for whatever ailed you. Even a broken heart.

"Let's get down to details. Xris, you and Ito and Rowan will conduct a raid on the munitions plant on TISor 13. Word is that's where their central computer system is located. Rowan will handle the computer end. Xris and Ito will find out what's being produced and if it's been designed with those damn Corasian blobs and their robot casings in mind. Once we get hard evidence, we can bust this thing wide open.

"Xris and Ito will land on TISor 13 first, stake out the factory. I've booked passage on the *IJD Lentian* for the two of you, arriving at TISor 4 in seven days. From there, you'll rent a spaceplane and fly to TISor 13.

"Rowan, you'll travel with Armstrong on the *Vigilance*, then link up with Xris and Ito planetside just before the raid.

I have no idea what sort of computer equipment these people are running, so bring everything in your tool kit."

Xris was disappointed that they weren't traveling together. Get Rowan alone for seven days and his two best friends would have him just about back to normal in no time.

"Excuse the interruption, Super," Xris spoke up. "But why not send Rowan along with us?"

Amadi was extremely irritated at the interruption. "We've intercepted some coded transmissions from the Hung. Our computers can't crack them. I want Rowan to work on them and he can do so only with the sophisticated equipment on board the *Vigilance*. I trust this meets with your approval, Agent?"

Xris ignored the sarcasm. The super was under a lot of pressure these days. "Sure thing, sir." He looked over at Rowan, who gave him a smile—a real smile.

"Good." Amadi grunted. "Now, where was I?" He peered at his notes. "Armstrong, your post will be on the *Vigilance*. You'll act as onsite mission commander—guide everyone into the factory and out again.

"Now listen to me." Amadi rested both hands on the desk, leaned over it. "I don't need to tell you how vital this mission is. Everything must go according to plan. Yes, I'm talking to you, Xris. You listen to the controller on this one and do exactly what he says or so help me you'll be back on Jackson's Moon busting cyberpunkers. Understood?"

Xris caught Ito's wink and swallowed the retort that would have only landed him in trouble. There wasn't much he could say in his own defense. He'd been right in ignoring the controller's warnings two times out of three, but it was the third—when he'd been wrong—that had nearly gotten them all killed. It was also the reason they now had a new controller. Xris heard that Polinskai had taken early retirement. He nodded glumly.

The super turned. "Captain Bolton, how soon will your ship be ready to leave?"

"Six days, sir. We've just finished ship's run-up trials, and need to take on all provisions and load the system's computers with the operational data for this mission."

"Very well, then, Captain. Six days it is. Armstrong, you and Rowan coordinate with the captain here for all transport details. You will establish contact with Xris and Ito on TISor 13 at oh-two hundred hours on the ninth. Rowan, you'll get a chance to fly one of the *Vigilance*'s new intrusion shuttles. You'll meet up with Xris and Ito on the surface, and Agent Armstrong will guide you in from his post on *Vigilance*. Anything else?"

Armstrong raised his hand. "I'd like to run over the details of the plan with the other agents after this, if that's convenient with them."

The super glanced around. The others shrugged, agreed.

"If there's nothing else, good luck!" Amadi dismissed the meeting.

Everyone stood as the superintendent and Captain Bolton left. When they were gone, Ito walked over to their new controller, held out his hand.

"Mashahiro Ito. I haven't met you before. Are you new in the agency?"

Armstrong shook hands. "No. I've been in for a few years now, working out of Central Headquarters. My specialization is the Corasians. I've been acting as our liaison with Naval Intelligence. I was due a change, so I requested a field assignment. They figured I could be useful on this case."

"Fed up with the politics, huh?" Xris was sympathetic. He, too, shook hands. "Name's Xris."

"No one can pronounce his surname, so we just skip it," Ito added.

For a man with not much muscle tone, Armstrong's handshake was surprisingly firm and strong. "Life in the capital *is* pretty stressful," he said in answer to Xris's question.

And that, thought Xris, is all we'll hear about HQ. For a while, at least. Though Armstrong doesn't look the type to open up. Pity. It'd be nice to know if the word floating around about disorganization and turmoil at the top is true.

Rowan shook hands with their new controller, mumbled "Nice to meet you," then asked abruptly, "What time's the briefing?"

Armstrong blinked and answered, "Twenty-two hundred, if that's okay with everyone? I thought—"

"Fine."

Rowan left, moving so rapidly that Xris fell over a desk in his effort to catch up. He caught his friend at the door.

"Hey, buddy, I thought we were going to talk. Look, I've got an idea. Come home with me to dinner. We've got six hours before the briefing with Armstrong. Marjorie's cooking something special—one of her famous 'welcome home' meals. She'd love to see you. She said she didn't hear from you the whole time I was away. You know how she worries. . . ."

Rowan was shaking his head, doing his best to escape out the door. But Xris was a big man, broad-shouldered and tall, and made a sizable obstacle.

His attempt foiled, Rowan halted, stared impatiently past his friend into the hall. "Thanks, Xris, but I just remembered an appointment—"

"Cancel it."

Rowan shook his head. "I'm afraid that's not possible. I'll see you at the briefing."

He tried to step around. Xris grabbed hold of his friend's arm. "Goddammit, Dalin, I'm sorry—"

Rowan looked directly at Xris for the first time since he'd entered the room.

"For what?" Rowan asked bitterly. "Being right?"

Slender, shorter than Xris, Dalin Rowan was wiry and agile. He feinted left, moved right, and was out the door before Xris could stop him.

"No luck?" said Ito, coming up behind.

"Hell no. He's acting strange, Ito. He could be in trouble. Big trouble. I heard—"

"Excuse me," Armstrong interrupted politely. He was standing behind them. "If I could get past? I need to put together a few things."

"Sure. Sorry." Xris moved one way, Ito the other.

Armstrong stepped between them, gave them a smile, and walked off down the hall.

"What have you heard?" Ito asked.

"Nothing," Xris answered. "Skip it."

Ito shook his head. "You heard he was on the take. I heard it, too, and I don't believe it."

"I *didn't*. Until I saw him."

"Rowan's straight arrow. You'll never convince me."

They both stood in the doorway, watched their friend step into the lift.

Xris took out a twist, stuck it in his mouth, chewed on the end. "Maybe one of us should . . . well . . . keep an eye on him."

"Damn it, Xris, we're talking about Rowan! Dalin Rowan!" Ito snorted. "If you want to tail a man who's been your best friend for ten years, who's saved your ass more than once, then go ahead. I'm going out for a drink. You coming?"

Xris went with Ito for that drink. But he was to wonder later—wonder over and over again—what would have happened if he hadn't. What if he'd tailed his friend, his pal, his buddy? What would he have seen? Rowan meeting with the Hung. Taking their filthy blood money. Selling his friends out.

Why? Why the hell didn't I go after him? Xris was to ask himself that question during the long, pain-tormented nights. And he always came up with the same answer.

Because he was my friend. A man doesn't tail his best friend.

But then neither does a man set his best friends up for the kill.

Armstrong was already in the briefing room when Xris entered. He sat down and waited. After a few moments, Ito wandered in, glanced worriedly at Xris, who had been moody and morose in the bar.

Xris smiled, nodded, indicated that he was once more in his right senses. An excellent meal—all his favorite food— and Marjorie's reassuring, levelheaded conversation had eased his mind. Dalin hadn't sold anyone out. He'd be fine. Some things a man had to work out on his own.

Ito grinned, relieved. He began to examine a map of TISor 13 that Armstrong had brought up on the large vidscreen.

Dalin came in, sat down next to Xris.

"I'm sorry," Rowan said abruptly. "But everything's going to be okay now. It's all . . . taken care of."

"What is? Look, Dalin, if you need cash, I've got a few extra credits in my account—"

"No, no," Rowan said hastily, with a bleak smile. "It's all arranged. I can't explain now. When this job's done, I'm going to be all right. I promise, Xris. Don't worry. It's going to be all right."

He looked at Xris anxiously, either begging him to drop the subject or desperately eager to talk. Xris couldn't tell which, and whatever he might have said in return never got said because at that moment Armstrong started talking.

Turning to the wall-mounted vidscreen, he called up a map of the munitions factory and surrounding areas.

"I've prepared some briefing notes; you can go over them at your convenience. I'll cover everything first, and then you can ask questions."

Using a red-light laser indicator, Armstrong pointed out a gray area near the munitions plant. "You'll make your approach from here. This swamp is the only easy point of access. The water and assorted plant life provide excellent cover right up to within three meters of the fence that surrounds the facility."

"Swamp!" Ito repeated, horrified. "Assorted plant life! What does that mean? And what about assorted animal life?"

Armstrong was soothing. "I've checked it out. According to our biometeorological research scientists, there's nothing *too* dangerous in the swamp."

"How the hell do they know? Have they been there?"

"No, but studies on swamps on planets with the same type of atmosphere and temperature would seem to indicate that the flora is standard for warm, wet environments. Nothing worse than skunk plants and plenty of vines. They don't think any of the vines are sentient."

"Don't *think* they're sentient," Xris kidded, nudging Ito under the table with his foot.

Ito paled.

"You shouldn't have to worry about the fauna, either," Armstrong continued. "Primarily your standard water lizards and tubor snakes and they don't like anything bigger than they are."

"Snakes . . ." Ito repeated in a whisper.

"Tubor snakes. Not poisonous. You'll be provided with the standard snakebite kit, just in case. To continue"— Armstrong hastened on, ignoring Ito's garbled protest— "you'll enter the swamp here and move to this point, closest to the fence. You'll exit the swamp, cut open the fence, and enter the vehicle loading dock—"

Xris grunted. "After we set off every sensor in the place, not to mention being fried by the electronic fence."

Armstrong shook his head. "Remember, Agent, this is a legal operation for the Hung. They have all the necessary permits; the community's even given them tax breaks. It's not against the law to produce and sell small arms and ammunition. And you can be certain that if said arms are making their way to Corasia, the Hung have it all very well disguised. No, gentlemen, you won't find any electric fences or force fields or fancy sensor belts. The Hung don't want to make the good folks of TISor 13 suspicious. Our preliminary reports indicate that this fence is chain-link. Its main function is to keep out the swamp creatures."

"What swamp creatures?" Ito demanded loudly.

Armstrong, with a wry grin, only shook his head.

"You won't find any 'live' guards, either. The plant employees live in a trailer park some eight kilometers from the facility. An automated system keeps watch at night, one of those with its own investigating 'bot. You know the kind—the 'bot can put out a small fire or report a major one. Kills large rodents, that sort of thing."

"Rodents." Ito shuddered.

"You'll have to disable the 'bot, if it locates you. As I said, you'll enter here, via the loading dock." Armstrong pointed. "That will put you inside the shipping warehouse. Proceed through the chemical storage room—here—and into the main assembly area. From here, you will make your way to the central control office—marked on this map with a circle. Your briefing packages contain copies of all of these maps. The main computer is located in the control office.

"Rowan will gain control of the computer system, establish a ground-space link to the *Vigilance,* and upload the entire memory core. We estimate transmission time at around eight minutes. Once you're finished, return the system to its original state and exit via the same route you entered. You should clear the compound by oh-three-twenty hours. You will then proceed to the *Vigilance*'s shuttle and return to orbit. We'll analyze the data and decide on a course of action. Any questions?"

Ito cleared his throat. "About those snakes . . ."

Laughter, even from Rowan. The meeting broke up. Xris offered to stand drinks. Ito said yes, just a minute, began anxiously searching through his briefing papers for the bioresearcher's report. Armstrong declined politely. Gathering his material, he left the briefing room. Rowan said sure, he'd join them in a moment. He'd just thought of a question he needed to ask Armstrong.

Xris dragged Ito away from the snake report. They took the lift to the top floor, to the employees' private lounge. They had their drink and then another. Ito finally went home. Xris waited a long time before he admitted to himself that Rowan wasn't coming.

The transport run to TISor 4 was dull. Ito and Xris had played businessmen on a marketing trip before and were very polished at it. They were good, so good that it was beginning to bore them. They didn't talk much. Xris divided his time between scanning his briefing notes and worrying about Rowan. Ito read a book titled *Poisonous Reptiles Indigenous to Class 4 Moons.* Arriving at space dock, they transferred to a planet-bound shuttle and headed for the commerce sector of the capital city of Greenlock.

Since there was only one city on TISor 4, calling it a capital was a bit grandiose. Greenlock did act as the capital for all of TISor's moons, though, so no one questioned its self-styled importance. The planet TISor was uninhabitable, a huge orange gas giant. Circling it were twenty-two moons, five of which had atmosphere and were warm enough to support life. Only TISor 4 was heavily populated. According to Armstrong's report, the other moons catered to a few low-budget resorts, several struggling factories, and lots of signs posted on lots of tracts of barren land boasting that they were "scheduled for future development." TISor 13 was the ideal location for a Hung factory. No one gave a damn what they produced or who they sold it to, as long as they provided jobs and forked over tax credits.

Xris and Ito checked into an old hotel on the end of what passed for the local social strip and waited until morning. Not much happened on TISor 4 at night, and the people liked it that way. The bars were quiet drinking holes, the entertainment industry was zero to nonexistent. Neither man felt much like being entertained. Xris called Marjorie. Ito checked in with Armstrong. The plan was still a go. No changes.

Armstrong had reserved a short-hop spaceplane for them. The courtesy hovervan from the rental agency arrived to pick them up early the next day. Xris and Ito showed their commercial pilot's licenses to a sleepy clerk, who barely glanced at them.

"Slot D," she said, yawning and handing over the codes needed to initiate the computer sequence that would fire the plane's engines. "I hope it starts," she added in a tone which indicated she'd be amazed as hell if it did.

They walked out onto the concrete tarmac and located their spaceplane—a shabby WR model in desperate need of a paint job. The plane had short wings, a small cockpit, and was unarmed. The central cargo area was only three meters long, but all in all the craft was exactly what they wanted. It certainly wouldn't draw anyone's attention, arouse anyone's suspicions.

"A good choice," Xris said, giving the outside a careful examination. "I've got to give Armstrong credit: He seems to know his stuff."

"Does that mean we get to keep him, Daddy? Huh? Please, please?" Ito begged, tugging on the sleeve of Xris's flight suit.

"Sure, son," Xris answered magnanimously. "But you've got to feed him and clean up after him." He grinned. "I'll stow the gear. You check the nav computer and see if it has any idea where TISor 13 is located."

Xris boarded the plane through the drop-down hatch that he trusted wouldn't drop down when they were deep in space. Ito checked the computer, began shaking his head and muttering to himself.

"Nothing much here, Xris. It provides the normal approach vectors, climate and weather reports—probably outdated—and a directory of inhabitants. I'm running the inhabitants against our known Hung member list, but I don't expect to find anything."

A few seconds passed as Ito cross-correlated the data with the list. "Nope, nothing here. I'll feed the standard inbound vector to the nav computer to take us in. Once we're in the atmosphere, you can fly us to our landing zone."

The computer made the necessary course corrections. The plane took off and they settled down to thirty minutes of unexciting flying. There were no landing authorities on the moons, so there was no need for radio traffic. And the computer wasn't the type that had been programmed to entertain the passengers.

"You hear about those XJ series computers Warlord Sagan's developed to put in his new Scimitars?" Xris asked. "I talked to one of the pilots. The planes are fast and more maneuverable than a Laskar belly dancer, but Sagan installed this computer XJ-type that's got a mind of its own. Actually argues with the pilot if it doesn't like what you're doing. Plus he says the damn thing never shuts up."

They discussed computers and the current unstable political situation, with the various Warlords plotting to fill the power vacuum left by the increasingly ineffective government of the Galactic Democratic Republic. People were grumbling and starting to talk about a return to the "good old days" under the Blood Royal. Since all the Blood Royal were—supposedly—wiped out by the purges during the Revolution, their return appeared highly unlikely.

The rush of atmosphere across the spaceplane's fuselage ended their friendly wrangling. Xris took over manual control of the spaceplane; Ito started calling out course corrections. They located the munitions plant, made one high-altitude pass over it. Xris had connected a small, portable computer to the space sensor array on the plane. Normally, the sensors were calibrated for use in close navigation in space. They didn't have the processing power or the resolution for high-altitude-to-ground surveillance. The addition of Xris's computer and the electromagnetic refracting lens apertures enabled the system to provide a scan of the area.

Xris shot several images, destined to be converted to tactical maps. Armstrong had provided maps, but these were probably outdated by several months. On a warm world, the terrain changed from season to season. There was no irritation worse—and sometimes no greater danger—than working with outdated maps.

TISor 13 was an interesting moon. An orbiting moon rarely rotated on its own axis, but this was one of them. According to Armstrong, the rotation made it difficult to determine planet-rise and planet-set without a computer. Most of the night wasn't truly dark, being illuminated by the moon's gas giant mother, which cast an eerie orange glow over the ground. Only about four hours were dark at any one time—this would play merry hell with their recon schedule.

Xris hovered the spaceplane into a dense woods, set it down in a small clearing. Surrounded by tall ugly gray-mottled trees, spackled with orange spots that were either some sort of disease or due to the orange light, the plane was easy to camouflage. It was already the same gray as the trees. Xris and Ito both changed into gray field coveralls, field webbing, and cloth hats. Xris carried a 44-decawatt lasgun in a side holster, a 22.3-decawatt lasgun in a shoulder holster, a synthusteel Eversharp fighting knife in his boot, two thurmite grenades and one tear gas canister in a pouch on his webbing, and a gas mask.

Ito carried the regulation 38-decawatt lasgun and a gas mask. His secondary armament consisted of a knife/fork/ spoon set and a Xirconian Army multiknife. He carried no other weapons, being burdened with the tool kit, which contained wire cutters, data-link with multiple interchangeable access ports (you never knew what computer you might have to interface with these days), minishovel, cutting laser, spreader clamps, and a can of spray neoprene rubber. Night-vision goggles rounded out both agents' gear, and then there was Ito's snakebite kit.

They waited for relative darkness before commencing. They had plenty of time; no need to hurry. The *Vigilance* wouldn't be arriving for another nineteen hours. Once the orange ball of fire had dropped below the horizon, the two agents moved out together. Their landing site was about two kilometers from the facility. The trees near the swamp were shorter and arranged in clumps, but the grass was long, nearly shoulder height, and had a slimy feel. The grass rippled in the night breeze like water.

Xris went first, walking slowly and crouching low to the ground. Ito did the same, some ten meters to his rear. Neither spoke. Every fifty meters or so, Xris stopped and pulled out his night-vision goggles and scanned the area. The place was assumed to be deserted, but Xris's credo was: *Assume, and get your ass shot off.* He saw nothing, however.

Following their map, they circled the entire facility, moving no faster than a crawl, stopping only when they found cover. A few security lights lit the outside of the building, but they were poorly placed, left large areas in deep shadow. About one-third of the lights had burned out and had not been replaced. The factory appeared to have been hastily constructed of the crude local brick and looked low-tech for a munitions plant, but there was no need for better. They weren't producing missiles for the Warlord's naval vessels, just small arms charges, grenades, and handheld rockets for the damn technologically illiterate Corasians.

Nearing the back end of the facility, close to the loading dock, Xris entered the warm, oozing water of the swamp. Behind him, he heard a splash and Ito's soft, disgusted grunt. The two agents crawled along the squishy bottom, propelling themselves forward by grabbing on to whatever was growing down there. This was the fastest method of traversing a swamp, though not the most pleasant. Try walking and you'd end up either sunk to your knees in muck or hopelessly tangled.

The trick was not to think real hard about what it was you were using for handholds. Once Xris grabbed what he thought was grass, only to feel it wriggle and slide out of his hand. The shiver up his spine made ripples in the water and he knew—from the sound of soft swearing—that Ito had encountered something similar.

But once again, Xris gave Armstrong credit. This approach—through the swamp—was the best and closest they could make. The swamp extended to within several meters of the chain-link fence. And Armstrong had been right about the fence, although Xris wouldn't have called it "ordinary." The fence was far simpler. No sensing devices, no magnetic anomaly detectors, no defense systems, no nothing. It was a plain hardware-store chain-link fence.

Xris touched Ito's arm, cautioned him to stay put. Xris slithered out of the swamp. Reaching relatively dry land, he belly-crawled up to the fence. He pulled out his boot knife, stood it handle-down on the ground, and then released it, letting the metal blade fall onto the fence.

No spark. Armstrong was right about that, too. The fence wasn't electrified.

Xris pulled out his night-vision goggles, took a long, careful look. Nothing moved anywhere in the facility. Retrieving his knife, Xris slipped back into the water. He and Ito spent an hour watching the loading dock and saw no signs of life except for something that might have been a cat slinking from one shadow to another. By now, the gas giant was on the rise again; Xris could see things swimming through the swamp. From Ito's muffled curse, he could see them, too. The two returned to their spaceplane.

Once inside, they peeled off their wet clothes. Ito wrinkled his nose, held his mud-covered coveralls at arm's length. "Man, that swamp stinks! And to think we've got to go back tonight. I swear, Xris, I saw a snake three meters long and as thick around as your leg. All that crap about it being more scared of me than me of it ... hah! The damn thing floated right in front of me, stared at me with its little snaky eyes."

"It didn't bite you, did it?" Xris asked, grinning, scraping muck off his face.

"No," Ito retorted, "but probably because it had just chowed down on a warthog or whatever kind of pork they grow around here. I'll be glad to get this job over. And if you think I'm bad, wait till Mr. Finicky white-lab-coat Rowan sets foot in that slimy soup."

"Maybe slogging around in muck'll take his mind off that female. I'll see if I can't find a nice fat cephalopod to drop down his back."

They changed into denims, spread out their equipment to dry in the hot sun. Xris routed the spaceplane's sensors through his computer, set the sensors to pick up any movement in the vicinity. The two went to sleep.

A light on the portable comm unit started to flash, accompanied by a beeping sound. Xris was immediately awake. He rose from the spaceplane's bunk, and slid his feet into his boots. He looked at the clock. 2700, Standard Military Time. Right on schedule.

He shook Ito, who could sleep through an artillery barrage. "The *Vigilance* is in orbit."

Ito fumbled his way out of his bunk. Xris sat down at the commlink. The channel was clear, and he entered the decryption code into the comm unit to begin to receive encoded messages. Earphones in place, he tested the link.

"Sunray, this is Delta One. How do you read me, over?"

Immediately, Armstrong was on the net. "Delta One, this is Sunray. You will proceed to the facility and begin your entry. Assume Blackjack situation—all control is exercised from this station. Do you understand, Delta One?"

Ito paused in midyawn, gave Xris a puzzled look. Xris shook his head, annoyed. He didn't know what was going on, either.

"Sunray, this is Delta One. Confirm that we are to begin our entry. We haven't linked up with Javelin yet. Has something gone wrong?"

Javelin was Rowan's comm call sign.

"Delta One, this is Sunray. You will immediately begin your entry. If Javelin doesn't arrive, do not wait. Do not execute any action without first clearing it with this station. Is that clear, Delta One?"

"Very clear, Sunray. Delta One, out." Xris sat back, glared, frustrated, at the commlink.

"I don't like this," Ito said.

"Me, either. We should wait for Rowan." Xris scratched irritably at a red welt on his arm; one of the local insects had bitten him. "Unless that computer system is dirt easy, there isn't much you or I can do to break in."

"What do we do?"

"Hell, there's nothing we can do! You heard Armstrong. We must assume Blackjack. No arguments, no questions." Xris kicked the console with the toe of his boot.

Ito was silent a moment, then said quietly, "You think it's Rowan, don't you? Something's happened."

"I don't know what to think!" Xris stood up, stomped around the small plane. Then he stopped, glared at nothing. "No, damn it. Whatever personal problems Rowan's got, he wouldn't let them get in the way of his job."

"You said it yourself—he's been acting pretty strange."

Xris didn't respond. He moved back over to stand in front of the comm unit. His fingers itched to touch the controls, call up Armstrong, demand an explanation—Blackjack or no Blackjack.

Not that Armstrong would tell him anything. The controller wasn't there in order to satisfy Xris's curiosity. The controller was in charge of the mission, and what he said went. Xris would only get himself into something deeper and darker than that damn swamp if he started disobeying orders again. Amadi wouldn't go easy on Xris this time. Xris would be stuck behind some desk somewhere. Besides— Xris's common sense took hold—if Armstrong was trying to grapple with an emergency, Xris might jeopardize the whole mission by attempting to reestablish contact.

"Maybe something's gone wrong with the shuttle," Ito said, reassuring. "That's a new type Rowan's flying in, you know."

Xris snorted. "Rowan's as experienced on flight systems as either of us. Maybe more."

"So what do we do?" Ito asked again.

"You heard the man." Xris went outside the plane, grabbed his coveralls, and started to dress. "Rowan's probably on his way. We'll link up outside the munitions facility."

Ten minutes later, both were ready, their equipment

strapped on. They put on earpiece headsets and keyed their data transmission to pass through the commlink on the spaceplane, enabling them to keep in touch with their orbital command vessel. The sky glowed an eerie orange. The gas giant was just setting. They headed for the swamp.

They slogged along side by side. No sign of Rowan. No word from the controller. Judging by Ito's tightly drawn lips and lowering brows, he was thinking the same thing as his partner.

Suddenly Ito came to a halt.

"This isn't right, Xris. We deserve some sort of explanation."

Xris looked up at the sky, instinctively and inanely searching for Rowan in the heavens.

"You know as well as I do that as far as the bureau's concerned, we don't deserve a damn thing outside of our paycheck. But," he added grimly, "you can bet I'm going to have a whole lot of questions to ask once we get aboard *Vigilance*. And the faster we do this, the faster we're back."

The night was much darker than it had been on their first trip to the facility. They could actually see the stars—a rare sight on TISor 13 and one that occurred only when one of the other moons was in position to completely block the light of the planet. The eclipse was one of the reasons Armstrong had chosen this date for their incursion.

The two agents stayed closer together this time, but moved faster. They had been over the ground once already and knew where they were going. Every fifty meters they hunkered down, pulled out their night-vision goggles, and scanned the area. The factory loomed ahead of them. They skirted the trees on the perimeter, heading for the building's back end.

The two slipped slowly and cautiously into the swamp, avoiding any noise. For the better part of fifteen minutes, they slid forward on their bellies, crawling through bottom muck, sliding over fallen trees and rocks.

Xris reached the tree stump closest to the loading dock fence and pulled out his night-vision goggles. Inside the compound, nothing moved; he could detect no heat sources that would indicate a living presence. Something heavy slid across his boot as he knelt in the water. Ito hissed and drew his lasgun. A snakelike creature, over ten meters in length, slithered past. It kept going, but Xris noticed that Ito didn't put his gun away. Xris knew how his partner felt. It wasn't the snakes. Something was wrong.

And still no word from Rowan.

Ito slid closer. Xris lifted his headset to hear.

"The more I think about it, the less sense it makes. We can't do a damn thing without our computer expert. Why don't you call in and request an abort on this one? We're allowed to do that much, even under Blackjack."

Xris toggled the transmitter switch. "Sunray, this is Delta One. Request permission to abort. Javelin has not linked up with this call sign yet."

"This is Sunray. Proceed. Out."

The two stared at each other. Ito shook his head. Cursing under his breath, Xris drew his lasgun, sloshed out of the swamp, and crawled to the fence. Seeing nothing in the compound, he motioned Ito forward.

Ito came slowly, dragging his tool kit bag behind him.

Xris pointed at the fence. He'd tested it yesterday, but he wasn't about to trust anything or anyone, especially now.

Ito pulled out a signal analyzer.

"It's not electrified and it doesn't have any sensor data flowing through it," he reported.

Xris nodded, sprayed neoprene on the section of the fence that he was going to cut. The rubber hardened into a black mass on the fence's metal links. Using laser wire cutters, he cut a hole in the fence large enough for them to pass through. The neoprene prevented the laser from building up a resonance within the wire, possibly setting off a passive sensor somewhere. The rubber also coated the ends of the wire, keeping it from snagging the agents' clothing when they crawled through. In case a quick exit was needed, they didn't want to worry about getting hung up on the fence.

Ito slipped through the hole onto the paved loading area. He ran to the front of a hovertruck that was backed into the dock, and quickly scanned the area. No signs of life. He motioned Xris forward.

Xris slid through the hole in the fence. Once inside the compound, he began inspecting the hovertruck—a basic container carrier, used to offload space containers from shuttles and move them to the factory. The power was shut off. The truck rested on its air-cushion skirts.

After a quick look, Xris again keyed the comm unit and whispered, "Sunray, this is Delta One. We are inside the compound and are preparing to enter the facility. Any further instructions?"

Armstrong's answer was immediate and terse. "This is Sunray. Proceed. Out."

"Sunray, this is Delta One. The area is deserted. We could hold here until Javelin arrives."

"This is Sunray. Proceed. Out."

Something was definitely wrong. Xris took a twist out of its waterproof case in his pocket, stuck the tobacco in his mouth, chewed on it.

"If you decide to pack it in, I'll back you up," Ito said in a low voice.

Xris considered, but not for very long. He and Ito had come too far to quit now. They'd been ordered in by their controller, who knew the situation. They didn't. They'd do the best they could without Rowan. After all, they only needed evidence of a probable Hung alliance with the Corasians in order to start an official investigation. A carelessly written memo might provide that much.

Xris swallowed the remainder of the soggy twist and nodded gloomily. Ito began to move, heading for the access door leading into the building. Xris stopped him.

"The door's probably got an alarm on it. This truck's backed in and sealed into the loading dock. If we go through the cab and cut our way into the cargo container, we should be able to just walk inside. Plus, it'll make this look more like a robbery attempt."

The door to the cab of the hovertruck was unlocked. The two climbed in, crawled over the seats. Ito took out a small cutting laser, opened up a six-inch hole in the back end of the cab. He peered through it into the trailer portion.

"Empty," he reported.

He started to cut a larger hole, but it soon became apparent that this was going to take too much time. Using a spreader clamp, Xris quickly widened the aperture to about a meter.

"You go first and check the truck's back doors. If they're unlocked, open them a crack and scan for movement inside the loading dock."

Ito wormed his upper body through the hole, ripped his gray fatigues on the jagged metal edges. Pausing, he rotated onto his back to gain leverage, dragged his legs through. He landed on the trailer floor and ran to the rear.

The doors were not locked. Ito pushed one side slightly ajar. Taking out his night-vision goggles, he peered into the darkness beyond. He motioned Xris to follow.

Xris was considerably bigger than his partner and had difficulty squeezing through the hole. He decided to go feet-first and was doing fine until he came to his chest and shoulders. For a panicked moment, he thought he might be stuck permanently, but a grunt and a heave bent the metal and propelled him forward, though he left a large amount of fabric and skin on the jagged edges.

Ito waited for him at the back end of the truck. "I figured I might have to leave you here, a little present for the Hung. I was going to tie a red bow around your ankles."

"Very funny," Xris muttered, wincing and rubbing his shoulders. "Shut up and move out."

Inside the loading dock, all was quiet. Maintenance lights cast a pale, sickly yellow glow over the entire area. The two jumped out of the truck, ran for cover behind a row of shipping pallets. Pausing, they looked around, matching their location to that on the mental map each carried inside his head.

The dock was filled with row after row of container pallets. To one side was a small office, probably for the shipping supervisor. At the back of the area was a divider wall, with several sets of double doors. The chemical storage room doors were marked bright yellow, with black warning signs posted on them.

Ito studied his scanner. "All clear."

Xris keyed his commlink.

"Sunray, this is Delta One. We are inside. Over."

"This is Sunray. Proceed. Out."

Ito took the lead. They left the loading dock through the double doors, entered the chemical storage room. It was completely dark. Only the red exit sign on the far side of the room provided any light, and the two padded silently toward it. Xris lit his nuke lamp, flashed it over a set of double doors fitted with electronic sensors.

He glared at it. "Damnation! This wasn't in the plans. Might be some sort of newly installed alarm system."

He could contact the controller, but if it wasn't in Armstrong's original plans, he wasn't likely to know anything about it, either. Rowan would. He could tell from the type of sensors used whether the door was rigged to alert someone on opening or if it was just an ordinary automated door.

Xris whispered, "Okay, Ito, my son, we bust through as fast as we can. You dive right and I'll go left. Got it? Let's move."

The two of them ran. The door started opening. They both sprinted through, dove for cover. Ito crouched behind a drilling machine, his lasgun arcing left and right. Xris was under a table, doing the same.

They saw nothing in the room but machinery gleaming in the yellow glow of the maintenance lights. Ito stood up and started toward the office containing the main computer.

Xris was just sliding out from under the table when suddenly his ears buzzed with static.

He stood up, tapped his comm. Ito was apparently experiencing the same thing, for he turned around, looked at Xris with a puzzled expression on his face.

The static dissipated; the channel went clear. A fear-distorted voice shouted, *"All Deltas! Joker's wild! For God's sake, get out of there! Joker's wild! Joker's wild!"*

"The abort code!" Xris yelled at Ito, who had heard the same and was already moving. "Get the hell out of here!"

But it was too late.

Behind them, in the chemical storage room, a small detonator attached to a storage container filled with refined high explosives triggered its charge.

The explosion hurled Xris backward. He landed under a large table with a laser drill press on it, just as the blast wave struck. The heavy table and machinery crashed down on top of him.

Ito was caught out in the open. The blast ripped him apart. He died instantly, never knowing what hit him.

Xris wasn't so lucky.

He writhed in agony. Blinding white agony . . .
Betrayed.
Fade to gray . . .
Rowan.
Black . . .

CHAPTER
5

We have to distrust each other. It's our only defense against betrayal.

Tennessee Williams, *Camino Real*

"So that's my story," Xris concluded, shifting his good leg into a more comfortable position. He made a conscious effort to appear relaxed, keep his hand—his good hand—from clenching, unclenching. That was his story, all right. Most of it—up to the ending. He left out the part about Rowan's betrayal. "Rowan arrived later in the shuttle, saved my life. He must have. Someone pulled me out of that burning factory—"

"But not Dalin Rowan," said Wiedermann.

Xris's eyes narrowed. The fingers of his good hand twitched.

"In this business," Wiedermann continued, "we are used to our clients lying to us. We expect it. We don't take offense. All part of the job. Dalin Rowan didn't save your life, because Dalin Rowan wasn't there at the time the factory blew up. And the reason Dalin Rowan wasn't there was because he *knew* it was going to blow up. Am I right?"

Xris took out another twist, put it in his mouth. "Go on."

"You spent a year in the hospital having most of your body parts replaced by metal—a god-awful year, if what I've heard about recovery from this sort of procedure is true. When you were finally released, you went home to your wife, but that didn't last long. Your marriage couldn't stand the strain. You walked out on your wife—"

"That has nothing to do with anything," Xris observed coolly.

"The next place you went was FISA, the bureau." Wiedermann either hadn't heard or wasn't interested in the interruption. "They offered you your old job back. But you didn't take it. You turned them down flat. You began asking questions. Questions about Dalin Rowan: Where was he? What had happened to him? What did the bureau tell you?"

Xris hesitated, then said, "According to Armstrong's report, Rowan left in the shuttlecraft. That was the last anyone heard from him. The next thing the bureau knows, one of Warlord DiLuna's ships reports that they received a distress call from *Vigilance* the day of the mission. The Warlord contacted the bureau, waited until they arrived—standard procedure, due to all the classified stuff we handled—then sent out a search-and-rescue team. They found the ship dead in space. *Dead*'s the right word. The crew had been murdered. Most died from asphyxiation—a deliberate air leak. The captain and bridge hands had been shot.

"Only Armstrong was still alive. He was trapped in the control room. He'd been supposed to die in the vacuum, but apparently the air leak triggered some sort of emergency device that shut the blast doors, sealing him up inside. When that happened, he guessed immediately what was going on and gave us the abort code. Too late. He was trapped inside the control room until the search-and-rescue team found him, about twenty-four hours later.

"It was easy to figure out what took place. One of the shuttlecraft was missing. Logs indicated Rowan took it. No one ever saw him again."

"You didn't get a chance to talk to Armstrong personally, did you?"

"No. He was killed shortly after that. Not surprising." Xris grunted. "Those who deal with the Hung have a habit of dying prematurely. But I read his report."

"And you believed it."

"Why the hell shouldn't I?"

"Yes, why shouldn't you? The bureau told you that what you had long suspected was true. Rowan had been on the take. The Hung had bought him. Dalin Rowan let you and your partner walk into that factory, knowing it was going to blow up. He wanted you dead. Why?" Wiedermann shrugged. "Probably figured you had caught on to him. You were going to expose him. That's the reason the bureau gave you, wasn't it?"

Xris didn't respond.

"The bureau claimed that they had been searching for Rowan all this time. No luck. They said he was probably living on some tropical paradise, richer than Snaga Ohme. You said you were going to track Dalin Rowan down if it took you the rest of your life. The bureau was extremely helpful. Extremely. How long did you look for Rowan?"

"A year," Xris answered, chewing on the twist. "Then I ran out of money."

"Find any trace of him?"

Xris shook his head. "It was like he dropped off the edge of the universe."

"In a way, he did," said Wiedermann softly.

Xris's fist clenched. "You *have* found him. Goddammit, you've *found* him!"

Wiedermann shifted his gaze, regarded Xris speculatively, curious to see his reaction to his next statement. "Yes, I found him. The bureau lied to you. They knew where he was all along. They know where he is."

Xris sat very still. LED lights flashed, tiny beeps and clicks ran up and down his cybernetic arm, indicating a systems check. One of the lights flared red instead of the usual yellow and green. Xris made a minor adjustment without thinking about it.

"That doesn't surprise me," he said after a moment. "For someone to disappear that completely, he'd had to have had help. But if he was on the take—"

"All the better. Gave the bureau leverage. Here's what we were able to find out. About nine months after the explosion, while you were in the hospital, the bureau cracked a big case—one of their biggest ever. They broke up the Hung, the largest crime syndicate in the inner part of the galaxy. One of their undercover agents had infiltrated the Hung's organization, raided their computers, probed their files, discovered everything about them. Contacts, bribes to government officials, tax evasion schemes, money laundering, phony corporations, dealings with the Corasians—he found out everything. Not only did this infiltrator raid their files, he made a few 'adjustments,' ruined them financially. That hurt the organization worse than their leaders doing prison time."

"Computers," said Xris. "Rowan."

"Right. He spent months patiently worming his way into the system, burrowing deeper and deeper, crawling through layer after layer. He knew all their secrets, every one. And he used those secrets to bring them down. He spent another couple of months on the witness stand, laying those secrets bare. Two attempts on his life were made during the trial. God knows how many others that were never made public. When the trial was over, Dalin Rowan walked out of the courtroom and was never seen again. The bureau gave him a new identity."

Xris frowned, thinking. "What about Armstrong?"

"Like you, he was trying to track Rowan down. Obviously, he succeeded. He was probably the one who led the agency to Rowan, who was already in bed with the Hung. Nice and convenient."

"And instead of blowing the traitor's head off, the bureau uses him!" Xris took the twist out of his mouth, leaned forward. "What have you got? A name, a planet? That's all I need. Give that to me and we'll call it a deal. I'll take it from here."

"Ah, this is where I enter a moral and legal dilemma," Wiedermann stated sonorously.

"Fuck it!" Xris swore. "I'm paying you enough to get over your moral and legal dilemma. I want to talk to him, that's all."

Wiedermann studied Xris, gazed at him long and intently.

The cyborg could see his own metal body reflected back to him in the detective's pale and watery green eyes.

"Having heard your story, I would say that you are entitled to that much," the detective conceded. "If anything goes amiss—"

"You won't be involved."

"Damn right, we won't be," Wiedermann snapped. "I've already established that you lied to us. Our lawyers have indicated to me that we'll be in the clear—"

"Clear for what? You worried about the bureau? Hell, this was almost nine years ago. We've gone through a major change of government since then. FISA's still around, of course, but I doubt if anyone's left in the department who remembers—"

"*Not* the bureau," said Wiedermann shortly. "I'll bring up the file."

He swiveled in his chair, rolled the chair over to one of the computers, and placed his hands on the keyboard. Data and a blurred picture scrolled rapidly past Xris's vision. A

printer whirred. Hard copy slid out into a tray, including—
Xris could see from his vantage point—a color photograph.
Xris waited with ill-concealed impatience while Wiedermann examined the documents, collated them, tapped them
into neat order on the desk, then handed them over to Xris.

The photograph was on top.

Xris looked at it, looked up at Wiedermann. "Who's
this?"

"Dalin Rowan. Not his real name now, of course."

Xris frowned, eyes narrowed. "What is this? A joke?"

"I never joke."

"Neither do I." Xris rose to his feet. Flinging the photo
and the rest of the data onto the desk, he leaned over it,
leaned into Wiedermann's face. "I paid you—paid you damn
well—to get information for me. As for what I do with that
information, that's none of your goddam business! You—"

"Please, sit down," Wiedermann said.

"Not until you give me my information! The real information!" Xris clamped his metal hand over Wiedermann's collar, bow tie and all, and twisted. The tie crumpled into a
wad. Wiedermann tilted his head back; his Adam's apple
bobbed up over Xris's fingers.

"That *is* the information," Wiedermann croaked, remain-
ing calm. "Read it, if you don't believe me. Frankly, I didn't
believe it myself. But when you think about it—"

Xris let loose, shoved Wiedermann backward. The cyborg
remained standing a moment longer, glaring, deciding what
to do. Slowly, he relapsed back into his chair and, grudg-
ingly, picked up the data, including the photograph. He
looked at it again.

Dalin Rowan had been two meters tall, with dark hair,
slender build, brown eyes, and a wide and infectious smile.
Above all, Dalin Rowan had been a he.

The picture Xris held was of a she.

Most definitely—a she.

"You have to admit," Wiedermann said in admiration,
"it's the ultimate disguise."

CHAPTER

6

On ne naît pas femme: on le devient.
One is not born a woman: one becomes one.
                    Simone de Beauvoir, *Le deuxième sexe*

"Darlene Mohini." Wiedermann had run off his own copy of the data in the file, was reading aloud. "Thirty-six. Unmarried. No children."

Xris snorted.

"She has a very neat little history. All completely phony, of course. Employment record, college transcript. I'm surprised the bureau didn't make her homecoming queen. Her fake history is seamless. Not a gap. As you can see, the bureau was even able to forge a past realistic enough for her to gain her security clearance."

"Rowan did that, not the bureau," Xris muttered.

He stared at the photo. It had been taken by a hidden cam as she was walking down a street. He searched for a trace of his friend beneath the makeup. The jawline, perhaps. The eyes were a possibility. If he could once see that smile . . .

Xris felt slightly dizzy, as if his internal computer system had gone on the blink, screwed up his chemical balance, was feeding him too much juice. He popped open his wrist, did a quick systems analysis. All registered normal.

"A disguise, you said." Xris shifted his gaze to Wiedermann. "Rowan goes around all day dressed up like a woman—"

"Ah, I didn't quite mean 'disguise,' " Wiedermann amended. "He's not merely dressing the part. Or perhaps I should say 'she.' We located the hospital where they performed the surgery."

Xris gaped. "What? You don't mean— Look, a change in identity means that a guy shaves his beard, not his legs! He gets a new driver's license. He doesn't have certain body parts whacked off and others added on!"

Wiedermann said nothing. He merely stared pointedly at Xris's metal arm. The wrist hatch was still open, the various lights blinking, the small computer screen scrolling through its readout on the cyborg's internal workings. Xris, flushing, snapped the hatch shut.

"That's different. This saved my life."

"What's your point?" Wiedermann gestured to the photo. "Dalin Rowan brought down people who were worth billions, ruined them financially, sent them to prison. If there is one person in this entire universe those people hate, it is Dalin Rowan. You think they can't touch him just because they're locked up?"

"All right. Yeah, I know. But still ..." Xris shook his head.

"You—his best friend—didn't recognize him."

Xris paused, thought about that. "You're right. I *wouldn't* have recognized him. Her."

Sure, Dalin Rowan had been worried about the Hung coming after him. But he was probably a lot more worried about someone else coming after him. Someone who'd known him so well ...

Xris stared at the photo. "It's starting to make sense," he admitted. He looked up. "I suppose you've got proof. I wouldn't want to make a mistake."

Wiedermann flipped the papers. "All in here. Including a DNA match—Darlene Mohini equals Dalin Rowan."

"DNA match? How the devil did you get a DNA match?"

Wiedermann grinned. "I understand that you are the leader of a mercenary organization. You do odd jobs for people. People who are—shall we say—high up on the social ladder. It was, in fact, rumored that you once worked for Her Majesty—"

"Okay." Xris raised his hand. "We've all got our professional secrets. Just curious, that's all." He flipped through the data file, found the information on the DNA, read through it twice. Again, he shook his head, said silently, You're a clever bastard, Dalin Rowan. No wonder I ran smack into a brick wall searching for you. But I've got you now, "old friend." I've got you now.

"And then there's the name." Wiedermann was rambling on. "That, to me, was the conclusive proof—from a philosophical standpoint, if you will."

"What about the name? Darlene?" Xris spoke with a slight sneer. "I think Rowan once had a girlfriend named Darlene, but—"

"No, not Darlene. Although the fact that both begin with the letter *d* and have two syllables, with the accent on the first in each case, is suggestive. No, it was the use of the name Mohini which I found significant. Your friend was a scholar, well read?"

Xris shrugged. "College degree. Advanced. Computer science—"

"Perhaps he dabbled in Earth religions such as Hindu? Well, never mind. Not important. According to Hindu legend, the god Shiva was so powerful that the other gods feared if he sank too deeply into meditation, the resulting energy could engulf and destroy the world. Therefore, in order to jolt Shiva from his meditative state, the other gods asked the god Vishnu to distract him. Vishnu did so by adopting the guise of a beautiful woman. Guess what her name was? Mohini." Wiedermann was triumphant. "Interesting, don't you think?"

Interesting. And, yes, damn it, it was like Rowan. Always trying to put some sort of cosmic spin on every ball, whether he sank it or not. Seeing himself as a god. Saving the world. But he'd gone too far. Decided he was above the law; above the ordinary, the little people. Above honor, friendship, loyalty. . . . Yeah, it figured, Xris tried to tell himself.

Except it didn't. Not Rowan.

Xris glared at the file, frustrated. He'd come expecting answers to his questions. More that, really, than expecting to find Rowan. If I could just understand. . . .

"So, you know where he . . . she lives . . . his . . . her place of employment?" Xris found this all very confusing.

"In the file."

The cyborg glanced through, gave a low whistle.

"Now you see my problem," Wiedermann remarked. "I don't give a damn about the bureau. I don't want trouble from the Royal Navy."

"You've got a point," Xris conceded.

Nine years ago, the galaxy had been under the control of powerful Warlords, who had each ruled his or her sector of space with enormous battle cruisers, destroyers, spaceplane carriers, fleets of spaceplanes. Since the return of the king, the Royal Navy was now the most powerful force in the universe—a force to be reckoned with, run by a man Xris knew well. Knew and admired. Lord of the Admiralty, Sir John Dixter.

Xris had worked for both Dion Starfire—now His Majesty the king—and John Dixter in the past. The cyborg tapped the paper with a finger, frowned. He didn't particularly like crossing swords with either Dion or Sir John on this one. Still, it couldn't be helped.

I'll have to be extra careful, that's all.

"Employee of 'RFComSec,' " Xris read. "What the hell is that?"

"Royal Fleet Communications Security Establishment. We're not certain, of course, but we figure it deals with coded transmissions ship-to-ship, and such like. Mohini lives on base in secure accommodations. The base itself is classified, off limits to unauthorized personnel. We couldn't even find out where it was located."

"Ideal," Xris remarked dryly.

"Certainly. Mohini has the entire Royal Navy to protect her. And they probably don't even know they're doing it. As I said, she was able to obtain security clearance. Probably low-level. We couldn't find out precisely what she does. Her job description reads 'CCA-2 FCWing.' "

"Any guesses?"

"Clerical work, maybe. We have no idea what CCA stands for, but a level-two employee—if that's what CCA-2 means—is usually pretty far down on the scale, wouldn't be likely to have top-security clearance, for example."

Rowan, a clerk. Xris tried to imagine him . . . her crunching numbers, tagging files, maybe doing a little programming for variety. . . .

He felt unaccountably sick inside; was almost sorry, at this point, that he'd gone through with this. He chewed the last bit of twist, swallowed the acrid tobacco juice, looked for someplace to deposit the wad. Wiedermann indicated a trash disposer unit on one side of the desk. Xris dumped the wad, picked up his file, prepared to leave. He needed to be out in the fresh air, needed to be by himself, needed to think.

"What do I owe you?"

Wiedermann rose to his feet. He was taller than Xris had

supposed, tall and excessively thin. When the detective stood, his shoulders slumped forward, his chest caved in.

"We'll send you our bill. It was a pleasure working on your case. A real puzzle. Your friend Rowan was clever, very clever. He didn't make many mistakes."

Just one, Xris thought. *He left me alive.*

"Do you know how we finally got on to him?" Wiedermann was prattling on. "His medical insurance forms. They're still on file. By law, you have to keep them on file for a certain number of years. I don't suppose you ever thought of looking at those?"

Xris had no comment, but he made a mental reminder of this slipup. Medical insurance. Why hadn't he thought of that? Probably the same company, the same policy that had covered him, obtained through the bureau. Rowan had never been sick a day in his life, but still . . .

"One of our operatives noticed your friend had been under treatment by a doctor during the trial. Could have been stress; probably what people were told. But in checking through the insurance files, our agent discovered that the doctor was administering a drug at frequent intervals. Except the drug wasn't a stress drug. Hormone shots. Female hormones. They have to inject the hormones several months in advance of the surgery. Swells the breasts, among other changes. Prepares the body *and* the mind, you see."

Xris didn't want to see. He wished Wiedermann would shut up. The cyborg edged his way toward the door.

Wiedermann trailed along behind. "Once we'd gone that far, the rest was easy. Then we ran into the death certificate. A nice touch. Almost stopped us cold."

It stopped Xris. He turned, stared.

"It was in the hospital computer," Wiedermann explained. "Dalin Rowan died on the operating table. Date, time. We nearly lost him there, but I figured out what he must have done. Dalin Rowan died the day Darlene Mohini was born. I knew what to look for and, sure enough, I found it—a woman checking out of that hospital who had never checked in. I included a copy of the death certificate for you. It's in the file. Thought you might be amused."

A death certificate. Rowan had written his own death certificate. Well, maybe that made things easier.

Xris reached the outer office, negotiated his way around the boxes of ancient, forgotten records of ancient, forgotten cases. He and Wiedermann shook hands. Wiedermann's grip was cold and damp, fishlike. Xris didn't prolong the good-byes. He stood outside the closed door. Opening the file, he located the death certificate, stared at it, not really seeing it.

He was back inside that hospital. Back inside the nights, inside the terrible pain. Back inside the days, learning how to walk, talk, see, hear . . . live all over again.

If you could call it living.

He snapped the file shut, was about to continue on his way out of the building when the door popped open.

"Oh, by the way"—Wiedermann peered out—"when you see Darlene Mohini, you might mention that if *we* were able to find her, so could others. Like the Hung. Her cover's blown. She's in real danger. You'll be sure to tell her that, won't you?"

"Yeah," said Xris, shifting the file to his cybernetic hand, getting a secure grip on it. "I'll be sure to tell her."

CHAPTER
7

The Way means inducing the people to have the
same aim as the leadership, so that they will share
death and share life, without fear of danger.
                    Sun Tzu, *The Art of War*

The large, private spacegoing vessel left Laskar at a leisurely speed. The ship—a typical research model, known
as *Canis Major Research I*—was not supposed to be
equipped to make the jump to hyperspace. Such modifica-
tions to university research ships were extremely expensive,
generally unnecessary, and would have excited comment, required the need for explanations. As it was, the killers were
able to slip off Laskar quietly, orbital-traffic control giving
them bored clearance.

Inside a small room on board the ship, one of the four
men—the one who had murdered Bosk—sat in front of a
computer terminal. He was working on the terminal and at
the same time speaking into a commlink. He stopped both
when the hatch slid open and one of his subordinates entered.

"Knight Officer. I've monitored Laskar's evening news,
sir."

"Yes, and—?"

"The fire destroyed the building completely. A single
body was discovered in the wreckage. The body was burned
beyond recognition, but only one tenant remains unac-
counted for and it is presumed that the body is that of an
Adonian known as Bosk. The fire was suspicious in origin,
believed to have started in the apartment of the dead man.
He was known to have ties with the mob. Neighbors reported that four men—armed—paid the deceased a visit

shortly before the fire broke out. They described the vehicle the suspects were driving. It was discovered abandoned a short time later, stripped and burned."

"The local authorities are satisfied that it was the mob?"

"Yes, sir."

"Case closed, then."

"I would say so. Yes, sir. The Laskar police will not get involved in mob business."

"Very good. Tell Knight Officer Captain he may depart when ready."

The subordinate nodded, departed.

The leader returned to work.

"You heard his report, Knight Commander?" the leader asked over the comm.

"Satisfactory. Continue. What is it you have found?"

The voice at the other end of the commlink was laconic, crisp, and obviously belonged to a machine. The speaker entered his or her words into the computer, the computer spoke them aloud. No one, not even the highest-ranking officer of the knighthood—of which Bosk's killer was one—ever heard the Knight Commander's voice. No one had ever seen the Knight Commander. No one knew his or her real name. All information was exchanged via commlink—voice only.

"Contrary to initial reports, Commander, it appears from Ohme's files that he actually constructed a working model of the negative wave device."

"Indeed."

"The device was crude, apparently, but operational. Ohme's records indicate that he performed a test on a living subject. And that the test was successful."

"A living subject." Knight Commander mused. "How is this possible? He wouldn't have dared test it on Derek Sagan. And if I'm not mistaken, there were no other Blood Royal known to exist at the time."

"That is true, Commander. This was just prior to Sagan's discovery of the whereabouts of the young king. Snaga Ohme did not have a Blood Royal on which to test his device, but that presented no problem for him. He couldn't find a true Blood Royal and so he created one. If you will recall, sir, Ohme had an extensive collection of weapons dating back to ancient times. Appropriate for a weapons dealer.

"Among his collection was a bloodsword. According to the notation in Ohme's catalog, the bloodsword was obtained during the Revolution, when most of the Blood Royal were eradicated. Inside this sword are the micromachines that are injected into the body of the Blood Royal when they insert the sword's needles into their hands. These micromachines connect the body and brain with the sword and are used to activate both the sword and its shielding device. A certain amount of these micromachines remain in the bloodstream and are activated every time the sword is used.

"Ohme removed the fluid containing these micromachines from the bloodsword and injected that fluid into his test subject. He then used the newly created negative wave device on the subject and recorded the results."

"Was the subject aware he or she was being used for such purposes?"

"According to Ohme's account, no, the subject was not aware. Ohme feared that the subject's awareness might influence the test results."

"He was probably right. Did the subject die?"

"No, Commander. Ohme didn't want to kill the subject, who might prove useful to him later. Ohme wanted to study the effects of the device on the micromachines in the subject's bloodstream."

"How did Ohme manage to keep such an experiment on the subject secret?" The mechanical voice held no inflection, but the officer could discern that his superior was skeptical.

"The subject was a male, in his late twenties, and, according to the record, a Loti."

"Slang term for habitual drug user, if I'm not mistaken?"

"Yes, Knight Commander."

"An expression that has its roots on Earth. The fruit of the lotus or *lotophagi,* as the Greeks termed it, was supposed to induce in those who ate it a state of dreamy forgetfulness, a loss of desire to return home. One might almost consider the entire human race as lotus-eaters. But they will remember their home." The voice was soft, ominous. "We will make them remember."

A pause, then the voice returned to business. "Surely such a heavy drug user as a Loti would be an inappropriate candidate for testing?"

"Ohme recognized this problem, sir, but determined that the drugs in the subject's system would have no influence on the micromachines and vice versa. It appears, from my preliminary investigation of the files, that Ohme was correct."

The Knight Commander was not convinced. "Ohme was a genius, there is no doubt about that, but he did not possess the patience and meticulous mind of a good researcher. He obviously chose this Loti because the man was convenient and not liable to ask questions. However, we must work with what we have. What were the results of his experiment?"

"Unfortunately, Commander, the exact results of the test are not recorded in the files. The last entry is dated the day on which Ohme was murdered. It reads, 'The experiment has been highly successful.' Nothing more. Bosk makes some attempt to fill in the experiment's results, but he was not in Ohme's complete confidence. Careful analysis proves that Bosk knew very little; most of what he added was mere speculation gained from observing the test subject, who lived and worked in Ohme's mansion."

Silence from the commlink. Then, "There is nothing more?"

"No, Knight Commander."

"Are you certain, Knight Officer?"

"Yes, sir."

"Damn!" said the Commander. "We need more information!"

Silence. The Knight Officer, having nothing further to contribute, maintained disciplined quiet. He made no suggestion as to their next course of action, would make none unless he was asked. Looking out the viewscreen, he watched the planet Laskar dwindle to a small green marble.

A wretched planet, corrupt, vile, he thought. But really no different from countless others in the galaxy. Humanity trashes its home, flees it, seeks out others, and ends up destroying them. It is only a matter of time before it will all end out here. Then the swarm of humanity will turn their faces homeward again. Then they will come to us and say humbly, "We are sorry." . . .

"It would be extremely valuable to us"—the Commander spoke suddenly and abruptly, startling the Knight Officer—"if we could get our hands on the test subject."

"Yes, Commander." The officer brought up the file containing information on the Loti. "Bosk had the same idea, apparently. He began to search for the man, but only in the most desultory and haphazard fashion. He soon gave up. The subject is an Adonian, as was Snaga Ohme. You are familiar with the Adonians, Commander?"

"A degenerate race of people who live solely for their own pleasure and gratification. Intelligent, charming, and completely amoral. Ohme was typical of his breed. I suppose this Loti is another?"

"A hired assassin, Commander. Specializing in chemical poisonings, as one might expect from someone who is dependent on chemicals. Ohme kept this Loti around to perform 'odd' jobs now and then. Ohme surrounded himself with his fellow Adonians. Bosk was another."

"As a race, Adonians are extremely attractive—the men *and* the women. Snaga Ohme could not stand to be long in the presence of an ugly person. The only thing that overcame his squeamishness on this point was money. Continue, Knight Officer."

"Yes, sir. This Loti had other advantages. He is firm friends—has an almost symbiotic relationship—with an empath."

"Not unusual," remarked the Commander. "Empaths enjoy being around Loti because their drug-induced tranquillity is rarely disturbed and thus the empath is not subject to disturbing emotions."

"The two were rarely apart, according to Ohme's notes. The Loti is the only one who can understand the empath. He acted as a sort of translator whenever Ohme needed to know what someone was thinking or feeling."

"What race is the empath?"

"Bosk claims no one knows. The empath was always cloaked in some sort of disguise. No one ever saw the face. Ohme had no interest in trying to find out."

"So long as the empath proved useful, Snaga Ohme wouldn't care."

"On studying the empath's description, Commander, I think it probable that we are dealing with a Tongan."

The Knight Commander was silent again.

"I have examined all the facts, Knight Commander. The empath is extremely short in stature. He is always disguised, which indicates that there is something unusual about his features or his body, and the Tongans as a race are as ugly as the Adonians are beautiful. He appears to have not only empathic abilities but telepathic abilities as well. Tongans are the only race to meet all these requirements."

"You know, of course, Knight Officer, that Tongans are forbidden on pain of death from leaving their home world?"

"All the more reason for the disguise, sir."

"Perhaps you are right. At any rate, such an unusual pair would be fairly easy to track."

"Bosk had no difficulty, at first. He and the Loti kept in contact. Both of them were eager to avenge Ohme's death. But whereas Bosk had determined that Ohme was murdered by Derek Sagan, the Loti was following a different theory. He was convinced that the murderer was a man known as Abdiel. Following this theory, the Loti worked in the Exile Café on Hell's Outpost, figuring that either Abdiel or someone who knew the old man's whereabouts must come to this place eventually. The last message Bosk received from him, the Loti was joining up with the late Lady Maigrey Morianna. They planned on entering the Corasian system—"

"So," said the Knight Commander, "the Loti was part of that small band of heroes. His Majesty owes both his throne and his life to them. Their leader was a cyborg—a rather unusual cyborg, as I recall."

"I have no information on that, sir," the officer admitted.

He was not surprised that these facts were known to the commander. The Knight Commander knew every prominent and/or infamous person in the galaxy; he was familiar with the political situations on innumerable major planets; he was privy to knowledge not readily accessible to ordinary citizens of the realm. Once, when the officer had first joined up with the organization, he had used such clues in an attempt to puzzle out the Knight Commander's true identity. That had been almost twenty years ago. Now the officer—a true fanatic—no longer knew or cared. He revered. And obeyed.

"No further information beyond that?"

"No, sir. Bosk indicates that he never heard from the Loti again and that attempts to find him proved beyond his means."

"I believe I know where to look. Return to home base, Knight Officer. Proceed with the construction of the negative wave device and await my commands. When the whereabouts of this Loti are discovered, you will be informed."

"Yes, Knight Commander."

"What is the Loti's name, by the way?"

"Raoul, sir. And the empath is known as the Little One."

"Raoul and the Little One," repeated the Knight Commander. "Yes, it is them. They are members of a mercenary team called Mag Force 7. Their leader is a cyborg known as Xris."

CHAPTER 8

. . . and, lips, O you
The doors of breath, seal with a righteous kiss
A dateless bargain to engrossing death!

William Shakespeare, *Romeo and Juliet*, Act 5,
Scene 3

The two minor government officials stood in the waiting area of the Modena Spaceport, looking up at a terminal displaying the arrival time for incoming flights. The time had not varied in the last thirty minutes—the transport would be half an hour late—but the officials continued to check it just the same, both of them acutely aware of the man in the dark suit. Leaning comfortably against a nearby pillar, he scanned intently the people gliding past on the moving sidewalk.

"What's he looking at *them* for?" the woman irritably asked her companion. "*We're* the ones he's following."

"Probably viewing them as targets on the shooting range," returned the man. "Look at the way he's smiling."

The woman shivered. "Don't. This is bad enough. Do you think he suspects us?"

The man considered. "No. We're only doing our job, after all. Meeting the ambassador from Adonia. I don't much like this scheme, but the cyborg is said to be one of the best in the business. We have to put our faith in someone."

"More than our faith. Our very lives!" The woman swallowed, put her hand to her throat. "I . . . I think I'll go to the restroom."

The man in the dark suit shifted his gaze to the woman, watched her enter, watched her return.

"He kept an eye on you," her companion muttered beneath his breath. "No, don't look. He's still watching."

"I can't stand this," the woman said. "I—"

She was interrupted by the arrival of a flight attendant. "Pardon me, sir, madam, are either of you booked for this flight?"

"We're meeting someone," the woman replied.

The attendant nodded, relieved. "I was afraid you were passengers. You've no idea what a nightmare we go through now. All the forms that have to be filled out. Checking documents. Not that I'm complaining, mind you," the attendant added hastily. "I am in complete agreement with the government's new regulations concerning civilian travel restrictions. It's just—"

The arrival of the transport saved the attendant from further indiscretions. She hurried off to unlock the door, admit the disembarking passengers, of which there were very few. The drab, unhappy world of Modena was not a pleasant place to visit these days.

"How do you suppose we'll recognize him?" the woman asked.

"I don't believe we'll have much trouble," the man answered dryly. "He's an Adonian, after all."

They had absolutely no trouble recognizing him.

It was rather as if the full color spectrum had just breezed in by transport and, on arrival, blown up. The Adonian was dressed in a tight, form-fitting jumpsuit colored a deep royal blue. Over this he wore a floor-length vest made of garish, rainbow-hued silk that billowed out behind him when he walked, revealing purple socks and emerald shoes. The sight was actually a shock to the central nervous system of the conservative Modenans. The two government officials, stunned by the impact, were momentarily unable to move.

The Adonian, seeing no one else in the vicinity and assuming, therefore, that these people must be waiting for him, flung himself in their direction and exploded in their midst.

"I assume that you must be waiting for me," he cried, smiling. "I am extraordinarily delighted to make your acquaintances."

The Adonian, with a graceful gesture of his hands, flipped

long black hair over his shoulders and gave everyone in the vicinity his charming smile.

"M-Mr. Ambassador." The man gave the formal greeting, though he was somewhat hesitant about it. Perhaps he was wondering uneasily if the appellation "Mister" was entirely correct.

"Your Excellency." The woman avoided the gender problem neatly by using a title acceptable to any sex. "Welcome to Modena."

The two bowed.

The ambassador was an Adonian male—at least that's the sex his passport claimed. His appearance raised cause for doubt, but the fact that he was an Adonian explained everything. Like most of his people, he was, quite literally, an extraordinarily beautiful human being. He was slender, of shapely build, with delicate bone structure and a lilting, mincing walk. His hair was waist-long and gleaming black. His eyes were large and lustrous—too lustrous. Close examination revealed them to be slightly unfocused, the pupils abnormally dilated. He swayed slightly, as though in a gentle wind, and gazed about him with vague, happy curiosity.

The man and woman exchanged glances. "He's on drugs," the man said out of the corner of his mouth, speaking Modenan. "A Loti!"

"What do we do now?" the woman demanded. "I thought you said this mercenary force was reliable!"

"We can't do anything *here*," the man returned grimly, with a sidelong glance at the man in the dark suit, who was staring with fixed interest at the new arrival.

"Thank you," said the Adonian suddenly. "I have landed safely and soundly on your fair planet. Your welcome is most gratifying. I consider this a fortuitous omen of future friendship between our peoples."

He extended a hand. The fingernails were long and polished; the fingers glittered with jeweled rings.

The man took the hand, but was totally at a loss as to what to do with it, since the hand's owner did nothing with it himself. Perplexed, the man transferred the flaccid hand to the woman, who returned the hand to the ambassador as quickly as possible. The sweet, pungent scent of gardenia enveloped them.

"I am Dolf Baejling, aide to the undersecretary of Foreign

Affairs of Modena. This is my associate, Mary Krammes. And now, Mr. Ambassador—" the man began.

"Raoul de Beausoleil," said the ambassador lightly. "Please call me Raoul, Dolf. Everyone does."

"I . . . I hardly believe that would be respectful, *Mr.* Ambassador," said Baejling, frowning.

"Respectful?" Raoul gave the matter brief thought. "I don't quite understand how you can come to respect me on such short acquaintance, Dolf, and I certainly have no respect for you. So we might as well be on a first-name basis, shouldn't we?"

Baejling frowned, insulted. Krammes laid her hand on his arm. "I don't believe he meant that quite the way it came out. We're being watched."

After an inner struggle and a surreptitious glance at the man in the dark suit, Baejling managed a grudging smile. He was about to suggest that they retrieve the ambassador's luggage when Krammes—nudging him—indicated a small and strange-looking personage who had apparently been standing close to Raoul the entire time but was only at this moment visible, due to the settling folds of silk.

"I beg your pardon, Excellency," Krammes said faintly, "but what—I mean, who is . . . what is . . ."

Raoul stared at the woman a moment as if endeavoring to remember where he'd seen her before, then—looking in the direction she was looking—he smiled.

"Ah, I beg your pardon." He waved his hand. "The Little One. My constant companion. He is with me. *Always.*"

It was impossible to determine the Little One's species, race, or anything about the creature, much beyond the fact that it was, apparently, alive. The Little One said nothing. He kept his hands—if he had hands—in the cadaverous pockets of an oversized raincoat. The turned-up collar hid the lower part of the creature's face, the fedora hat hid the upper. All anyone could see of the Little One were two bright and penetrating eyes, gazing solemnly out from the shadow cast by the hat.

"How . . . how do you do?" Krammes said, not quite knowing how to address the apparition.

The Little One gazed unblinking at the two.

Krammes gulped. Baejling made a snorting sound and the two exchanged alarmed glances. The ambassador, meanwhile, was studying the spaceport with languid curiosity.

But when Raoul turned to Baejling, the aide was disconcerted to note that the Loti's eyes were not quite as lustrous and unfocused as Baejling had first supposed.

"Remarkably empty for such a large planet, isn't it, Dolf?" Raoul observed. "Your people don't indulge in spaceflight, I take it."

Baejling glanced at the rows of empty plastic chairs, the nearly deserted hallways, the closed restaurants and shutdown vendors' stalls. The few people who were in the spaceport walked swiftly and kept their eyes on the ground, as if by refusing to acknowledge anyone else's presence they could successfully hide their own.

"Off-world travel's restricted, Excellency." Baejling spoke carefully, mindful of the man in the dark suit. "Our government believes that the people of Modena have no need to leave their home world."

"Isn't that marvelous," said Raoul, struck by the notion. "How very . . . domestic."

Baejling's frown deepened. He cleared his throat, looked hopefully at the open door leading to the spaceplane.

"The other members of your party—" Dolf began.

"We're it," Raoul said cheerfully.

Baejling protested. "We were expecting a colleague of yours. A cyborg . . ."

"I beg your pardon, Dolf? You spoke so softly, I failed to catch most of what you said." Raoul leaned near. Gardenia fragrance rolled off him.

Baejling coughed. "A man named Xris."

"Ah!" Light dawned. "You are referring, no doubt, to Xris Cyborg. He was not able to come. He is otherwise engaged. He sent us instead." Raoul gave his diminutive friend a tap on the fedora. "We are sufficient for the task."

Dolf Baejling did not exude confidence at this statement. Mary Krammes sighed, glanced sideways at the man in the dark suit, twisted her hands together. Raoul bent down gracefully to confer with his companion, though not a word was spoken. Raoul straightened, with a jangle of bracelets.

"Pardon me for mentioning this, Dolf. As I am unfamiliar with the local customs, what I am about to question may be nothing more than Modenan curiosity, but the Little One informs me that the gentleman standing over by that pillar is taking a great deal of interest in us."

Baejling did not even bother to look. "He is one of our respected secret police," he said in a careful monotone. "The government of Modena takes very good care of its citizens. He is here to ensure our safety as well as yours, Mr. Ambassador."

"My safety? Are you certain?" Raoul asked, touched. "I must say, that is very kind of him. And he *is* rather attractive, in a thuggish sort of way."

"The secret police are extremely interested in everything that the people do," Dolf said meaningfully, hoping Raoul would take the hint. "They accompany us . . . everywhere. Now if you would—"

But Raoul was not to be deterred. He gazed steadfastly at the man in the dark suit. "He's not all that 'secret,' is he? For secret police, I mean. I thought those fellows usually hid in luggage bins, popped out at you from dark alleyways."

"Be careful what you say!" Mary Krammes whispered, clutching Raoul's arm. "He and his kind run the country now. They can do what they want. They have only to answer to *her.*"

"Her?" Raoul was intrigued. "Who is her?"

The Little One shuffled his feet, tugged on the silken folds of the vest. Raoul glanced down, listened, then nodded. "Ah, yes. Madame President."

"Damn it, keep your voice down!" Dolf cautioned angrily. He paused a moment to regain control, then said stiffly, "If you would excuse us, Excellency, I need to confer a moment with my colleague. I fear that a problem has arisen in regard to your hotel suite."

Raoul gave gracious assent. Baejling drew Krammes to one side. The two began to talk in an undertone in their own language.

Casting an interested glance at the man in the dark suit, Raoul smoothed his hair, fluttered his eyelids. Then he redistributed the bracelets on his arm, sliding three up above the elbow, four below. Not liking the effect, he moved the third back down below the elbow again. This accomplished, he opened a velvet drawstring bag he carried on his wrist, drew out a mirror, studied his own reflection.

Running the tip of his little finger around his lips in order to repair minute smudging of his lipstick, he said to the Little One, "What are they discussing?"

No one was quite certain how Raoul and the Little One communicated. So far as anyone knew, Adonians did not possess telepathic abilities. Telepaths tended to emerge from races noted for their well-developed sensitivity to the feelings of others. No one had ever accused the Adonians of such a characteristic, the Adonians being notable galaxy-wide for their almost complete and total self-absorption. How these two talked was, therefore, a mystery.

While Raoul sometimes spoke to the Little One aloud, the Little One was never heard to speak to Raoul, or to anyone else, for that matter. Only Raoul could understand and interpret what the Little One said, and how Raoul managed to do that was beyond the ability of everyone—including the leader of Mag Force 7, Xris—to figure out.

The two had been part of Xris's elite commando team for almost four years now. Xris theorized that the mind-altering drugs taken by the Loti had somehow made Raoul susceptible to the Little One's thoughts. This was the only explanation for the phenomenon—that and the fact that the two had formed an unusual and exceedingly strong bond.

"Isn't that interesting?" Raoul murmured in response to his partner's silent flow of information. "Dolf wants to send us packing. He doesn't trust us, doesn't believe we're capable of carrying out the contract. If we bungle the job, he fears that he and the woman will be arrested, probably killed. The Krammes woman reminds him that to get rid of us now would look extremely suspicious. How would they explain the fact that the Adonian ambassador suddenly changed his mind about establishing diplomatic ties with the Modenan government and went home? Xris Cyborg will not be pleased if they break the contract. Yes, I suppose we would get to keep the deposit. . . ."

Raoul brushed back an errant strand of hair that had fallen over his face.

"Here they come," he said quietly. "Have they reached a decision?"

The Little One gave a violent nod which caused the fedora to slip down over his eyes.

The two returned. Baejling was breathing heavily, gave the appearance of a man who has been in an argument and lost. Mary Krammes was pale and tight-lipped. She had triumphed, but was obviously having second thoughts.

"Thank you for your patience, Mr. Ambassador. We will escort you to your hotel. Your luggage will be sent over. If you and your ... uh ... companion would accompany us to the car ..."

"Is the hotel far from here, Dolf?" Raoul continued admiring his own reflection in the mirror. "Within walking distance?"

"Yes, Excellency," Baejling answered cautiously, wondering what new weirdness was about to be perpetrated. "But the car is quite comfortable—"

Snapping shut his mirror, Raoul returned it to the velvet bag. "My companion and I would prefer to walk, Dolf, dear, if that does not discommode you. We would love seeing the sights of your fair city. I had so little exercise on the flight over. I must have gained a kilo at least. Walking keeps the calves shapely, did you know that?"

Raoul took Baejling's arm—though it had not been offered—and drew the man close. Baejling flinched, choked in the gardenia fumes, but he couldn't very well insult the Adonian ambassador.

"Besides," Raoul continued languidly, "this cozy walk will give us a chance to get to know each other better. I have heard rumors to the effect that the hotels on Modena are crawling with *bugs*."

Baejling stiffened. "I assure you, Excellency, that you are being accorded the finest accommodations—" He stopped suddenly, gave the Loti a penetrating look. "Ah, I ... um ... believe it would be a fine day for a walk. I must warn you, though, that the traffic noise is terrible. It's sometimes difficult to hear yourself think. You see, Excellency," he added, "everyone walks this time of day. Everyone." He cast a significant glance at the man in the dark suit.

Raoul lifted a plucked eyebrow, smiled. "Perhaps I can be of some assistance."

Baejling looked alarmed. "I don't think that would be wise—"

Raoul ignored him. Releasing Baejling's arm, the Adonian walked rapidly on ahead, his high heels tapping the floor, the silken vest flowing behind him like gaudy butterfly wings. The Little One ambled along after, occasionally tripping over the long hem of his raincoat. Baejling and Krammes, slow off the mark, hastened to catch up.

The man in the dark suit saw the group leaving. He prepared to follow, was suddenly intercepted by Raoul. The

Adonian veered, turned, and walked right up to the policeman, who was staring at him in astonishment.

Krammes went white. Baejling swore under his breath.

"What the devil is that whacked-out Loti doing?"

One hand on his hip, Raoul let his painted eyes rove over
the policeman's body, starting with the head, moving linger-
ingly down, gliding back up. The policeman flushed an ugly
and embarrassed red.

"Here, now—" he began roughly.

"Don't be coy. I saw you watching me." Raoul gave the
man a simpering wink. Reaching into the velvet bag, he
drew out a gold case, flipped it open. "My card."

The policeman gave the card a cold stare.

Not the least disconcerted, Raoul tucked the card into the
man's suit pocket, gave the pocket a caressing pat. He gazed
up at the man through provocatively lowered eyelids. "I'm
staying at the Grand Modenan Hotel, near the presidential
palace. Ask for my room number at the desk. I'll be in . . .
all night."

Pursing his lips, Raoul kissed the air between the two of
them, favored the policeman with a melting smile, turned,
and strolled off to rejoin the astounded Baejling.

"It is my considered opinion that the gentleman will no
longer follow us," Raoul said gravely.

The policeman did *not* follow them from the spaceport.
But, as Dolf mentioned grimly, that meant little. The police
undoubtedly had backup agents in place.

"They're keeping an eye on us because we're meeting
with an off-worlder. Although"—Mary Krammes managed a
smile for the first time since Raoul had met her—"I imagine
that they no longer consider you and your companion much
of a threat."

The four were seated in an outdoor café located along one
of the tree-lined boulevards of the capital city of Modena.
The volume of traffic along the major streets was heavy. The
air was filled with the screech of brakes and the honking of
horns. Modenans still drove wheeled vehicles, since hovercraft were banned in the city proper, with the exception of
the police, whose streamlined vehicles could be seen whiz-
zing above the congested streets, sirens adding to the din.
Unaccustomed to the smell emitted by gas-powered autos,
Raoul held a scented handkerchief to his nose and refused

all food. The location had one advantage. No one could overhear their conversation. They could barely hear each other.

"This woman, Madame President, is a monster," Dolf was explaining. "Our President is a good man. Probably too good. That's how she was able to get her clutches into him. He met her shortly after he was elected to office. All of us saw what she was after. But he was blind, poor fool. He was in his fifties, unmarried. One of those scholarly types who just never seemed to get around to relationships. She's in her thirties, intelligent, charming—"

"Beautiful," Mary Krammes added.

"Yes, she's beautiful." Dolf shook his head. "And deadly. She married him, and almost the very next day she was grabbing the reins of power. She had her organization already in place, ready to move. She put her people in top-level positions—Ministry of Defense, Law Enforcement, Justice Department. She either bought off the right senators or blackmailed them. Those who denounced her simply disappeared. Now the senate tamely approves all her new legislation.

"You've seen the result of the travel restrictions for yourself. She's shut down all vid stations, closed up all the newsmags who opposed her. Those who spoke out were arrested. We've heard rumors of concentration camps, mass grave sites. Entire families have disappeared; their relatives don't dare ask about them for fear they'll be next. Something's got to be done.

"She's surrounded by bodyguards, of course. She travels in an armored car, when she travels at all, which isn't much. She has to keep her claws in her husband."

"He's a wreck," Mary added sadly. "Poor man. He was a fool, but he's paying for his folly now. You hardly ever see him in public. She makes him appear on occasion and then he's a puppet, dancing to her piping. He never opens his mouth but that he looks to her for approval."

Raoul attempted to appear deeply interested and profoundly sympathetic, but his gaze wandered. He stared at the trees, the flowers, the drab people walking by—all of whom returned the favor by staring hard and suspiciously at the colorful Adonian. Finally, when this occupation grew tiresome, he sneezed, dabbed his nose with the handkerchief, and stifled a yawn.

"Pardon me," Dolf said irritably, "but have you been listening to anything we've said?"

"Frankly, no, Dolf," Raoul returned languidly, blinking his mauve-colored eyelids. He fluttered a delicate hand. "Why should I? You have hired the Little One and myself to murder the wife of your president."

"Good God, man!" Baejling paled. "Keep your voice—"

"Bah! No one can hear us. You have a guilty conscience, that's all. Which is why you are taking all this time and trouble to explain to me and my companion your own justifications and motivations. Personally I don't give a damn about you or your country or your problems. And neither does the Little One. Why should we?"

The raincoated figure indicated, with a shake of the fedora, that such was the case.

Mary Krammes stared into her empty wineglass. Dolf Baejling took out a neatly folded handkerchief, toyed with it.

"I suppose you're right. It's just that I've never done . . . I've never even imagined . . ." He mopped his sweating forehead.

"It's for the good of the country," Mary Krammes said automatically as if she'd been repeating the words over and over again, even in her sleep. "That woman's death is for the good of the country."

Raoul shrugged. "Of course, that is what all traitors have said, since the beginning of time."

Baejling rose stiffly to his feet. "We should proceed to the hotel, Excellency. Tonight is the Embassy Ball. You will be formally introduced and presented to the President and Madame President. You can meet her, get a good look at her. Tomorrow you deliver your letters of mark—"

"All forged, you know. Quite a good job. We have a member of our team. His name is Tycho. He—"

"Tomorrow." Baejling hung on grimly. "You will proceed to the palace tomorrow—"

"Oh, we won't be staying that long," Raoul said complacently.

Baejling sat back down again.

"What? But—How? Surely you're not thinking of"— Baejling swallowed, lowered his voice to a hoarse whisper—"assassinating Madame President during the ball!

She'll be surrounded by bodyguards! Her supporters. They'd catch you. We'd all be shot on the spot!"

Raoul gazed at Baejling long moments. The Loti's drug-fuzzy eyes slid into focus, became fixed and cool, without pity, without compassion.

"I am an expert at my work. The Little One is an expert at his. You either trust us and allow us to proceed as we think right or you terminate our employment this moment."

Baejling looked sick. Mary Krammes, white to her lips, said something to him in her own language. He nodded heavily, wiped the handkerchief over his head again. Lifting his previously untouched wineglass, he downed the drink at a gulp.

Raoul glanced out of the corner of his eye at the Little One. The Adonian's eyelashes flickered. He smiled serenely. "Well, what will it be, Dolf, dear?"

Baejling's hands clenched into fists. "Do it," he said harshly.

"Is . . . is there anything you need . . . from us?" Mary Krammes asked faintly.

"No, Mary, darling, thank you," Raoul said. "We have everything we need. However, I assume that you two will be in attendance?"

"Yes. Yes, of course."

"Good. And now, I do believe that we should be proceeding to the hotel. This beastly smell is giving me a pounding headache. And headaches cause wrinkles. As does stress. You should really do something about that, Dolf. Those frown lines around your mouth—most unattractive. I could give you some cream I found on Avedai Arden. Oil of cucumber. Rub it in three times daily. . . ."

Raoul took hold of Baejling's arm, sauntered off, talking of his favorite subject next to clothes—cosmetics. The Little One shambled after, small legs forced to take two steps to the humans' one. His shoulders, beneath the raincoat, heaved up and down.

Mary Krammes, hurrying along fearfully behind, wondered if the strange little creature was laughing.

The Embassy Ball was a glittering affair, held in the Grand Ballroom of the Presidential Palace. Men and women, dressed in their very finest, most elegant clothes, drank champagne and ate small, fancifully decorated and bland tidbits, which were being circulated throughout the ballroom by tall, fancifully dressed waiters. Since all present knew that the waiters were spies for the secret police, the conversation among the guests tended—like the food—to be elaborate and innocuous.

Talk picked up considerably with the arrival of the Ambassador from Adonia. Raoul was in full regalia; he might have gone onstage as the Sun God or even a sun itself. He was dressed all in gold, from a rayed golden headdress, to golden doublet and knee breeches and hose, to golden slippers—low-heeled, since he might possibly be going into action. Every centimeter was crusted with golden bangles and/or sequins. His eyelids were painted with gold and he wore metallic gold lipstick, of which he was evidently worried about smudging, for he kept his lips always slightly apart, was careful never to bite them or pass his tongue over them.

The Little One, trundling along at Raoul's side, wore the same raincoat and hat—a small and shabby satellite orbiting a gorgeous sun.

The majordomo pounded his staff on the polished marble floor, made his sonorous announcement. "His Excellency, the Ambassador of Adonia."

Raoul extended a shapely, gartered leg, bowed low, sweeping a large feathered fan across his body. Rising to what he assumed were admiring murmurs from the audience, he glanced about vaguely, accosted a passing footman, who indicated the reception line, where the President and his wife and other dignitaries waited to greet their arriving guests.

Raoul floated that direction, spreading charming smiles and clouds of lilac perfume. He passed down the line, blithely ignoring the cold and withering stares of the ministers of Defense and Morality. He gave the men what passed for an Adonian handshake—dabbling his fingers lightly in the palm. With the women, he brought their hands near his lips but never bestowed a kiss on any of them, undoubtedly to protect his flawless lipstick.

But, when introduced to Madame President, Raoul behaved quite differently. Awed by her beauty, he murmured a few words of polite and correct greeting, then actually deigned to press his golden-coated lips against the skin of her extended hand.

Madame President found this all highly amusing. She

made a polite response to Raoul, then, switching off her translator with a feigned, casual gesture, she said something to her husband having to do with "fairies and fags." All of which the Little One passed on to Raoul.

Raoul, smiling coyly, advanced to pay his respects to the President. The Adonian ambassador was apparently not all that impressed with Mr. President, who was shriveled and shrunken, a withered husk covered by wrinkled skin. Raoul, gazing at the man, speculated seriously on vampirism in modern times.

Madame President, meanwhile, was delightedly and laughingly exhibiting to her neighbors the gold lipstick impression left on her skin. She would, she claimed loudly, never wash this hand again. Her comments drew polite laughter from all those within hearing distance, as well as from those who could not possibly have heard but considered it politic to laugh anyway.

Raoul wended his way through the crowd. He discovered Baejling and Krammes huddled together in a distant corner of the gigantic ballroom, attempting to appear nonchalant and comfortable, with the result that both managed to look extremely suspicious.

"Ah, here you are!" Raoul sang out loudly. "I've been searching for you everywhere. Don't kiss me, either of you. You'll muss me."

"What the devil are you doing?" Baejling demanded in a furious undertone. "You're drawing everyone's attention to us—"

"There's something I must tell you," Raoul whispered, adding loudly, with an admiring glance, "You're right about one thing, Dolf. Madame President is a remarkably beautiful woman." He gave a rapturous sigh. "I'm quite smitten. Is my lipstick smudged, Dolf?"

Baejling gave him a disgusted glance, started to turn away. Krammes tugged on her partner's sleeve. Several of the waiters were eyeing them closely.

Raoul removed his mirror from a gold lamé shoulder purse, studied himself critically. "I'm smudged! How beastly!"

"Hot in this room, isn't it?" Baejling said loudly, adding in a low voice, "Look, we're calling this off. We've had word that the secret police are on to us. Why don't you—"

"Ah, a bit late for that," said Raoul quietly. "The deed is done."

Baejling darted a swift glance at the reception line, where Madame President—looking extremely fit and healthy—continued to receive guests.

"What is this? Some kind of sick joke?"

Raoul removed a small vial from his purse, then began dabbing the contents on his lips.

"In about six hours," he said, speaking softly, under cover of music from a small orchestra, "your Madame President will start to feel extremely unwell. About an hour after that, she will be in excruciating pain and convulsions. In twenty-four hours, she will no longer be able to move her lower extremities. In forty-eight hours, she will be dead."

The Little One pulled a handkerchief out of one of the raincoat's pockets, handed the cloth to Raoul.

"Thank you, my friend," he said gravely, and began to wipe his lips.

Baejling's jaw sagged. "How—"

"The lipstick," Raoul said simply, taking extreme care to remove the last vestige. "The poison is in the lipstick. One of my favorite techniques. I wear a protective base coat underneath and I am quite careful, of course, never to ingest any myself. But it is always wise to take precautions. I am drinking the antidote for it now."

He consumed the contents of the vial, then examined his lips critically. Certain that every trace of the golden, poisoned lipstick was gone, he returned the mirror to his purse.

The Little One held open a plastic bag marked HAZARDOUS WASTE. Raoul deposited the handkerchief and the empty vial inside. The Little One snapped the bag shut, thrust it into a pocket. Baejling and Krammes watched the proceedings in dazed disbelief.

Raoul reached into his purse, drew forth a second vial of the clear liquid. He held it out.

"What's this?" Baejling eyed it suspiciously, refused to touch it.

"The antidote," Raoul said with a sly smile. "Administered anytime in the next twenty-four hours, it will save Madame President's life. The choice is yours. She will not be in such extreme pain that she cannot negotiate. You might, perhaps, be able to strike a bargain with her. The antidote in exchange for an extended trip on her part to a distant moon. If the lady proves recalcitrant"—Raoul shrugged—"you let her die."

He pressed the vial into Baejling's hand. The man's fingers closed over it nervelessly.

Krammes clutched at him. "This gives us a chance! We don't have to be murderers—"

"Unless she refuses. Or orders us shot anyway. The safest course to follow would be not to tell her. Let her die."

"A difficult decision." Raoul was sympathetic.

Baejling stared at the antidote, then lifted his haggard gaze to Raoul. "Damn you."

Raoul smiled sweetly. "Our work is guaranteed or your money will be cheerfully refunded. And now, if you both will excuse us, we have a transport to catch."

"You won't be able to leave. There are no transports for off-world—"

"Ah, I have the distinct feeling that one will soon be making an unscheduled departure. Not to worry. We can take care of ourselves. Farewell. It's been lovely. Give me a kiss good-bye, Dolf."

Shuddering, Baejling backed up a step.

Laughing, Raoul turned on his golden heel, sauntered leisurely through the crowd. Taking his time, he paused to drink a glass of champagne. The Little One trotted doggedly along behind.

"So very civilized. Didn't want to do the dastardly deed yourselves, did you?" Raoul raised his glass in a toast to Krammes and Baejling. "Here's to what you kiss next, my dears."

CHAPTER 9

Assess the advantages of taking advice, then
structure your forces accordingly, to supplement
extraordinary tactics. Forces are to be
structured strategically, based on what is
advantageous.

Sun Tzu, *The Art of War*

"What the hell's keeping that damn Loti?" Xris demanded.

Switching on the screen in the center of the table—a screen that provided a view of the large bar area of the Exile Café—he scanned it for some sign of the flamboyantly dressed Adonian.

"Relax, will you, Xris? He'll make it. He said he wanted to say hello to a few old friends from back when he used to work here. You didn't say it was urgent, you know," Harry reminded him. "This *is* just a planning session, isn't it?"

"Yeah, yeah." Xris was roaming restlessly around the room. "It's just . . . I want to get on with it, that's all."

The others present exchanged glances, raised eyebrows, asked silently what was up. Most specifically, all looked to Harry Luck, who had been with Xris and the Mag Force 7 team the longest.

Harry shrugged his shoulders, made a face. He didn't have a clue, indicated silently to the rest, *You know as much as I do.*

Each one of the members of Mag Force 7 had received a coded transmission to meet on this date in the Exile Café on Hell's Outpost—a desolate chunk of rock that could barely be dignified with the term "moon." Drifting on the fringes of the galaxy, Hell's Outpost was made unique by the Exile Café, described politely as "a meeting place for professionals in search of employment." All the galaxy knew, however, that the Exile Café did not cater to the sort of professionals likely to scan the vid classifieds.

But even if one was not looking to hire or to be hired, the Exile Café was an excellent meeting place. A large bar area located on the ground floor provided decent liquor and edible meals. The waiters and waitresses were attractive and would provide their own form of entertainment for a price. Weapons could be worn but not used—on penalty of immediate death. This was a place of business and those who came here were serious.

Rooms in the Exile Café were guaranteed private by the management, who boasted that not even the Royal Navy took such precautions to keep identities concealed and conversations secret. The user paid for such luxuries, of course, but the people who frequented the Exile Café could generally afford it.

And thus the members of Mag Force 7 who were present were wondering what they were doing here. Planning sessions were usually held in Xris's condo on Alpha Gamma. Mag Force 7 was a mercenary team, handpicked by Xris himself. They were licensed by the government, had a well-deserved reputation as being the best in the business. They had done jobs for the topmost of the top levels in government. Xris was on a first-name basis with the Lord Admiral, Sir John Dixter, and had once saved the life of the fleet adjutant, Mendaharin Tusca. It was rumored, but not known for certain, that Xris had once been secretly employed by Her Majesty the Queen.

Mag Force 7 didn't need to take on shabby or dirty little jobs. And though they took care to keep a client's business secret—if that's what the client wanted—they had never before taken the extraordinary precaution of meeting at the Exile Café.

Xris took another turn around the room. Harry—whose specialty was piloting every craft that flew, floated, or ran on wheels—watched his boss in perplexity. The two had been together a long time—years, in fact. Other members in the original team had come and gone. Died on the job, some of them: Chico, killed by the Corasians on Shiloh's Planet; Britt dead in the tunnels of a Corasian slave labor mine. Lee had quit the team to get married. Harry was the only one left of the old bunch. He'd never seen Xris—usually as cool as the metal he was mostly made of—nervous, on edge.

A lilting voice came floating through the commlink. "It is—" A pause, as if the person speaking had to think about it.

"Raoul," said Harry, grinning.

"Raoul," decided the voice. "And the Little One."

Xris switched the screen from the bar area to the hallway outside the meeting room.

Raoul, resplendent in an eye-piercing fluorescent green unitard, smiled blissfully and waved to the cam.

Xris activated the controls, admitting the Loti, the rain-coated Little One, and a heady wave of perfume.

Raoul wafted inside the room. "Xris Cyborg," he said gravely, gliding over and giving Xris a light kiss on his left cheek. "I am extremely pleased to see you again. The Little One also extends his most gracious compliments."

The raincoat shook itself, like a dog readjusting its fur.

Xris, accustomed to the typical Adonian form of greeting, submitted to the Loti's kiss with a good grace, but only after he'd taken a close, scrutinizing look at Raoul's lips. Not that Xris feared Raoul would deliberately poison his boss, but the fact that he was wearing lethal lip gloss occasionally slipped the Loti's drug-fogged mind.

"Peach-flavored, nothing more." Raoul flicked his tongue over his orange-tinged mouth.

Xris grunted. "You're late."

"I am? For what?" Raoul was astonished.

"The meeting. I didn't bring you here to celebrate old home week," Xris added wryly.

"Meeting . . ." Raoul cast a vague glance around the room, suddenly noticed there were other people present. He gave them a charming smile, fluttered his fingers at them. "The team assembled. I am extremely pleasured to see you all again. The Little One, as well. We are sorry to have kept you waiting." He turned to Xris with a reproachful air. "We were not informed that our presences were required in a timely and immediate fashion."

"The meeting was called for thirteen hundred hours—"

"But you didn't tell us we had to *be* here by then," Raoul pointed out with an aggrieved air. Green eyelids—to match his unitard—fluttered. "I do not see how this can be my fault, Xris Cyborg."

Xris opened his mouth, shut it on what would have been a caustic remark. The last thing he wanted to do now was hurt the Adonian's feelings. The thought of Raoul's face, streaked with tears and green eyeliner, was too much. Besides, what Raoul had said was true. The Loti operated on his own time system, which bore little or no relation to any other time system currently in use anywhere in the galaxy. Xris had never quite figured it out. When timing was critical to the operation, Raoul and the Little One were always where they were supposed to be at the precise second. But to casually mention to Raoul that he should be attending a meeting at 1300 hours . . .

Raoul's eyes were starting to shimmer. "In the days of my former employment in this location—due, if you will recall, to the untimely and most treacherous death of my late former employer, Snaga Ohme—I made a considerable number of acquaintances here at the Exile Café, all of whom were quite pleased to see me again. But if you would have told me, Xris Cyborg, that you had called a meeting of the team—"

"Very well, Raoul," Xris interrupted testily. "It's all my fault. I apologize for you being late."

"And I forgive you," said Raoul graciously.

He brushed his finger lightly across the cyborg's flesh-and-blood arm, then minced across the room to take a seat with the rest of the team, who were now grinning at each other.

Xris waited with exemplary patience for Raoul to settle himself. When the Adonian had his legs crossed and his hair arranged on his shoulders and his lip gloss reapplied and when the Little One had plopped himself down on the floor and pushed the fedora back to reveal the bright, gleaming eyes, Xris called the meeting to order.

"As you've probably all guessed by now . . ." He paused a moment to take out a twist and light it, then had to wait further while Raoul put a scented handkerchief over his nose. "We have a job. It's going to be a tough one. Dangerous . . . and something more."

He took a drag on the twist, blew smoke. The LED lights winked on his arm, emitted a quick series of beeps. He glanced down, made a minor adjustment, looked up. "There could be some possible ramifications. Legal ones. I'm telling you all this up front, so that if any one of you wants to drop out, you can go with my blessing."

"What are you getting at, Xris?" Harry asked. "Hell, we've all broken our share of laws before now."

Xris nodded, held the twist in his hand between his thumb and forefinger. "*Local* laws. This job is going to require us to break into a top-level, secret, secure Royal Naval military facility."

"Shit," Harry Luck said, almost reverently.

The Little One, curled up at Raoul's feet, stirred and shivered beneath his raincoat. Raoul murmured something, patted the empath soothingly on the fedora. The Loti regarded Xris with a peculiarly intense and suddenly focused stare that was extremely disconcerting.

Xris shot a glance at him and the Little One, frowned. "Whatever information that damn empath is draining off me, he better keep it under his hat."

Raoul coughed delicately into the handkerchief.

Xris, glaring, took a last drag on the twist, snubbed it out, and tossed it in a receptacle.

"You'll be paid double," he went on, "but if anything goes wrong, we're going to have our tails caught in one hell of a tight crack. I'll take full responsibility. But I want you to know what you're in for. So"—he started to light another twist, caught Raoul's eye, and thrust it irritably back into the case—"that's it. If you want out, leave now. The less you know, the better."

The others exchanged uneasy glances. It wasn't that they were worried about the job. They were more worried about their boss.

"I forgot to mention one more thing," Xris went on before anyone could say a word, "this is a kill job. I'm going to be taking out a man—woman. I'll do the killing myself. It's sort of legal. There's been a warrant out for his arrest for years. But essentially I'll be taking the law into my own hands. If anything goes wrong, you could be charged with accessory to murder."

"Is it permitted, Xris Cyborg," Raoul said quietly, "to ask the name of our client? Who is the one hiring us to kill this person?"

Xris took the twist out, began to chew on it. "Me."

"Ah!" Raoul breathed a deep sigh. Settling back in his

chair, he clasped his hands, sparkling with rings, over his shapely legs. "And is it also permitted to ask what crime this man and woman have committed that you have marked them for death?"

"Not a man *and* a woman," Xris said impatiently. "A woman."

"You said a man and a woman, Xris Cyborg."

"I made a mistake. A woman. As for what he did, he was responsible for the death of a friend of mine. And for a lot of other deaths. Maybe thousands. Because of him, the Corasians got their robot claws on some of the latest in firepower—weapons they used against our people on places like Shiloh's Planet."

The Little One jerked suddenly as if in pain.

"Shut up," said Xris softly, taking the twist from his mouth. "Just shut up."

The Little One cringed and shrank back against Raoul's legs.

"*He* was responsible for the deaths?" Raoul was puzzled. "Whom is it that we are discussing? He who?"

"I meant she!" Xris snapped his teeth viciously down on what was left of the twist.

"First he is a he, then a she, then a he again, and now back to a she. I beg your pardon, Xris Cyborg"—Raoul shook his head gently, so as not to muss his hair—"but I am extremely confused."

"Look, Xris," Harry spoke slowly, reluctantly, "I'm not one to question your judgment. If you say this ... uh ... person's got to die, then that's good enough for me. But if there's a warrant out, why take the chance on being sent to the terminator? Why not just arrest ... this person?"

"Because he's dead," Xris said.

Raoul gave a faint moan, pressed his hands to his temples.

"Legally he's dead. In reality, he's still alive, but I'd have a hell of a time proving it. Not that the case would ever come to trial," Xris continued bitterly. "They'd see to that— FISA. They've got their own dirty little secrets to hide."

"My gawd!" Harry's jaw sagged. "The Royal Navy *and* the bureau!"

"You can leave," Xris said coldly. "There's the door. No one's keeping you."

"Look, Xris. I'm sorry. I didn't mean— It's just that—"

"Xris Cyborg." Raoul stood up. Taking care to avoid stepping on his diminutive partner, the Loti walked over to Xris, laid a gentle hand on the cyborg's good arm. "You are not being sensible. Not being logical. And this is very much *not* like you, my friend. You are permitting this woman who is a dead man to run away with your emotions. You know that everyone in this room is most loyal to you, Xris Cyborg."

The others in the room nodded earnestly, openly voiced their support.

"Precisely." Raoul neatly cut them off. "But, as the saying goes, you must look at yourself from the rear in order to tell if your panty hose are crooked."

"Does all this have a point?" Xris demanded.

"My friend, if you came to yourself with this job and told yourself what you have told us . . . you must admit, Xris Cyborg, that you would tell yourself to go play in hyperspace. If you would reveal the truth to your friends—tell us, for example, the fact that this dead man/woman is the one responsible for the explosion which left you—"

"All right!" Xris snapped sullenly. He glared at the Little One. "So much for trying to keep anything private around the mental sponge."

"He means no harm. And I think that you will feel better if you will ease your soul of this—"

"Your lipstick's smudged," Xris pointed out.

Raoul paled. "Is it? Very badly?" His hand went to his mouth.

"Smeared all over your face."

Raoul was stricken. "If I might be excused—"

"The bathroom's over there." Xris indicated a door.

Grabbing his makeup kit, the Adonian departed.

Xris could not look at the rest of the team. He walked over to the window, stared out moodily. "The crazy Loti's right. I came into this ass-backward. To make a long story short—"

"You don't need to tell me any more, Xris," Harry interrupted. "I know all I need to know. Count me in. And you don't have to pay me double. The usual pay's good enough."

"I'm in, Xris," said Jamil Khizr. "You can pay me whatever you consider I am worth."

He was worth plenty, and he knew it. So did Xris. The handsome, black-skinned human had been a heavy weapons instructor in the Royal Marines. He had caught Xris's attention during a raid on Tarmigan, when Mag Force 7—acting under cover on request of the Lord of the Admiralty—had infiltrated the marine unit posted there in order to flush out a spy.

Major Khizr had been of enormous help, showing a real talent for this type of work, talent that was being wasted in firing off practice rounds and droning classroom lectures. When Xris made him an offer, Jamil responded by resigning his commission that very day. Unmarried and professing to like it that way, Jamil was interested in one thing: money.

Tycho spoke through his translator. "I'm cashing in my chips."

Xris, after a moment, realized the alien meant that he should be included in the deal, not that he was about to get shot in the back. Translators normally reduced most alien languages' more colorful imagery to clichés in order to better facilitate human understanding. Unfortunately, either Tycho's translator had a glitch in it somewhere or the alien's imagery was more colorful than usual, for the results were often interestingly garbled.

The wiry Tycho was of a race that was so exceptionally thin that most humans mistook his people for insectoids, an impression that was enhanced by the alien's ability to alter at will the color of his skin—anything from porcelain white to ebony black to brown to forest green. His people were thus known, unofficially, as "chameleons." Such an ability was an advantage in his line of work. Tycho was a highly trained assassin, who came recommended by former Warlord Bear Olefsky.

An expert shot—Xris had never seen a better—Tycho had once taken out the infamous Bergermeister of Demselhaus, the capital city of the Olefsky Hegemony, from a distance of six thousand meters with a modified needle rifle. Being double-jointed, Tycho was also capable of climbing up, into, over, or underneath almost any obstacle. He was also a financial expert and handled the monetary affairs of Mag Force 7.

The man seated to Tycho's left stood and bowed. "I, too, would be honored to be included, Xris. To catch the bastard who injured you would be most pleasing in the eyes of the Master of the Universe."

Dr. Bill Quong was the newest member of the team, and one of the most remarkable. He was an expert at fixing or altering any type of machine currently in use anywhere on any planet in any galaxy. In addition, he could also fix most "broken" living organisms, human or alien. He held advanced degrees in mechanical and hydraulic engineering, and was a doctor of medicine. He'd had little luck holding a job, however. Quong—or Doc, as he was known—had an unfortunate tendency to treat machines like people and people like machines. Xris hadn't hired the doctor for his bedside manner, however. One of Quong's major responsibilities was keeping the cyborg's mechanical half in good working order.

Xris looked around at his team, started to say something, couldn't. He shook his head, shut his mouth.

Feeling a tug on the hem of his pants leg, he looked down. The Little One was looking up.

"You're in, too?" Xris said, smiling.

The fedora nodded violently. The Little One raised a small, clenched fist.

"Thanks," Xris said quietly. "Thanks all of you." He drew a deep breath, motioned them to gather around a table. Switching on a hologram, he said, "Here's the plan—"

The bathroom door opened. A ruffled and indignant Raoul emerged.

"My lipstick was not either smeared!"

CHAPTER
10

She's a phony. But she's a real phony!
  Truman Capote, *Breakfast at Tiffany's*

"Must have been a trick of the light," Xris told Raoul soothingly.

"Ah, certainly."

Happy once again—a visit to a mirror always improved Raoul's spirits—the Adonian started to head for a sofa.

"I was just about to explain the operation." Xris intercepted Raoul, indicated the holographic image. The other team members—grinning hugely—gathered around.

Raoul blinked. "But I was going to do my nails."

"You and the Little One have a critical role to play," Xris said patiently. "I'd appreciate it if you'd join us."

"You could explain it to me later."

"We only have the room for six hours, and once we leave here, we don't discuss the plan, even among ourselves."

"I understand, my friend," Raoul said quietly, noting the steel edge in the cyborg's voice. "Perhaps I could do both at once."

The other members of the team made room for Raoul. He pulled up a chair, brought his makeup kit, and proceeded to carefully paint opalescent polish on his fingernails while listening to Xris. The Little One curled up on the floor, head pillowed on Raoul's purse, and went to sleep.

The empath never participated in planning sessions, never looked at a hologram or a map, never took any sort of instruction from anyone except Raoul. Early on, when the two first joined the team, Xris had harbored misgivings about this arrangement; he was never quite certain whether or not

Raoul was absorbing anything said to him or was off in some Loti drug-induced dream world of his own. Yet the two always managed to come through when needed.

Xris glanced at Raoul, who was taking care to spread the polish evenly on each nail, his glistening jet-black hair falling over his shoulders and completely obscuring one corner of the holographic model of the space station.

The word *reliable* came into Xris's mind and he almost coughed. He supposed a person could get himself a nice quiet sanitarium room with a view and a caretaker to go with it for referring to a Loti Adonian as reliable. Yet, in all these years, during which the two had worked on some very dangerous and delicate assignments, Raoul and his small, mysterious cohort had never let Xris down. He'd have to remember to ask how their job on Modena had gone. It was a mark of his confidence that he'd taken it for granted it had "progressed in a manner most satisfactory," as Raoul would say.

Raoul suddenly looked up from his work. His eyes met Xris's and their gaze was steady, intense, not the dreamy, unfocused gaze of the Loti. Raoul smiled, a secret, knowing smile for just the two of them. And he did know—he knew the truth, knew everything about Dalin Rowan/Darlene Mohini. The Little One, who was also a telepath as well as an empath ("It comes with age among his people," Raoul had once explained), had peered out from under the brim of the fedora and seen right inside Xris. Hell, the Little One probably knew more about what Xris was thinking and feeling than Xris did himself. And in some strange and inexplicable manner the Little One had transferred his knowledge to Raoul.

Was Raoul for real? Xris wondered, not for the first time, as he returned Raoul's smile with a reluctant, grudging half smile of his own. The lipstick, the clothes, the nail polish; the foppish behavior, the affected mannerisms. Certainly they were typically Adonian. So very typically Adonian that it was almost *too* typically Adonian. It was too real ... surreal. And the drugs. Was Raoul a true Loti? Or was that, too, some sort of charade? In emergencies, he could react with split-second timing, something no true Loti could accomplish. He was inventive, creative, a genius with chemicals—traits the pleasure-seeking, indolent Loti did not possess. Yet the unfocused eyes, the dilated pupils, the blissful, unperturbed, most assuredly drug-induced euphoria were all typical—again, to the point of being atypical.

But if his was an act—why? What was the purpose?

Xris could almost suppose that Raoul, behind those painted, drug-drenched eyes, was laughing at them all. . . .

"Yes, Xris Cyborg?" Raoul's eyelids fluttered lazily. "What is wrong? Not the mascara!"

"Your hair's blocking part of the space station," Xris said, pointing.

"I beg your pardon." Raoul flipped his hair over his shoulder and, breathing a sigh of relief to know that his mascara wasn't smudged, continued with his nails.

Xris shoved aside a vial of nail polish remover that was sitting in a docking bay, and began. "What you are looking at is a holographic image of RFComSec. In case you can't translate the acronym, RFComSec stands for Royal Fleet Communications Security Establishment."

Harry gave a low whistle.

"Yeah, I know," Xris said. "For obvious reasons, it wouldn't be a good idea for any of you to know how I managed to obtain this layout. So don't even bother. Or," he added for Raoul's benefit, "if you know, keep your mouth shut."

Raoul glanced up, smiled, returned to more important work.

Xris continued. "Inside this space station is where the Royal Navy formulates the codes and ciphers that keep their secrets secret. It's also where they work at decoding other people's secrets. Security is as tight as Raoul's buns."

The Adonian nodded his head to indicate he appreciated the compliment.

"The space station sits squarely in the middle of nowhere. It's near one of the Lanes, but most hyperspace traffic zips right past, never realizing the station's there. No inhabited star systems within a couple of hundred light-years. RFComSec is heavily shielded and completely self-sufficient, except for one small detail, which I'll go into later. This large complex in the center here"—he indicated the hub of what looked like a gigantic wheel—"is the headquarters, the work area. These spokes radiating out from it provide housing, shops, gym and recreation areas, that sort of thing. Our man—"

Raoul lifted his head.

"Woman," Xris corrected himself grimly, "lives and works on the station, rarely leaves. According to the files, she's only left twice in the seven years since he . . . she's been assigned to it. Those trips were duty-related."

"Perhaps," Raoul suggested mildly, studying his nails with a critical air, "if we called her by name, this would alleviate the confusion in your mind, Xris Cyborg."

"Which name? She's got two."

Raoul shifted his gaze and again the eyes were disconcertingly focused. "The name you attach to her in your thoughts. The name of the person she was to you. For that is the person who must die."

Xris said nothing for long moments, just chewed on the twist. Finally he said, "Rowan. We call her Rowan. That's who she was and, as far as I'm concerned, who she is."

Raoul nodded complacently, repeated "Rowan" to himself several times, spread his fingers, and waved his hands in the air to dry the nail polish.

Xris again indicated the holograph. "Best-case scenario would be to catch Rowan alone in her apartment, which is located somewhere in this block. But that's out, for several reasons. Getting onto the space station itself is going to be damn difficult. Once we get there, we're going to have a limited amount of time, so we'll have to move fast. One thing the military doesn't give out is the addresses of its people. We could spend hours wandering around the station searching for her housing unit, only to find out when we get there that she's not at home.

"But she works in a place called FCWing. Once we're inside, we tap into the computer, ask it where to find FCWing, and let the computer lead us right to him. Her."

Raoul rolled his eyes, gave a delicate sigh.

Xris pretended he didn't hear. "If Rowan's in an office by herself—no problem. I'll need five minutes alone—"

"Five *minutes*! To take out a mark?" Harry was a bit thick-headed.

Xris stared fixedly at the holograph. "I need time for a short conversation."

Harry looked uncomfortable. "Sure, Xris. Sorry. I wasn't thinking."

Xris turned, walked away from the table over to the trash receptacle located beneath a fully stocked bar. He spit the soggy wad of tobacco into the trash, then helped himself to a brandy—Mataska 7 Star. The seven-hundred-year-old variety. He poured himself a glass. Looking in the mirror, he could see the others exchange questioning glances, with the exception of Raoul, who calmly blew on his nails.

Xris swallowed the brandy, returned to the hologram. "Any questions so far?"

Raoul raised a hand. "What happens if this Rowan is not alone, my friend?"

"Then I'll know for certain there's not a God," Xris returned quietly. "I'll need one of your special concoctions." The cyborg indicated his weapons hand. "Something I can smear on a needle, inject into the flesh. Slow-acting, no antidote."

Raoul was thoughtful, intrigued. "I have just the thing. It is known as—"

"I'll leave the details to you." Xris indicated a large digital clock placed in a prominent location on the wall. "We're running short on time and we've got more important details to cover."

"Such as how we get onto the space station," Quong observed. "I take it blasting our way through is not an option."

"We'd never make it within torpedo range. The base is well armed with strong defensive capabilities. It switches on its marker lights only when a ship is near, to aid in docking. And the only ships that ever dock are Royal Navy, plus a select few. A very select few. A fleet of Corasian mother ships would have a tough time taking that space station out."

"But you have a plan," said Harry, grinning.

"I have a plan." Xris bent near the hologram. "As I said, the base is mostly self-sufficient. Mostly. They have one little problem that requires outside intervention."

Xris straightened, shook another twist out from the case, and lit it. "Fleas." He inhaled the noxious smoke.

"Fleas!" Harry guffawed.

"They don't consider it a laughing matter. It seems that about twenty years ago, some colonel's kid sneaked a stray dog on board the space station. The dog was infested with a particularly virulent type of flea. Not only is this flea harder than hell to kill, it carries a highly infectious, flulike disease. It's not fatal to healthy adults, but it puts them out of action for a considerable length of time. Came damn close to shutting down the entire RFComSec operation for about a month the first time the plague hit.

"Since then, the Navy's tried every trick known to men and aliens to eradicate the pest. The best they can do is keep it under control. This requires a team of specially trained exterminators to come in once a month."

"*Every* month?" Jamil asked, skeptical. "Is this reliable?"

"Every Standard Military month," Xris said, "for the last twenty years."

"Twenty years! Why doesn't the Navy just do it themselves?"

"The Royal Navy is *not* in the bug-killing business," Xris returned. "Besides, this extermination company invented the system that keeps the fleas dormant. No one's quite sure how it works and the exterminators won't tell. They hold patents on the entire system and they have an open-ended exclusive contract to take care of it.

"Here's what we do know. The exterminators place robots that release the chemicals in minute doses all over the station to control the fleas on a continuous basis. If the 'bots run across flea-breeding grounds, they actively seek out the fleas and their larvae and eradicate them using a chemical spray and microlasers. Every month the Olicien personnel bring the 'bots in to a central checkpoint for maintenance and chemical replenishment."

"Nice profitable operation they've got going," Tycho observed through his translator. "Paid for by our tax credits. I'll bet they stick the Navy for a fortune!"

"Quit worrying about your tax return. At any rate, this is one time the Navy's *not* going to get their money's worth. As I said, the exterminators visit once every SMT month. Every month they fly their own craft, which leaves from their own home world. They make the jump, arrive on the space station. The crew goes in—just like they've been going in once a month for twenty years."

"Same old same old," Harry said softly. "I'll bet no one even bothers to check their IDs."

"Yeah, but is it the same crew all the time?" Jamil wondered. "If so, we've got problems."

Xris shook his head. "No, they've got other contracts to handle. Plus the usual amount of employee attrition and turnover. We may have a tough time explaining why *all* of us are new to the job, but I'm sure that's something our knowledgeable Adonian salesman can handle." He looked at Raoul, who grimaced.

"I do not enjoy playing salesmen, Xris Cyborg."

Xris was sympathetic. "I know, but you're so good at it. And I think it's about time that Olicien Pest Control tries to sell the Navy some additional services. Their charming representative will keep the security systems officer on RFComSec engaged in bug-related small talk—"

Raoul shot Xris a reproachful glance.

"—while the rest of us take care of business. At this point, we face a problem. The exterminators are supposed to remain in one secure area. The security officer keeps tabs on them by following their movements on his screen. Any deviation from the norm and we'll have the whole blasted Navy on us. And," Xris added, taking another drag on the twist, "it's highly probable that once I locate Rowan, I'm going to have to leave the area to get to her."

"I am a good conversationalist," Raoul said gravely, "but I do not believe I am capable of distracting a person with airy chatter—even on a subject as fascinating as fleas— while his monitor is flashing alarms and urgently attempting to gain his attention."

"I don't expect you to." Xris snubbed out the twist. "When the Little One picks up the first indication that this officer has spotted something wrong, you give him a quick fix. Nothing lethal—I don't want any innocent people killed. Just something to send him to la-la land while we finish the job."

Raoul nodded complacently, admired his nails. "I see no problem in this, Xris Cyborg."

"There is one little thing I better mention, Raoul," Xris said slowly.

Not liking the cyborg's tone, Raoul looked up in alarm. "What is that, my friend?"

"You have to wear . . . coveralls."

Raoul's eyes widened. "*Baggy* coveralls?" he whispered, aghast.

"Bright yellow."

Raoul shuddered.

Xris was relentless. "With a large black beetle on the back."

Raoul shut his eyes, unable to contemplate the horror. "I will take that double pay, after all."

Xris looked around at the others. "That's the general plan. Now we'll cover the details. Any questions so far?"

"What happens if we get there and this Rowan's taken the day off or is working the night shift?" Jamil asked.

"She won't be," Xris said shortly. "I have her work schedule."

"Damn!" Harry was admiring. "What'd you do, Xris, ask Lord Admiral Dixter to hand over the Navy's classified files?"

"Something like that," Xris said easily. "Any more questions?"

They discussed how they were going to hijack the craft, what they were going to use to subdue the exterminators before they could be stripped of clothes and equipment. The team tried to anticipate anything that could go wrong and formed a variety of contingency plans to deal with various scenarios.

Xris brought the meeting to a close. "Our time's almost up. When we leave here, we don't mention any of this. Not a word. From this point on, we separate. You four split up. I'll keep the Loti and the empath with me. You'll find the date, time, and location of our meeting place in a coded file in your own individual computers. That will also give you the location of Olicien Pest Control. Raoul, you and the Little One will arrive early, ahead of the rest of the team, in order to conduct your research. You're going to have to learn a lot about fleas."

Raoul gave a heart-wrenching sigh. "The sacrifices I make for my career. And the Little One"—he glanced at his slumbering friend—"will find this most distasteful. He has the strong aversion to insect life-forms that is so prevalent among his kind."

"He'll get over it," Xris said, who had no idea what "kind" the Little One was and who knew better than to ask, having been through that once with Raoul and gaining nothing from it except a throbbing pain behind the eyes. "Wake him up. I've got some additional instructions for you both."

The others filed out, pausing to ask final questions or obtain clarification on some minor details. The last man had gone before Raoul roused the Little One. The empath shook himself, straightened his raincoat, and stared up from beneath the brim of the fedora at Xris.

The cyborg reached across to the control panel, shut and sealed the door.

"Now here's the plan for Olicien—" Xris began, then interrupted himself. "What the hell does *he* mean—staring at me like that?"

"The Little One says you are unsettled in your mind, Xris Cyborg, and that is most unlike you. Not even when you were contemplating that foolhardy venture to launch a one-man rescue of your wife from the Corasian prison camp—"

Xris frowned, interrupted the flow. "If this is leading somewhere, get to it. We don't have much time and I still have to pack up the equipment."

"Not even during that dark time were you this . . . this . . ." Raoul fluttered his hands, searching his fog-ridden mind for a word. "Deranged."

"Deranged." Xris clamped his jaw down angrily on a twist. "He thinks I'm deranged."

"Perhaps that is not the word I meant. Possibly you would prefer *unhinged*?"

"I'd prefer you both out of sight *and* out of mind!" Xris glared at the Little One. "But I suppose that's impossible, since you're traveling with me. This is the last I want to hear of it, or you can both make the trip home locked up snugly in the storage compartment. Now here are your orders—"

"We are telling you this for your good, Xris Cyborg." Raoul was defensive. "Usually your brain is like a laser beam—clear, focused, flashing in a straight line toward your goal. But now, my friend, you are a laser beam in a room full of reflectors. You bounce off one and are distracted by another. You are zapping all over the place."

"Thanks for the analysis," Xris said. "Send me a bill."

"The bill may be a large one, my friend." Raoul's eyes were extraordinarily clear, intense. Disconcerting. "And we—the others and myself—are the ones who will pay. You are too emotionally involved. This could lead you to commit rash and hasty acts. You are already making mistakes."

"Clear out." Xris ground the words between his teeth and the twist. "Both of you. Now. I'll meet you at the spaceplane."

He pointed at the door.

"In just a moment." Raoul appeared to have taken root. The Little One entrenched himself behind the Loti's legs. "You must listen to us."

Xris sighed. Unless he wanted to get physical—which Raoul would have probably enjoyed—there would be no budging the Adonian. The fastest way to get rid of him and the empath was to simply let them have their say. And, although he was fairly certain no one could plant any listening devices aboard his spaceplane without his knowing it, he was up against some of the best in the business—the bureau, the Royal Navy, *and* the Hung. Sure he was acting paranoid. It was unlikely any of these groups would have found out about him yet, but—as the saying went—just because you're paranoid doesn't mean someone's not following you. Best to let Raoul unburden himself inside a secure room.

"I could always shut down the circuits that control my hearing," Xris muttered to himself. But he didn't. He had a strange need to listen, like poking at an aching tooth to feel the pain.

"Okay, but make it quick. Why am I . . . unhinged?"

"Number one. You did *not* ask John Dixter for those files on the space station, as you led Harry to believe. You obtained the files illegally, by raiding the Royal Navy's computers, using the access code John Dixter gave you the time we did some work for him. You betrayed a friendship *and* a trust and you are not pleased with yourself. Such an action bothers you deeply."

"It does not. I had to do it. I'll explain later. Rowan's a security risk." Xris indicated the chronometer set into his wrist. "You've got five more minutes."

"Number two. In your mind, you have already judged, tried, and convicted your former friend and partner. This Rowan must die. He—or she, as the case may be—deserves death. That is what you have decided and this decision is unalterable."

Xris removed the twist. "Yes."

"Then let me kill her," Raoul said softly.

Xris shook his head. Dropping the twist, he ground it beneath the heel of his steel leg.

"A mistake." Raoul sighed a delicate sigh. "You are not a killer, Xris Cyborg. Not a killer in cold blood, like myself. I have no conscience—thank the maker of pharmaceuticals—but you do. It would be far easier and far safer for the team if I were to be Rowan's executioner."

Again Xris shook his head. "I need to have a little talk with Dalin Rowan."

"Talk!" Raoul was impatient. "Recall the dictum of the late Warlord Derek Sagan. 'Do not talk—shoot!' It was a saying of which he was very fond and which kept him alive far longer than one might have considered possible under the circumstances. You put us all in jeopardy, my friend."

"You can always walk, Loti. You and the sponge."

The fedora—the hat was now all Xris could see of the Little One—quivered.

Raoul's eyes began to shimmer. "How can you say that? We are your friends, Xris Cyborg."

A tear trickled down the rouged cheek.

"Now, don't start crying," Xris said, exasperated. "You'll ruin your makeup. Your nose will swell. You can't go out of here looking like that."

"I don't care," Raoul returned with unexpected passion. He grasped hold of Xris's good arm. "Tell me you will at least consider what we have said."

Startled by the Loti's unusual outburst—Raoul was generally placidity personified—Xris gently removed the bejeweled hand.

"I'll consider it," he promised. "Now I'm going to give you your orders. Do you think you're calm enough to handle them?"

Raoul removed a lace-trimmed handkerchief from his purse, dabbed carefully at his eyes. "Yes, Xris Cyborg. I am once more in control of myself."

Whatever that means. Aloud, Xris continued, "You'll be traveling to Olicien Pest Control corporate headquarters—"

"Is this when I'm a salesman, wearing coveralls?"

"No. This is before you're a salesman. This is how you get to be a salesman. First, you have to find out all you can about the Olicien Pest Control Company and how they operate. You are the representative for a company who owns floating platforms—"

"Where do they float?" Raoul asked in a muffled voice, blowing his nose.

"In space," Xris said with elaborate patience. "Your company is having a pest problem and your platforms need servicing. The Olicien people will say, 'Certainly. Only too pleased.' They will then provide you with the location of the franchise which services space stations, tell you to contact them directly. This will be the franchise which services RFComSec. They have only one. You will ask for a tour of this franchise, mentioning that several other members of the corporation will be joining you."

"Ah, I see!" Raoul smiled.

Xris thought it just as well to make certain. "This Olicien Pest Control Company has franchises in every major city on Alinus Misk. Only one of them devotes itself to outer space work. You're going to find out which one and arrange for us to get inside. Once there, we do a quick, quiet takeover, hijack their vessel, and that's that. Understand?"

Raoul fluttered the handkerchief. "Of course."

"Use commercial transport. Anything else would look suspicious. I'll take you back with me to Alpha Gamma. You can leave from there. Maintain contact. You know the routine."

"Very well, Xris Cyborg. The Olicien Company on Alinus Misk. The bug place sounds perfectly ghastly. But we will be there."

"I know you will. And listen." Xris paused a moment, then said quietly, "I won't let the team down. I'll do what I have to do."

Raoul shrugged, smiled his euphoric smile as though he hadn't a care in the universe. "Time will tell, won't it, Xris Cyborg?"

Shepherding the Little One, who had relaxed considerably, the Loti headed for the door. Xris was quick to hit the controls, open it.

"One last question." Raoul teetered on the threshold.

Xris remained patient. A glitch in his system was the probable cause of the fingers on his metal hand clenching. "What?"

"About those coveralls—"

"Yes. You have to wear them." Xris gave the Loti a push, shut the door.

Left alone, the cyborg returned to the table to pack up the holographic equipment. He deleted the image of the space station, was about to shut down the power when, on impulse, he touched a control, brought up another holograph.

A man. Dalin Rowan.

Xris had taken Darlene Mohini's photograph, fed it into the computer, made a few changes, and found his friend. At that point, he'd begun to believe.

"Why did you do it?" he asked the silent image. "Set us up for the kill? I just need to know why!"

A red light above the clock began to flash. A female voice advised Xris politely that his time was up. Other clients were waiting for the room. The door slid open and would not shut again—management's way of saying it was time to leave.

Xris killed the image, packed up his equipment, and left.

*

CHAPTER 11

So if you know the place and time of battle, you
can join the fight from a thousand miles away.
                                    Sun Tzu, *The Art of War*

"Sir, Knight Commander has received your message. He
is on the comm."

The officer nodded in silence, retired to his private quarters.

"Knight Commander. The circulation of the descriptions
of the Loti and the empath known as Raoul and the Little
One has produced results. At twenty-two hundred yesterday,
SMT, a member of our order observed the two of them in the
Exile Café. The cyborg Xris was also present. The three left
together in the cyborg's spaceplane."

"Where is the Loti now?"

"We are unable to ascertain, Knight Commander. Their
plane made the jump to hyperspace."

"If one of our knights had this Loti under observation,
why didn't he capture him?"

"They were inside the Exile Café at the time, Knight
Commander. No violence is permitted. The rules are very
strict on that point and are rigidly enforced. Besides, the cyborg was with him and the cyborg is a formidable opponent."

The Knight Commander appeared to consider this. "True.
Well, there will be another time. God will deliver him into
our hands."

"Assuredly, sir. And this does provide us with conclusive
proof that the Loti is part of the cyborg's mercenary team."

"I had reached the same conclusion. I have received information that this team was involved in secret dealings with Her Majesty the Queen on the woman's pagan, Goddess-worshiping planet of Ceres. The Loti, Raoul, and the empath known as the Little One traveled to the planet on commercial transport. I obtained records of their entry. I am transmitting these to you now. Since we lost him at the Exile Café, these might be useful in tracking him down."

The officer waited in silence for the files. The Knight Commander continued talking.

"It is quite probable that the Loti has a number of passports registered to him under various aliases. This time, as you see, he used his real name—if Raoul *is* his real name—and listed his planet of origin as Adonia. The Little One probably uses the same passport every time, since he has been granted 'mixed breed' status. Planet of origin is listed as 'unknown.'

"My guess is that these two were involved in the inexplicable illness and subsequent sudden disappearance of the wife of the President of Modena. Eyewitness accounts put the two at the reception during which Madame President fell ill. The two left before we could send a squad to capture the Loti, and at that point we lost them."

"I do not think they will be difficult to track, sir," the officer replied. "The cyborg has several different dwelling places. We have posted men at all of them. We have also arranged for Raoul's home on Adonia to be kept under constant surveillance."

"Excellent. We must be patient, however. Wait for them to split up. As you say, the cyborg Xris is a formidable foe. Not only that, he has friends in the highest places. We do not yet want to call undue attention to ourselves. Therefore, do not attempt to apprehend the Loti in the cyborg's presence. There will come a time when this Raoul and his small companion are alone. Strike then."

"Yes, Knight Commander."

"Contact me immediately when you have effected the Loti's capture. Any questions?"

"Yes, sir. What are we to do with the creature known as the Little One?"

"He is of no use to us. Kill him."

CHAPTER
12

In battle, confrontation is done directly, victory is
gained by surprise.

Sun Tzu, *The Art of War*

Christy's Cracked Egg Restaurant was large, crowded—especially for this early in the morning. According to
Xris's research, the all-you-can-eat breakfast buffet was extremely popular, attracting large numbers of people—ideal
for Xris's purpose. When he entered, no one even glanced
twice at the cyborg. Dressed in a business suit that covered
his mechanical limbs, a sun visor hiding his cybernetic eye,
and a foam-flesh and plastiskin cosmetic hand attached to
his arm, Xris looked the part of an Aurigan executive.

Having informed the 'bot who steered him to his table
that there would be four joining him, Xris loaded his plate
with the local fare and sat down to eat and wait.

Tycho was next to arrive. The tall, skinny alien did attract
a few curious stares, but the customers soon returned to their
meals, having more interest in Aurigan mush—considered a
delicacy. Located on one of the major trade routes, the capital city of Auriga was home to a large intergalactic population. Not much surprised the citizens of Auriga.

Tycho located Xris, sat down.

"Steer clear of the mush," Xris advised in a low voice.

A vegetarian, Tycho gave the mush a look, grimaced, and
told the 'bot he would be having only carrot juice.

"Any trouble with the weapons?" Xris asked.

It was not necessary to keep his voice down. A cheerful
people, Aurigans enjoyed talking—the louder, the better.
Consequently, the restaurant was a din of noise, with every

Aurigan in the place shouting shrilly and gleefully at every other Aurigan. Xris had turned his hearing down to the bare minimum necessary and still the row was deafening.

Tycho shook his head. His long-fingered hand could have wrapped twice around the glass of juice. He sipped at it. "No problems. I expected none. So long as I do not bring the rifle on board the spacecraft with me, I am rarely stopped. After all, it looks the same as any other beam rifle. I carry the duonamic sights hidden on my person in a shielded case."

Xris nodded. Duonamic sights were the hallmark of the professional assassin and were illegal in most parts of the galaxy. With those sights, which detected any form of radiation from heat to light, as well as Doppler movement, Tycho could not only see through walls, he could shoot the person standing on the other side.

"There won't be any need for gun play," Xris said. "It's going to go smooth. I'm feeling lucky. I'm due this."

Tycho looked at him strangely. "It's well to be prepared. Better safe than sitting in your canoe without a paddle."

Xris could feel another lecture coming on, wasn't in the mood; and so he didn't respond. He ate his mush more for the sake of putting food into his body than because he was hungry. He was too tense, too wired to be hungry. What he truly wanted was a twist, but smoking was forbidden in the dining establishment. He went back to the original subject.

"Where did you leave the rifle?"

"In the hovervan. Harry's parking it now. I met him and Quong outside. The Doc had to go powder his nose. They should both be here any minute."

"They're here now."

Standing in the entrance, partially blocking it with his large body, Harry was scanning the crowd. Tycho waved his long arm. Quong emerged from the bathroom and the two joined the rest of the team. Harry left immediately to fill his plate at the buffet table. Quong selected fruit and cereal. Returning to the table, he eyed Xris in concern.

"Are you feeling well?"

There were times, Xris decided, when having your own private medic was a distinct disadvantage.

"Yeah, Doc, I'm fine."

"You don't look it." Quong was blunt. "I'd like to run a systems analysis—"

"I said I'm fine. Just a little keyed up, that's all. Adrenaline pumping."

Xris took out a twist. "I'm not going to smoke it," he informed the waiter 'bot, who had located and zeroed in on the forbidden object with the speed of a sublight torpedo.

The 'bot continued to lurk about, obviously convinced that Xris was going to light up the moment its electronic eye was turned, and finally Xris gave up and put the twist away. The 'bot retreated and Harry came back with two plates.

"Fried meat, fried potatoes, eggs. You're going to need a heart replacement before you're forty," Quong observed testily.

"Sure, Doc." Harry was unperturbed. "Good thing I've got you around to take care of me."

"Not when you abuse your system like that. Besides, of what use is a new heart if the arteries leading to it are clogged? I am fifty years old and in far better physical condition. . . ."

The argument went on, as it did almost every time the two sat down for a meal together. The discussion about cholesterol levels flowed around Xris. He found it irritating, had to bite off a snide comment.

Fortunately, Jamil had just entered. Xris waved to his friend, who was looking extraordinarily handsome in his expensive business suit. As he passed through the restaurant, several women, with typical Aurigan forthrightness, yelled at him to join them. Jamil smiled, made polite responses, and sat down beside Xris.

"Breakfast?" Xris asked.

"The food's not bad," Harry mumbled, his mouth full.

"I've eaten already," Jamil answered, adding casually, "She makes a great omelette."

Harry gulped, swallowed. "*She?* How the hell do you manage? You just got here last night!"

"He keeps himself in excellent physical condition," Quong intoned. "Women appreciate that."

"Fine, then." Xris interrupted what was likely to be either an argument about clogged arteries or a discussion of Jamil's sex life. "Harry, did you check in with Raoul and the Little One last night?"

"Yeah." Harry nodded. "I met the Loti in the bar of the fancy hotel he's staying in. Olicien's putting them up in style."

"Did Raoul manage to get a layout of the Olicien place?"

Harry patted his suit pocket. "I've got the diagram here. Raoul paid them a visit yesterday. The bug people gave him a personal tour *and* took him to dinner. Adonian charm, you know. The franchise is family-owned, small. This RFComSec contract is their biggest account and, since they've got the equipment to service space stations, they're eager to land others like it. Oh, and by the way"—Harry winked—"as far as they're concerned, RFComSec is a Naval 'refitting and maintenance station.' "

"That's what they've been told to say, obviously. Does Raoul think the Olicien people know the truth?"

"Not a chance. Oh, they know it's a Naval base—"

"All the people running around in uniforms would probably tip them off," Xris said dryly.

Harry grinned. "Yeah. According to the Little One, no one at Olicien has the least suspicion that they're dealing with anything as big as a *top-secret* Naval base. Not even the personnel who go up there. The empath gave them the once-over. To them, the space station's nothing more than a floating body-repair shop."

"What's the timetable?" Jamil asked, preparing to set his chronometer.

"It's oh-eight-hundred now. We travel there, get ourselves into position by oh-nine-hundred, which is when you and Harry are supposed to meet Raoul at the Olicien HQ." Xris looked at Harry, who confirmed.

"I went over that with Raoul last night. He says it's all fixed up. Jamil and I are high-level company executives. He's arranged for us to meet with their manager at oh-nine-hundred."

"Fine. The spaceplane with the exterminators on board leaves the Olicien grounds at ten hundred. The exterminators are scheduled to arrive at the space station at thirteen hundred."

"Three hours?" Harry was impressed. "They must have hyperdrive."

"They do," Xris said. "I took a look at the plane yesterday, spent some time chatting with one of the mechanics. Said I was looking for work. The plane—"

"You short of credits, Xris?" Harry asked anxiously. " 'Cause I'd be happy to loan you a few."

Xris scratched his forehead. Harry was a good fighter, an

excellent pilot, and the best hovercraft driver in the business. But, over the years, the big man had taken one too many stun-blasts to the head.

"No, Harry." Xris was patient. "I'm not. But thanks anyway. We're dealing with your standard light-cargo spaceplane, with a few major exceptions. These include hyperspace capability and an XP-28 computer upgrade."

"Compliments of the Royal Navy, no doubt. Your tax dollars at work, gentlemen," Tycho muttered through his translator.

"The Olicien plane's crew never deviates from their time schedule," Xris continued, "so neither can we. They've got a thirty-minute window to make their landing on the space station or the trip's scrubbed for the day, rescheduled. Security reasons, obviously. RFComSec wants the exterminators there when the place is quiet—which suits us fine."

"I am all in favor of quiet," Quong agreed.

"Raoul and the Little One join us at the Olicien plant at oh-nine-hundred. That gives Quong and Tycho and me an hour to hijack the plane, load all the equipment. Plenty of time, even if something goes wrong, which it won't."

"He's feeling lucky," Tycho observed.

Xris ignored him.

"Meanwhile, Raoul and Harry and Jamil take over the Olicien facility. Will you need access codes for the spaceplane, Harry?"

"With hyperspace drive *and* an XP-28, you can bet on it. The bug people won't want to chance anyone taking joyrides in that baby. XP-28—my favorite computer system." Harry rubbed his hands together in anticipation. "This is going to be a treat."

"How long to secure the facility?" Xris looked at Jamil.

"Ten minutes. Twenty if we have to search for code cards and reprogram them."

"I'll give you thirty, just in case. Meet us at the plane at oh-nine-thirty. How long do you figure preparation for take-off, Harry?"

"Not long. Most likely the course will already be laid into the computer. Ten minutes."

"And we've got thirty. That gives us some breathing room. Everyone ready? Then let's move out."

Xris motioned to the 'bot, who trundled up. The amount they owed flashed across its screen. Tycho entered the credit account number. The 'bot thanked them and hoped they had a wonderful day.

"We intend to," Xris told it as they left.

They climbed into the hovervan. Harry asked the computer for directions to Olicien Pest Control. A three-dimensional map appeared on the screen. They drove off.

Jamil studied the layout of the facility. Raoul had learned—under duress—how to draw a fairly clear diagram. But he found the task tedious in the extreme and Xris had never been able to break the Adonian of the habit of embellishing the mundane work with fanciful doodles. Jamil was forced to trace his route from the entrance to the manager's office through several large beetles; two eyes and a smiling mouth had been added to the *O* of "Olicien."

Quong worked on Harry's "contraption"—a device meant to look like a souped-up bug killer, but which had other, far more interesting applications. Xris removed his business suit, put on body armor which had been modified to free up his cybernetic arm and leg, detached the useless cosmetic hand. From a compartment built into the leg, the cyborg removed one of his weapons hands, attached it to the arm.

Quong looked up from his work. "Which one is that?"

"Small rocket launcher."

The rockets were heat-guided. Xris's servoelectric eye processed the target's image and downloaded it to the rocket just before launch. The small rocket would zero in on its prey with unerring efficiency.

"Heavy-duty for this job," Quong observed.

"I trust I won't have to use it," Xris said quietly.

Quong said something else, but Xris pretended he didn't hear. Once he was outfitted and had done a systems check, he took out a twist, moved over to sit next to the van's open window for a smoke. He also pretended not to see that the others had exchanged glances all around. They were worried—not about the job, but about him.

Damn it, just let me alone! he told them silently. When this is finished, it'll all be okay. And this is going to finish it. I know it. I'm due. I'll be okay.

He watched the smoke from the glowing twist whip out the window, watched the end of the twist burn red in the rushing wind.

Quong finished work on Harry's bug "contraption," set it

aside, and changed into body armor and fatigues. Tycho was
wearing his armor beneath his civvies. A type developed
specially by his people, the body armor was completely
transparent, to accommodate his changes in skin coloration.

Chameleons are not accustomed to wearing clothing,
which interferes with their natural ability to blend in with
their surroundings. They are not, therefore, shy or modest. It
had taken the other team members a short time to get used
to Tycho's transparent body armor. Now they no longer noticed. But the sight of the naked chameleon often came as a
shock to other, more inhibited humanoids.

Once everyone was dressed, they settled back into their
seats. Tycho assembled his beam rifle. He and Quong discussed the current rise in Royal Treasury bonds and whether
or not Tycho thought the rise would continue and Quong
should invest now or wait. Jamil checked his weapons and
sang along in his rich baritone with the music from the local
radio station. Harry enjoyed the drive. No one attempted to
talk to Xris, although he could feel their anxious gazes slide
over him, then slide quickly away. He smoked another twist.

They left the central city, buzzed over the suburbs, and
entered a large industrial park, which appeared to be trying
to hide the fact that it was an industrial park by camouflag-
ing itself with trees, pruned hedges, and a few placid ponds.
The buildings housing the various businesses were indistin-
guishable from one another—long, low warehouses trying
valiantly not to look like warehouses.

A sign posted at the entrance to the park warned that
space vehicles took off and landed on this site. Hovercraft
were advised, for their own safety, to keep close to ground
level and stay in the marked lanes.

"According to the map, we're coming up on it, Xris,"
Harry reported, peering intently at the various signs adorned
with various company logos.

Xris left his seat in the rear of the van, came to sit beside
Harry.

"You can't miss it. The building's painted bright yellow
and there's a giant plastic bug on the front lawn. By the way,
the spaceplane's painted the same color."

Harry shook his head. "Hell of a thing to do to an XP-28.
They're sensitive, you know."

"I know." Xris was sympathetic. "You two can commiser-
ate over it."

Harry slowed the van. The others stared with interest out the window.

"Keep going," Xris advised. "The airstrip is another kilometer on ahead, at the end of this tarmac. You can see the hangar—"

"It's hard to miss," Jamil said dryly.

"I've seen some ugly shades of yellow, but that's the worst," Quong stated. "Don't you go turning color to match." He poked Tycho in the ribs.

"I don't believe that would be possible." Tycho shuddered.

The van flew along the marked route past the Olicien facility, heading for the hangar.

"The takeoff site's about a kilometer from the hangar, which puts it two kilometers from the main building. The hangar sits between the building and the spaceplane, so there's not much chance that anyone happening to look out a window of the main Olicien building would see anything funny going on with their spaceplane. Just in case anyone did see us and took it into his head to report us to the local cops, Quong's going to disrupt their communications, both phone and vidnet."

"Just as long as the Doc doesn't disrupt ours in the process," Jamil said. "Remember the Guaranty Fidelity Bank security job?"

Quong stiffened. "That will not happen again, I assure you, Major Khizr! The device I have with me blocks microwave transmissions only. Our comms work on the VHF band. Therefore, Major—"

Xris was quick to intervene. When the doctor got formal, trouble loomed.

"Look"—Xris pointed—"they've got the spaceplane out."

The others could barely see the plane. Jamil produced binocs. Xris adjusted the lens in his cybernetic eye, brought the distant plane into sharp focus.

"I can see four people from this angle. Here's where we leave the marked route, Harry. Take us to that low rise over there, the one that overlooks the tarmac."

Harry peered through the windscreen, nodded.

"Drop us off there," Xris ordered.

Harry steered the hovercraft for the hill, brought the vehicle down for a gentle landing. Quong produced his scanner, did a quick search for other craft. They were alone. No other vehicles nearby.

Xris opened the back end of the van, climbed out. Quong, from inside, handed the equipment to him. Tycho—rifle in hand—jumped to the ground and immediately began studying the area, looking for the best possible site. When everything was unloaded and Xris had run through the checklist, he looked at his chronometer.

"Oh-eight-forty-five." He turned back to the van. "On your way, Harry. Communications inside Olicien go down at oh-nine-hundred. We'll see you at the spaceplane at oh-nine-thirty. Jamil—remember the code cards. Good-bye and good luck."

Xris slammed shut the double doors. The van lifted off, headed back in the direction of the bright yellow building that was Olicien central.

"Move out," Xris ordered Tycho. "Keep us covered. Stun setting."

The tall alien nodded. He was already beginning to alter skin color, was now a mottled brown to match the brown bushes and scrub trees that dotted the barren hillside.

Xris and Quong gathered up their equipment, started walking down the slope. They headed for a creek that ran at an angle between the small hill and the spaceplane. The two splashed into the shallow water, proceeded upstream toward the tarmac and the spaceplane.

Xris stopped every few meters or so, scanned the area. He had lost sight of Tycho, but that wasn't unusual. The alien was probably hunkered down in the brush. He'd be the exact color of the hillside itself by now.

Xris turned his attention to the van, which was just pulling into the parking lot of the Olicien facility. Harry and Jamil both climbed out, straightened their ties. Briefcases in hand, they entered the main door of the building.

0855.

Quong halted, took off his backpack. He removed a collapsible metallic dish, placed it on the ground on the edge of the creek bank, aimed the dish at the vidnet antenna on top of the Olicien building. Using a spectrum analyzer, he scanned the communication airwaves for the frequencies in use, downloaded the information into the dish.

Looking back at the analyzer, he said, "All blocked."

0901.

Xris removed a grenade from his leg compartment, set its delay for six SMT hours, activated the detonation mechanism, and placed the grenade beside the metallic dish. He made it a practice to always take out the garbage.

Xris spoke into the commlink.

"Tycho, this is Xris, do you read me?"

"I read you loud and clear. I am in position. There are four targets on the tarmac in front of you."

"I see them. I'm going to give them five minutes. With luck they'll move to the far side of the plane. If not, you'll have to take them out."

"Understood."

Xris didn't want to have to cross the tarmac in full sight of God, the giant plastic beetle, and the crew of the spaceplane. He didn't want a bunch of comatose bodies littering the ground, either. The sight of fellow crewmen dropping over was almost certain to cause someone to panic and then all hell would break loose.

"Come on," he said to the crewmen under his breath. "Leave, damn it."

Almost as if obeying his order, three men walked around to the far side of the plane. A fourth remained, however, working on a maintenance panel on the winglet.

"Go along, kid," Xris told him. "Go follow after your buddies."

Quong stood beside him, squinting against the sunlight, unable to see anything more than the plane itself.

"Oh-nine-oh-five, Xris."

The Doc was holding a short-barreled autogun. It could fire two hundred bursts per second and was known as a "corridor broom" for its capability of making a clean sweep of any small area. It had no stun capabilities, but it was Doc's favorite weapon. Xris could trust Quong not to use it unless there was absolutely no other way out. And that wasn't going to happen.

Xris was feeling lucky.

The mechanic shut the panel. Bending down, he picked up his tool kit, started walking away.

"Xris!" Tycho was back. "Go for it! I've got you covered!"

Xris began running across the tarmac. Running was not an easy task for the cyborg, and one he generally tried to avoid. The metal part of his body worked faster and better than the physical; the flesh-and-blood half seemed a drag on the artificial. Consequently, his run was awkward and ungainly. He felt uncomfortable, unstable, and off balance. In the back of his mind lurked the fear that he might stumble and fall and something vital inside him would short out. He had visions of himself lying helpless on the tarmac.

Not today, said a voice. Today's the day. After all these years, it's finally coming together.

Xris relaxed, let the physical part of his body glide into synch with the metal, and loped across the landing strip. Quong was at his left, keeping pace easily. The middle-aged doctor wasn't even breathing hard.

The spaceplane stood on a tripod landing system. The plane was a new model based on an old design dating back to the dawn of spaceflight, but over the centuries no one had come up with anything as reliable and efficient. Two wings swept back from the fuselage, forming the delta-wing configuration necessary for in-atmosphere travel. It was big enough to accommodate passengers and cargo, was equipped with shields and reinforced superstructure to withstand the rigors of hyperspace.

Xris gestured. Quong headed for the nose of the spaceplane. Xris ran to the tail section.

The four crewmen were bunched together, gathered around a large maintenance 'bot, cheerfully discussing something being displayed on a computer screen. None of them was armed; not surprising.

This was all so easy. So damn easy.

Xris rounded the plane's tail, eased to a walk. He raised his weapons hand, aimed.

"Good morning, friends." Xris shouted above the conversation to make himself heard. "If you all keep very still, no one will get hurt."

At the sound of a strange voice, four heads jerked around. One of the men, who recognized Xris from their talk yesterday, grinned as if he thought this was a joke. The grin slid from his face when he got a good look at Xris's arm, noticed the metal projectiles that had replaced the cyborg's left hand.

Quong appeared from around the plane's nose, the autogun leveled.

The crewmen began to yammer. Typical Aurigans, they wanted to discuss the matter. A motion from Xris's metal hand silenced them. They raised their arms in the air.

Quong kept the men covered. Xris hurried to the hangar, looked inside. The hangar was extremely dark, especially after the brightness of the sunlit tarmac. His natural eye went temporarily blind, but his artificial eye instantly refocused and adjusted filters.

Only one man was in the hangar, and he was seated before a small computer, shouting commands at it. In addition, some sort of machine with a loose bearing was making a deafening racket. The man hadn't heard anything that had gone on outside, apparently. Xris walked right up to him, poked the hard steel of his weapons hand into the base of the man's skull.

"Don't say a word," Xris ordered. "Move your fingers away from the keyboard. Now."

It was possible the computer was tied to a central system inside Olicien. A verbal or typed warning could sound the alarm. The mechanic was too shaken by the sudden feel of cold steel on his flesh to do anything, however. He went rigid with fear. Xris eventually gave up trying to get the mechanic to raise his hands. The poor guy couldn't move.

Xris motioned. "Bring 'em inside."

The other four crewmen marched into the hangar, their hands on top of their heads. Quong dragged the fifth man out of the chair, added him to the group, and herded them into the center of the hangar.

Xris was back on the comm. "Tycho, this is Xris. All is secure. Move in."

"I'm on my way."

Xris left Quong on guard duty, went back outside. He touched a control on his arm. A door on the side of his mechanical leg popped open, revealing a holding rack for tools and weapons. Xris detached his weapons hand, placed it in the correct slot, and replaced it with a tool hand. The compartment door closed.

Making some minor adjustments, Xris walked to the maintenance 'bot, read the message on the monitor: *Maintenance check complete. All systems within operational parameters.*

"Couldn't have timed it better if I'd tried!" Xris gloated, and actually laughed.

He looked out over the tarmac, searching for Tycho. A flash of sun off the barrel of the beam rifle was the only clue to the alien's location. Tycho's skin had turned black, in order to blend in with the tarmac.

0910. Smooth. Very smooth.

Xris moved to the loading doors located on the other side of the spaceplane. They were sealed shut, locked. He found the security keypad, studied it. The numbered and ominously glowing pad was designed to allow access only to those who had authorized fingerprints and punched in the correct code. An alarm would sound if anyone else so much as breathed on the wrong key.

Xris touched a control on his mechanical hand. A durasteel cutting drill extruded from the center digit. He activated the drill, plunged the whirling bit into the "9" button on the keypad. The drill cut through wires and into a metal plate behind. Sparks flew. The keypad went dark. He held his breath.

No siren howled. Slowly, the hatch began to rise.

Tycho appeared at Xris's side, seeming to materialize out of the tarmac itself.

"Nice work, boss."

"It's a standard Morubundi K-33 Keypad. Any teenager with a screwdriver could have taken it out. Navy probably required them to install some sort of security system and Olicien bought the cheapest on the market."

"You can't blame them," said Tycho. "What are the odds that something like this would happen to them?"

"I guess this is just their lucky day," Xris said, grinning.

He headed back into the hangar, rejoined Quong and his prisoners, who were now slumbering peacefully on the cement floor. Quong exhibited a can of hypno-spray. Xris nodded.

Tycho set up his rifle on top of a storage bin, aimed the weapon at the double doors leading into the Olicien facility. Quong began to strip off the crew's yellow, bug-adorned coveralls.

0915. All going according to plan.

And then his comm buzzed.

Quong and Tycho looked up, faintly alarmed.

"Xris here," Xris answered briefly.

"Is this Mr. Borg's office? Is that you, Mable?" Harry's voice. "Uh, put me through to Cy, will you, sweetheart?"

Someone must be listening in.

Xris took out a twist, put it between his lips. "This is Mr. Borg. What's wrong, Harry?"

"It's Raoul, Cy. You heard from him?"

"No, not a word. What's the matter?"

"He's not here, Cy. Raoul never showed."

CHAPTER
13

"Shit!" said Xris loudly and with feeling.

The response came over clearly on Harry's cel'link.
Harry looked at Jamil, who shook his head. It was not exactly the response likely to come from the chief executive of
an outer space floating platform corporation. Harry looked
askance at the Olicien receptionist, afraid she, too, had heard
the expletive.

But the receptionist had begun talking to Harry and Jamil
the moment they entered the door and hadn't paused, except
to draw breath. She continued to talk now, and probably
hadn't heard, though she was starting to slow down and was
obviously getting a bit too interested in Harry's conversation. Jamil distracted her, asked a question about Raoul that
got her started again. Harry moved closer to the door, tried
to see out to the tarmac.

"This is weird, Xris," Harry said in a low voice, under
cover of Jamil's conversation. "We've waited for Raoul as
long as we can."

"Did you try his comm?"

"No response. What's really strange, he was supposed to
meet one of their people for breakfast at the hotel. He never
showed."

"Something's gone wrong."

Harry glanced at his watch. 0918.

"The question is, boss, do we go ahead?"

"We've gone too far to quit now. Proceed as planned. I'll try to raise Raoul. Out."

Harry stared a moment at the link, then replaced it in his briefcase, snapped the case shut. Jamil was watching him. Harry nodded once. Jamil flickered his eyelids in understanding.

"We'd like to meet with your manager anyway, if we could. Undoubtedly Mr. de Beausoleil will be here momentarily."

"Certainly. I'll let Mr. Darminderpal and Ms. Kohli know you are here. Too bad about Mr. de Beausoleil. I'd try calling him again, but our links don't appear to be working at the moment. Our commlink company is so impossible. This is the second time this month. Such a fine-looking young man, and so polite. We had a nice conversation yesterday. And his funny little friend in the raincoat. Never says a word, does he?" The receptionist, still talking, gazed curiously at Harry, who had begun to unpack the "contraption" from its case. "Why, what on Alius—"

"We thought we'd bring along the device we're currently using for exterminating the little critters," Jamil explained. "This unit just isn't doing the job for us. We figured your people should take a look at it."

Harry fit his arms into shoulder straps, hoisted a battery pack onto his back. A short length of hose trailed out the right side of the pack. He attached the hose to a large metal ring, attached three metal tubes to the ring, forming a triangle. Finally, he clicked into place a pistol grip with a triggering device. He flicked a switch. The battery pack hummed. The ring with the tubes began to rotate.

The receptionist stared at it, then began to giggle. "Why, you could destroy bugs the size of the one out there on our front lawn with that thing!"

"Why, yes. Yes, ma'am, we could," said Harry gravely.

The "contraption" was, in reality, a disguised 4.2-megawatt laser pulse cannon with triple rotating barrels. Specially designed and built by Quong, the cannon could take out the building, and everyone inside.

"I'm sure Mr. Darminderpal will be fascinated by it. He has a collection of extermination devices from all over the galaxy. . . ."

Continuing to talk to them, the receptionist managed, at the same time, to inform a Ms. Kohli that she had visitors.

This done, the receptionist turned her attention and her conversation back to the prospective new clients.

Harry reached into his suit pocket and pulled out a small spray can. "Then there's this product. We've tried applying it to our skin, but the damn bugs actually seem to enjoy the taste. Perhaps you're familiar with the brand?"

He held the can for the receptionist to see. As she leaned forward, peering intently at the label, Harry sprayed the contents of the can directly into the woman's face. She gasped involuntarily, inhaling the spray. Not that inhalation was necessary. As soon as Raoul's hypno-spray made skin contact, the victim was comatose.

The receptionist flopped forward across the desk.

Harry lifted her, propped her up in the chair, turned the chair away from both the hall and the front door.

Jamil took a quick glance out the door, locked it shut. "No one outside," he reported. "But we have company inside."

A woman in a brown suit was walking toward them. Jamil moved swiftly. "Good morning. I'm Kevin Coleridge. This is my colleague, Jeff Fuqua."

"How'dya do?" Harry bobbed his head.

"Jeff, why don't you wait here for Mr. de Beausoleil?" Jamil glanced significantly at the front door.

Ms. Kohli stared at the cannon. "What's that thing?"

"I'll explain later. We might even give you a demonstration. Where's your office? Nice building you have here. Such an interesting color."

Jamil took hold of Ms. Kohli by the arm, propelled her politely but firmly back down the hallway. "It seems that our Mr. de Beausoleil is late. We're operating on a rather strict time schedule. If we could go ahead with our meeting . . ."

"Of course, Mr. Coleridge. Come back to my office. I've sent for Mr. Darminderpal, our senior technician. Oh, just a moment. I forgot . . ." Pausing, the woman turned to the receptionist. "Madeline?"

Harry was bending over the desk, apparently having the most interesting conversation with the receptionist and managing to block the view of anyone in the hallway.

"Madeline, please hold my calls." Ms. Kohli didn't wait for a response.

She entered the office, moved aside to let Jamil pass in front of her. A thin man, clad in yellow coveralls, was standing at the window, staring with fixed intensity outdoors in the direction of the tarmac.

"That's odd . . ." the man began.

Jamil gave a loud and hacking cough.

Startled by the sound, the man turned his head.

Jamil was on him instantly, grabbing the technician's hand and shaking it heartily. "How do you do, sir? I'm Coleridge. Kevin Coleridge."

"Darminderpal." The man gave his name vaguely. He turned his head, looked back out the window.

"What is it?" Kohli asked.

"I thought I saw a stranger out there—"

"My business card."

Jamil reached into his pocket, took out a can of hypnospray and blasted Darminderpal in the face. The man gagged, gargled. His eyes rolled. He slumped forward. Jamil caught the flaccid body, lowered it to the floor.

"Don't move or make a sound," Jamil ordered, holding the spray can in front of Ms. Kohli.

Gliding past her, Jamil shut and locked the office door. Then, pocketing the spray can, he pulled a .22-decawatt lasgun from a shoulder holster. He glanced at his watch. 0930. They were running late.

"Keep very quiet and no one will get hurt. Your friend on the floor is just taking a nice little nap."

"What do you want?" the woman asked fearfully.

Jamil gestured with the gun toward a wall safe. "Open it."

Kohli shook her head.

"Is the money really worth your life?" Jamil demanded, his voice hard, gruff. "What about his?" He turned the gun on the comatose technician.

"But—but . . . there *is* no money." Kohli extended her hands in a pleading gesture. "You have to believe me! We only k-keep cash on payroll day and this isn't—"

"What? . . . Damn!" Jamil blustered. "Raoul really screwed this up good. He said *this* was payroll day!"

The woman just stared helplessly at him.

Jamil waved the gun. "Then if there's no cash, you won't mind opening the safe, will you? Or would you rather see me open up your tech's head?"

Kohli gulped, mumbled, "No, please. Don't hurt—"

"Move!"

She moved, opened the safe with her hand print and a coded entry.

Jamil shoved her roughly to one side. Peering in, he swore loudly. "My God! You're telling the truth. Nothing but plastic." He snatched up the spaceplane's code cards. "Let's see how much you have in your accounts."

He thrust the card into the computer.

"But those aren't credit cards. They only operate—"

"Operate what?" Jamil demanded, though he knew perfectly well.

The woman bit her lip, shut her mouth.

Muttering to himself, pretending to be frustrated over his inability to discover a bank account, Jamil was, in actuality, swiftly altering the code on the cards. This done, he removed them from the computer, slid them into his pocket. "Ah, hell! I'll work on this later. Wait till I get my hands on that Adonian!"

He pulled the aerosol can out of his pocket. "You're going to take a little nap now, like your friend. You might want to sit in the chair first."

The woman sank down in the plush chair behind the desk. Jamil sprayed her in the face. She blinked once, and slumped forward.

Jamil slid the lasgun back into the holster. Opening the office door, he glanced quickly up and down the hall.

"Yes, I know the way out, Ms. Kohli. Thanks. We'll be in touch."

Shutting the door, Jamil walked swiftly down the hall.

"Any trouble?"

Harry rose to his feet. "Nope, all quiet. You?"

"Their senior tech spotted one of our guys out by the plane. I sprayed him before he got a good look. Let's get out of here. We're already late."

"Did you get the cards, make the code change?"

"In here." Jamil slapped his pocket.

Harry unlocked the front door. They both walked out into the bright sunshine.

"Keep me covered," Jamil ordered.

Harry posted himself outside the front door.

Jamil opened his briefcase, removed a large canister. On the way into the company, he had looked for and found the building's central air-conditioning unit, located on the roof. Jamil climbed the maintenance ladder attached to the building's exterior wall. Once on the roof, he placed the canister beside the air intake system, pulled the ring tab on the top of the canister. White smoke began to rise and was immediately sucked into the system's intake. Jamil climbed down, rejoined his partner.

Harry was on the comm. "Xris, we've got the code cards. We're now leaving the building. Jamil's released the gas. Everyone inside should be sound asleep by now."

"Good work. When you come, bring the van. There's been a change in plans. Out."

The two exchanged glances, then each looked at his watch.

0940. It was rather late for a change in plans.

When the van pulled up to the hangar, Xris was there to meet it. The cyborg yanked open the door on Jamil's side.

"I'm going to find out what's happened to Raoul. I'll take Harry with me. You and the others load the gear in the plane. Search through the company's flight records—you'll find them in the hangar office. Find the latest codes and approach vectors for today's run."

Jamil jumped out. Xris, barely waiting for him, climbed inside the van. Tycho and Quong, wearing bright yellow coveralls, stood near the spaceplane.

"What about the clock?" Jamil shouted over the roar of the hovervan's engine.

"Screw the clock!" Xris yelled. "We need Raoul and the empath! Don't worry. We'll make up the time en route."

He slammed shut the door. Jamil backed hurriedly away.

Inside the van's cab, all was quiet. Harry was looking unhappy.

"Just drive, damn it!" Xris said irritably.

Harry drove, wheeling the vehicle around so swiftly that the blast from the air jets nearly knocked Jamil off his feet.

"Where's his hotel? Near here, I hope."

"Yeah, Xris. Not far. But—"

Xris brought up the computer map. "What's the name? I'll punch it in. Get the fastest route."

Harry looked even more unhappy. "Uh, that's just it, Xris. I can't remember the name of the hotel. But"—he perked up—"I do remember his room number. Ten-nineteen."

Xris removed the twist from his mouth. "You what?"

"I don't remember the name of the hotel, Xris," Harry

said miserably. "I'm sorry. I'd had a few drinks. It just didn't register. But the room number. I know that."

"That's going to be a fucking big help. Do you know how many hotels there are in this bloody city?"

Xris didn't often swear. Harry's hands tightened on the wheel. He stared straight ahead. A muscle in his jaw twitched.

"I know about where it is, Xris," he said suddenly. "And I know what it looks like. It's a fancy building. I'll know it when I get there."

Xris drew in a deep breath, let it out slowly. "All right. I guess that'll have to do."

"I'm sorry, Xris. I didn't think it would be important."

"Just drive, Harry. Just drive."

0945.

Harry recognized the hotel—the Grand Aurigan—easily. It was big and elegant. Valets swarmed around the front entrance, eager to relieve travel-weary guests of all their burdens, including their means of transportation.

"Valet parking, Xris," Harry said, slowing the van to a crawl about a block away from the hotel.

"We can't risk that," Xris replied. "We're going to need to leave here fast. Drive around."

They located a side entrance, with only a doorman on duty. Vehicles of all types lined the street. There was no place to park. Harry dropped the van to street level.

"Stay here. Keep the engine running and your comm on," Xris instructed, jumping out.

He had removed the tool hand, replaced it with the flesh-foam hand, but had not bothered to change out of his fatigues. The doorman glared at him.

"He can't hover there," he said.

"I'll only be a minute," Xris told him, heading for the door.

"But—" The doorman started to argue.

Xris shoved the man aside, yanked open the door. When the elevator didn't arrive fast enough to suit him, the cyborg found the stairs, took them two at a time to the tenth floor.

He emerged through a fire door, began scanning room numbers. A woman with a small child passed him, both in swimsuits, evidently on their way to the pool. Otherwise, the corridors were quiet, empty.

"No one around," Xris reported to Harry over the comm. "I was half expecting to find the hallway jammed with cops. But nothing appears to be wrong."

"The damn Loti took an overdose," Harry returned. "You'll probably find him spaced out of his mind. Or maybe he met someone in the bar last night. Or some *thing*. I hate to think what you might be walking in on."

It's possible, Xris agreed, just not probable. In all the years he'd worked with Raoul, the Adonian had never let the team down. Xris halted in front of a large double wooden door with 1019 in brass digits.

He listened. His augmented hearing would have picked up the flutter of Raoul's false eyelashes.

No sound.

Xris scanned the hall. No one in sight except a cleaning 'bot down at the far end. Removing his lasgun from his shoulder holster, Xris lightly tapped on the door with the barrel.

"Raoul!" he called.

He hoped—hoped like hell—the door would open. He'd find the embarrassed and apologetic Loti trying to kiss him.

The door remained closed.

"I'm going in," Xris told Harry.

Gun in hand, Xris kicked his steel leg into the door, burst it open. Splinters flew. The lock snapped. He dashed in, his gun moving in a tracking arc, looking for targets. He saw nothing more alarming than one of Raoul's hats.

The room was made up. The beds hadn't been slept in. Raoul's luggage was open, clothes strewn about—on the bed, on the floor. A red taffeta cloak was draped over the vid. Xris might have concluded immediately that the place had been trashed, but Raoul's bedroom back home looked exactly the same, only worse. Even an overturned lamp was nothing out of the ordinary, if Raoul happened to be suffering through a bad hair day.

And then, "Damn it all," Xris said softly.

"What is it, Xris?" Harry heard the cyborg's ominous tone. "What've you found?"

Xris didn't answer. Walking over to a cream-colored wall, he examined the large wet splotch, touched it. Then he swore.

"Blood. And it's fresh."

"You need me up there?"

"No. Stay with the van."

Xris found several more red spots on the carpet, still more in front of the bathroom. Gun raised, he slowly pushed open the bathroom door with the toe of his boot, looked in the mirror on the wall to see if anyone was inside.

No one was. At least not that he could see from this angle.

Xris shoved open the door, whipped around it.

"Dear God in heaven!" he said, appalled.

"Xris! What is it? You okay?"

"I'm fine," Xris said bitterly. "It's the Little One."

The small figure lay huddled in the bathtub. Blood was spattered all over the walls and the sides of the tub; the raincoat was soaked red, especially around the collar. The fedora was askew on the battered head.

Gently, Xris removed the hat, to try to get a better look at the injuries. He recoiled in revulsion and shock. Not from the sight of blood or the brutal punishment the small body had taken; Xris had seen people beaten up before. It was the sight of the small body itself.

"Xris?" Harry was getting nervous. "You better hurry. That doorman's been raising hell about our parking in a no-park zone. What's going on? Is the little fellow dead?"

"Beats the hell out of me," Xris said, baffled. "At first I thought his face was smashed in. Now I'm beginning to think he was just born this way."

Kneeling beside the body, Xris put his hand on what he presumed was the neck. He thought he could feel a pulse, but if so, it was faint and thready.

He glanced swiftly around the bathroom, looking for a towel to stanch the bleeding, saw an object on the counter.

His lips tightened. He changed his mind about the towel. Shoving the lasgun into its holster, he went back to the bedroom, yanked a blanket off the bed, returned to the bathroom. He worked swiftly, trying to be gentle, but aware that time was ticking away.

Time for the job. Time for the Little One's life.

He wrapped the small, bloodied body in the blanket, lifted it easily in his arms. Making certain the blanket covered every part of the Little One, Xris carried the empath out of the hotel room. He took the stairs again, figuring the odds of meeting anyone on the fire escape were slim.

"Harry, I'm coming out. I've got the Little One with me. See if you can distract that doorman."

"No need to worry, Xris," Harry returned. "I think he's gone to get the cops."

Xris made it down the stairs and out the door, practically knocked over a couple entering the building. They looked at him and his burden in startled surprise.

"Sick kid," Xris said, barreling past them.

Harry was waiting outside the van. He had the back doors open. Xris laid the Little One inside, then jumped in himself. Harry had already returned to the driver's seat. The van lifted into the air, soared down the block just as the doorman, in company with a traffic cop, rounded the corner.

"So what's happened?" Harry glanced back worriedly at the blanket-covered body. "Is the Little One dead? Where's Raoul?"

"I don't think the little fellow's dead, but he's not all that alive, either. We'll take him back to Quong. If anyone can fix him up, it'll be the Doc. As for Raoul . . ." Xris paused, then said, "I found his makeup kit on the bathroom sink."

Harry gave a low whistle, shook his head.

"The room was a mess, like there'd been a fight," Xris continued. "All his clothes are still there."

"Raoul wouldn't go to his own funeral without his makeup kit," Harry observed, glanced sideways at Xris. "Except in this case, maybe?"

"I don't think he's dead." Xris drew the blanket closer around the Little One, tucked it in. "We'd have found Raoul in the same condition as the Little One. The Loti's been snatched. Someone kidnapped Raoul."

Harry was silent a moment, pondering. Then he said, in all seriousness, "But, Xris . . . who would *want* him?"

CHAPTER
14

It is a bad plan that admits of no modification.
                    Publilius Syrus, *Maxims*, 469

Who in the universe would want Raoul?

"A good question," Xris admitted.

"You think it's got something to do with this job?"

The thought had already occurred to Xris. He'd discarded the notion before he was halfway out the hotel room.

"Not logical. The people at Olicien sure as hell didn't expect us, did they?"

Harry neatly maneuvered his way around a lumbering truck. "Nope. They were *real* surprised."

"And if the Royal Navy was on to us—say Wiedermann went crazy and tipped them off—they'd be after *me*. Raoul's made a lot of enemies over the years, but most of those would want him dead. Why take him alive?"

"Information," Harry guessed. "About us."

Xris shook his head. "You ever try to get information from a Loti? Half of it you *can't* believe and the other half you don't *want* to believe. But that's not the problem."

"Yeah." Harry grunted. "The job."

The job. What to do without Raoul and the Little One? Raoul, the charmer, the talker. Raoul, who was supposed to distract the security guard at RFComSec, then shoot him full of dope to keep him from sounding the alarm. And the Little One, who was supposed to read the guard's mind, alert Raoul to possible danger.

Xris glanced down at the small body. Blood was starting to soak through the blanket. If the Little One survived, he wasn't going to be reading anyone's mind today. And who would he communicate with if he did? The Little One never "talked" to anyone except Raoul.

Xris swore softly to himself. He should abort the job right now. End it. Give it up. Call it off. The Olicien people would think it was a bungled robbery, leave it at that. Breaking into RFComSec was too dangerous without Raoul and the Little One.

Too dangerous.

And yet, Xris said to himself, when will I have this chance again?

Olicien would be on their guard after this. Plus the Royal Navy—eternally paranoid—would undoubtedly conclude that this "robbery" had something to do with their top-secret space station. They'd tighten security until not even His Majesty could get on base without being strip-searched. What's worse, the Navy might start asking questions. . . .

Xris took out a twist, absently chewed on it, stared out the van's window. He was seeing not the Olicien Pest Control factory, which was looming ahead, but another factory. A factory in a swamp. A factory that had become a tomb.

A tomb for the living, as well as the dead.

For though they termed him "alive," the living Xris, the Xris he had been, was buried in the rubble alongside what remained of Ito.

The van glided to a halt, set down on the tarmac. The rest of the team surged out of the hangar. Xris shoved open the doors.

"Doc!" he called. "Take a look at the Little One. Harry, start the plane up. The rest of you get on board; Doc and I'll be along in a second. Someone's kidnapped Raoul. We'll have to go without him."

Harry came around to the back end of the van. Doc was already inside, examining the Little One. Tycho and Jamil looked at Harry, looked at each other, looked at Xris.

"We *are* going," Xris said, his voice tight. "We've gone too far to stop now."

The others nodded, left. Xris couldn't tell whether they agreed with him or were simply too well disciplined to argue.

Not that it mattered.

He turned back to the van.

"Holy Master!" he heard Quong say, and the man sounded awed.

"Well, Doc? How is he?" Xris tried to curb his impatience to be gone.

Quong turned. His almond-shaped eyes were wide; his mouth gaped.

"Xris, did you know? He"—the Doc gestured at the Little One—"he is a Tongan! I've never seen one before, but I'd stake my professional career on it."

"I don't care if he's Derek Sagan's grandmother," Xris said acidly. "Is he alive?"

"Yes, but—"

"Can you help him?"

"I *think* so." Quong sounded dubious. "I don't know that much about Tongan physiology. No human in our profession does. You see, no one's ever had a living specimen to study. Or a dead one, for that matter. No human has ever been allowed on the planet and, so far as I know, not a single Tongan has been permitted off-planet. This is a rare opportunity—"

"Save it for your thesis!" Xris snapped. "Let's get him onto the plane!"

"Certainly, Xris." Quong was calm, efficient. And he was once again eyeing Xris with concern. "If you could carry him. Be careful. Try to support the head. . . ."

Xris reached down, lifted the Little One in his arms, and stalked off to the spaceplane.

"Good morning, XP-28." Harry eased himself into the pilot's chair in the spaceplane's cockpit. "My name is Harry Luck. I'm the new pilot. You might want to adjust your voice activation to my verbal patterns."

"Good morning, Pilot Luck. Please enter your Olicien authorization number to transfer pilot functions."

Harry took the code card Jamil had obtained in the Olicien offices, slid the card into the console. A series of letters and numbers appeared on the computer screen, flashed on and off. Then came the word: *Proceed.*

"Pilot Luck," said the computer. "Welcome aboard. You must be a new employee. According to my bioscans, the entire cleaning crew is new. One of your people is injured. Why is this person being brought on board? I recommend that he be left on the ground for treatment."

Xris arrived in the cockpit, pointed grimly to the plane's

chronometer. 1030. They were already behind schedule by thirty minutes.

"I have received and duly noted your recommendation, XP-28," Harry said calmly. "One of our people is a doctor. He's treating our friend now. But thank you for your concern. I'm uploading the flight plan, approach vectors, and the authenticity codes for the flight to the space station. Oh, and we're running a bit late. Bypass the fuel conservation program, if you have to, in order to reach RFComSec on time."

The computer hummed to itself a moment, then said, a bit stiffly, "Yes, Pilot Luck. I suppose you will be taking manual control now?"

Harry leaned back comfortably in his chair. "No, no. You handle it."

The computer's screen actually appeared to glow with pleasure.

"It is obvious you are a true professional, Pilot Luck. Unlike others I could mention. I perceive no difficulty in making up the time. In fact, I could get us there twenty minutes *ahead* of schedule."

"Uh, no," Harry said hastily. "They might not be ready for us. We'd only have to sit in the docking bay and wait."

"I understand. Please strap yourselves in. We will be taking off in ten minutes. I'll be leaving you now, to begin prelaunch cycle."

"It's all yours," Harry said complacently.

The computer busied itself. The hatch sealed shut, lights came on. Life-support began its comforting hiss.

"Some pilot you are," Xris muttered, taking advantage of the delay to change into the bright yellow coveralls. "Sitting there doing nothing. I thought you hated letting computers run things."

Harry shrugged. "In some cases. In this one, I've made the computer my friend."

"True. I thought we were in for a fight there."

"We would have been, with an old XJ model. Those independent-minded computers were a pain in the ass. These XP-28s . . ." Harry gave the computer a pat on its console. "You just have to know how to handle them. Most pilots don't. They refuse to relinquish control. Which makes no sense. The computer can handle the mundane stuff—takeoff, landing, routine flights—more efficiently than any human pilot. And, as you can see, it gets a real ego boost. I always work this way with an XP-28. From now on, I can do no wrong."

Xris grunted and ripped a seam out of the shoulder. He was far bigger than the last man to wear this bug outfit.

Harry cast an admiring glance at the cargo plane's cadaverous, ugly, utilitarian interior. "This plane is a beauty, Xris. I don't suppose we could keep it? I could give it a new paint job."

"We're going to be in enough trouble already. If anything goes wrong at RFComSec, every ship in the Navy will be on the alert for this craft. We'll use it to throw off pursuit. Once we reach home, we'll set the plane on autopilot and send it back."

"A real shame." Harry sighed.

Xris took over the copilot's seat, swiveled around.

The plane's interior was dark, green, and smelled of chemicals and grease. Since the plane's main function was to transport cargo on short hops, passenger comfort was not a priority. There were no windows, except in the cockpit. Large tracks, designed to wheel heavy equipment on and off, ran from the tail section, down the center, almost to the cockpit. Passengers and crew sat on metal-frame seats bolted to the bulkheads or rested in metal-frame cots attached in the same manner. It was in one of these that Xris had laid the Little One. They had stowed the bug-'bot (as Tycho called them) maintenance machinery in the rear. Everyone was now strapped in, ready for takeoff.

"How's the Little One, Doc?"

"He'll live. His people apparently have remarkably thick skulls. A blow like that would have pulverized mine. His is cracked, but not seriously. He's lost a lot of blood and he's going to be unconscious for a while, but he'll wake up with no more than a nasty headache."

"Not in the middle of the raid, I presume?"

"Unlikely. We'll be leaving him on board?"

Xris nodded. The spaceplane lifted off, began rocketing through the atmosphere. The Olicien Pest Control Company was suddenly a bright yellow patch on the fast-receding ground. No one spoke until the plane had cleared the planet's atmosphere, was heading for the Lanes, where they would make the jump to hyperspace. Star-studded blackness surrounded them. At that point, the computer switched off the main thrusters and it was possible to hear again.

Jamil asked the questions that were on everyone's mind. "So what's the change in plan? How do we manage without the charmer and the empath? Who's going to keep the guard occupied?"

"Harry will take Raoul's place," Xris said.

Harry blinked. He looked as if he'd been hit over the head with a plastisteel pipe. "What? Me? But—"

"It makes sense," Xris continued. "I want you to stick close to the spaceplane so that if anything does go wrong, you can reach it before all hell breaks loose. As for the guard, just talk to him, that's all."

"But I don't have the drug!" Harry protested. "Raoul was supposed to drug the guy!"

"You've got the hypno-spray—"

"Yeah, right. Some iron-guts Marine lets me waltz up and shove an aerosol can in his face! Right!" Harry was bitter.

"You'll think of something," Xris said curtly.

Unstrapping himself, he headed back to the rear cargo bay to double-check the equipment. The others exchanged glances. Discussion over. Quong shook his head.

"Pilot Luck," said the computer, "we are coming up on the Lanes. Would you care to review my calculations for the jump to hyperspace?"

"Uh, yeah. Sure." Glumly, Harry returned to his duties.

The spaceplane made the jump. The team members were, for the most part, silent. Xris had not returned from the rear cargo bay area. They could see him, an indistinct shadow brightened by occasional glints of ambient light off metal. They could all smell the rank tobacco smoke. They all concluded—rightly—that he wanted to be left alone.

Quong remained near the Little One. The empath had not regained consciousness. The doctor took the opportunity to examine his comatose patient. Speaking into a handheld recorder, he entered all his newly discovered information on the physiology of a Tongan.

Jamil found a cot, stretched out for a nap.

Harry, hunched morosely in the pilot's seat, was playing games with the computer.

Tycho came forward, tossed a vid cassette in Harry's lap. "Here, I found this when I was back at the bug place. I figured I'd give it to Raoul, but it looks like maybe you could use it."

Harry picked up the vid, glanced at the title and groaned. *Fleas: The Immortal Enemy.*

CHAPTER 15

When the speed of rushing water reaches the point
where it can move boulders, this is momentum.

Sun Tzu, *The Art of War*

"Pilot Luck, we are entering the one-light-year exclusion
zone around the RFComSec space station. I have already obtained preliminary clearance through flight operations, but security would like to speak to the person in
charge. They have scanned us," the computer added with
maddening complacency, "and they have some questions."

Harry glanced at Xris, seated in the copilot's chair.

"Relax. I expected as much." Xris leaned forward. "Put
me through."

The computer complied and the next voice they heard was
RFComSec.

"Olicien Two Five Niner, this is Approach Control. Are
you receiving me?"

Xris spoke calmly. "This is Olicien Two Five Niner. We
are on approach to your station on our regularly scheduled
pest extermination visit. We've given you the security
passwords and clearances. Is there a problem, Approach
Control?"

"No, Olicien Two Five Niner. All that's fine. But according to our scans, you're not the regular crew, plus you're
short-handed. There's normally seven."

"Approach Control, the regular crew has been stranded on
Clinius. They were doing a job on that planet when their
ship was struck by lightning. Fried the electrical circuitry.
My crew was the only crew with the requisite clearances to
act as replacements for this one trip."

Xris chewed on a twist. If Approach Control was the least bit suspicious and tried to check up on them through Olicien, this trip was going to be a short one. But he was counting on the fact that this sort of incident couldn't be all that unusual. In twenty years of flea eradication, there must have been times when the regular crew didn't show. Damn it, it wasn't that big a deal!

Let it go right, Xris pleaded silently with Fate. You owe me this one. Let it go—

"Olicien Two Five Niner, you are cleared to Shuttle Bay One."

Harry exhaled loudly. "You know the procedure, XP-28. Take us in."

Quong came forward into the cockpit, a subcutaneous inserter in his hand. "Gentlemen, it is time for me to insert the communicators."

Harry grimaced, rubbed the back of his neck. "Jeez, I hate those damn things! It hurts like hell going in and I always end up with a rash. I think I'm allergic. Why can't we just use our regular commlinks?"

"Because the real exterminators wouldn't have sophisticated equipment like that," Xris answered. "We didn't find any type of communication devices in the equipment they had ready to load on board. It's likely they just use the station's internal communication system. Make sure, when you talk into these, that no one hears you."

"I know. I know," Harry grumbled. "But won't they hear us anyway? I mean, with all the fancy scanning equipment they've got on board, aren't they likely to pick up our signal?"

"The odds are against it." Jamil joined them in the cockpit. "Remember, the arrival of the exterminators on RFComSec is a common occurrence. People are used to it; they're complacent. They won't be looking for trouble and unless you're scanning specifically for this type of transmission, you won't find it."

"It's a chance we'll have to take. Which means we keep communication down to the bare minimum. High urgency/ need-to-know only. Besides"—Xris patted Harry on the knee—"you're going to keep the guard so enthralled with your scintillating conversation that he wouldn't notice a direct hit from a plasma cannon."

"Yeah." Harry snorted. He flinched when Quong placed

the cold metal inserter on his skin behind his ear, yelped when the device went in. "It's the sound I hate. Thump! Like it hits bone or something."

"It's all in your head," Quong said, and laughed loudly at his own joke.

He was the only one. Harry didn't get it. Xris didn't hear it. He was staring fixedly at the space station.

"Xris . . ."

He glanced around. "What? Did you say something, Doc?"

"I'll need to make adjustments to your receiver to put you on the same frequency," Quong repeated patiently. He'd said the same thing three times now.

Xris tilted his head. The Doc depressed a tiny button in back of the cyborg's left ear, opened a small panel. Using minuscule, delicate tools, Quong made the necessary adjustments.

"Okay, boss. Give it a try."

"Right, listen up. Does everybody hear me?"

Harry nodded, grumbled. "Yeah. It tickles. I hate that damn tickle."

Tycho's voice reverberated in Xris's ear. "Check."

Jamil came in next.

Quong confirmed his with a quick nod. He snapped shut the panel.

"What do you want me to do with the Little One?"

"Leave him here. He'll be all right, won't he?"

"Yes, but that wasn't what I meant. Surely someone on that station is going to ask why only five of us show up for work when they've scanned six life-forms on board."

Xris swore to himself and at himself. *I should have considered that, already made plans. I'm slipping. Too emotionally involved. Yeah, I'm emotionally involved!*

He made a pretense of running a systems check on his cybernetic arm.

"Good thinking, Doc. Bandage up the little guy's face real good. Hide the bloodstained raincoat and hat. Cover him with a blanket. I'll feed them a line if they ask."

Quong departed. The others stood around, staring at him. Concerned.

Xris glanced at them irritably. "You guys got nothing better to do?"

They filtered out.

"Coming up on the thousand-kilometer marker, Pilot Luck," the computer reported.

The thousand-kilometer marker was a small navigational buoy placed in the approach lane to guide incoming vessels. Acting as guide was apparently not its only function, however. Strobe lights began to flash.

"We are being scanned, Pilot Luck," XP-28 informed them.

"I thought we'd already been scanned," Harry protested.

"They're looking for weapons," Xris said briefly.

"Well, they won't find any on board this plane," Harry stated with an accusatory glance at Xris. "They're all stacked neatly in that bloody hangar back at Olicien."

Xris smiled, shrugged. Leaving the weapons behind had been—and obviously still was—a sore point. When he'd first mentioned that the team would have to enter the facility weaponless ("Naked!" Tycho said indignantly), Xris was afraid he'd have to either call off the project or find a different team. Harry had balked, Tycho and Jamil had argued vehemently. Even Quong, who generally obeyed orders with cold-blooded mechanical precision, had expressed doubts.

"If everything goes according to plan," Xris had argued patiently, "we won't need weapons. I don't want to take the chance of an innocent person getting hurt. We'll be long gone before anyone ever figures out something's wrong. We stroll in, stroll out. An hour after we've left, Dalin Rowan drops dead. Cause: unknown."

This part of the plan had not met with general enthusiasm.

"And if something *does* go wrong?" Jamil had asked.

"The station is crawling with armed Marines," Xris had replied lightly. "You won't have any trouble finding weapons."

"We just can't shoot anyone," Jamil had said glumly.

"Right."

The cargo plane flew slowly past the marker.

Xris reached in his pocket, pulled out a twist, and lit it. The statement that there were no weapons on board wasn't quite accurate. Tycho had brought along the duonamic sights. Xris was armed. His weapons hand and its assorted devices were packed into his leg compartment. Shielded, of course, but a truly sophisticated scanner might just pick them up. . . .

Olicien Two Five Niner set off no alarms.

RFComSec rotated like a pinwheel in space. The central hub, bristling with communications antennae, transmitters, receivers, was brightly lit. Four arms extended from the hub to an outer ring. This ring—the living area for the three thousand residents of RFComSec—was dark by comparison. Only a few sporadic tiny specs of light, shining through windows, glittered against the darkness.

"Cutting engines," the computer announced. "We will coast in until the magnetic tractor beams lock on."

A slight jolt indicated that this had occurred.

"Olicien Two Five Niner," came a voice, "you are now under station control."

Soon, Xris told himself, almost shaking with excitement. In maybe thirty minutes or less, I'll be face-to-face with Dalin Rowan.

He could swear that he could see Ito's face floating in front of him.

At the hub's center, a door one hundred meters wide and fifty meters tall began to open. The spaceplane glided into the aperture. The plane's metallic skin shimmered with the reflected energy of the atmospheric integrity force field, which maintained the atmosphere inside the station during the time shuttle bay doors were open. Once the craft was inside, control personnel guided the spaceplane slowly to the middle of the bay, rotated it, and set it down.

Looking out the plane's viewscreen, Xris read, in Standard Military, the words: *Unsecured. Quarantine.*

"Damn!" he muttered, blowing smoke. "Quarantine! We've been scanned. Why the hell are we being quarantined?"

"Maybe they're looking for bugs?" Harry chortled. He prodded the cyborg. "That's a joke."

"Computer, is this standard procedure?" Xris snapped, in no mood for humor.

"Yes, sir. We normally enter this area. The plane and its cargo are checked by security. The equipment is scanned here, then the plane is moved over to the loading dock. It's routine."

Routine! Xris stared at the yellow markings, at the steel doors that were now rumbling shut. Ito's face disappeared.

I should have asked about the routine, Xris told himself. The one member of the flight crew who has been here— probably a hundred times or more—is the XP-28 flight computer. I should have taken the time during the flight to find out from the computer exactly what the landing procedure was. It's what I would have done on any other job. Another error in judgment.

"Go on back, tell the rest what's going on, and see if they need help with the equipment," Xris told Harry. "I'll be there in a minute."

Harry hesitated, then said softly, "Sure, Xris." He unstrapped his harness and left.

"So far, I've been lucky," Xris said aloud to nobody. "The next mistake I make could be the last mistake I make."

He unclipped the shoulder harnesses holding him into the copilot's chair, stood up, and moved back to the cargo area.

"Don't worry. There won't be another," he said to himself—and to the memory of Mashahiro Ito.

The team was assembled, all wearing their yellow coveralls with the large black beetle and OLICIEN PEST CONTROL emblazoned on the back. The Little One, his extraordinarily ugly and battered face concealed by bandages, slept soundly on the cot. Quong had bundled the empath in bulky blankets to conceal his small stature. The bloodstained fedora and the raincoat had been safely stowed away in a locked compartment.

"Everyone know what he has to do?" Xris glanced around.

They all replied in the affirmative. Calm. They were all confident, self-possessed, calm. Xris envied them.

"This is it, then," he continued. "Harry, go back to the cockpit. Take the plane to the loading dock, then head up to central security ops and start shmoozing about fleas. Computer, open the cargo bay hatch."

The hatch opened. The loading ramp descended to the deck of the shuttle bay. A Marine lieutenant, backed up by a detail of six armed soldiers, was there waiting for them. The ramp thudded into place. The lieutenant motioned for the pest control team to join him. They all clumped down the ramp.

"Who's in charge?" the lieutenant asked.

"I am," Xris said, stepping forward. He extended his good hand. "Aaron Schwartz."

The lieutenant shook hands cordially, glanced at Xris with only minimal curiosity. The Marine had obviously seen his share of cyborgs.

The yellow coveralls effectively hid Xris's metal leg. He

had attached his tool hand, however, equipped with drill and screwdriver and other instruments—routine, with one small exception. The thumb was a special design, housed a tiny needle. When activated by contact, the needle popped out, injected a delayed-action lethal drug.

"I see you've got a new team this time, Schwartz." The lieutenant was relaxed, jovial, obviously thankful for any excuse to break the monotonous duty on this isolated space station. "So Kloosterman and Lypps got stranded on Clinius, did they? Poor bastards. Dullest planet in the galaxy. And you got tagged for this detail."

"Yes, sir. We were the only ones available who were cleared for the job." Xris gestured behind him. "You want to look over our equipment?"

The lieutenant gave it a bored glance. "Maybe a quick look. Just to make sure you guys aren't trying to smuggle jump-juice in here." He laughed.

Xris gave a polite chuckle.

The lieutenant did a head count. "Our scans indicated six life-forms. Who's still on board?"

"My pilot is waiting to move the plane over to the docks, and I've got an injured crew member. The load shifted when we made the jump. He got clonked a good one."

The lieutenant was concerned. "I'll summon a medic."

"Won't be necessary, sir, thanks. He's out cold."

"But it won't be any trouble," the lieutenant persisted. "Our doctor could check him over while you work."

"One of our guys is an EMT. He bandaged him up. It's not really necessary to bother your medical staff. Besides, technically he was injured on Olicien property. The company's responsible. Your people would have to fill out a diskload of forms, what with worker's comp, insurance, medical release waivers. It wouldn't be worth the hassle just for a bump on the head."

"You've got a point." The lieutenant considered the situation a moment, wrote down something on his electronic notepad. He showed it to Xris, offered an electronic pen. "I've made a notation that I offered medical treatment and that you refused. If you'd sign here . . ."

Xris did so, solemnly scrawling the name "Aaron Schwartz" on the line indicated.

"There. That should satisfy the authorities." The lieutenant smiled, relieved. "Sergeant, take your detail on board."

The soldiers trooped up the ramp. Jamil and the others moved to one side to let them past. A few of the Marines gave Tycho an odd look. The chameleon's skin had, unfortunately, changed to the same obnoxious yellow color as his coveralls.

Five minutes later, the Marines exited the plane. The sergeant made his report.

"Nothing out of the ordinary, Lieutenant. All the equipment checks out. The injured man seems okay. He's asleep. I didn't want to disturb him."

The lieutenant turned back to Xris. "Very well, Schwartz. Move your plane over to loading dock 28L. The sergeant here will escort you gentlemen to that location to unload your gear, then on to Engineering. Clear?"

"Yes, sir. Thanks." Xris yelled up to Tycho, who had keyed the intercom button on the door control. "Tell Harry he has clearance to move into loading dock 28L. We'll meet him there."

Tycho solemnly repeated the message via the spaceplane's comm, although Harry had already heard everything over his own internal commlink.

The spaceplane lifted from the deck and glided smoothly forward.

The lieutenant spoke a few words to the sergeant, then headed for the exit. The sergeant ordered one of his men to stay with the team, and dismissed the rest.

"Good hunting, Schwartz," the sergeant said, smiling.

"Thanks for the help, Sergeant."

The sergeant left. Xris and his team, accompanied by a young Marine, were marched over to loading dock 28L. They found the plane there ahead of them, settled on the deck in the designated area. Harry lowered the cargo ramp.

Jamil, Tycho, and Quong located several floating air-carts, activated them, and took them up the ramp into the spaceplane. Harry joined Xris on the deck. The escort Marine stood several meters away, his beam rifle carelessly slung over his shoulder. He was relaxed, interested in the proceedings, which were a change from boring routine. He certainly wasn't expecting trouble.

In low tones, Harry asked, "Everything go okay?"

"So far."

Tycho and Jamil appeared, pushing air-carts loaded with equipment down the ramp.

Quong shoved the last cart out of the plane. He reached over to the control panel to close the hatch.

Xris waved, caught the Doc's attention. The hatch took twenty seconds to cycle through before it opened. Those twenty seconds might mean the difference between life and death if they had to make a fast exit.

Quong left the hatch open, the ramp in place, and joined the others on the loading dock.

"We're all set to go, boss," Jamil said loudly.

The Marine glanced back at the spaceplane. "You're not going to shut the hatch, sir?"

Xris grinned. "Why, kid? You afraid someone's gonna steal my plane?"

The Marine stared, momentarily taken aback. Then he laughed, somewhat shamefacedly. "No, sir. I guess not. If you'll follow me. Oh, and, uh, sir. I'm sorry, but smoking's not permitted anywhere in the space station."

Xris had the twist in his mouth. He started to offer his customary explanation that he wasn't going to smoke the damn thing, then decided it would be easier to put the twist away. He didn't want trouble of any sort.

He and Harry helped push the heavily loaded carts. Xris paired himself up with Jamil, the only ex-military man among them. They exited the loading dock, entered the space station interior.

Wide double doors led into a faintly lit access corridor. Pipes and cables were visible overhead, providing heat, power, oxygen, and other services. The walls were painted white. Emergency oxygen stations and fire-fighting equipment were mounted in compartments in the wall every twenty meters. The team moved along in single file behind the Marine.

They passed two more sets of double doors, marked by signs in Standard Military. The first read SS-SIGINT 2–2 and the other HS-SIGINT.

Xris, mentally going over the layout of the space station, tried to get a fix on their location. "What does that mean?" he asked Jamil, not bothering to lower his voice. With the rattle of the equipment and the whoosh of air from the cart, the cyborg wasn't worried about being overheard.

"*SigInt* stands for 'Signal Intelligence,' " Jamil returned. "I don't know what the other letters mean."

"Let's hope it isn't important."

The access corridor opened into a large, brightly lit work area. Overhead cranes were built into tracks in the ceiling. Huge metal-paneled doors lined the walls. Yellow and black floor markings were covered by puddles of greenish motor oil.

"Please wait here, sir," the Marine instructed. "I'll inform Commander Drake that you've arrived."

The Marine left.

"This is Engineering," said Jamil.

Xris marked it on his mental map.

Moments later, pistons hissing, the metal doors along the right side began to open. Looking through them, Xris spotted some of the most important units in the space station—water pumps. Water was a highly valuable resource in space, second only to air. The air exchangers were located here, too, along with the myriad other machines all designed to keep the living inside the space station alive.

The Marine returned, accompanied by a short, stocky, muscular man wearing regulation coveralls with commander's tabs on the collar. He smiled broadly, shook hands all around.

"Greetings, gentlemen. I'm Bradley Drake, chief plant engineer."

"Aaron Schwartz. We're here to perform the routine maintenance on the exterminator drones and to restock their chemical supply."

"Sure, same as usual," said the commander. "You guys are new here. Do you know where to find everything?"

"Actually, no. The regular team was stranded on Clinius, no way to brief us. If you could show us where the 'bot control station is located and, uh, this man here"—he indicated Harry—"needs to be escorted to the central security station."

Xris could almost see everyone in the team tense up. This was the crucial part of the entire operation. If the commander balked, they were in trouble.

As it was, Drake did appear startled by the request. "Why do you need a man at security? That's not normally part of your routine."

Xris nodded. "We're installing a new software maintenance release in the exterminator 'bots. If they stray during testing, they're liable to set off your alarms, and we don't want some trigger-happy Marine to vaporize them. I don't suppose the Navy'd be thrilled about having to pay for replacements."

"Right, right. I see your point. The private"—Drake indicated the young Marine—"will take your man to security. I'll let them know he's coming. You'll find the bug-'bot station over there, by Air Exchanger Three next to the bulkhead. Let me know if you have any problems."

The commander returned to his office. Harry, looking nervous, grabbed a tool box and left with the Marine.

Xris motioned for the rest of the team to follow him, headed for the service area—a computer station located near a major air exchange unit. Three large air conduits, over a meter in diameter, entered the exchanger. From there, the conduits branched out, stopped at various access ports throughout the station.

"You're in charge, Quong," Xris told him.

The Doc moved over to the computer, began tapping on the keyboard. After studying it a moment, he turned to the others.

"According to Xris's information, there are twenty-eight exterminator robots roaming around the facility, inside the air ducts. We bring them down through that conduit there to check their programming, update it if necessary, and replenish their chemical supply. Jamil, you and Tycho remove the air duct access ports. I've called 'bots one, two, and three down for servicing."

A large metal conduit, attached to the air ducts, canted downward at a gentle slope, ending at deck level. A large metal plug sealed it shut. Tycho and Jamil removed the plug just as the first 'bot rumbled down the conduit and exited onto the floor. The 'bot was cylindrical in shape, moved on crawler tracks, and didn't look particularly intelligent.

Jamil hooked up the hose from the chemical tank on his cart to 'bot one. As he refilled its tanks, Tycho ran the self-check program built into the unit. That was routine. What wasn't routine was the placement of a microchip specially designed by Quong. Minuscule in size and perfectly harmless—unless activated—one microchip inside the 'bot's complex inner workings would never be noticed.

By the time the team had finished with the first 'bot, numbers two and three had arrived. Quong ordered robot one back into the duct. Tycho placed identical microchips in 'bots two and three.

'Bot five had just been serviced when Xris heard a beep in his ear. He looked around. Station personnel were moving through the work area, going about their business. No one was paying any attention to the exterminators.

Xris activated the comm. "Xris here."

"Harry here. I'm in the can just outside security. I'm surrounded! Two guys are working the computers and monitors *and* that damned Marine's still with me. Nobody told him he could go home, so he's sticking to my ass like one of those fleas I was reading about. I'm surprised he's not inside the stall with me. What the hell am I supposed to do now?"

Raoul, where are you when I need you? Xris asked silently. The charming Loti would have sent the Marine out for coffee and a sandwich, kept the security officers sniggering at the latest Adonian ribald jokes, while artlessly leading the conversation around to FCWing. ("I heard the juiciest rumor about one of *our* employees and one of *yours*. Doing something more than killing bugs, if you know what I mean! He worked in . . . let me see . . . somewhere called FCWing. Yes! In the women's restroom, no less!")

And while the security officers were thinking about FCWing, the Little One would have sucked their minds dry.

"Harry, we've been through this." Xris remembered to be patient. "Tell the security personnel you've got to keep an eye on these 'bots and in order to do that you have to know where the conduits run. Have security pull up floor plans, and study them. When you come to one called CCA-2 FCWing, let me know where it's located."

"Okay, right." Harry sounded glum. "I'll give it a try. Out."

Xris shook his head, turned to Quong. "This may take a while, Doc. Once you've serviced 'bot fifteen, slow down a bit. Buy us some time."

Quong passed the word to Tycho and Jamil, who began to ease up. They had just serviced 'bot twenty, with no word from Harry, when Quong tapped Xris on the shoulder.

"Here comes trouble," the Doc warned under his breath.

Commander Drake had emerged from his office. "You guys are running a little behind schedule."

"It's this new software upgrade," Xris explained. "It's taking a while to install—" His commlink buzzed in his ear.

"Xris!" It was Harry.

"Maybe you should explain this to me." Drake was talking at the same time.

Xris looked blank. "Did you say something, Commander?"

Drake raised his voice. "I was saying maybe—"

"Sorry, Commander!" Xris shook his head violently, tapped on his ear. "My hearing unit appears to have shorted out. If you don't mind, I'll go fix it. Aleko here will answer your questions."

Tycho, taking the hint, pounced on Drake, began talking.

"We're updating the maneuver routines in the robots, Commander. The plan is to allow one 'bot to go to the aid of another 'bot if it finds a large breeding nest. We figure that this will increase the effectiveness of the program immensely. Have the fleas been bad lately?"

Xris moved off, keeping a close watch on Drake. Fortunately, the commander was more interested in fleas than in malfunctioning cyborgs.

"Xris here. What's up, Harry?" Xris asked in a low voice, cupping his hand over his ear.

"I think I've got a fix on that location for you. Lima Three Niner, Deck Eight. If FCWing's not there, it's real close."

"Right. Harry, pay close attention to the monitors. There's going to be some activity up there, so be prepared to handle it. I can't talk anymore. We've got company." Xris cut off Harry's protest.

"We've been having a problem with the fleas down here," Drake was saying to Tycho. "The filters catch them in the air exchangers and they're breeding—"

Xris returned. "If you don't mind, Commander, we *are* running behind schedule and my men need to get back to work."

"You want me out of the way." Drake smiled broadly. "I understand. Stop by my office before you leave, if you have time. The other crew usually does. I've got hot tea, fresh doughnuts."

"Sure thing, sir. Thanks," Xris said, and watched the commander walk off.

A nice guy. Xris hoped like hell nothing would go wrong. He turned to Quong, who was scratching at his neck.

"With all this talk of fleas, I'm starting to itch."

"It's all in your head. Listen, I've had word from Harry. Lima Three Niner, Deck Eight."

Quong ran a check. "That area's serviced by 'bot eleven—one Tycho's already 'fixed.' "

Xris breathed a sigh. That would save time. His luck was holding.

"I'll start the malfunction cycle." Quong pulled out a handheld minicomputer from the pocket of his coveralls.

He tapped in several commands, extended the small antenna, and transmitted instructions. Several seconds later, the microchip that Tycho had installed into the 'bot's control circuitry responded.

"All systems go," the Doc announced.

A minute passed. Xris glanced at Quong.

"Don't worry, Xris. It'll work."

Tycho and Jamil continued to perform their chores on the 'bots, but both kept an eye on Quong's computer.

Another minute passed. Xris looked back at Drake's office. The door remained shut. Another minute . . .

Commander Drake burst out of his office, waving his arms to attract their attention. He began shouting at them when he was still about twenty meters distant.

Xris ceased work, loped toward him. "What is it, Commander? What's all the excitement?"

"Security called. One of your 'bots is malfunctioning! It's dumped its chemicals. The stuff's dripping down out of the ceiling into the offices! Is it poisonous? Should I evacuate personnel?"

"No, sir!" Xris said hastily, not having foreseen such a drastic response. "No need to evacuate anyone. The chemicals are perfectly safe. Unless you're a flea," he added with a grin that he hoped didn't look as corpselike as it felt.

Drake wasn't amused. "Well, toxic or not, that gunk's liable to get into the computer systems. You better take care of it."

"Yes, sir. We can probably fix it from the station."

Xris moved back to Quong. Drake tromped along behind, breathing down his neck. "One of the 'bots is malfunctioning. See if you can bring it up on the screen."

"Sure thing. Where is the 'bot located, Commander?"

"FCWing."

"And where's that, sir?"

"Lima Three Niner, Deck Eight. It should be in the ducting off junction three-eighty-one."

Quong brought up the control routine for 'bot eleven. He tapped keys, gloomily shook his head.

"It doesn't seem to be responding. I can't gain control from here." He glanced at Xris. "You'll have to go fix it by hand."

Drake frowned. "That's a secure area. I'm not sure—"

"Excuse me, Commander," Jamil intervened. "But if this 'bot is dumping its chemicals, it's probably shorting out. Which means it could lose its programming and take off on its own. If it starts wandering around the air ducts, we might never find it. It might crash into something vital."

Drake looked worried. "Right, I see your point." He thought a moment. "Why don't you give me instructions on how to fix it. I'll go—"

"It takes special tools. I'll have to train you—"

"There's no time for that, Schwartz," Quong yelled. "The 'bot's starting to veer off course!"

Drake looked frazzled. He could handle an enemy bombardment. A runaway bug-'bot was something new in his experience. "Hell! Wait a minute. I'll get someone to escort you."

The commander bellowed. Everyone in the area halted, froze. The commander bellowed again, this time added a name.

A short man in Navy coveralls jerked his head up, waved in response, came trotting over.

"Technician Collins." Drake performed hurried introductions. "Schwartz here's got a malfunctioning 'bot. Take him up to FCWing. Help out if he needs it."

"Yes, sir. Schwartz, if you'll follow me . . ."

Xris had to restrain himself from grinning widely at the others. Looking serious and stern, he grabbed a tool box from the cart, followed the technician.

Behind him, Commander Drake called out, "Good hunting, Schwartz."

CHAPTER
16

When the speed of the hawk is such that it can
strike and kill, this is precision.

Sun Tzu, *The Art of War*

Outside the work area, Xris and his escort entered a corridor with dim lighting, white walls that ended in a T-junction. The tech turned left, punched an elevator button.

"Deck Eight," Collins commanded when the lift arrived and he and Xris were inside.

The doors opened onto another corridor that looked exactly like the first, except that this one had a large "8" stenciled on the wall and a sign reading: SECURE AREA. AUTHORIZED PERSONNEL ONLY.

"I'll need to stay with you at all times, sir," said the tech.

Yes, well, that was going to be a small problem.

Xris smiled, nodded, said nothing.

Collins took the first corridor they came to, which branched to the left. He stopped in front of the second door on the right. The computerized sign above the door read FCWING.

Alarms on Xris's cybernetic arm started beeping, LEDs flashed red.

The tech glanced at him in astonishment.

Xris jerked up the sleeve of his coveralls, made a quick adjustment of the fluid levels to the hydraulics. His heart was pumping like a photon combustion chamber.

"All fine now," Xris said.

The technician raised an eyebrow, but placed one hand on the security pad to the right of the door, held up a pass with the other. "Collins, Maintenance, Access Two Eight One Alpha Two."

The door opened.

The tech entered, Xris almost tripping on his heels.

The room was softly lit, glowed with the eerie light of innumerable computer screens of various shapes and sizes. Xris's augmented hearing caught the soft hum of the machinery that was banked along a wall to his right.

The center of the room contained several work desks. Xris recognized standard data- and commlink receivers and transmitters, digital state diagrams, and three-dimensional holographic data abstraction diagrams—all had been hastily shoved aside. A puddle of orangish, greenish liquid—dripping from the ceiling—had accumulated on the desk and was slowly starting to ooze to the floor.

A man, standing beside the desk, was staring up at the ceiling in baffled astonishment. A woman was on the comm, yelling at security.

Xris gave the woman a close scrutiny, comparing her to the picture of Darlene Mohini burned into his brain.

It wasn't her.

He glanced swiftly around the room.

On the left-hand side was a wall with a single door. The wall was plastered with electronic scratch boards. Across them were drawn mathematical equations, bits of computer code, diagrams, and sketches of equipment. Perhaps it was wishful thinking, but Xris could have sworn he recognized the neat, precise handwriting. He looked again at the door.

It was shut. But another computerized sign on the wall beside it flashed: CCA-2.

Xris heard Wiedermann's reedy voice echo in his mind.

Her job description reads: CCA-2. Clerical work, maybe. We have no idea what CCA stands for, but a level 2 employee . . .

"I'm from Olicien Pest Control," Xris began. The words came out a croak and he was forced to stop to cough, clear his throat. "It looks as if you've found our malfunctioning 'bot."

"Is that what it is?" The man, staring at the ceiling, shook his head. "I never would have guessed."

"Who would? One of those damn bug-'bots," said the woman, from her position next to the comm. "And *you* said it was the toilets backing up."

"So? What do I know?" The man glared at Xris. "You gonna fix it or what?"

The woman remained standing next to the comm. Xris discovered that his metal hand had clenched into a fist. He made a conscious effort to relax. He had to get rid of these two and the tech.

Dalin Rowan was in that office. Xris knew it as surely as he knew he was trapped inside his damn metal body. And he wondered why, with all the commotion, Rowan hadn't come out to investigate. A thought chilled him. Maybe Rowan was on coffee break. Lunch break. Gone to powder her nose . . .

Xris had a sudden memory of his friend—hunched over a computer, rapt, enthralled, completely oblivious to anything happening around him. Once they'd been caught in a firefight, forced to shoot it out with some goons. Rowan, breaking into the computer, had been negotiating a maze of security traps in an effort to crack the system. The goons attacked. Laser beams flashed around him. He kept working. He'd won a commendation for bravery. Only he and Xris and Ito knew—and often joked about it later—that Rowan hadn't even been aware a firefight was going on.

"Who's in there?" Xris asked, pointing at the CCA-2 sign.

The woman followed his gaze. "That's Major Mohini's office. We didn't want to interrupt her work. But perhaps I better tell her—" She started toward the door.

"No, that won't be necessary," Xris intervened. "The problem's out here."

Moving to the desk, he noticed a splotch of green on the sleeve of the man's uniform. "You didn't get any of this on your skin, did you?"

The man glanced down. "Well, some of it splashed onto my hand and the back of my neck, but—"

"Is it toxic?" The woman was alarmed.

Xris had no idea whether it was or not, but this was too good to pass up.

"Look, I don't want to frighten you," he began in a calm, soothing tone guaranteed to scare the hell out of everyone. "But you better get to the washroom. Scrub that stuff off. Use strong soap. Does it burn or itch? You're not dizzy, are you?"

"Well . . . maybe a little . . ." The man was gulping, rubbing at his hand. "And it . . . it *is* beginning to burn—"

Xris turned to the other two. "Take him to the john. Wash

that stuff off him. Then get him to sick bay. You both better go with him. He may feel faint."

The woman hurried to help her friend.

"I'm nauseous," he said in a quavering voice. "I'm not sure I can walk."

"Lean on me," the woman told him.

"You better go, too," Xris told the tech.

"But I'm not supposed to leave you—"

"If he keels over, she'll never be able to hold him up." Xris moved closer to the tech, spoke in low, urgent tones. "You've got to rinse the skin with water and soap within five minutes or that stuff can seep into the bloodstream. And then . . ." He shrugged.

The tech wavered.

"I feel sick." The man rocked on his feet.

Either the stuff *was* toxic or he was extremely susceptible to the power of suggestion. The woman struggled to support him, but she was short and he was tall.

"Crewman! Give me some help here!"

"Yes, ma'am." Obeying orders was deeply ingrained. The tech turned to Xris. "Please stay here until I can send someone to escort you, sir. It's for your own safety."

"Sure thing," Xris promised. "Oh, if they don't see me at first, tell them not to panic. I may be up inside the air ducts."

The tech waved his hand in acknowledgment and ran off. The door shut, sealed behind him.

Xris climbed onto the desk, reached up, removed a couple of ceiling panels. If security entered the room, they'd spend the first few moments searching for him up there. Once the panels were gone—leaving a gaping hole in the ceiling— Xris jumped down, turned to the door marked CCA-2.

"Jamil," he said over the comm. "I'm in FCWing. I sent my escort off and I'm alone now, but I won't be for long. Everything okay with you down there? Still got company?"

"Everything's quiet. Security reported you found the malfunctioning 'bot. The commander was thrilled. He went back into his hole."

"Good. Listen, I've located Rowan. In an office off a main room up here. This is a secured area. My escort had to show a pass and use a palm print to enter. The door to the office is shut. I don't see any card slots or palm pads or code buttons, just a plain ordinary door control. Is it likely to be rigged?"

"If it's like other military bases I've been on," Jamil returned, "the answer's no. Why bother? If you've got clearance that far up, you're not the type to go around snooping through other people's offices. My guess is the door won't even be locked."

"I hope like hell you're right." Xris switched comm channels. "Harry, I've located Rowan and I'm going in."

"Xris!" Harry was whispering, sounded tense. "Security's sending someone up—"

"Take it easy, Harry. It's under control. I only need five minutes. Out."

Xris had to pause a moment to stop shaking. The green CCA-2 flared bright, blurred around the edges. He started walking and it seemed to him that he had been making this walk, taking these steps, ever since that moment when he first woke up in the hospital and knew that his life was over.

He checked the needle in his thumb, made sure the mechanism was working. He reached the door, hit the control.

It slid silently open.

A woman sat in a swivel chair at a desk. Her back was turned to Xris. All he could see was a tumbled mass of shoulder-length curly brown hair. Above her swirled a mathematical model. She was staring at it intently, using a computer holographic pointer to make changes in the algorithm.

Xris cast a quick glance around, searching for electronic eyes, security cams.

Nothing. The room was essentially baren, devoid of life. No photographs of family, a lover, not even a pet. No green plants to relieve the gray sterility of her surroundings. Nothing except computer equipment. But all of it was impressive. Expensive state-of-the-art machines, the very latest in technology.

A little warning went off in Xris's mind. This was some fancy setup for a mere clerk.

He stepped inside the room. A touch of the control and the door slid shut behind him. The woman never moved, didn't appear to have noticed his entry.

The way she was sitting, the tilt of the head, the very movement of the hand—all familiar. So very familiar.

Tiny alarm beeps went off in Xris's arm. He ignored them.

"Rowan." He tried to say it twice, but his voice failed. The third time it came out strong. "Rowan. Dalin Rowan."

The hand holding the pen froze in midair. The woman didn't move for a long moment, the space of a thudding heartbeat. Then, slowly, taking care to make no sudden motions, she put the pen down on the desk.

"Hello, Xris," she said quietly, and turned around.

Her face contorted in pain when she saw him. Xris kept tight control of his own face, determined to show no emotion, not even the fury that was suddenly engulfing him like white-hot flame.

He looked for Dalin Rowan in the woman's features and he found him. Rowan was there, although it looked as if someone had taken an eraser and rubbed off all the sharp, masculine edges, made them rounded, blurred. But the eyes were the same: intelligent, a bit red from overuse, and—oddly—sad and resigned.

"You know me," Xris said and his voice grated harshly. "And I know you. So I guess we both know why I'm here."

Rowan nodded, sighed. Her hands were folded calmly in her lap. "I've been expecting you. Or them. The Hung." She shrugged. "I didn't know which would find me first."

She smiled, lopsided. "Ironic. All these years, I've listened for the footstep behind my back. When it finally comes, I don't hear it." Rowan looked up at him steadily. "I'm glad it was you, Xris. Glad and . . . strangely enough . . . relieved." She glanced around. "It's all over at last."

Xris was at a loss. This was certainly not what he'd expected. He'd been imagining the fear. The look of guilt. The frantic plea for understanding, for life—which he would take grim pleasure in denying. He hadn't expected resignation, sadness. It was starting to unnerve him.

He brought up the mental picture of Ito.

"You're going to die, Rowan." Xris held up his metal hand, wiggled the thumb. "There's a needle here. When I touch you, it'll inject poison into you. It's a pity," he added, working himself back into his comfortable anger, "but you won't feel any pain. Not like Ito. Not like me. You'll be unconscious for about an hour—long enough for me to leave—and then you'll die. Of unknown causes. This leaves no trace, and there's no antidote."

Rowan listened to all this gravely, as she once used to listen to Xris outlining a plan for a bust. When Xris was finished, she sat motionless, looking up at him. She said nothing, no word in her own defense.

Xris was becoming exasperated. "Why? Just tell me why. If you needed money that bad, you could have come to me. I didn't have much, but what was mine was yours. You knew that! Damn it, Rowan, we were friends! Why didn't you talk to me?"

And now her gaze lowered. Her hands trembled. She shook her head. The long brown hair fell forward, hiding her features. Still, she said nothing.

"I see. Maybe you needed more than we had. So you set me and Ito up." Xris grunted. "I guess I should be glad—"

"Xris!" It was Harry's voice. "Security's in FCWing! They're looking for you!"

"Hey! Olicien Pest Control!" The shout came from outside the closed CCA-2 door. "Are you up inside the ducts there? Come down here a minute."

Xris didn't bother to respond. He was cold, brisk, efficient. He took a step toward Rowan, metal hand reaching for the woman's arm.

"You can scream for help," he said, "but it won't do you a damn bit of good. Sorry it has to end this way between us, Rowan—"

If she had screamed, jumped up, rushed him, she would have been dead. Rowan remained seated, watching him with those calm, sad eyes. She held perfectly still, and that probably saved her.

That and her next words.

"Joker's wild, Xris. For God's sake, get out of there. Joker's wild."

He heard, once again, a frantic and unrecognizable voice: *All Deltas! Joker's wild! For God's sake, get out of there! Joker's wild! Joker's wild!*

Xris paused, his hand not four centimeters from the woman's arm. "Yeah? The abort code for the mission. What's that supposed to prove. You knew it. Armstrong would have given it to you."

But Armstrong wouldn't have given Rowan that little added cry of panic that had echoed in Xris's mind during the terrible days of pain that followed. That wasn't part of the abort code.

For God's sake . . .

Rowan stood up, moved nearer, courting death. "They

told you I killed the crew, stole the shuttle, left you and Ito to die. If I had betrayed you, why would I have transmitted the abort code? And *I* was the one to transmit it that day."

"Bug man!" The voice outside the door was starting to sound impatient, suspicious. "Are you up there? Harrison, go on up and check."

Xris stared at this woman who was Rowan and who wasn't Rowan. Something inside him gave way—a dam bursting, a seething cauldron boiling over, a festering sore draining. He wanted to believe. Dear God, he wanted to believe!

But Rowan was smart, creative. He—she'd had all these years to think up a clever lie.

"We have to talk, Xris!" Rowan put her hand on his arm, the deadly arm. "You have to hear what I found out. You have to let me explain!"

"He's not up here, Captain," came the report from outside the door.

"Security! Intruder alert. Unauthorized personnel at large in FCWing."

Alarms sounded.

The cyborg's metal hand twitched. He moved it back, away from Rowan. Then he nodded once, abruptly.

She touched the control. The door slid open.

"Captain. Call off the alert. The gentleman's here—"

"Jamil!" Harry was shouting into the comm. "I can't raise Xris! All hell's breaking loose! You guys head for the plane. I'm going after him."

"Harry, don't—" Xris began, then stopped.

All he could hear over the commlink was Harry shouting, someone else swearing, glass breaking, and lasgun fire.

And then Harry's comm went dead.

CHAPTER 17

The prayer of the chicken hawk does not get him the chicken.

Proverb, Swahili

Xris's hand—his good hand, flesh-and-blood—closed over Rowan's arm. He jerked her back into the room, hit the door controls. The door slid shut.

"Is there another way out of here?"

"Yes," Rowan answered, short and sweet, not wasting time for explanations. Just like the old days.

Could he trust her—like the old days?

He'd soon find out.

His leg compartment flipped out. He pulled out his lasgun, fired, effectively soldered the door control.

"Where's the other door?"

"At the opposite end of the room, to your left."

"I see it. Does it lock?"

"Yes, but the guards could override it."

"I'm sure you could fix it if you wanted to. And believe me, you want to." Xris aimed his lasgun at her.

Rowan smiled, shrugged, and sat down at the computer. "There," she said after a moment's work. "We can get out. No one else can get in. Not without plastic explosives," she added.

"Funny." Xris snorted.

Outside, he could hear voices: "Security, I've found the intruder. He's in FCWing, Major Mohini's office. The door controls have been frozen. We can't get inside."

A phone on Rowan's desk began to buzz insistently. She looked at Xris.

He picked it up.

"What we have now," Xris told whoever was on the other end, "is a hostage situation. I've captured your major. I'm armed. One move to break in here and your major's dead."

He hung up, ripped the phone off the desk, tossed it— wires dangling—into a corner. "Derek Sagan was right," Xris muttered to himself. "Shoot—don't talk. I'd have saved myself a hell of a lot of trouble if I'd just gone ahead and shot her!"

He heard the captain repeatedly calling, "Security!"; then, "I can't raise anyone. Something's wrong. One of you men go check central security ops."

Harry must be doing something constructive. Xris hoped his pilot was not getting himself killed at the same time.

"Jamil." Xris was back on the comm. "What's going on down there?"

"Xris!" Jamil sounded relieved. "Where—"

"Answer the question!" Xris snapped.

"We made it to the spaceplane two jumps ahead of Commander Drake and a squad of Marines. We're okay, but they're sure as hell not going to let us fly out of here."

"Hang tight," Xris growled. "I'm working on it."

Like hell he was. Trapped inside a computer room with his one-time best friend who had maybe tried to kill him, while half the Marines on the space station were lined up outside waiting for him.

"I can help," Rowan offered. "Just tell me the setup."

Xris hesitated, studied her. Logic told him not to trust this woman; she was battling for her life. But it was Rowan talking and they were together again, their backs against it, outnumbered, everything going wrong that could go wrong. And in the brown eyes that were Rowan's eyes was the same bright excitement of long ago—the delight in the challenge, the exhilaration of the adrenal rush, the fun of beating the odds.

Besides, when it came down to it, what choice did he—or his team—have?

"Remember this," said Xris, lifting his metal hand, wiggling the thumb with its deadly needle. "If you let me down, so help me, I'll—"

He didn't finish. It wasn't necessary.

"I understand," Rowan said quietly.

"Here's the deal. I've got a man stuck in security. I've got three more men trapped inside our spaceplane, which is located on loading dock 28L. None of my men is armed. They have orders not to kill."

Rowan raised her eyebrows. "You're kidding."

All was quiet outside the door—too quiet.

"No one dies," Xris said. "We're in enough trouble already."

"You bet you are," Rowan agreed. She was seated at the computer, fingers dancing across the keyboard. "See if you can raise your man in security."

"You're coming with me, you know," Xris told her. "I want to hear that explanation of yours." Then he was back on the comm. "Harry, Harry, can you read me?"

Rowan paused, looked earnestly at him. "Taking me would put you in one *hell* of a lot of trouble, Xris. More than you could ever imagine."

"You're coming with me," Xris said with finality. "Either you come or I blow your cozy little setup here sky-high. I'm sure the Navy would be real interested in knowing that once upon a time you used to pee standing up."

Rowan looked at him a moment longer, then—unexpectedly—she chuckled, low in her throat. Still laughing, she went back to work.

Xris was back on the comm. "Harry! Harry, come in—"

"Harry here! Xris, are you all right?"

"Never better," Xris answered wryly. "What the hell is going on down there?"

"Security had a make on you. So I knocked 'em out. Like you said."

"Then what was all that racket? The hypno-spray—"

"Hypno-spray? Jeez, Xris. I forgot all about the damn hypno-spray. I just used my fists. Oh, uh, and I've got a lasgun now. A couple of 'em, in fact."

"Damn it, Harry—"

"They'll be okay, Xris. When they come to."

"Is that your man?" Rowan interrupted.

"Unless someone makes me a better offer," Xris returned bitterly.

"Can he reach the spaceplane from his location in three minutes?"

Xris relayed the message, received an answer in the affirmative. "But they've probably got the plane guarded," Xris added.

"Maybe one or two Marines posted outside the door to the loading dock." Rowan shrugged. "After all, they know you're not going anywhere."

"But we are, aren't we, old friend?"

"Yes, old friend," Rowan replied, with that lopsided smile. "We are. Tell your man to move out. He's got three minutes, starting now."

Xris gave the order.

Rowan, breathing a sigh, sat back in her chair.

"What do we do now?" Xris asked.

"Wait."

Xris pulled a twist out of his pocket, lit it.

"Smoking's not allowed," said Rowan, amused.

"Add it to the list of charges." Xris eyed her. "I never thought I'd say this, but you don't make a bad-looking woman. Just what is it we're waiting for?"

"An enemy attack," Rowan returned gravely.

"Fortuitous timing."

"Yes, isn't it. Ah!"

The deck shook beneath Xris's feet, nearly knocking him over. He grabbed hold of the edge of Rowan's desk.

Rowan stood up. "That will be the enemy now. Coming?"

Red lights were flashing, Klaxons sounding.

Rowan negotiated her way through the maze of computer equipment, heading for the side door. Xris, lasgun in his hand, followed.

"What *was* that?"

"I set a plasma venting system to overload, caused an explosion on Level CC, Section 2. Don't worry. No one was around. That section's been abandoned for years. Unused living space. The hull's been breached—according to the computer—by an enemy Corasian torpedo."

"Let me guess: There are no Corasians within a zillion light-years of this place."

"I shouldn't think so," Rowan returned calmly. "But according to the computer, there's an entire enemy fleet out there, complete with mother ships."

"But the scanners—"

"Shut down."

"Hell, all anyone has to do is look outside the damn window. They'll *know* we're not under enemy attack."

"True," said Rowan. "But it's going to take them at least two hours to convince the computer otherwise. In the meantime, all the blast doors have been shut, which means most people are trapped in their own areas. The Marines are under orders to report to their combat stations—if they can get to them."

"But they'll be able to manually override the controls."

"Not anymore." Rowan had reached the door. She looked at Xris. "There'll be guards outside waiting for us."

Xris waved the lasgun. "You're my hostage, remember? Just a minute. If the blast doors are shut, how do we get out?"

"We have manual security override," Rowan answered. She had her hand on the controls, but she didn't open them. "You wouldn't have asked me such questions in the old days, Xris."

"Ito hadn't been blown into a fine red mist in the old days. And I wasn't a machine. I'm letting you live, Rowan. Don't ask me to trust you into the bargain." He jammed the lasgun into her side. "Open the door. And watch what you say and do."

She nodded, touched the controls.

The door slid open.

Five Marines, beam rifles leveled, were waiting for them out in the corridor.

Rowan raised her hands, stepped out. Xris crowded close behind her, using her body as a shield.

"I've got a 22-decawatt lasgun," he told the Marines. "It's set to fire the second the pressure of my finger relaxes. You so much as stun me and the major dies."

"He's not bluffing," Rowan said swiftly. "He's a mercenary, working for the Corasians. Part of the enemy attack force. Now, if you'll just let us pass—"

The captain of the Marines looked uneasy. "You know we can't do that, Major Mohini. We have standing orders to shoot you, rather than allow you to fall into enemy hands."

Rowan glanced back over her shoulder. "I'm sorry."

Xris glared at her. "Why, you—"

The lights went out. The windowless corridor was suddenly, intensely, unbelievably dark.

Xris's infrared vision clicked on; he could see warm bodies. The Marines, on the other hand, were completely blind. The cyborg took out the captain with a blow of his metal hand to the jaw, sent the man reeling. A kick of his steel leg sent another Marine to the floor.

Grabbing hold of Rowan's arm, Xris dragged her after him, began running down the corridor.

Leaderless and unable to see, fearful of hitting each other, the Marines were calling for security to turn on the emergency backup lights.

Security wasn't responding.

"Lights out—your work, too?" Xris asked Rowan. "Taking a chance, weren't you?"

"Not really." She shrugged. "I know you. I figured you'd have some sort of infrared."

They came to a blast door. Rowan punched in a code on the keypad. The blast doors shuddered, slid open. Xris and Rowan slipped through. Rowan hit the controls on the other side, the doors slid shut. This corridor was still brightly lit.

"The elevators won't be working. We'll have to take the fire stairs. Oh, shit."

People were milling about in the hallways. One, spotting Rowan, started toward her.

"Major, what's going on? We can't reach secur—"

"What the devil are you people doing out here?" Rowan demanded. "Don't you hear the damn alarm? We're under enemy attack! Get to your posts!"

Some returned to their offices. Others remained huddled uncertainly in the corridor. But at least her orders gave them something else to talk about.

Rowan shoved open the fire door, began running down the narrow metal stairs. Xris clattered after her.

"Were those soldiers serious?" he yelled over the noise they were making. "About shooting you?"

"Yes!" Rowan yelled back. "I told you. You're going to be in a lot of trouble."

He grunted, said nothing, saved his breath for running.

They exited out into the work area near the bug-'bot station. And there was Harry, looking nervous, lasgun in hand, waiting for them. He was so relieved at the sight of Xris that the cyborg was afraid for a minute Harry was going to hug him.

"Where is everyone?" Xris cast a swift glance around.

"Some Marines were all bunched up around the door leading to the loading dock and our plane. I hung around, making myself scarce, wondering how I was going to get past them. Then the floor began to shake and the alarms went off.

That commander fellow talked to someone, then said something to his men about the hull being breached and they had to get up there right away. He left a couple of Marines on guard and the rest left. I took care of the Marines. I used the hypno-spray this time," Harry added hurriedly.

They ran through the deserted work facility.

"XP-28's got the engines warming up," Harry continued. "But unless you want me to blast that plane through a nullgrav steel door, we're not going anywhere in a hurry. And then there's the tractor beam."

"All taken care of," Rowan said briskly.

Harry looked at the woman running along beside him in considerable astonishment. He nudged Xris. "Who's that?"

"Rowan. Dalin . . . Darlene . . ." Xris gave up.

"Just Rowan," she said, with her crooked smile.

"The person you were gonna kill," said Harry.

Xris didn't see any need to answer that.

Harry grinned, rubbed his hands. "That's great," he said. "Really great! I win the pot."

Xris glanced at him, puzzled. "What pot?"

"The bet. With the others. I said you couldn't kill her, Xris."

Fortunately for Harry, Xris was too busy at the moment to respond. They dashed past the comatose forms of two Marine guards and entered loading dock Lima 28. The spaceplane was lit up, engines throbbing, ready for takeoff.

"I've got Xris, Jamil," Harry said into the comm. "Lower the ramp and prepare for takeoff." He cast a dubious glance at Rowan. "I sure as hell hope you know what you're doing, lady."

The ramp lowered. They hurried on board.

Harry went straight to the pilot's chair, Rowan right behind him. Xris came right behind her.

"She's Rowan. I'll explain later," he said in response to startled looks from the rest of the team.

"Strap yourselves in tight," Harry ordered. "We could be in for a rough takeoff."

Rowan sat down in the copilot's chair. Xris kept as near her as possible, strapping himself into the seat closest to the cockpit. He still held the lasgun in his hand. Rowan glanced at it, then looked away.

"This is what I've done." She spoke to Harry coolly. "I've set the docking bay door controls on automatic. When the spaceplane approaches them, they'll begin to open. Once they've started to cycle, the control tower can't prevent the blast doors from rising. That's a safety feature."

"Okay, so we can fly out of here. What about that damn tractor beam?"

"I've rerouted all power from the tractor beam to the food processing panels and recycling plants. It'll take them awhile to figure that one out."

"All right," Harry said slowly, assimilating the information, "so we fly out *and* away from the tractor beam. Then the Navy locks us on target with the big guns and shoots us down."

Rowan shook her head. "The lascannons are all being aimed at the Corasian invasion fleet."

Harry gasped. "What? A Corasian invasion—"

"Never mind!" Xris snapped. "Just get us out of here!"

"You're going to fly into a Corasian invasion fleet? Xris, that's sui—"

"It's not real!" Xris shouted.

"He's right," Rowan said soothingly. "It's not real. I'll explain later. You can take off safely now."

But Harry was not to be rushed. "What about patrol planes? We"—he tapped the cargo plane's console—"have no shields, no guns."

"There'll be a few patrol planes out there," Rowan admitted. "Not much I could do about those. But most of the squadron pilots have discovered that *their* docking bay doors won't open. I activated a maintenance program that—"

"Skip it." Xris knew from experience how long some of Rowan's explanations could last. "Get us the hell out of here *now.*"

Harry glanced over. "You trust her, boss?"

"It doesn't much matter, does it? We can either fly out of here or walk out with our hands on top of our heads. Which is it going to be?"

Xris had avoided the question of trust and everyone in the plane knew it. The others exchanged grim glances.

"Well, when you put it that way . . . XP," Harry ordered, "bring main engines on line and fire maneuvering thrusters."

"Excuse me, Pilot Luck," said the computer respectfully, "but I am programmed to remind you that we have not received permission to leave—"

"Take over manual control," Xris commanded.

"Sorry about this, XP," Harry said, giving the computer a conciliatory pat. "But switch flight control over to manual. That's an order."

"Yes, Pilot Luck. I was only doing my duty. I trust that will be so noted in the log."

"Oh, sure, sure," Harry said absently.

He was absorbed in his job now, oblivious to all else. The expression on his face even altered from one of almost perpetual befuddlement to intense, focused concentration. He seemed to flow into the spaceplane, almost like the legendary Blood Royal, who had reputedly been able to connect themselves with their own spaceplanes through the micromachines in their bloodstream. Harry had no micromachines in his blood. He connected with the plane by feel and thought, by instinct and intuition.

The spaceplane lifted off the landing pad, turned, headed for the gigantic metal doors.

The cockpit speaker crackled to life. "Olicien Two Five Niner, you are *not* cleared for takeoff. Repeat, *not* cleared. Return to your assigned parking area."

Harry shut off the speaker and aimed the nose of the spaceplane at the blast doors. He fired the thrusters. The doors shivered. The plane flew nearer, nearer, picking up speed.

"As fast as we're flying," Tycho observed to no one in particular, "we won't be able to stop."

No one answered.

Xris glanced at Rowan, who was staring at the doors with a pale, set expression on her face. Maybe this is how she's going to end it, he thought suddenly, his stomach muscles tightening. Go out in a ball of fire. And this time she'll make sure of me, as well.

The plane's speed was increasing. Harry steered for the bottom of the blast door, planning to swoop out the moment he had enough room.

If that moment came. . . .

They were within two hundred meters, rocketing toward nullgrav steel doors that could absorb a direct hit from a meson without buckling. The spaceplane would smash into the blast doors, explode, and maybe leave a black char mark that would probably wash off with a little soap and water.

One hundred and fifty meters. Jamil's ebony skin glistened with sweat. Quong's eyes were closed, his mouth moving, either in prayer or reciting algebraic equations; he did both in emergencies. Tycho's thin fingers gripped the arms of his chair; his skin had turned a sick pink—not due to color alteration, but to strain.

One hundred meters.

"Ah!" Harry breathed softly in satisfaction.

The blast doors shivered, began to rise—at a crawl.

"Come on, baby," Harry said to the doors. "Faster."

The doors were now a little over a quarter of the way up.

"I'm going for it," Harry shouted. "Hang on."

The plane shot through the opening and soared into the black vacuum of space.

"Did you hear a scraping sound?" Tycho asked, his translator squeaking. "I heard a scraping sound. I'll bet we've left a streak of yellow paint on that damn door."

"I think I left a streak of yellow down my pants leg," Jamil muttered.

"We're not out of this yet," Harry cautioned. "There's a Katana fighter coming for us. Not on visual yet, but you can see it on the screen."

Xris looked—a blip on the sighting screen was converging on them.

"Where's the nearest Lane?"

"The one we took coming in. Out past the thousand-kilometer marker." Harry glanced at the screen. "We'll be in range before then. And this cargo plane has all the maneuvering capability of a Solosian elephant. No offense," he added, for the computer's benefit.

"None taken, Pilot Luck," responded the computer. "I am aware of the plane's limitations. And it is my duty to report that the Navy fighter is requesting us to shut down our engines and stand by for towing."

"I'll take that under advisement. In the meantime, increase speed. Give me everything you've got."

"Yes, Pilot Luck," said the computer, adding, after a moment, "I must admit, I find this rather exhilarating. I was once assigned to a short-range Scimitar myself, when I was in the Navy."

"Were you?" said Harry, his gaze divided between the thousand-kilometer buoy, blinking up ahead, and the Katana itself, which could now be seen through the viewscreen. "Then perhaps you could tell me why it's not firing at us. We must be dead in the pilot's sights."

"Pilots are not permitted to fire this close to the station, sir, unless under enemy attack."

"And maybe the soldiers were bluffing back there," Xris said, eyeing Rowan. "Maybe they don't want to blow up Major Mohini."

"It's possible." Rowan appeared thoughtful.

Tracer fire flashed past the viewscreen.

"Warning shot across the bow," Harry said. "XP, plot the jump. I want to be ready the moment we hit the Lane."

"What course?" XP asked.

Harry looked questioningly at Xris.

"Olefsky's system. The rendezvous site. If Raoul manages to extricate himself from whatever predicament he's in, he'll know to meet us there."

Harry nodded, provided the computer with the coordinates. Another shot from the Katana streaked past the viewscreen, this one so close that it seemed to blaze right through the cockpit, temporarily blinding all of them.

"Coming up on the thousand-kilometer marker," Harry reported calmly.

"Pilot Luck," the computer said, "the Katana warns that it has orders to attempt to disable us."

"Fine, fine." Harry waved his hand vaguely. "You ready for the jump?"

The thousand-kilometer marker flashed past.

"Yes, sir."

"Good. Start cycle. In four . . . three . . ."

The plane shuddered, rocked. Everyone held on for dear life.

"We have been hit, Pilot Luck," the computer said unnecessarily. "Ending jump cycle."

"Damn it! What damage?"

Rowan looked at the screen where a model of the spaceplane was being displayed. "Tail section, but it's minimal. Nothing else hit."

"Thank the Creator it wasn't the engines. Restart jump cycle. Four . . . three . . . two . . . one."

A sickening sensation of being turned inside out. A momentary horrifying notion that all your guts have been sucked out through your nose and mouth and are now twisting in the air outside your body. And then just before you pass out—or, in some cases, right after you come to—you look out the viewscreen and notice that someone has switched off all the starlight.

But they'd made it.

"Questions," Xris said, endeavoring to unstrap himself from his chair. "Have to ask . . . questions." He was dimly aware of lights flashing on his arm, warning alarms, then he felt heavy. Far too heavy. "Questions . . . Rowan . . ."

Doc's face floated above Xris. He heard the word, "Malfunction—"

Then it seemed that the empty, silent, and immensely comforting black blanket of hyperspace wrapped around him, tucked him in for the night.

CHAPTER 18

Incoming fire has the right of way.
                    Murphy's Military Laws

The adjutant strode rapidly into the Lord Admiral's chambers, banging the heavy ornate door and causing the eyebrows of the admiral's aide—one Sergeant-Major Bennett—to lift in disapproval.

"Where's Dixter?" the adjutant demanded unceremoniously.

"Good morning, sir," Bennett said with a withering stare. "If you are referring to Sir John Dixter, he—"

"Never mind, I spotted him. Thanks."

The adjutant sprinted across the large office, knocking askew several antique pieces of furniture. This offense brought a shocked Bennett to his feet.

"Really, Commander Tusca!" Bennett entered the race, moving to intercept the adjutant before the adjutant could intercept the Lord Admiral.

"General Dixter! I mean, my lord! Sorry, sir, I forgot there for a moment."

The adjutant—a well-built human male, small-framed, with black skin and tightly curled black hair—brought himself up sharply in front of the Lord Admiral.

"What is it, Tusk?" Dixter smiled. He didn't mind being reminded of the old days—the days when he'd been a leader of a band of mercenaries. It was one reason he'd invited a former mercenary to serve as his adjutant. That and the fact that Mendaharin Tusca—or Tusk, as he was known—was Dixter's closest friend.

"An urgent call from RFComSec, sir."

"My lord, your appointment with His Majesty," Bennett murmured, hovering.

Dixter hesitated.

"Epsilon Red, sir," Tusk said. "Top priority. Urgent."

Not even Bennett could argue with an Epsilon Red. "I'll inform His Majesty that you're dealing with an emergency situation, my lord."

"Yes, thank you." Dixter frowned. Turning, he accompanied Tusk back through his office, out a door, down a corridor, and into the comm. A startling contrast—coming from the lemon-scented, highly polished oak-desk environment of the admiral's office to the cold bright electronic buzz of the central communications operations for the Royal Navy.

"Any idea what this is about?" Dixter asked Tusk.

"No, my lord." They had just entered the comm and Tusk always made an effort, when around other members of the Lord Admiral's staff, to use the correct form of address. "The commander insisted on speaking to you personally. It must be somethin' big, though. They've run up every flag they could find: Epsilon Red, level one, top priority, urgent, most secret. *And* the transmission's being scrambled from Hell's Outpost back again. They sure as hell don't want any eavesdroppers."

Dixter fished around in a pocket for his antacid tablets. Finding them, he gulped down two. "RFComSec never has emergencies. They're not *supposed* to have emergencies. They're out in the middle of an uncharted region of space for the sole purpose of *not* having emergencies. Which comm station?"

"Over here, my lord." A captain rose to her feet, made room for the Lord Admiral. "RFComSec standing by, my lord. Admiral Lopez."

"Thank you, Captain."

She moved discreetly away. Tusk was about to make himself scarce, but Dixter indicated that his adjutant was to stay.

A harried-looking face appeared on screen. The stars on his uniform indicated an admiral, a rear admiral.

"John. Good to talk to you again. It's been too long. A damn shame it's like this, though."

"Good to see you, Roderigo. You're right. It's been too long. Pardon me for saying I wish it was longer. What's up? What've you got? Corasians?"

The rear admiral grimaced. "Funny you should mention

that. It's not the Corasians. I almost wish it was. It's Major Mohini. Major Darlene Mohini. She's been taken hostage, kidnapped."

Dixter stared in silence at the screen, scanning the name in his mind, trying to remember. Then, "Good God!" he said, and sat down in a chair. "How did it happen?"

The rear admiral ran his hand through his thinning hair. "It was a professional job. You know that damn flea problem we have? A team of five commandos disguised themselves as exterminators, broke through our security. They went straight for Mohini, so they knew who they were after and how to find her. You want to hear the real kicker, John?"

"Not really, Rod," Dixter muttered under his breath. "But I suppose you're going to tell me." Beneath the cover of the console, he rubbed his stomach.

"Mohini was in on it. Had to be. The commandos knew the layout of the place, the routine. And no one except a genius like the major could have so thoroughly screwed up all our computer systems. We've just now managed to convince our mainframe that the whole Corasian fleet isn't parked outside our space station."

"Damnation." Dixter swore softly. His fingers drummed the console. "This is one hell of a mess, Rod."

"Don't I know it." The rear admiral was looking worried, as well he might.

"There'll have to be an inquiry," Dixter said slowly, thinking as he went. "If it wasn't the major herself, you've got a security leak somewhere. Do you have vids on the commandos?"

"Security cams got some good shots. So did one of our pilots, by the way. He fired one of the new 'tick' tracking devices at the spaceplane. Says it was a direct hit on the tail section. We'll know where and when the commandos come out of hyperspace. Here are the vids. I'll be standing by."

The admiral's face was replaced by a shot taken by a security cam hidden in the ceiling. It showed an attractive woman, wearing a naval uniform, being forcibly escorted from her office by a man in bright yellow coveralls. Several armed Marines had them surrounded.

The man was saying, "I've got a 22-decawatt lasgun. It's set to fire the second the pressure of my finger relaxes. You so much as stun me and the major dies."

At that point, Dixter said, "Good God!" again.

And this time Tusk joined him.

Both of them stared in shocked disbelief at the vidscreen.

"Sir . . . that's Xris!"

"It can't be," Dixter said flatly. "Computer, give me still shots, enlarged, with enhancements, of each second of that vid. I want a voice print, too. Then search the files and see if you find a match for the photos and the voice."

The computer went to work. Tusk and Dixter watched the vid again.

"It's the cyborg," said Tusk after the second time through. "I'd know Xris anywhere. I should. He saved my life, sir," he added pointedly.

Dixter was grim. "I don't like this any more than you do, Tusk. Xris and his team have done good work for us. If you remember, he was almost killed trying to protect Her Majesty. But he *is* a mercenary. He works for money. Maybe someone offered him . . ."

He stared at the vid again, then shook his head. "That would explain the security leak. Xris had low-level access. I gave it to him."

"What good would low-level do him?"

"A lot, apparently," Dixter said wryly. "Maybe just providing him with the fact that the damn space station has fleas!"

"He wouldn't do that, sir. Xris wouldn't betray you. Damn it, I know him!"

"Match," sang out the computer suddenly, with what Tusk considered an irritating note of triumph. "Photo I.D. Cyborg. Name: Xris. Planet of origin—"

"What about the voice?" Dixter snapped, interrupting the flow of statistics.

"Match. Voice print I.D. Cyborg. Name: Xris. Planet of origin—"

Dixter ordered the computer to be quiet.

Tusk shrugged helplessly. "There *has* to be some explanation, sir!"

Dixter said nothing, turned his attention back to his rear admiral. "We think we have an I.D., Rod."

"You do? Damn, that was quick. And we've just received a report from the 'tick.' The plane's course will have it coming out of hyperspace in about six hours. The question is, do we shoot to kill, knowing they've got Major Mohini aboard? Or do we try to capture them and risk losing them?"

Dixter was silent, thinking.

Tusk was thinking, too, about the time he'd been shot all to pieces, about Xris coming to his rescue, hauling him through heavy enemy fire to safety.

"This is *Xris,* sir!" Tusk couldn't help saying.

Dixter cast him a stern glance. "I am aware of that, Commander."

"Sorry, sir." Tusk knew he'd gone too far, overstepped the line.

Dixter sighed, stared at the photo I.D. of the cyborg, who had more than once put his life on the line for a number of people John Dixter cared about.

"Major Mohini must not be allowed to remain in enemy hands," he said slowly. "Give her captors every opportunity to surrender. If they don't, orders are: Shoot to kill."

"Yes, my lord." The rear admiral signed off.

Dixter looked suddenly old, tired. "Now we wait."

Tusk was studying the still photos, staring in bafflement at Xris and the attractive, intelligent-looking woman he was holding at gunpoint.

"Who is this Major Mohini, sir?" Tusk asked. "And why is she so damn important?"

Dixter told him.

CHAPTER 19

> . . . because the only people for me are the mad
> ones, the ones who are mad to live, mad to talk,
> mad to be saved. . . .
>
> Jack Kerouac, *On the Road*

Raoul was not happy. He was not enjoying himself—an unusual and alarming state of affairs for a Loti.

Lying naked on a bed, his hands and feet locked in steel paralyzers, was a situation that—under different circumstances—might have afforded Raoul a certain amount of pleasure. The room in which he was incarcerated was actually quite charming, tastefully decorated, with ambient lighting and a view of the stars outside his window. The bed was comfortable, the sheets delicately scented. But even these amenities—and the interesting situation in which he found himself—could do nothing to raise the Loti's spirits.

"I attribute this, first, to the large and undoubtedly unsightly bump on my forehead." Raoul mourned aloud. "And second, to the fact that I have been deprived of sustenance for a period which must surely exceed four-and-twenty hours."

By sustenance, he did not mean food. He had, in fact, been given a meal, watched over by an extremely ugly man, who had removed the paralyzers long enough to permit Raoul to spoon down something that seemed to be an excuse for soup. The man would not speak and he refused to bring Raoul wine with his meal. Raoul, therefore, had been unable to eat. Accepting this with philosophical indifference, the ugly man had replaced the paralyzers, taken the food, and left the room, sealing the door shut behind him.

"I am grounded, my friend," Raoul lamented. "I am a cold chicken. Or is it turkey? I am forced to confront reality. The horror," he added in a shuddering whisper. "The horror . . ."

One might have questioned just how "grounded" the Loti truly was, considering the fact that he was talking to the Little One, who was light-years away. But Raoul had to talk. He was accustomed to talking and he was accustomed to talking to his friend. Now he was bereft of his companion, alone, and extremely puzzled. Why in the name of all that was hallucinogenic had someone done this to him?

Perhaps he had enemies . . . perhaps there were people out there who didn't like him. . . . Poisoners do not make friends easily. Raoul knew this as a sad fact. It was a long time before Harry Luck could bring himself to eat a sandwich comfortably in Raoul's presence. But surely he had never done anything bad enough to merit such treatment! And the Little One hadn't done anything at all. And yet they'd hurt him. Hurt him badly.

Thinking of his small friend, wondering what had happened to him, Raoul couldn't stop himself from sliding into the darkness of depression.

Or reality, whichever came first.

Desperate to escape by any means possible, Raoul altered history, invented the comforting fantasy that the Little One was still with him. This achieved several key objectives. First, Raoul was able to apologize profusely to the rest of the members of Mag Force 7.

"Tell them I was undevoidably attained," he begged solemnly, too sober to make sense.

Second, and most important, he took comfort in the knowledge that the Little One was with him. And by the time Raoul had spoken to his friend for a while, fantasy tiptoed across Raoul's admittedly blurred lines. In what remained of Raoul's mind—a mystery to everyone, Raoul included—the Little One was listening to him and perhaps even responding.

"I wish I could tell you where I am, my friend," Raoul murmured. "But I cannot. All I know is that I am on board some type of spacegoing vessel and I know this only because I can see nothing but a black void punctuated by stars outside a window. The stars are moving. I am moving. I therefore consider it likely that I am moving through space."

He was arrested by a sudden thought. "Either that or the bump on my head is worse than I thought."

He sighed a dismal sigh.

"I am sorry, my friend. I became distracted. To continue, I am apparently being flown through space with a bump on my head. It is due to the bump that I have no recollection of where I am, very little of what happened to me. The entire night last night was a ghastly experience. Now I know why you"—here Raoul swallowed—"my poor Little One, were upset a great portion of the evening. You were undoubtedly aware of the dark thoughts being directed against us. But being unable to define your fears—these men were quite clever in concealing their evil designs—you, my unfortunate friend, were not able to warn me.

"The last thing I remember is these dreadful hulking beasts bursting into our room at an ungodly hour, dragging me bodily out of my bath, and . . . and hurting you."

Raoul blinked back tears. The memory was blurred, but it was terrible. He recalled hearing a thin, high-pitched wail, remembered seeing a shadowy hand smash down on a small and defenseless figure. The wail abruptly ceased. Despite this, the hand descended again and again, several times. It was at this point that Raoul rather indistinctly recalled feeling an unpleasant but oddly stimulating emotion.

"Rage. Anger. Fury. I hurled myself at the attackers," Raoul reported with quiet pride. "They ripped my silk kimono, but I persevered. And it was then, I rather imagine, that I received the blip on the headbone. Because the next thing I remember is waking up here, with an ugly hairy man bending over me."

Raoul shuddered again at the recollection.

"I am telling you all this, my friend," Raoul continued plaintively, "because I need you to explain to Xris why I did not arrive at the Olicien Pest Control factory in my yellow coveralls. It was the first time I have been where I was not supposed to be instead of where I was."

That statement momentarily confusing even Raoul, he paused to try to figure it out, gave it up as a bad effort.

"Ah, but I am certain Xris went in search of me. I am certain he found you, my friend, and that you are all right. Yes, I know you're all right!" Raoul repeated, his lips trembling. "You must be. I can't bear to think of you lying there, hurt, alone. . . ."

It seemed to Raoul that he heard a voice, a whisper, inside his head. It was familiar, reassuring, and it even provided instructions.

"Find out the name of the ship," Raoul repeated to himself. "Very well. If you think it will help."

The door slid open and the ugly man walked inside.

Raoul turned his head into the pillow. "Really, my friend," he whispered to the Little One, "this person is simply too frightful to bear! I am surprised he has the nerve to show such a face in public!"

The ugly man said nothing. Crossing the room to the bed, he removed the paralyzers that bound Raoul's ankles and wrists.

"Would you do me the favor of informing me why I have been absconded with?" Raoul asked pleasantly, keeping his eyes averted. His stomach was queasy enough as it was. The voice in his head prodded him. "Ah, yes. And what is the name of this ship?"

The ugly man did not answer. He grabbed hold of Raoul roughly by the shoulder and dragged him to his feet.

The room tilted. Raoul tilted with it.

The ugly man held out a hospital gown. It was gray, many times washed, pressed, and sterilized. It was held together with three ties and a snap. "Here, Loti, put that on."

Raoul laughed politely.

"I said put it on."

Raoul regarded the alleged garment with shock. "You can't be serious."

The ugly man tossed the gown at him. "We don't have much time. The doctor's waiting. If you don't put it on, I will."

"Go ahead, by all means," Raoul said, returning the gown. "You can't possibly get any uglier. And by the way, while you're undressing, what is the name of this ship?"

The man growled and took a step forward, and then Raoul understood.

"Ah, you mean you would dress me! Thank you," he said, snatching the gown, "but no."

Fumbling at the ties, accidentally ripping one off, struggling to separate the sleeves, which adhered to the gown as though they'd been glued to it, Raoul was at last semi-dressed.

The unsightly garment was the ultimate torture, and the

experience almost shattered him. At the sight of himself in the mirror, Raoul suffered excruciating pain, very nearly gave way to despair.

The ugly man shoved Raoul toward the door.

Whether due to the erratic motion of the spaceship, the bump on his head, or his lack of what the Loti usually referred to as "support," Raoul discovered that walking was an adventure in itself. Attempting to locate the door, he wandered into a corner. The ugly man was forced to place hairy hands on Raoul again, steer him back on course.

"Whoever is flying this ship must be swilling jump-juice," Raoul said thickly, careening through the half-open door and out into a brightly lit corridor. "I don't suppose he'd share?"

The ugly man did not answer. He did not appear to be having any difficulty walking the undulating, heaving, and twitching deck, but guided Raoul's floundering steps with a rough and uncouth touch.

It was when the walls started to throb, pulsing to the rhythm of a gigantic beating heart, that Raoul began to fall apart.

"Something's wrong with the engines!" He came to a giddy stop, looked around in terror. "Can't you hear it? Ka-thump. Ka-thump."

The ugly man paid no attention. Another shove started Raoul moving, brought him to a sealed door. The ugly man opened it with a touch on the controls, then retrieved Raoul, who had drifted off down the corridor. Returning with the Loti, the ugly man herded Raoul in through the open door.

The name of the ship! said the insistent voice inside Raoul. *Find out the name!*

"I can't." He moaned, weak and barely conscious. He'd caught another glimpse of himself reflected in a large steelglass window. "I can't."

A woman clad all in white, with a white cap over her hair, white rubber gloves, and a white sterile mask over her face stood beside a medicbot.

"Put him here," said the woman.

The ugly man did as requested, forcibly seating Raoul in a chair.

Raoul stared at the woman in the mask. "What happened to your mouth?"

The woman's eyes, visible above the mask, narrowed. "Loti!" she muttered in disgust. "Leave us alone."

The ugly man protested. "He's been given the detoxifiers and he's on a real downer. You might need help with him, Doctor."

The woman sniffed, shook her head. "I can manage this wretch. And I don't want to risk contaminating the samples. Wait outside the door. You can carry the bloodwork to the lab."

The man nodded, left. The door slid shut.

The woman turned to the 'bot. "You may begin. Start with the blood, then do the bone marrow."

The medicbot went to work. Raoul sat back in the chair. The 'bot produced a laser extractor, placed it into position, switched it on. The woman watched closely, then sat down at a computer terminal, began to make voice entries. The voice inside Raoul was sympathetic, but demanded action.

"Speaking of names"—though no one had been—"what is the name of the ship?" Raoul asked the 'bot.

It did not answer.

Raoul watched, fascinated, as his own red blood flowed into the extractor. From there it was deposited into various tubes and vials, all of which the 'bot carefully labeled and arranged on a tray.

At length, growing light-headed, Raoul allowed his gaze to wander.

"I am in a room, my friend, in which there are several white beds, separated from each other by curtains hanging from tracks on the ceiling—"

The woman with no mouth, absorbed in her work, glanced up. "What did you say?" she asked irritably.

"What is the name of the ship, madame?" Raoul was extremely polite. It was, he thought, a reasonable question.

The woman snorted, returned to the computer.

Raoul shrugged, continued. "They are taking my blood away from me and putting it into little tubes. I don't have the slightest notion why. Unless I am being held prisoner by vampires. . . ."

This fascinating and titillating thought carried him through the next few moments by providing certain entertaining fantasies. Then a particularly nasty jab from the 'bot returned him to what passed for reality.

His gaze—which had been wandering aimlessly around

the room, flicking over various serious-looking machines—
landed on a cabinet made of steel with a code-key locking
device. Raoul blinked, focused both his eyes and his attention. He lurched forward in his chair, occasioning a scolding
from the medicbot.

The woman with no mouth turned. "Please sit still," she
ordered. "The extractor is very sensitive equipment." Then
she noticed Raoul's fixed and rapt expression.

"What is in the cabinet?" he asked.

"Supplies," the woman answered, frowning.

"Ah . . ." Raoul sighed, sat back in the chair, and stared at
the locked cabinet.

"Test samples completed," announced the 'bot.

The woman collected the vials, finished the labeling, and
called the ugly man back into the room.

"Take these to the lab," she said.

The ugly man took the vials and disappeared.

The woman approached Raoul. She had pulled down her
mask.

Raoul jumped, stared at her vaguely. "Have we met?"

She drew up a chair, took out a small vidcam, placed it in
front of Raoul, ordered it to activate.

"The subject is an Adonian of undetermined age. He is
also, purportedly, a Loti. I am beginning the interview now."
She looked at Raoul. "You were once in the employ of the
weapons dealer Snaga Ohme."

"Ah," said Raoul sadly. "My late former employer. A
charming man. But most unfortunate. He managed to get
himself murdered, you know—"

The woman was not interested. "How long were you with
Snaga Ohme?"

Raoul shrugged. "What is time but an ephemeral butterfly,
flitting through the dead garden of our wretched existence?"

The woman asked other questions, interminable questions,
which Raoul answered absently with whatever came into his
head. His gaze had returned to the steel cabinet.

The laboratory door slid open; the ugly man walked inside.

"Knight Officer wants to know how the interrogation is
going."

The woman switched off the vidcam, handed it to the
man. "He can judge for himself." She sounded pleased. "I
would say the evidence is conclusive."

"The blood samples have been evaluated. They test positive."

The woman gave a stiff nod. "I will await Knight Officer's orders."

The ugly man glanced at Raoul. "Good riddance," he said, and left.

Raoul sank back in his chair. Time passed. The woman appeared impatient. She paced back and forth. The medicbot whirred about the room, cleaning up.

Then a voice came over a comm. "The interview is satisfactory, Doctor. You may terminate the subject."

"Yes, Knight Officer," the woman answered.

"Terminate the subject," Raoul repeated dreamily.

That means you, twit! They're going to kill you! the voice inside Raoul's head shouted. *Do something!*

Yes, I should do something. I should, Raoul thought, fight for my life. Yes, that is what I should do.

But he was feeling weak-headed and lethargic, completely uncaring. Various notions of attacking the woman flitted into his skull, danced around there aimlessly, and eventually fluttered out. Fighting required so much effort. . . .

"You will take care of Xris for me, won't you, my friend? He and the others will be terribly lost without me. You can communicate with him by—Ah!"

Raoul sucked in his breath. The woman had gone over to the cabinet. Removing a plastic card from the pocket of her white coat, she inserted the card into a slot, punched in a series of numbers on a keypad.

Raoul watched through half-closed eyes.

The cabinet was, as he had supposed, filled with small bottles. Each small bottle was filled with a chemical substance.

Life might be worth living, after all.

The woman removed a vial containing a reddish orange liquid. She emptied the contents of the vial into an infusor that was attached to the 'bot's mechanical arm.

"Inject him," she commanded.

The medicbot trundled toward Raoul.

Halfway there, however, the 'bot rolled to a stop. Its mechanical head swiveled around.

"I have run a routine analysis on this drug. Are you aware, Doctor, that the injection of this substance will be lethal to the patient?"

"Of course I'm aware," the woman returned, irritated. "Continue with the injection."

"I cannot, Doctor." The medicbot ground to a halt. "My programming will not permit me to kill a patient."

"Then give the damn thing to me." The woman seized the injector from the 'bot.

Raoul watched the woman draw near. A dim, terror-filled haziness seemed to slow time, to stretch it like an elastic band. Seconds lengthened to hours, hours to eternities. The speed of sound slowed. The woman's loud, thudding footfalls reverberated through Raoul's body. A squeaking bearing on the 'bot grew louder and louder until it was a shrill, screeching scream.

A voice boomed over the comm. It had a strange, echoing quality to it, which made it difficult for Raoul to understand what was being said. He heard the words, some part of his brain understood; other parts watched them drift past.

"Synchronize chronometers to Zulu Time—now. Mission go/nogo will be transmitted in sixty-six hours. Mission completion, barring nogo, will occur by eighty-one hours. You have your orders."

This made no sense to Raoul, but it jolted the woman. She stopped, stared at the comm as if she would have liked to interrogate it.

The ugly man reentered the room. He was in haste and appeared greatly excited.

"Have you terminated the subject yet, Doctor?"

"I am about to do so now," the woman responded. "I had trouble with the 'bot. I heard the announcement. The mission is starting. May the one true God be with us."

"God *is* with us," the man answered reverently. "Something's happened with the Royal Navy—"

The doctor was alarmed. "They've discovered us!"

"You're paranoid." The ugly man scoffed. "How could they? No, I don't think that's it. Knight Officer isn't talking specifics, but he says the military's got big problems and that this proves God is working for us in this matter. Work on the device has been completed, except for the final test run. Speaking of the test, the termination order for the subject is canceled."

The woman stood about six centimeters from Raoul. She continued to hold the injector in her hand. Raoul—attracted by the bright reddish orange color of the poison—stared at it in fascination.

"Why is that?" The woman sounded annoyed.

"Further examination revealed the possibility of undamaged micromachines in the subject's bloodstream. If this is true, it will make him the ideal candidate for the last run-through of the device. We won't have to sacrifice one of our own. Knight Officer wants you to look at the blood samples, to see if you reach the same conclusion."

"Interesting," the woman said in thoughtful tones. "Of course. I will be right up."

Turning, walking away from Raoul, she laid the injector on a countertop. Raoul stared at the injector, its color the only bright spot of warmth in the cold, sterile room.

"What are we going to do with the Loti in the meantime?" the ugly man asked. "When he goes into total withdrawal, he will be a confounded nuisance. A raving lunatic. We'll have difficulty managing him."

"I will give him a strong sedative, render him comatose. After that"—she shrugged—"the test itself will kill him."

"Report to the lab as soon as he goes under. I will send one of the squires to keep an eye on him."

The woman returned to Raoul, laid a long-nailed and cold-fingered hand on his shoulder. "Stand up," she ordered. "Go lie down on that bed."

Raoul obeyed, meandered off in what appeared to be the general direction of the bed. The medicbot intercepted him halfway to the steel cabinet, gently turned him around, gently steered him to the bed.

Raoul lay down. He had the vague impression that they weren't going to kill him after all. He supposed he should be happy about this, but what had truly perked him up, caught his attention, were the words "strong sedative."

"Give him forty ccs." The woman was issuing instructions to the medicbot. "I presume your programming allows you to do that," she added sarcastically.

"Yes, Doctor," said the 'bot, and whirred toward Raoul.

Raoul watched it approach with blissful anticipation.

The 'bot placed the injector on Raoul's upper arm. The drug flowed into him. Raoul experienced a sudden feeling of intense drowsiness that very nearly put him to sleep.

He closed his eyes.

"There, that should take care of him," said the woman,

and Raoul was dimly conscious of the fact that she left the room.

The medicbot, no longer needed, shut itself down.

After several moments, Raoul opened his eyes, sat up. He yawned, stretched, looked about him with interest. Feeling relaxed, alert, as after a good night's rest, he jumped down off the bed.

The injector lay forgotten on a tray. Raoul took it, studied it, sniffed at it, made his analysis, and hid the injector beneath the pillow of the bed. He walked over to the computer, scrolled back through the doctor's entries, read them with interest.

What is the name of the ship?

The voice was much clearer now and Raoul recognized it. Hopeful, exhilarated, he searched the lab room, found nothing. He hastened back to the computer files. Nothing there, either.

Frustrated, Raoul glared at the computer, began folding and unfolding the hem of the detested hospital gown.

It was then he noticed the markings stenciled on the bottom. Laundry markings.

Raoul smiled blissfully. Returning to the bed, he lay down, rested his head on the pillow.

"The name of the ship is *Canis Major Research I,*" he reported to the Little One, then settled back to enjoy being heavily sedated.

CHAPTER
20

. . . And thereby hangs a tale.
William Shakespeare, *As You Like It,* Act 2, Scene 7

Xris woke with a start and the panicked feeling that always hit him when his systems shut down. The sound of a snore was highly comforting. He glanced over to see the Doc, sitting upright, his head lolling backward, asleep in one of the metal frame chairs.

Tycho, who didn't handle jumps well, was stretched out on a cot, feebly twitching and groaning. The Little One was a bundle of blankets. Above the usual rattlings and thrummings of the plane, Harry's loud voice could be heard discoursing on the subject of fleas.

Xris did a careful systems analysis. Everything checked out. Quong must have fixed him up. Standing, Xris walked forward into the cockpit.

Jamil, looking intensely bored, was listening to Harry. Rowan was pretending to listen. In reality, she probably hadn't heard a word, sat staring out into space.

Xris began to chew on a twist. "Hello," he said. "How's everything going?"

"Fine, everything's fine," Harry said cheerfully.

"You okay?" Jamil asked gruffly.

Xris nodded, changed the subject. He hated talking about the times when he "crashed," as Quong put it.

"What's our ETA?"

Harry glanced at the instruments. "Six hours fifty-four minutes and seven seconds."

"Good. Now why don't you and Jamil go take a walk."

Jamil, casting a glance at Rowan, was already on his feet. Harry just sat there, looking blank.

"Take a walk, Harry," Xris repeated. "Beat it."

"C'mon, Harry." Jamil prodded the big man. "You can show me that video."

"Oh, uh, sure. If you really want to see it. You know, I never knew bugs could be so interesting. Why, were you aware that the flea is known for its agility in leaping—"

The two wandered off back into the interior of the cargo plane.

Xris leaned against the console, chewed on the twist.

Rowan continued to stare into space.

Xris stirred, shifted his gaze to join hers. "Give me one good reason," he said quietly, "why I shouldn't throw you out there."

She finally looked at him.

"Where do you want me to start?"

Xris waved his hand. "Oh, how about when you decided to betray us to the Hung?"

Rowan sighed. "I didn't, Xris. You have to believe me. I didn't."

Xris remained silent, was unconvinced. He finished off the twist, took out another.

"I admit I made mistakes, Xris. I know that now. I knew it then, but by the time I realized . . . I should have talked to you . . . I wanted to . . ."

Shutting her eyes, she shivered. The spaceplane was cold and her uniform—a crisp white blouse and knife-pleated black slacks—was intended for the sheltered, temperature-controlled space station. Xris realized he was still dressed in the yellow coveralls. He glanced around, found a down-filled jacket—Harry's, to judge by the enormous size—and tossed it to Rowan. She wrapped it around her slender shoulders, hunched into it.

"I've often wondered if it would have made any difference," she continued. "Maybe if I'd opened up to you that day of the briefing, before we left for TISor 13 . . . met you in the bar, like I promised, talked about—" She abruptly skipped that part. "Maybe I would have been less preoccupied with myself. I might have seen the warning signs. . . ."

She stared at him bleakly. Her hands lay limply in her lap. "I couldn't! I wanted to, but I couldn't! Damn it, Xris, can't you understand? You'd been *right*! You'd been so goddamn right. And I hated you for being right. I didn't want to hear you say, 'I told you so'!"

Xris took the twist out of his mouth. "Yeah, I figured that. I wanted to apologize. Your private life was none of my business. I should have kept my mouth shut. It's just—" He shook his head.

"You were trying to save me from myself," Rowan said, smiling the lopsided, sad smile. "I know that. I knew it then. And I knew the truth about her, too. I just didn't know the truth about myself."

She was silent a moment, seemed about to add something. She did add something, eventually. But Xris had the feeling it wasn't what she'd intended.

"I wanted to be loved. It was nice, having someone to come home to at night. I wanted what you and Marjorie had. . . ."

Xris tossed the chewed-up twist onto the deck.

Rowan glanced at him, looked away. "I heard. I'm sorry."

"So you were saying you should have talked to me," Xris prompted, cold and hard.

"Yes," said Rowan, "I should have talked to you. . . ."

Dalin Rowan sat in his seat in the shuttlecraft, pretending to study the material he'd been given yesterday, during the briefing at agency headquarters. He was pretending to study it because the new controller—what was his name? Armstrong. Mike Armstrong—was seated beside him and obviously wanted to pass the time in conversation.

Ordinarily, Rowan would have enjoyed the opportunity to talk with someone who had worked in HQ, who could have filled him in on the latest changes, promotions, who was in, who was out. But not now. Not today. He didn't want to talk to anyone. Not even his best friend.

Rowan was hurting. When he'd been a new recruit to the agency, he'd received training in hand-to-hand combat. He'd been pummeled, stepped on, kicked, thrown, stomped, and mauled. There hadn't been one part of his body that didn't hurt. It was how he felt now, except the hurt was inside, not out. And though he told himself it was his ego that had taken the beating, not his heart, the pain was there and it was real. He knew, too, that he was indulging himself in his pain, luxuriating in it, getting some sort of a perverse satisfaction out of it. He was doing his best to prolong it.

You're being a real asshole, Rowan told himself. You shouldn't have stood Xris up last night. This wasn't his fault.

Yes, but he's enjoying this, came the ugly rejoinder from some croaking demon inside Rowan.

He knew that wasn't true. Xris probably hurt as much for his friend as Rowan hurt for himself. But the demon wouldn't shut up, wouldn't let loose. And because he knew he was treating Xris unfairly, Rowan felt guilty as well as hurting. Irrationally, he blamed Xris for adding to the pain.

Someone touched his arm. Rowan gave a violent start, nearly dropping his electronic notebook.

"Sorry! Didn't mean to startle you." Armstrong was obviously astonished at Rowan's reaction. He made a vague gesture. "You can see *Vigilance* from the viewscreen now. Thought you might want to take a look, the ship being new and all. . . ." His words dried up.

Rowan flushed. "Yeah, thanks. I should put this stuff away anyhow. I guess we'll be docking soon." He switched off the notebook, thrust it into the metal space traveling case, and tried to appear interested in the new space cruiser.

And then, in spite of himself, he *was* interested. *Vigilance* was the newest weapon in the agency's arsenal. The ship was equipped with the latest in sensing and communications devices. Its main function was to act as an orbiting command post for planetside operations. The relatively simple raid on TISor 13 was to be the test run.

"Sorry I haven't been very good company," Rowan apologized. "It's just . . . well, I've got a lot on my mind."

"Sure. I understand," said Armstrong, and then promptly proved he didn't by adding, "From what I've heard, this job should be relatively simple for a computer genius like you."

It was the type of compliment Rowan detested. It made him sound like some sort of freak. And then he wondered just exactly what Armstrong had "heard." And was the reference to "genius" a subtle sneer? Rowan forgot about his own internal miseries, studied Armstrong more closely, taking a good look at the guy for the first time since they'd met yesterday.

What he saw was unprepossessing. Probably in his late forties, Armstrong had sandy hair, tanned skin with a smattering of freckles that gave him a friendly, youthful appearance. He was of average build, average height, apparently average intelligence—an all-around average sort of guy. And from his vacuous smile, Armstrong had intended his remark to be a compliment. Obviously not the subtle type.

A good steady man to have on the team, probably make a good controller. But he wouldn't ever be a friend. Not like Xris. Not like Ito.

Rowan was disgusted with himself. Suddenly he wanted to talk to Xris. Needed to talk to him. The logjam of self-pity and anger was beginning to break up inside. He knew what he had to do now. It would be a comfort to let the pain pour out.

I'll have my chance, he promised himself. When this job is finished and Xris and Ito and I are flying back on *Vigilance* together, it'll be like old times, sitting, talking over a beer. I'll tell them everything. . . .

The shuttle docked with *Vigilance*. The two agents gathered their belongings, prepared to disembark. Captain Bolton was on hand to meet them.

"Welcome aboard the *Vigilance*. Your berths will be up forward off the forward mess. Stow your luggage. Then meet me on the bridge. I'll give you a tour of the ship."

With a cool nod, Bolton returned to her duties.

"She must be a good captain," Rowan said, shifting his luggage from his right hand to his left. Most of what he carried was equipment intended to help him break into an unknown computer.

"How can you tell?" Armstrong asked. "And which way is forward?"

"This way. Follow me." Rowan led off, Armstrong trailing along behind. "As for Bolton being a good captain, you can generally tell by the feel of the ship. The crew carrying out their duties efficiently, briskly."

"No one's lurking about in dark corners plotting mutiny. Is that it?"

"Something like that," Rowan agreed. "First time on board a working spaceship?"

"Is it that obvious? I must say, it's a bit different from your standard passenger ship, isn't it? Everything's so . . . well . . . small."

"Efficiency, not comfort."

As Rowan said this, both he and Armstrong had to flatten

themselves against the bulkheads to allow an apologetic crewman to slide past.

They continued on down the corridor, Rowan leading the way. The ship even smelled new. The walls were a creamy off-white in color, and he could detect the odor of fresh paint. There were, as yet, no streaks or marks on them, although several of the access panels were already smudged with fingerprints. Neat red stripes outlined cabinets containing emergency equipment, such as fire-fighting gear, vacuum suits, oxygen bottles, and first-aid equipment. All the doors were automatic sliding panels, with override controls built into the bulkheads.

The corridor dead-ended. Rowan indicated a ladder leading upward.

"Great," Armstrong muttered. He began to climb awkwardly, dragging a small duffel bag behind him. "I'm glad I packed light."

Rowan followed, moving almost as slowly and awkwardly as Armstrong. After a laborious climb, the two men reached the top, paused to watch a crewman slide down the ladder with ease, not even bothering to use the rungs. Looking up, she flashed them a grin. Both men looked at each other, shook their heads dolefully, and continued on.

"This is the forward mess," Rowan said. "Hopefully we have a cook this trip. Living off frozen and/or dehydrated meals can be hell." He took a brief survey, nodded his head. "This is fine. Really first class. Even a bar." He opened cabinet doors, peered inside. "Well-stocked, too."

Armstrong smiled politely, glanced at the bar without interest.

Doesn't drink, Rowan decided. "Do you play cards? Ante-up? Bridge?" He indicated several tables, surrounded by comfortable-looking chairs. The mess was the focal point of life for the crew, who used the room for meetings and recreation as well as eating. "We'll have enough for a foursome when we hook up with Xris and Ito."

"No, sorry." Armstrong shrugged. "Never learned. Where did you say our rooms are?"

Taking the hint, Rowan led the way to their quarters. He showed Armstrong his, then left to find his own. The cabin was small, contained a single bed and a sink. Drawers were built into the bulkheads. Rowan emptied his clothes onto the bed and began tossing them into the drawers.

"So Armstrong doesn't drink and he doesn't play cards," Rowan muttered to himself. "Just as well. We won't have to include him in our all-nighters. Not a bad sort, though. Just boring."

Captain Bolton came over the ship's comm to announce that they'd be leaving the system in ten minutes. A knock on the door was Armstrong, wondering how to find the washrooms.

"It's known as a 'head' aboard ship," Rowan told him, and advised him to try the end of the corridor.

Armstrong thanked him and left.

Clothes put away, Rowan began to unload his computer equipment. He checked it, repacked it into a backpack carrier, stowed it away. He'd have it out again tonight, checking it again. Before they entered orbit around TISor 13, he'd recheck his equipment a dozen times. Ever since that botched assignment in the Omacron Interior, ruined because some bastard had broken in, removed all his interface cables without his knowing it, Rowan had become obsessive about making certain that whatever went into his pack stayed in his pack.

This completed, he lay down on the bed and realized that he didn't want to get up. He was relaxed, more relaxed than he'd been in a month, and he knew he could sleep—something else he hadn't done for a while. His financial woes would sort themselves out—surely, after all these years of being a responsible customer, his creditors would take a tolerant attitude. As for Kim, well, she was gone and that was that. The hurt was fading rapidly and that should tell him something. If he had loved her—truly loved her, the way Xris loved Marjorie—then the hurt wouldn't let loose. In a way, this was good.

The knock on the door jolted him awake.

"Yeah?" he called.

"Me, Armstrong." The voice came through the door. "Ready for the tour?"

"No, not really," Rowan grumbled, wondering for a moment if he could get out of it. You've seen one bridge, you've seen 'em all. Armstrong was interested, of course. As controller, he'd be working on board this ship. To Rowan, it was a means of transportation, nothing more. Still, he didn't want to offend Captain Bolton. "I'm coming."

He splashed cold water on his face, ran his hand through his hair, and opened the door.

The bridge was the usual blinking display of electronic equipment and control panels—all the very latest. Any other time, Rowan would have been fascinated. Now, the bright lights blurred in his eyes. Captain Bolton formally welcomed the two agents to the bridge, and gave them a guided tour. She explained the navigation and helm positions, communications station, and the command station. Rowan deftly turned a yawn into a sneeze.

"In this room, Agent Armstrong, is the controller station."

The captain opened a sealed door off the port side of the bridge. Armstrong entered, took a long and interested look around. He asked questions, she answered. Rowan, after listening a few moments, lounged back against the door, let the conversation flow past him. Armstrong was sharp, intelligent, obviously knew what he was doing.

"Monitors . . . infrared . . . sensing . . . ground communication" floated around Rowan. He smiled and nodded whenever either of them looked at him; had no idea what was going on. He'd take time later to study the setup when he went to work on the Hung codes—after about twelve hours' sleep.

"Excellent," Armstrong was saying. "I'll try a few simulations just to shake it down. Then I'll program the station for our upcoming mission and load the tactical imagery. That is, if I have time. How long until we jump?"

"We'll move out of this system and into open space in the next four hours, then make the jump around oh-three-hundred. I'll sound general quarters fifteen minutes previous, so that you can return to your berth and prepare for the jump. After we come out, we'll travel under linear drive to the TISor System. That will take around twenty-four hours."

Armstrong nodded absently. He was already seated, starting work.

Captain Bolton watched him a moment, then turned back to Rowan.

"Would you care to see anything else, Agent?" she asked.

"Yeah." Rowan yawned. "The insides of my eyelids."

The captain laughed. "Strap yourself in your bed so that we don't have to wake you for the jump."

"Sure thing. Thanks, Captain. See you, Armstrong."

The controller didn't even look up. Rowan returned to his

room, fell onto the bed, strapped himself in, then remembered he hadn't taken off his shoes.

"The hell with it," he started to say, but before he had finished the sentence, he was asleep.

"Agent Rowan, report to the bridge."

Rowan struggled to wake out of a deep slumber. He had the impression the voice had been calling for him repeatedly; it had managed to work itself into his dreams. He tried to get out of bed, wondered for a frantic instant why he couldn't move, remembered that he was strapped in. He fumbled at the belts and webbing, stood up groggily, and lurched over to the comm.

"Rowan here."

"Message from the captain, sir. We will be entering the TISor System in approximately one hour."

"Thanks."

He'd been asleep for over twenty-four hours. No time now to work on those Hung codes. He'd do it on the trip back.

Rowan dug out clean clothes, went to shower, eat breakfast, and drink about six cups of coffee. Following this, he felt sufficiently restored to qualify as a member of the human race. He returned to the room, collected his equipment, checked it over and, finding everything as it should be, headed for the bridge.

The bridge aboard a small ship such as this one was unique in that it was the only area on board with a large steelglass viewscreen. The screen might seem superfluous to some; instrumentation gave highly accurate and detailed readings about what was outside the ship. A few races (notably the eyeless Corasians) relied totally on instruments, didn't bother to go to the expense of adding costly viewscreens. But humans needed them. The screen provided the crew with a visual duplication of what their instruments were telling them—essential to humans, who receive a disproportionately large percentage of their sensory input through their eyes.

Entering the bridge, Rowan paused, stared, awestruck. The view entering the TISor System was magnificent. The numerous moons shone with the reflected light of the system's sun and the radiance of its orange gas-giant planet. Times like this, he wondered if the people who were touting the now fashionable worship of God were really on to something.

Vigilance slipped into orbit around the thirteenth moon. Rowan entered the controller room to check in with Armstrong. The agent was already on the comm channel talking to Xris and Ito.

Rowan cast a cursory glance over the equipment. He hadn't had time to study it; but then, it wasn't really his concern. And there was always the return trip.

Armstrong gave him a brief and businesslike nod, then returned to his conversation with Xris.

"Everything okay down there?" Rowan asked Armstrong when the conversation had ended.

"Yes. You may proceed. You'll find the day's codes in the computer. I'll send you the cipher key. The shuttle is standing by."

"Uh, I don't suppose I could send Xris and Ito a message—something rude and crass. You know. Between friends."

Armstrong gave him a cold look. "That's strictly against regulations."

"Sure, I know. It's just— Oh, hell. Never mind."

Rowan walked off, headed rearward for the shuttle bay.

I might have figured Armstrong for a by-the-book bastard, Rowan thought. Probably all that time at HQ. Must be something they put in the water.

He found the crew chief inspecting the shuttle. The woman had a worried frown, was shaking her head.

"How's she look, Chief?" Rowan asked.

"Well, sir, I'm not certain. I *think* everything's okay. It's just that I've been locked out of all of the maintenance routines on the onboard computer."

"Did you ask Armstrong?"

"He said that was regulation—security purposes. I guess he doesn't trust us. We're on *your* side, you know." The chief was angry, insulted.

That might be regulation—Rowan wasn't certain—but if so, it was a bit heavy-handed. He reminded himself to have a little talk with Armstrong when they came back. Regulations were fine, but they shouldn't interfere with a good working relationship with the ship's crew. Rowan did his best to smooth things over.

"I've never flown one of these new intrusion shuttles before, Chief. Very impressive. Would you show me around?"

Two shuttlecraft were docked in the bay. Somewhat mollified by his interest, the chief gave Rowan a tour of the craft he would be flying, pointed out its significant features.

Rowan listened politely. He'd never flown an intrusion shuttle before, but he had studied them extensively.

"Everything looks okay to me, Chief. Including the computer."

"I checked the computer out before we left, sir." The chief was still defensive. "It was working fine then."

"Then I'm certain it's working fine now. Don't worry about Armstrong. He's just been reassigned from HQ. He'll loosen up."

"If you say so, sir."

The chief looked doubtful, but she smiled and waved good-bye, headed back into the shuttle bay control room.

Rowan boarded the shuttle and moved to the cockpit. Shuttles were launched and recovered by magnetic tractor beams. Unlike spaceplanes, shuttlecraft were not designed to handle the tricky maneuvering required to land or take off from spacecraft. The chief, on board the mother ship, was in control of the shuttlecraft during launches and landings.

Rowan keyed the commlink. "Sunray, this is Javelin. How are my comms? Over."

Armstrong answered from the mission control room. "Sunray here. All comms check out. Proceed with your launch and descend to the moon's surface. Sunray out."

Rowan transferred control of the shuttle to the crew chief for launch. The chief acknowledged and started the suction pumps that removed the air from the shuttlecraft bay.

When hard vacuum had been achieved, the shuttle bay doors opened. Magnetic tractor beams lifted the shuttle off the deck. Slowly, it moved out into space. As the shuttle cleared the bay, it was no longer in the ship's artificial gravity environment, and Rowan went weightless. His webbing held him in his seat, but he hated the sensation. Spaceplanes and larger spaceships were equipped with artificial gravity field generators. Shuttles were not. At least not the shuttles purchased by the agency.

"Cheap bastards!" Rowan muttered.

This won't last long, he told himself. When he drew near the moon, its gravity would begin to take effect. Soon he'd be sitting in the pilot's chair like a normal person, not like some helium-filled balloon tethered to a string.

When the shuttle was one thousand meters off the aft of the ship, the chief bid Rowan good-bye and good luck.

"Sunray, this is Javelin." He reported in. "The shuttle is under my control, and I am beginning my descent. Please feed the coordinates of the ground ops and the cipher key for tactical communications into my nav computer."

"Javelin, stand by to receive ground ops coordinates and cipher key."

Again, routine procedure. The cipher key was the codes that would be used by the team during the operation. For security reasons, the codes were changed on a daily basis and were issued to the operatives immediately prior to the job. Xris and Ito would have already received the day's codes.

"Roger, Sunray. Receiving ground ops data now. Thanks. Javelin out."

The shuttle turned in a graceful arc and headed for the thirteenth moon's surface. Upon entering the moon's atmosphere, the shuttle encountered upper-level turbulence, began to buck and rock—a most uncomfortable and unnerving experience. But at least now the moon's gravitational pull was compensating for the shuttle's lack of gravity. Rowan sank back down in his seat and felt better.

The descent was a long and boring process. He had nothing to do. The computer would handle the entry until the shuttle had dropped to the moon's stratosphere, at which point he would take over. Rowan sat back and played tourist, admiring the spectacular view of the gas giant and its many moons. He kept his mind as empty as the darkness around him, refusing to let anything intrude on the job at hand. He was looking forward to seeing Xris and Ito, though. They'd be a bit leery of him, but a handshake, a nod, a smile, and his friends would know he was back on track.

"Entering the stratosphere," the computer reported.

"Taking over manual control," Rowan informed the computer, and began to line up with his projected bearing of descent. He turned to the left.

The shuttle did not.

Rowan checked his instruments. They registered the correct turn, but the shuttle was flying in the same direction, at the same angle of ingress.

"Computer, release flight control to me."

"Flight control is already in pilot's control."

"Computer, your systems registered a turn, but the shuttle has not turned. Explain."

"Flight and navigation computers have registered a turn of forty-one degrees. Your new bearing is twenty-one degrees, angle of descent thirty-one degrees, speed of . . ."

Rowan didn't need to hear his speed, which was rapidly increasing. What the hell was wrong?

Nothing—according to the computer.

"Computer, bring up maintenance routine two-one—flight controls."

A text message flashed across the display console: *Access denied.*

Rowan swore. The shuttle was now nearing dangerous velocity. The hull temperature was rising due to friction with the moon's atmosphere.

"Computer, how long until impact with the moon's surface?"

"Four minutes thirty-one seconds."

The hull temperature indicator continued to rise.

"How long until hull has lost integrity?"

"Two minutes three seconds."

Rowan activated the comm. "Sunray, this is Javelin. Mayday! Mayday! Mayday! My nav computer is out and I can't bring up the maintenance routines in order to correct it. Manual is out. Please advise."

No response. Only static. The comm was working; no one was home.

"Damn it, Sunray! *Mayday! Mayday!* Where the hell are you?"

The static on the line was now being drowned out by the rumble of the shuttle's hull, creaking with the stress of its accelerating descent.

I've been locked out of all of the maintenance routines on the onboard computer. The chief's voice echoed in Rowan's mind.

Sabotage. Deliberate sabotage. That was the only explanation. Someone wanted him dead.

Rowan took a deep breath. He didn't fight the instinct to panic; rather, he put panic to good use, as he'd been trained—keep calm, use the adrenal rush to aid your thought process. Unstrapping himself from the webbing, he left the cockpit and headed for the rear compartment, grabbing his backpack on the way.

"Computer, give me a time check every twenty seconds until hull degradation."

He searched for, quickly located the access panel to the maintenance computer.

"One minute forty seconds until hull degradation."

The bolts were hand-fasteners, meant to come off quickly in case of emergency—such as this. He yanked the panel free. The computer was a sealed unit, but it had a small display screen and test points, allowing access for repairs.

"One minute twenty seconds until hull degradation."

Rowan opened the backpack and dumped its contents on the deck. Grabbing his small handheld computer, he attached leads to the test points, toggled the control switch from voice to keyboard access, typed in a command.

The maintenance computer remained blank for several seconds, then read: *Manual mode. Enter command.*

"One minute until hull degradation."

Rowan took a few seconds to think. He had to assume that all high-level commands had been frozen out by the saboteur. It was unlikely, however, that his killer would have bothered—or maybe even thought about—freezing out low-level commands.

"Let's try 'self-test,' " Rowan said, typing in the commands.

The computer started running its diagnostics procedure—which could take far longer than Rowan had left to live. He stopped it.

"Reboot from backup," he ordered.

The system hesitated, and then restarted.

"Forty seconds until hull degradation."

The maintenance computer began loading its programming from stored backups.

Rowan cursed the time that it took. He switched the computer to voice mode.

"Maintenance computer, do you hear me?"

No response.

"Maintenance computer! Wake the hell up!"

He'd done all he could. A strange thought crossed his mind. Only a few days before, he had seriously thought about killing himself. Now he was fighting desperately to survive. It was as if God was teaching him a lesson.

"Twenty seconds until hull degradation."

"Come on, damn it!" Rowan swore beneath his breath. Sweat poured off his body. It was hotter than hell in the shuttlecraft.

And then the maintenance computer's display area lit up. "Successful reboot."

Rowan could have kissed it. "Maintenance computer, respond!"

"Maintenance here. What's the problem?" Even the voice was different from the voice of the flight computer. These shuttle designers thought of everything.

"Maintenance computer, the flight computer has malfunctioned. Pilot authorizes you to take over flight control *now*!"

"Maintenance computer here. I have now taken over flight control."

Rowan sighed in relief. "Reduce shuttle speed to full stop and reduce rate of descent to ten meters per second!"

Main engines cut. Forward breaking thrusters fired. Inertial dampeners kicked in. Everything in the compartment lurched forward. Rowan and all of his equipment slid across the deck to the foot of the forward compartment bulkhead.

Bruised and battered, he regained his feet, staggered across the listing deck to the console.

The timer had stopped.

"Good work, maintenance," Rowan said, hoping his thudding heartbeat would return to normal sometime soon. "Restore all onboard computers to their original backup programs and inform me when that is complete."

Rowan switched to the comm. "Sunray, this is Javelin. Do you read? Over."

No response.

He sat and thought. Someone had tried to kill him by locking him out of the computer. The chief said the computer was fine when she checked it on the ground. Which meant that the killer had tampered with the computer *after* the chief had checked it. Which meant the killer was on board *Vigilance*. And either the killer had silenced Armstrong or else . . .

Good God! Xris and Ito!

Whoever tried to kill me wouldn't be likely to stop there, Rowan realized. The only reason to kill me is to halt this mission!

He had to warn them, tried the frequency he'd been given. "Delta One, this is Javelin. Come in, Delta One."

Nothing. No response.

Rowan tried again and again until at last he was trying only out of sheer frustration. Either he'd been given the wrong cipher—Xris and Ito wouldn't respond to anything except the correct daily codes—or Rowan had been given the wrong coordinates. Or maybe both. It was all starting to fit together. . . .

"Pilot, navigation and flight computers have been restored."

"Thank you, maintenance. Return control back to the primary computers and maintain surveillance of all computer activity. Tell me if any other nonstandard code shows up."

The restart of the nav computer had wiped its short-term memory. The landing coordinates on TISor 13 were no longer displayed. The sensor array still held a fix on the mother ship, however. Rowan had two choices. He go could on—not being certain where to land or what to do after he landed. Or he could return to *Vigilance*. From there, he could obtain the correct frequencies and check the cipher codes, get in touch with Xris.

And, hopefully, find the bastard who'd done this. He headed back to the ship—as fast as the shuttle would fly.

Vigilance came into view, silhouetted against TISor's sun. Lights were on, everything looked normal.

"Shuttlecraft to *Vigilance*. Come in, *Vigilance*."

No response from the bridge.

Why wasn't he surprised? His heart rate had slowed; now it was sinking.

The shuttle bay was open, but no friendly tractor beams reached out to guide him inside.

He nudged the shuttle forward slowly, crept into the shuttle bay.

The other shuttle was gone.

Rowan landed the craft on the deck. The chief was not at her post in the control room. None of the crew was around, at least that Rowan could see from the cockpit. No one to shut the shuttle bay doors. He struggled into his vacuum suit.

Rowan exited the shuttle and moved to the airlock, a 38-decawatt lasgun in his hand. Entering the airlock, which separated the shuttle bay from the main portion of the ship, he hit the button to cycle the atmosphere.

Nothing. A red warning light flashed insistently. No air on the other side of the airlock.

Rowan pulled the override handle and opened the door leading to the ship's internal compartments. The warning light had been right. No air. Finding a comm panel, he tried to raise the bridge.

No response. He hit the emergency button on the panel, setting off alarms all over the ship. He could hear no sound in the vacuum, but the alert lights flashed red. This part of the ship was in hard vacuum, and the emergency alarm had not been activated. He kept going.

Entering the shuttle bay control room, Rowan found someone—the crew chief. Dead. Her hands were clasped to her throat, her eyes bulged, her lips were blue; she'd died of asphyxiation.

Rowan shut the shuttle bay doors and exited the control room. Moving down the corridor, he found more bodies. Everyone was dead, all suffocated.

A terrible accident? Possibly, but Rowan didn't think so. Ships were equipped with all kinds of fail-safe devices to prevent just this sort of tragedy from occurring. Someone had overridden them, deliberately bled the air from the ship.

He entered the bridge. The scene was almost the same— almost. Everyone was dead. But these people had been shot to death, lasgun blasts to the chest and head.

Captain Bolton sat in her command chair, a look of surprise frozen on her face. There was a hole in her chest—a lasgun blast at short range. The blood had started to run, but had frozen in midstream.

If there had been any doubt in Rowan's mind, he was convinced now. Murder and sabotage. Someone wanted this operation to fail and had gone to terrible lengths to achieve that goal.

And Xris and Ito were on the ground, with no idea that they could be walking into a deadly trap.

Unless somehow Armstrong had managed to warn them. . . .

Rowan started to hit the pad to open the door to the controller's station, then stopped. A green light on the panel indicated that there was atmosphere on the other side of the door. He pushed the override button, held on fast to a nearby console with one hand, his lasgun with the other.

The door slid open. The rush of air nearly blew him off

his feet. When he could move, he darted inside, more than half expecting—or hoping—to find Armstrong's bloody body slumped over the control panel.

Armstrong wasn't there.

Rowan entered and shut the door. Air immediately began to pump into the small room, restoring pressure.

The controller's workstation was set to automatic mode. Rowan sat down at the computer, attempted to bring up the communications log.

A message flashed across the screen: *Access denied.*

Again, all high-level commands were frozen out.

Rowan slammed his fist down hard. He didn't have time for this! And then, as the air and the pressure inside the room began to return to normal, he could hear Armstrong's voice.

"This is Sunray. Proceed. Out."

A recording. A goddam recording!

Rowan ran back to the bridge. Dragging a body from the chair, he sat down at the comm workstation and pulled up the automatic communications log.

There it was. Thank God! All the comm parameters had been stored in the ship's log.

"Computer, restore the last communications parameters set by the mission controller, and set up transmitter two to use these same parameters."

Rowan couldn't shut down the controller's computer, but he could talk on the same frequency, using the day's codes.

"All Deltas! Joker's Wild! For God's sake, get out of there! Joker's Wild! Joker's Wild!"

He waited to hear Xris's voice, demanding angrily to know what the hell was going on.

Silence. The silence was sickening.

"Maybe they didn't hear," he said to himself, and sent the message two more times. He was going to send it a fourth when he forced himself to stop.

There was nothing more that he could do. He sat in the chair, glaring at the orange gas giant—floating serenely in space—in bitter frustration. They'd been betrayed, and there was no question in Rowan's mind who was responsible. The frustration and his fear for Xris and Ito gnawed at him. He had to do something. He activated the ship's emergency distress signal, which would beam out into space, requesting help from the nearest vessel. Then Rowan returned to the rear of the ship.

Before entering the shuttle bay, he stopped at the weapons storage locker, picked up a plasma rifle with scope, and a box of thurmaplasma grenades. Stowing the weapons in the cargo compartment of the shuttle, he flew the shuttle back out, again under his own control.

Now, how to find Xris and Ito?

Rowan accessed the *Vigilance*'s sensor computer, got a fix for the last transmission from the surface of the moon, entered the coordinates into the nav computer. Then there was nothing to do but wait. The shuttle trip this time was not a lot more pleasant than his last. His own life wasn't in danger, but apprehension and fear twisted his insides, made the waiting unendurable.

He tried to tell himself that everything would be all right. Maybe—please dear God!—Xris had decided to flout the controller's authority, go off on his own. Neither he nor Ito would want to enter that factory without the third member of the team, without Rowan.

"I'll find Xris hip-deep in some swamp, madder than hell, ready to take on the entire agency. And Ito yammering about snakes. But I'll find them," Rowan repeated. "I'll find them alive."

The flight took two hours, seemed like two hundred. He reached the location, overflew it by about one hundred meters. He didn't immediately land.

There was no need. He had his answer.

The factory was a pile of twisted, smoldering steel. Fires still burned. As he watched, a small blast took out a far corner. Thick smoke smudged the morning sky.

No fire trucks. No one around to put out the blaze or rescue any casualties.

"Probably paid off," Rowan said bitterly. "Or called to the other side of town. Or maybe this jerk-water place doesn't even have a fire department."

He landed the shuttle inside the fence line, set off his own emergency beacon. He was going to need help. He hoped like hell he was going to need help.

He was still wearing the vacuum suit, which would protect him from the heat, though not from falling beams, radiation leaks, or exploding ammunition. He put on the helmet, took it back off, and detached the breathing apparatus. He would need to be able to hear, if someone called for help.

He'd need to be able to answer.

Strapping the oxygen tank to his belt, he put the mask to his face, emerged from the shuttle, and looked swiftly around.

He saw the hole in the fence. He damn near cried in fury and frustration.

"They went in," he said softly. "They went in! And now you know it's hopeless. Absolutely hopeless. No one inside that place could have survived. And you *know* that Xris and Ito went inside."

Dogged, refusing to listen to himself, Rowan took a deep gulp of oxygen and plunged into the inferno.

CHAPTER
21

Forsake not an old friend. . . .
     Ecclesiastes, Chapter 9, Verse 19, Apocrypha

"I never did find Ito," Rowan said. She spoke quietly, telling the story in monotone, never once looking at Xris, but staring into the past with dark and pain-filled eyes. Her face was pale, drawn, and haggard.

If she's lying, she's doing a damn good job, Xris thought. But then, we were all of us trained to lie.

"I found you," she continued, and for the first time since she'd started speaking, she shifted her gaze to him. "I don't know how. Those who believe in God would say an angel led me." She smiled that sad, lopsided smile.

Xris snorted. He'd been sitting on the edge of the console during her narrative, and he was startled to discover that his flesh-and-blood leg had gone to sleep. Grunting, he stood up, tried to restore the circulation.

"You expect me to believe that?"

"I guess not," she said, shrugging. "But it's true. I *did* find you in that hellhole. Accident. Coincidence. Logical reasoning. Angels. Who can say? Maybe they're all one and the same anyway.

"I was standing somewhere near what had once been an outer wall, yelling for you, yelling for Ito. I caught a glimpse of movement. It was your hand poking out of the rubble. You were lying under some sort of heavy worktable. The table protected you from the blast. It saved your life. . . . That was about all it saved."

Rowan paused, grew paler still. "My God, Xris. I'd never seen anything like it. Bones crushed, the broken ends sticking through your flesh, blood ... so much blood.... One eye ... one side of your face ... gone. Just gone. But you were breathing. You were still breathing.

"I didn't know what to do. There wasn't anything I could do. I was afraid to move you. Some ship would hear my distress signal. Someone would come. I kept telling myself that. I told you that. And I told you then just what I've told you now. I told you the whole story.

" 'We'll get Armstrong, you and I, Xris,' I said to you over and over. 'We'll make him pay.'

"Maybe ... some part of you heard me?" She stared at him, pleading.

Xris didn't answer.

Rowan shrugged. "I supposed not. I kept hoping ..." She let the sentence hang, sighed. "Anyway, that's about it. The next thing I remember, a soldier was standing beside me, yelling for a medic. Warlord DiLuna's battle cruiser—the *Athena*—had picked up the distress call. The medics worked on you for a long time on the ground, then they transferred you back up to *Athena*. I went along, made my report to the captain. She ordered *Vigilance* to be towed, sent out her soldiers to search for Armstrong. He must have landed on TISor 13. The shuttle was small—one of those ship-to-ground transports. It couldn't have made the trip to any of the other moons—"

"It could have been picked up by another ship," Xris said.

Rowan sat forward eagerly, her eyes suddenly bright. A tinge of color stained her pale cheeks. "You believe me!"

Xris shook his head. "Just a reflex action. I suppose that there'd be some record of all this coming and going in *Athena*'s logs?"

Rowan sank back down, her shoulders slumped. Wearily, she leaned against the console. "I don't know. Maybe. Maybe not. You see," she said quickly, forestalling Xris, "a day after we'd been on board *Athena*, Amadi from the bureau arrived. He had a closed-door session with the captain. He called me in, asked me what I'd seen, what I'd heard. I told him and then I said I wanted one thing from him, one thing only. I wanted Armstrong.

"Amadi said I could have him. It would mean going undercover, infiltrating the Hung. I agreed. You were in a coma, Xris. They'd amputated your left leg, your left arm.

They told me they could keep you alive, but you'd be more machine than man. The decision would be up to Marjorie.

"I said good-bye to you there, on *Athena,* and I left with Amadi. As we were leaving, I saw the *Athena* hit *Vigilance* with a plasma fusion torpedo. The ship was vaporized, nothing left. The families were told that the *Vigilance* had been struck by an asteroid. No survivors, bodies never recovered. That may be on *Athena*'s log, but again it may not. The captain may have been told to forget she'd ever seen *Vigilance,* you, or me. The bureau was a pretty powerful force in those days."

"All very convenient for you, isn't it, old friend?" Xris said, chewing on the end of a twist. "Records expunged. Armstrong dead. I supposed that was your work?"

Slowly, she shook her head. "I was a little too late. His own people took him out. He'd served his purpose. They didn't trust him. Once a traitor, always a traitor."

"Tell me about it." Xris sneered.

Rowan flushed deeply, the color returning to her face in a rush. She was on her feet, confronting him. "Damn it, Xris, we were friends! Friends! *How* could you think I'd betray you?"

Her angry voice carried through the cargo plane. Harry and Jamil stopped talking. Quong, jolted out of a sound sleep, peered around, muttered groggily.

"Everything all right, Xris?" Jamil called.

"Sure, yeah, fine."

Xris eyed Rowan. "So, you go undercover, send a few of the Hung's top boys to the gas mines on Nogales 4, and then you pop out to buy a new wardrobe and a body to match."

Rowan's face was now cold, pale. She no longer expected to be believed. Perhaps she no longer cared. She continued to face him, her eyes level. "That job was hell, Xris. I worked undercover for nine months and I knew every moment that passed was going to be my last. I'm not asking for sympathy. I did good work. I broke them. But in the process, something broke inside me.

"When I was finished, I told the bureau I wanted out. The feeling was mutual. They wanted rid of me, too. I knew the truth about Armstrong, you see. I'd become an embarrassment. Amadi offered me a new identity, but I knew that changing my name and shaving off my beard wasn't going to be any kind of protection."

"From the Hung . . . or from me?" Xris asked.

"I heard you were out of the hospital, asking questions about me. I wanted to see you, Xris. I wanted to tell you the truth. But it would have been too dangerous. Not for me," she added before he could comment, "for you."

He stared at her.

"Haven't you figured it out yet?" She was impatient. "It was the bureau who set me up, Xris! They set me up to take the fall. I didn't see it coming. I didn't realize until it was too late. And if I didn't play their game, they would have killed me, you, Marjorie. Anyone who knew anything. You see, I not only found out about the Hung, I found out about their connection with the bureau."

It was all starting to make sense. Xris watched a light flash on the console. "When you said 'they' killed Armstrong, you didn't mean the Hung, did you?"

"That was when I decided to do this." Rowan gestured to herself, to her body. "Dalin Rowan had to die. He knew too much. If he died, the rest of you might live."

"Why didn't he die for real, then?" Xris demanded harshly.

"Because he intended to come back from the dead," she said softly. "One day, he was going to return and make things right."

"Why didn't he?"

She was silent a moment, then said, "You don't feel any pain when you're dead, Xris. Resurrections hurt."

He could have said something to this, was about to when the computer interrupted. "We will be coming out of hyperspace in mark: thirty minutes and counting."

"Harry!" Xris yelled.

"I'm on my way." Harry entered the cockpit. "Excuse me, ma'am," he added awkwardly, blushing, as he tripped over Rowan's feet.

"I'll move," she offered. "My throat's dry. Talking too much." She smiled faintly, said something about getting some water, and left the cockpit.

Xris stared at nothing. He had a twist in his hand but had forgotten about it. Harry looked extremely uncomfortable, as if he wanted to ask a question but couldn't think of any way to phrase it. He punched a few buttons in a desultory fashion and darted glances at Xris out of the corner of his eye.

Ignoring him, Xris sat down in the copilot's chair, began to strap himself in.

Rowan didn't return. Probably needed some time to herself. Time to recover from a painful ordeal? Or time to think up more lies? After all, she'd had almost ten years to devise that nifty little story.

He had to find out if she was telling the truth.

Xris motioned to Quong.

Yawning and stretching, the Doc wandered over. "How are you feeling?"

Xris waved that away. "Look, is there any way we can communicate with the Little One? I could really use the empath's help about now."

Quong shook his head. "I doubt it. He and Raoul seem to have developed some sort of strange symbiotic connection. I'm not certain the Little One even understands what we are saying. My guess is that he gets everything filtered through Raoul. If I knew more about Tongans, maybe I could suggest something. But I don't. I doubt if any human does."

"Then we have to find Raoul. At least the Little One ought to be able to tell us something about what happened to his buddy. Maybe he could answer yes-or-no questions. You know—one blink of the eye for yes, two for no."

"I'll give it a try," Quong promised, but he didn't sound hopeful. Shaking his head, he went to examine his small patient.

Xris clenched his fist, his good fist. Damn it! Trust the Loti to get himself snatched right when he might be useful!

Harry was warning everyone to strap themselves in.

"Coming out of hyperspace in one minute. Counting down. Fifty-nine. Fifty-eight . . ." The computer chanted the time.

Coming out of the jump was not nearly so traumatic as going into it. Everything seemed to slow, to move in slow motion, but Xris had read that this was a psychological reaction to the process. Of course, the ship was essentially slowing down, but the human mind was not capable of comprehending the change. The main difference one noticed was that one minute there was nothing visible and the next minute, the viewscreen was filled with stars.

Stars and . . .

"Holy shit!" Harry gasped, swore.

A Naval battle cruiser, sleek and huge and powerful, came

into view. Compared to the immense cruiser, the Olicien Pest Control plane was as small and helpless as the black beetle painted on its bright yellow hull.

"They *can't* be after us!" Harry protested, his eyes bulging.

A warning shot streaked past the viewscreen.

"Oh, yeah?" Xris demanded. "That one was close enough to smell! Take us back into hyperspace."

"But how did they know—"

"Just do it, damn it!" Xris shouted.

"The missile cruiser *Starfire* requests that we cut our engines and prepare to be towed," said the computer. "May I add that I'm not enjoying myself anymore? I think it would be advisable—"

"Computer, switch to manual," Harry commanded. "Now!"

Sullenly, the computer did so. "It's going to take a minute to make the calculations—"

Jamil crowded into the cockpit. "I'll tell you how they found us. That wasn't any missile that hit us back there at the space station! Navy Katana pilots can shoot straighter than that. It must have been some sort of tracking device!"

"Through hyperspace? That's impossible!"

A second warning shot skimmed past them, so close that the cargo plane bucked and rocked.

"Ask your girlfriend!" Jamil said grimly, and before Xris could make an angry retort, Rowan appeared.

"He's right, Xris! The Navy's been working on a device capable of tracking ships through hyperspace."

Xris glared at her. "You knew about this!"

"Xris, please—" Rowan began.

"Skip it. How does the thing work? Can we get rid of it?"

"The device attaches itself to the outer hull. It doesn't actually track the plane, like a homing device. It doesn't need to. It has one simple function, and that is to tap into our plane's computer, download our coordinates, and transmit them. Once our plane has made the jump, the coordinates can't be changed, and so the Navy knows when and where a plane will come out of the Lanes."

"You know a lot about it," Xris said.

"I invented it," Rowan answered. She was silent a moment, then added, "I'm glad to see it's working."

Xris snorted, but he caught himself almost smiling. The old Rowan all over again. . . .

"Your tax dollars at work," Tycho was muttering.

"Evasive maneuver! Hang on!" Harry shouted.

The stars whirled. The cruiser disappeared. Everyone clung to whatever they could find to cling to. A thud, a yelp, and a curse came from the vicinity of the cargo bay. Quong must not have heard the warning.

Xris was on his feet. "Computer, how soon can we make the jump into hyperspace?"

"We will not be going into hyperspace," said XP-28 in self-righteous tones. "We have no shields, no weapons. I have decided that it would be in our best interests to surrender. I have locked out manual control."

"Harry, take over!"

"I can't, Xris. It's getting some sort of signal from that cruiser out there! I can't override—"

"I can, Xris," Rowan said quietly. "You know I can."

Xris stared at her, grim, doubtful.

"Spaceplanes," reported Jamil, peering out the viewscreen. "Flying to intercept. We won't outmaneuver *them*. We better do something fast."

"Trust me, Xris," Rowan pleaded.

Xris spit the soggy wad of twist out on the deck. "If you screw us, you'll die with us. Because I'm not about to surrender."

He was bluffing and he figured Rowan knew he was bluffing. The old Rowan would have. But this one only nodded and turned to the computer.

"XP-28"—she rested her hands on the keyboard—"goodbye."

"What the devil is going on?" Quong appeared in the cockpit, highly indignant, a large and swelling bump on his forehead. "And why am I always the last one to know?"

"I'll explain later—" Xris began.

"Hang on, gentlemen," Rowan warned.

Her eyes shone; her face was flushed. Her fingers tapped swiftly, lightly. She was enjoying herself. And she was, Xris found himself thinking incongruously, a damn attractive woman.

"Making the jump in five, four . . ."

There was a mad scramble; everyone rushing to find seats, fumbling with the complicated straps and webbing.

"Another rough jump!" Tycho groaned.

"I hope you realize this is upsetting my patient," Quong snapped, hurling himself into a chair.

"He'd be a lot more upset in the brig," Xris returned.

Stars flashed before his eyes and so did most of his life. They were making the jump. And this one, as Tycho had said, was rough.

When Xris could breathe again and was relatively certain that his body parts—real and mechanical—had all returned to their respective locations, he unstrapped himself with a shaking hand.

"Everyone make it?" he asked.

Tycho, his hand over his mouth, was on his way to the head.

Xris returned to the cockpit. Harry, mopping his face, looked a bit green around the gills, but appeared otherwise fine.

Rowan was reclining back in her seat. She was pale; her eyes were closed. Her brown hair was damp with sweat and starting to curl around her face. But she was smiling, obviously extraordinarily pleased with herself.

Xris stood over her.

"You're no level-two government clerk. The Navy doesn't make clerks majors. The Navy doesn't threaten to shoot clerks rather than let them fall into enemy hands. And the Navy sure as hell doesn't take the time and trouble to plant homing devices on clerks to find out where they're going. Just what the hell do you do for RFComSec, 'old friend'?"

Rowan looked gravely up at Xris, and told him.

CHAPTER
22

He was a gentleman on whom I built
An absolute trust.
      William Shakespeare, *Macbeth*, Act 1, Scene 5

"Chief crypto analyst." Tusk stumbled over the words, then said, "What the hell does that mean, sir?"

"It means we're in a bad situation. Potentially, a very bad one." Dixter was back at his desk in his office. He had placed an urgent call to the king, was waiting for His Majesty to return it. "Major Mohini is our top-level code maker and breaker. She was responsible for designing and setting up the high-level secure communications used by every ship in the fleet. And now she's been kidnapped. Think about it, Tusk. Think about it."

Tusk did. He stared at the picture of the woman he held in his hand, said several words appropriate to the situation, then added lamely, "Begging your pardon, sir."

"No need to apologize." Dixter sighed, ran his hand through his grizzled hair. "I've been saying the same myself. Do you realize that right now, at this moment, our security is breached? Whoever has the major could potentially gain access to the movements of the fleet, the current position of every ship of the line. Worse then that"—Dixter's voice lowered—"they could send out false commands. Scatter the fleet all over the galaxy. Order our ships into Corasia, for God's sake!"

Tusk was on his feet, pacing about the room. "But *why*, sir?" Coming to an abrupt halt, he put his hands on Dixter's desk, leaned over it. "Why would Xris—Why would anyone—What motive—"

"Revolution," Dixter said dryly, "for one."

Tusk gave a low whistle, slowly straightened. He considered the matter, then shook his head. "No, sir. Not Xris."

"We can't ignore the evidence!" Dixter slammed his hand down on top of the vid shots. "And I can't afford to take chances! That's why I ordered them shot down."

Tusk turned away, walked over to the window. The view of the Glitter Palace—residence of Their Majesties, King Dion Starfire and his Queen, Astarte—was magnificent. The palace's crystal walls were streaked with the reds and purples and oranges of a spectacular sunset. Tusk didn't see it; any of it.

Once again, he was back in the Corasian galaxy, was lying wounded, helpless on the ground beneath his shot-up spaceplane. Corasians had him surrounded: lasfire streaked around him. And then Xris appeared, coming out of the smoke. Using his extraordinary strength, the cyborg lifted the injured pilot in his arms.

We've got a better chance inside the plane than out, Xris told him.

You, maybe! Tusk vaguely remembered arguing. *Not me. Go on. Leave me!*

He saw the cyborg's grim smile, the brooding, scarred face. He felt the strong arms, comforting, protecting . . .

A firm hand rested on his shoulder. "I'm sorry, son," Dixter said quietly. "I know he was your friend."

"Damn it all, sir," Tusk said, blinking back tears, his voice choked. "I just don't believe it! Not Xris!"

"Good men have gone bad before now, Tusk," Dixter said, his voice softened. "Every man has his price, they say. Every man . . . and every woman."

The comm buzzed. Both men jumped, turned.

"Rear Admiral Lopez, my lord," Bennett reported.

Dixter hurried to the comm room, Tusk right behind. All nonessential personnel had been ordered out. The rest remained at their posts, carrying on business as usual, though with a heightened tension. Everyone knew something was wrong; no one yet knew what. All eyes glanced at Dixter as he entered, immediately shifted back to their brightly lit screens.

Dixter sat down in the chair, faced the screen, saw the expression on the admiral's face, and sighed. "That bad, eh, Rod?"

"We had them, John," the rear admiral reported. "The 'tick' worked just like it was supposed to. The Olicien spaceplane came out of hyperspace right under our guns— *Starfire*, missile cruiser. Captain James Manto ordered them twice to surrender, then sent a signal to the onboard computer which should have locked it up. But someone was able to override it. The next thing Captain Manto knows, the plane has disappeared back into hyperspace. And now the goddam homing device has shut down. Of course," he added wryly, "you know who designed it."

Tusk breathed a soft, relieved sigh.

Dixter glared at him.

"Sorry, sir," Tusk said, half ashamed of himself. "I know this is serious, but—damn it—Xris *must* have some logical explanation."

"I can hardly wait to hear it!" Dixter muttered. "But this leaves me no choice. Captain?" He turned to the communications chief. "I am calling a holo-conference with all flag-grade officers in the fleet now—Alpha One priority."

Everyone in the comm room exchanged glances. No one even pretended to work. Dixter started for his office, Tusk in accompaniment. Once they were alone, in the small corridor that separated Dixter's office from the comm room, Tusk leaned near.

"You were relieved, too, sir. Weren't you?"

"In case it hasn't occurred to you, Commander," Dixter said grimly, "we may be facing armed rebellion, a revolution. Or a mass assault from the Corasian Empire. The next order I'm about to give will throw the fleet into disarray, disrupt Naval operations in every sector of the galaxy."

Dixter fumbled in his pocket, produced more antacid tablets, threw them in his mouth, and crunched them down.

Pausing at the door to his office, he said quietly, "Yes, maybe I was." Then, shaking his head, he added, "But I shouldn't have been."

With that, he entered.

"Bennett, I will be holding a holo-conference with my flag officers."

Bennett's gaze flicked over the Lord Admiral's uniform. The aide counted two coffee stains on the sleeve and what appeared to be the remnants of a bran muffin on the breast.

"I'll send to your quarters for your other uniform, sir."

"No time for that!" Dixter snapped, heading for the conference table.

Bennett planted himself in front of the Lord Admiral. The aide said nothing, but stared pointedly at the bran muffin crumbs.

Dixter looked down.

"Do what you can, then," he said impatiently.

Bennett moved in, brushing and buttoning and straightening seams.

Caught, Dixter waved his hand toward the vid panel. "Tusk, get everything set up."

"That is the best I can manage under the circumstances, my lord," Bennett said severely. "I suggest you keep your hands folded and your arms on the table." He indicated the coffee stains.

"I wish that was the worst I had to worry about." Dixter grimaced, tugged at the constricting collar. "How are we coming, Tusk?"

"Taking roll call now, sir."

"If you will excuse us, Sergeant-Major."

The aide left the room. Tusk, seated at the console, nodded, indicated they were ready. Dixter sat down at the large conference table. Clasping his hands together, he placed his arms on the desk.

The holographic images of fifty-one officers of rear admiral rank or higher appeared around the conference table. Some looked sleepy, had obviously been dragged out of their beds. One alien was still fumbling with her translator. Others, sensing that something big was up, looked alert, apprehensive. One of them—Admiral Lopez—looked sick.

Dixter drew in a deep breath. "Ladies and gentlemen. As of this moment, I am implementing Operation Macbeth."

Drowsy officers woke up. Those who had been waiting for something big obviously hadn't been expecting anything as big as this. Around the table, expressions went from startled to amazed to baffled.

"This is *not* a drill," Dixter continued. "I repeat, *not* a drill. You will immediately relay the order for the implementation of this operation to all ships and units under your command. I—"

Admiral Krylyn, commanding the Komos Sector, interrupted. "What the hell's going on, John? I've got some of my ships on a pretty dangerous mission into Corasia and I can't just—"

"I'm sorry, Souchmak." Dixter gave a small shrug. "No exceptions."

Several others started to speak, to ask questions, to protest. Dixter cut them off. "One final command will be issued from HQ within the next thirty minutes. You have your orders. Transmission closed."

The images winked out, leaving behind an odd, empty impression.

Dixter sat in the conference chair, staring at the table. Tusk looked at him worriedly.

"Are you feeling all right, sir? Maybe you should go lie down. Or get something to eat."

"I'm fine," Dixter said, grimacing. "I've got to go report this to His Majesty."

"Before you leave, sir, remember that I'm the new kid on the block. This one wasn't covered in any of the manuals. What is Operation Macbeth?"

"The plan was devised following the Ghost Legion incident, in order to handle similar incidents—a challenge to the crown or civil war. Such a disruption might mean that elements of the Royal Military could be in revolt. Or some outside force might attempt, through false orders, to remove ships from strategic locations. Therefore, as of now, no ship is to move or initiate communication. They are authorized to first warn, and then fire on, anyone attempting to communicate with them."

"Good God!" Tusk said softly, considering the ramifications. "They can't talk to each other. They can't talk to us. If they do, they get shot! This'll mean chaos, sir!"

"I agree, son, but I've got no choice. The way it looks now, our top code breaker has gone over to the other side— whatever the other side is. We don't even know that much!"

Tusk was silent, awed at the implications of this drastic act. He tried to imagine what it would be like—to be captain of a destroyer, hundreds of lives on board, suddenly cut off, isolated, alone in space. Even distress signals—especially distress signals—would be suspect; more than one ship had been lured to disaster by phony calls for help.

"How long will this last, sir?"

"We should have new codes developed within seventy-two hours, at which time I'll cancel Operation Macbeth.

Each ship has its own stand-down command, unique to that vessel. Each has to be contacted individually, by voice, its code verified. Which could take another forty-eight hours."

Bennett reappeared. "My lord, His Majesty will receive you now."

"Thank you, Bennett." Dixter rose slowly to his feet, flexed aching shoulders. "I don't mind telling you, Tusk, that I hated like hell issuing that order. My old friend, Admiral Souchmak Krylyn, has several ships involved in a delicate operation on the Corasian frontier. I've risked countless lives by doing this."

He stopped in front of Tusk, gazed at him steadily. "And now I want you to do something you're going to hate."

"I think I know, sir. The final command." Tusk, uncomfortable, waved his hand in the direction of the corridor. "Look, sir, I'm sorry about what I said back there—about being relieved that Xris had escaped. I guess I didn't realize how serious this was."

"Understood." Dixter's grim face relaxed momentarily in a smile, which almost immediately disappeared. "You will draft an executive order to go out galaxy-wide. To all law enforcement agencies and to all commands: The cyborg Xris, every member of his team—we should have photo I.D.s of them by now—and Major Darlene Mohini are wanted criminals, to be arrested on sight or their deaths confirmed if capture is not possible. Is that clear, Commander?"

"Yes, my lord," Tusk answered.

"After that"—Dixter sighed—"shut us down."

CHAPTER

23

Like pilgrims to th' appointed place we tend;
The world's an inn, and death the journey's end.
                John Dryden, *Palamon and Arcite*, Book 3

"The 'tick' is deactivated," Rowan reported.

Leaning back in the chair, she lifted her arms above her head, stretched, then put her hands behind her head, stretched again. Xris watched. He'd seen Rowan perform that stretching maneuver a hundred times. Maybe a thousand. But it was like watching an actor portraying his friend. Darlene Mohini as Dalin Rowan. Or Dalin Rowan as Darlene. Xris missed his friend, he realized suddenly. Missed him very much.

"I think I got to the 'tick' before it transmitted our destination," Rowan continued. "But we won't know until we get there." She started to say something else, was interrupted by a yawn. "Sorry. It's been a long day."

A couple of lifetimes, Xris said to himself. He looked questioningly at Harry.

The big man shrugged helplessly. "Beats me, Xris. I tried to follow what she was doing, but she lost me on the second command."

"Coming out of hyperspace in thirty minutes," reported a subdued and slightly altered XP-28.

"I guess we'll see what happens when we get there," Xris said through the twist clenched in his teeth. "We can always make the jump again if we need to."

"Oh, please! No!" Tycho groaned.

"I'm to the point where I'd almost rather be shot," Jamil muttered.

Glumly, they strapped themselves in and waited.

The cargo plane came out of hyperspace and into black, starlit loneliness. No carriers, no destroyers; not another spaceplane within instrument range.

"Take us home," said Xris.

Home was a spacious lodge located in the mountains of Sol-garth, ruled over by the gigantic and jovial human known as Bear Olefsky.

Formerly a Warlord under the Galactic Democratic Republic, Olefsky was a longtime friend of the current ruler, His Majesty, Dion Starfire. Certain gossipmongers among the vid-mags had romantically linked Olefsky's daughter Kamil with the king. But, with the queen pregnant and about to give birth and the king looking and acting extremely happy over the event, the gossip had faded away.

Xris knew the truth of the matter; he'd been involved in the middle of the potential scandal, managed to get himself shot up in the process. He admired Queen Astarte, had once thought himself in love with her. But then almost every man who came in contact with Queen Astarte fell in love with her. The feeling had been easy to dispel. He was half a man. She was fully a woman, one of the most beautiful and powerful women in the galaxy, a woman expecting a child, a woman completely devoted to her husband. But the danger Xris and Astarte had faced together had forged a bond between them. When Astarte and Dion offered to give Xris an estate as a reward for his services (he'd turned down a knighthood), Xris chose this site, near Olefsky's castle, as the location for what was now his favorite home.

Built of timber and stone taken from the land itself, the lodge stood on the side of a mountain, its many rooms sprawled across the mountain's face. Trees surrounded it, and because the lodge was made of the same trees and formed of the same stone as the mountain behind it, the dwelling was well camouflaged. Xris called it Journey's End.

Xris had access to the Bear's own private landing site, located over thirty kilometers away from the lodge, for his own spaceplanes. Hoverjeeps were used to transport them to the lodge; no other vehicle could make the rough trip.

Harry landed the spaceplane on Solgarth without incident. The region was isolated, with a small population. Air traffic control was nonexistent in this area. Once on the ground ("And so thankful to be here!" Tycho said fervently), they unloaded their gear. Quong carried the Little One from the cargo hold, took him to one of the hoverjeeps Xris kept parked at the landing site, and settled the empath comfortably in a backseat. Then, without saying a word, one by one they each quit their tasks, gathered together on the tarmac, and stared at the spaceplane.

Mountains soared above them; pine trees surrounded them; white clouds scudded across a cobalt-blue sky. The tarmac was made of slate. Amid the grays and greens and blues of nature, the bright yellow cargo plane, with the black beetle on the side, shone like a garish, lumbering sun.

"You can probably *see* it from the sun," Tycho remarked.

"What do we do with the damn thing?" Harry asked. "Bury it?"

"We do what we always planned to do," Xris returned. "Set it on automatic pilot and send it home."

"That leaves us without transportation," Jamil observed.

Xris glanced over at several long-range Scimitars and a Schiavona gunship, belonging to Bear Olefsky, parked on the tarmac. "If we need a plane, we can borrow one. For the moment, we're not going anywhere. Not until we figure out what's happened to Raoul. Speaking of which, Doc, how's the Little One?"

"He is doing quite well. Remarkable, I would say, except that such swift recovery may be perfectly normal for a Tongan. I would like to do a research paper on him. I would keep his identity secret, of course." A dreamy, wistful look appeared in Quong's eyes. "It would cause a stir in the medical community. I would most assuredly be asked to present it at the Royal College of Surgeons—"

"What I mean, Doc," Xris said tersely, interrupting the dream, "is when can I talk to him? When will he be conscious?"

Quong was startled. "He is conscious now. Somewhat groggy from the injury, but conscious. How do you plan—"

"Good. Harry, you get rid of the interstellar beetle. The rest of us will load the gear into the jeeps."

The others in the team exchanged glances. It was guaranteed Xris had some plan in mind, but in his current dark mood, he wasn't likely to share it. The rest dispersed about their duties. Harry continued to stare gloomily at the spaceplane.

"Maybe they'll be able to trace it back to us somehow."

"I'll scramble the log," Rowan offered. "By the time I'm finished with it, that plane will think it's been to Corasia and six other galaxies."

"Yeah, you could," Xris said. "Or you could fix it so that it would lead someone right to us."

"For God's sake, Xris!" Harry exploded angrily. "Lay off her! If she'd wanted to lead them to us, she could have left that damn 'tick' to do the job. Come on board, ma'am."

Rowan looked uncertainly at Xris, who gave a grudging nod.

Is it a matter of trust? he wondered, watching the two of them walk to the plane. Or is it a matter of not wanting to lose the hate that's kept me alive all these years? Without that, what do I have left?

He turned around to find Jamil, Quong, and Tycho staring at him.

"I'm tired. We're all tired," Xris said by way of explanation.

They said nothing, returned to their chores.

They're losing faith in me, Xris realized. And I can't blame them. Damn it, I'm beginning to lose faith in myself! I've never had a job go this wrong. If I was superstitious, I'd almost say it was cursed.

He'd been right about one thing, though. They were all exhausted. Turning back, he saw Rowan stumble wearily on the uneven tarmac.

"Allow me, ma'am," Harry offered, catching hold of her, steadying her.

She thanked him. The two continued on toward the spaceplane, but not before Harry had cast Xris a final reproachful look over his shoulder.

"Great! So now *I'm* the bad guy," Xris said bitterly.

Removing the butt end of the twist from his mouth, he tossed it on the stone, ground it out beneath his heel.

"You have to admit, Xris, your friend did a neat job of saving our skins." Tycho came over to stand beside the cyborg. "She didn't have to do it. Harry's right. She could have arranged it so that we'd be locked up in some brig right now. Not only would she be safe, she'd be a hero. Instead

... well ... she's in this up to her neck. Right along with us."

"Do you believe the story she told you? About Armstrong and what happened at the factory? ... Sorry," Jamil added with a rueful smile, "but I had to listen to something other than Harry's lectures on the lives and habits of fleas. Her explanation sounded logical to me."

"Yeah, but then it would, wouldn't it?" Xris said, frowning. He didn't like talking about himself, his past, didn't like his wounds open for public viewing. But he owed his team something for this, even if he could offer nothing more than unloading the metal casing that housed his soul. "She's had years to come up with it. I don't know." He shook his head moodily. "I just don't know. And she still could have betrayed us. I don't feel safe, not even here."

"I know what you mean," Quong said, glancing around uneasily.

The woods were silent, but it wasn't a comfortable silence. Even animal sounds were hushed. That could be the result of the spaceplane's landing; probably was. But everyone stirred restlessly, kept looking around, fearful of ambush. Jamil even peered up into the sky, as if he might catch a glimpse of Naval battleships cruising among the clouds.

"A lot of people know about Journey's End, Xris. Your friend Dixter, for one. He's been a guest here." Jamil shook his head gloomily. "The Marines are probably on the way."

"They'll have to get through Olefsky first. He's a major power in this part of the galaxy and no one, not even the Lord Admiral, will want to offend him. Still, you've got a point. We should get ready to move out." Xris opened up the commlink. "Harry, make it quick. We could have company."

"Rowan says five minutes," Harry reported, then added, "She sure is a nice guy."

"Yeah," Xris muttered. "She sure is."

He saw again in his mind Harry take hold—politely—of Rowan's arm. Rowan thanking Harry—politely—and then gently, politely, moving away. For the first time since they'd come together, it occurred to Xris to wonder if his friend was now a woman as in ... well ... *a woman*. Or was this disguise only skin deep? His file said he'd taken female hormone shots. Xris wondered what that meant exactly. He'd have to ask Raoul, who was most assuredly informed on the matter. Adonians were said to change sex as easily and as often as they changed clothes.

Rowan acted like a woman, but then he had always been a good actor, one reason he'd done so well infiltrating the Hung. He was forced to play his roles as if his life depended on them and he'd been playing this role for almost seven years now.

But which was Rowan inside: male, female? Did she even know? Did she care?

Xris suddenly recalled a part of the report he'd received on her. She had rarely, in seven years, left the space station. She lived alone. No husband. No lovers. No close friends.

Alone.

Maybe that answered his question.

Shaking his head, Xris shouldered his share of the equipment, headed for the hoverjeep.

CHAPTER
24

Mute and magnificent . . .
　　　　　　John Dryden, *Threnodia Augustallis*

The hoverjeeps pulled up in front of the house. Climbing out, Xris looked toward the wooden balconies on the upstairs floors, more than half expecting to see pantyhose hanging out to dry—a sure sign that Raoul had returned.

The balconies were empty, the house locked up.

"Damn," Xris muttered, and looked at the Little One.

He was disconcerted to find the Little One looking back at him.

The battered and bloodstained fedora was perched at an odd angle on the empath's bandage-swathed head. Only one eye was visible, and that because someone—probably the Little One himself—had shoved the bandage up in order to see. That one beady, gleaming eye was staring at Xris intently and it suddenly occurred to the cyborg that the Little One needed to communicate with him as urgently as Xris needed to communicate with the empath.

The Little One knew—through the strange, almost symbiotic relationship—where Raoul was and what was happening to him! Xris was sure of it.

But how to get that information out of the small person, who had never been heard to utter a word? Who might not even comprehend what they were saying?

But he would certainly know what they were thinking.

"Take the jeeps around to the garage," Xris ordered, climbing out. "Get rid of any tracks we may have left. Once we're inside the house, we keep the blinds lowered. Don't switch on any lights. I want anyone approaching this place to think it's still deserted. Check the sensors on the back door before you enter. Rowan, you're with me. Quong, bring the Little One."

"Pictures," suggested Quong as they climbed the stairs, waited on the front porch for Xris to check the sensor readings. "Primitive man communicated with pictures."

"Primitive men weren't empaths," Xris returned. Then, "Sensor readings check out. No one inside." He unlocked the door, touching his hand to a security pad.

The door opened directly onto a spacious living room: airy, open, with beam ceilings, an entertainment center, a fireplace in the middle of a sunken pit surrounded by comfortable leather-cushioned couches. Large floor-to-ceiling one-way windows provided the spectator with a spectacular view outside, yet prohibited anyone from seeing inside. Off the living room was a kitchen.

The bedrooms, game rooms, offices rambled off in different directions, some upstairs, some down. An observatory on the top doubled as a conning tower, lookout station. Xris's office was directly off the living room, faced into it. Inside he kept his computers, his books, and his own personal arsenal and collection of antique weapons: an old gas mask, a commando knife, a flashlight, a grenade belt and pouch, his own lucky grenade. That grenade, by *not* detonating, had once saved Xris's life.

"The house is beautiful, Xris," Rowan said, gazing around in satisfaction, appreciation. "It's what you always dreamed of building."

She might have said *what you and Marjorie always dreamed of building,* but she didn't, for which Xris gave her points.

Xris motioned for Rowan to sit down. Quong fussed over his patient. The Little One perched on the very edge of the couch, his feet not touching the floor. Rowan pulled her shoes off. She yawned and, before Xris could stop himself, he was yawning, too.

"We should all get some rest," Quong said severely.

"Yeah, in a little while," Xris returned. He sat down opposite the Little One.

Quong was frowning. "I might remind you, my friend, that—after all—this *is* Raoul. . . ."

Xris gazed at Quong steadily. "He's a member of the

team, Doc. I don't abandon a member of the team. *Any* member."

Quong lifted an eyebrow, said nothing more.

Xris began to think of, to concentrate on Raoul.

Immediately the Little One became animated. He clapped his small hands; the single eye visible beneath the fedora glistened.

"Do you know where Raoul is?" Xris asked, speaking slowly and enunciating each word clearly, with no particular object in mind other than that it was what one tended to do when talking to someone who spoke a foreign tongue.

He must have also raised his voice level, because Quong observed tersely, "He's mute, Xris. He's not deaf." There was a pause. "At least, I don't think he's deaf."

The fedora bobbed up and down enthusiastically.

"Where is Raoul?" Xris asked.

The Little One excitedly pointed at the ceiling.

"Upstairs?" Xris tested. "In his room?"

The fedora shook violently. Xris breathed a sigh. At least now he knew the Little One could understand what was being said to him.

"You mean up ... up in the sky. The stars. Space."

The Little One clapped his hands again, rocked back and forth excitedly on the couch.

"Great. Just great. On average, how many inhabited star systems would you say there are?" Defeated, Xris pulled out a twist, bit down on the end.

"Look, Xris." Rowan touched his arm.

The Little One was shaking his head, waving his hands.

"*Not* a star system," Xris said.

The Little One indicated it was not.

The other members of the team entered one by one, all of them looking worn out.

"Nothing to report," Jamil said, stretching and flexing his aching muscles. "We covered our tracks. Harry made sure the security cams are in place and working. The gear's unloaded, stowed away. Any objections if I take a nap?"

Xris shook his head.

"I'm gonna get a beer," Harry said. "Anyone else want one? You, ma'am? Anything I can get for you? A glass of white wine?"

Rowan glanced at Xris, bit her lower lip to keep from smiling. "No, thank you."

Harry wandered off to the kitchen. Jamil went upstairs. Tycho flopped his long body onto the couch, closed his eyes, and turned off his translator. His skin color gradually assumed that of warm brownish red leather.

"Raoul's *not* in space," Xris tested again.

The Little One waved off the assertion.

"Raoul *is* in space. He's—"

"On a ship!" Rowan guessed.

"He's being held prisoner on a spaceship!" Xris felt as if he were playing charades.

The Little One made fists of his hands, smashed them together—apparently, a sign of approbation.

"Well, that narrows it down to a billion or so," Quong observed helpfully.

"Xris"—Rowan was excited—"if the Little One could give us a name, I could get into the Navy's registry files. If the ship's got hyperspace capability, they have to register a flight plan. If not, they'd still be fairly easy to locate. ISDS—Interstellar Ship's Directory System—keeps track of everything that moves through space. We know the kidnappers were on Olicien's home planet just a day or two ago. They might have left a trail, asked for clearance for landing, gone through customs—"

Xris shook his head. "Not likely. Probably set down in some deserted airfield, like space pirates."

"I'm not so sure," Rowan argued. "On a heavily populated system like Auriga, landing at a deserted airstrip could put them a thousand kilometers away from the city. And why run the risk of attracting the wrong kind of attention? At a busy spaceport, they could easily smuggle their victim on board, offer some kind of excuse in case anyone asked. Maybe he's been taken ill or was on the juice—anything. I'll bet they came and left as legitimate, law-abiding citizens. And I'll bet I can find them in the files."

"Except that the Navy's probably shut you out of those files by now."

Rowan smiled. "This is me we're talking about, Xris. But I *do* have to have the ship's name."

And that proved impossible. The Little One obviously wanted to tell the name to them as much as they wanted to hear it, but he couldn't manage to get it across. Xris began by handing the Little One a computer drawing pad and an electronic pen.

The Little One recoiled in horror, refused to even touch them. (This was the first indication Dr. Quong had that the Tongan are terrified of modern technology.)

Rowan tried an ordinary pad of paper and a pencil, drew a few symbols to get the idea across.

The Little One took hold of the pencil awkwardly, wrapping his entire hand around it. He scrawled a heavy line on the paper, ripped it, then tossed both pad and pencil away in frustration.

Harry sat down with his beer, began coming up with spaceship names. *"Enterprise, Fortitude, Hercules ..."*

The Little One stared at him blankly.

Xris called a halt. "Face it. This is hopeless. We could be here for the next twenty years doing this."

"Maybe I could rig up some kind of computer mind-link," Rowan suggested, thoughtful. "Empaths and telepaths usually have extremely strong electronic impulses in their brains. It might take days and it would be crude, at best, if it worked at all. I don't know. Dr. Quong, what do you think?"

"I think—"

A warning Klaxon sounded, accompanied by a computerized voice. "Sensors have been tripped in grid M-1. Repeat. Sensors have been tripped in grid M-1."

Xris took the twist from his mouth.

"Moose?" Harry asked, and set down the beer.

"The sensors are set to pick up only humanoid lifeforms," Xris said calmly. He opened his leg compartment, took out his weapons hand.

The alarms continued to sound.

Tycho woke up, fumbled with his translator.

Jamil came running down the stairs, clad only in his undershorts. "What is it, Xris?"

"I don't know yet, but it should be on-screen. Go check it out."

Jamil left, heading for the security room.

"Sensors have been tripped in grid K-1," reported the voice. "Repeat. Sensors have been tripped in grid K-1."

"M-1. K-1." Harry went into Xris's office, stood looking at a map of the property, tracking a line with his finger. "They're moving this way, and fast."

Jamil's voice came over the comm. "The cam's dead in grid M, Xris. It went black just when I got in here.

Switching to grid K. I have ... No. That cam just went dead."

Xris performed a systems check on his arm. He had attached the automatic fléchette-round shotgun. When you didn't know what was coming, the shotgun was the best choice.

"Sensors tripped in grid D-10," reported the computer.

Everyone, with the exception of the Little One, had gathered in Xris's office, was huddled around the map.

Tycho followed the line. "On this route, they're headed for the front door."

"Probably a diversion. The main force is likely coming at us from the back. Jamil, you see anything?"

"Not a damn thing! They must be crushing these cams with a TRUC!"

"Nothing more you can learn there, obviously. Report back here. Tycho, head up to the tower."

The alien nodded, selected a beam rifle equipped with a sniper sight from the well-stocked arsenal, headed for the tower.

"Sensors tripped in B-7."

Jamil returned, carrying two more beam rifles, one of which he tossed to Quong.

Xris continued giving orders. "Harry, cover the back door. Doc, the east wing."

"Xris." Rowan was on her feet. "What can I do?"

"Go down the basement," Xris said.

"What?" Rowan stared at him.

"Go down the blasted basement!" Xris told her. "The door's there, off the hall."

Motioning to Jamil to take a far window, the cyborg moved over to a window that provided a view of the front door.

Rowan hadn't moved. She had a stubborn, determined look on her face that Xris knew all too well.

He left his post. Grabbing Rowan by the arm, the cyborg pushed her forcibly toward the basement door. "The walls and door are reinforced nullgrav steel. They can withstand about anything, including a direct hit from a lascannon."

Xris opened the door. Rowan halted, planting her feet firmly and refusing to budge.

"I'll pick you up and throw you down there if I have to," the cyborg said grimly.

"You don't trust me. I swear to you, Xris—"

He cut her off. "You're right, old friend. I don't trust you. But that's not the reason. I need you alive and well, Major Mohini. You're the ticket out for my men. If anything happens to me, you tell Dixter it was between us—you and I. My men were just following orders. They had no idea what was coming down. You'll tell Dixter that."

She stared at him a moment, then said, "Sure, Xris." She entered the door, stood on the top step. "I'll tell him."

"Sensors tripped in grid A-5," said the computer.

Xris started to leave, to shut the door. He paused, not looking at her. "You can't ever go back. You realize that. Your cover's blown. I'm sorry about that. I didn't mean to—"

What *had* he meant? Meant to murder her. He shook his head.

"It doesn't matter," Rowan said, with a slight shrug. "It doesn't matter at all. Take care of yourself, Xris."

"I'm not easy to kill. As you know."

He shut the door.

"Xris!" Jamil shouted. "I can see movement."

Tycho's voice came over the comm. "Xris. I've got them in my sights. I recognize one of them. It's . . ." He paused, then said, "You're not going to believe this."

Jamil lowered his rifle, grinned. "Guess who?"

Xris relaxed. "Not the Royal Marines."

Jamil shook his head.

A thundering crash nearly staved in the front door.

"The neighbors, come to call."

Xris hurried to open the nullgrav steel door before it shattered.

CHAPTER
25

That proverbial saying, "Bad news travels fast and far."

Plutarch, *Morals of Inquisitiveness*

A giant of a man, Olefsky not only had to duck to slide his head beneath the doorframe, he had to rotate his enormous body, and then was forced to squeeze his way through the door. When he succeeded, he shook himself in a manner similar to that of the large shaggy hunting dog that trotted at his side. His two sons followed, grinning sheepishly and bobbing their heads.

"My friend! By my lungs and liver, it is good to see you again!"

Bear Olefsky enfolded Xris in an embrace that completely engulfed the cyborg, squeezing the air from his body and setting off an alarm on his breathing apparatus. Releasing Xris, the Bear regarded him gravely.

"But not perhaps under these circumstances. Have you been watching the galactic news?"

"No," Xris wheezed, making adjustments. "We've been preparing for an assault. We thought you were the Marines. Why the devil did you take out our security cams?"

Olefsky, brow furrowed, glowered around at his two boys. The Bear towered over Xris by about a meter and the Bear's sons—though only fourteen or fifteen—were taller and broader than their father. Both young giants held their father in mortal dread, however. At his glare, they turned extremely red and shuffled their big feet, though it was obvious they had no idea what crime they had committed.

The Bear barked questions at them in their own language.

Both boys made feeble protests. Olefsky listened in patience for a few moments, then ended the defense with a motion of his big right hand. Following this, he cuffed each boy soundly and ordered them out of the house. Hanging their heads, the boys tromped out, both of them managing to knock over several small pieces of furniture on the way. The dog, evidently thinking it was in trouble as well, cringed and licked the Bear's hand.

The Bear shook his head, heaved a sigh that nearly blew the Little One—who had crept up to stare at the dog—off his feet. "Ah, I must make certain that these boys of mine see more of the universe. But with fifteen sons . . ." He shook his head again. "I apologize, friend Xris. These two lumbering dunderheads"—he jerked his thumb in the direction of the porch, where the two boys waited—"found one cam and thought it was the evil eye, planted on you by some sorcerer. They bashed it with a rock. As for other cams . . . You said there were others?"

Xris nodded.

The Bear tugged at his long curly black beard. "I regret to say that they did not see any others. Neither did I. Were they located on the ground?"

"Never mind, Bear," Xris said, putting a twist in his mouth to keep from smiling. "No harm done."

Glancing outside, he could see Olefsky's boys picking bits of bark and twigs from their animal-hide clothing. The Bear's clothes were covered with leaves. A small branch—caught in the fur of his cape—trailed behind him. Now that he looked, Xris could detect shards of broken glass on the Bear's leather boots.

Fairly certain that they were no longer under attack, Xris called Harry and Quong back from their posts, brought Tycho down from the tower. Jamil joined them, still in his underwear. He glanced at Bear, saw the big man's stern face and dark expression, and sighed.

"Looks like we're going to be awake for a while. Anyone else want coffee?"

Rowan emerged from the basement. Her eyes widened at the sight of their guest.

Xris performed introductions, though, he noticed, these weren't really necessary. Rowan recognized Olefsky from the newsvids and it was obvious—from the sharp, scrutinizing gaze Bear fixed on her—that though he may not have known her, he knew something about her. Not a good sign.

"Send me a bill for the cams," Olefsky said, waving his hand. "What was I saying? Ah, yes. The—"

The Little One, with a strange, inarticulate cry, suddenly hurled himself at Xris, flung his arms around the cyborg's legs.

"What the—" Xris stared down.

Now that the empath had Xris's attention, the Little One let loose his hold. He ran across the floor, raincoat flapping, and this time flung his arms around the dog's neck, nearly dragging the large animal to the floor.

The dog, accustomed to a household that always seemed to possess at least one toddler, took the mauling patiently, stood with its tongue hanging out, grinning.

"We'll get you a pet next week," Xris said, his mind on the Bear. "Now, sir, you were saying—"

The Little One ran back, caught hold of Xris's pants leg, tugged on it, and pointed urgently to the dog.

"I'll be damned," said Rowan suddenly, and left them abruptly, heading for Xris's office.

Something had clicked. Xris knew that much from the intent, introspective expression on her face. He watched her sit down in front of the computer, order it to come on, bypass his security with absentminded ease. Asking her questions now would get him exactly nowhere. She wouldn't even hear him. She'd left this world as completely as if she'd made her own personal jump into hyperspace. She was now inside the machine.

The Little One abandoned the dog, trundled into the office after Rowan. He stood at her elbow, careful to make no sound, not disturbing her. Olefsky, obviously mystified, ordered the dog out of the house.

Xris took out a twist, lit it. "Sorry about the interruption, sir. He's fond of animals. You were saying?"

The Bear eyed Xris narrowly and with a hint of coolness. "The galactic news. You are all over it, my friend. What are you up to?"

Xris didn't know quite how to answer. Bear Olefsky dressed in animal skins; his shaggy hair and beard were uncut, uncombed, unkempt. Skulls, scalps, and other less recognizable, more repugnant trophies adorned the wide belt that encircled his broad middle. He and his shieldwife lived in a castle with no central heating, no running water. His people were fierce and warlike, spent their lives cheerfully bashing each other over the head or banding together and flying off to bash other tribes in their star system over their heads.

Olefsky was a powerful force in the galaxy, however. His people adored him. And though he preferred fighting with spear and shield, he commanded a fleet of starships that he used in defense of his systems. He was a personal friend of the king and queen and was exceptionally loyal.

"It's a long story, Bear," Xris said finally, lamely.

"I think it must be," Olefsky rumbled.

Rolling casually over the furniture, leaving a trail of destruction in his path, the Bear approached the large-screen vid. One room in the Olefsky castle was filled with high-tech electronic equipment, manned by two of Bear's older (and more educated) sons. The Bear himself had as little to do with such modern horrors as he possibly could.

"How does it work?" he demanded, reaching out a hairy hand.

"Allow me, sir," Quong offered hastily.

He brought up the continuous news channel. Galactic reporter James M. Warden's digitized, chiseled features filled the screen. After sitting through several minutes of news on the king and queen, news on the prime minster and the Parliament, followed by vid idols and a feature on the latest fashions, which made everyone present think of Raoul, the news report cycled back around to the lead-off story.

"The Royal Navy announced a surprise galaxy-wide 'readiness' test today. When asked by this reporter what exactly this meant, a spokesman for the admiralty was extremely vague, citing Naval security. She did add that all ships of the fleet were on full alert and would be for the next seventy-two hours."

Warden smiled. A sardonic slant to his mouth and a quirk of the eyebrow let the viewer know that "this reporter" didn't believe a word. He leaned slightly forward, drawing the viewer into his confidence. "This reporter has obtained exclusive information, from a highly placed source in the Cabinet, that this alert is *not* a test. The admiralty has assured us that no threat of danger exists to the citizens of this galaxy, yet we remind you, viewers, that the Navy has never before conducted such a 'readiness' test and one can only ask, why is such a test being conducted now? We understand that members of the Parliament were not informed, that they are demanding an explanation from the prime minister, and that a protest has been lodged by the Loyal Opposition. We will keep you apprised of this situation as it develops.

"In what may be a related matter, a galaxy-wide manhunt is under way for this man"—a photo of Xris flashed across the screen—"and other members of a commando team calling themselves Mag Force 7.

"Described as well-trained mercenaries, these men are wanted 'for questioning concerning the alleged break-in of a Naval establishment.' The leader is a cyborg, known only as Xris. A former federal agent under the old regime, he left that job to form his own mercenary unit, which has done work for—so we understand—some extremely *high-ranking* people."

Warden paused to allow the audience to catch his meaning, then continued. "These men are considered armed and highly dangerous. If you see any of them, you are urged to take no action yourselves, but to contact your local law enforcement agency."

James M. Warden leaned forward again in his chair, placed his hands on the table. "A Naval establishment attacked, a crack team of mercenaries wanted for 'questioning,' the surprise 'readiness' test of the Royal Navy. Coincidence, viewers?"

Warden closed with his standard line. "I think not."

"You see there!" Olefsky waved at the vid. "By my bowels and spleen, you are the most notorious criminals in the galaxy!" His gaze narrowed. "I could summon my soldiers. You should be cooling your heels in my dungeons."

Xris started to say something to the effect that it would take an entire regiment of the Bear's soldiers to capture him, if he decided to fight. But he wouldn't fight and Olefsky knew it, so why bother? Xris kept his mouth shut.

"You still won't tell me what is going on," Bear said, his tone grim.

Xris stared moodily out the window. "It's all a mistake. A misunderstanding."

The Bear frowned, tugged at his beard.

"I can explain everything to the Lord Admiral," Xris added. "Ten minutes with Dixter and we'll be in the clear."

The Bear was shaking his head.

Rowan appeared in the doorway. "Xris," she said excitedly, "I think I've found something."

Xris was about to follow her when he discovered he wasn't going anywhere. Bear's massive hand had clamped down on the cyborg's good shoulder.

"I'm going to call Dixter right now," Xris promised.

"It is not as easy as that, I am afraid, my friend," Olefsky replied. "You heard this news about the Naval 'readiness test.' I'll tell you what is truly going on. I have been informed. Operation Macbeth, it is called."

"Macbeth!" Rowan repeated, stunned. "Good God!"

"Operation Macbeth"—the Bear rumbled on—"is designed to thwart a revolution. All communication between ships is silenced. Anyone who tries to communicate with a ship of the line will be fired on."

"It's because I know the codes," Rowan murmured, looking dazed. "Of course. I never imagined that they would go this far, but I don't suppose they have any choice. I could take over the fleet! Macbeth would be the only way to stop me."

"But we're not trying to take over the damn fleet," Xris said impatiently. "And if I can just talk to Admiral Dixter—"

"That's the point, laddie," said the Bear. "You can't talk to Dixter or anyone else in the Royal Navy. No one can, not even myself. Not for seventy-two hours."

"What a bizarre situation!" Rowan spread her hands in a helpless gesture. "The Navy shuts down communications because I could betray them, and because communications are shut down I can't communicate with the Navy to let them know I'm not a traitor. What do we do?"

The Bear gazed at them from beneath thick, lowering brows. "Turn yourselves in to the authorities."

"That's not a bad idea, Xris." Jamil spoke up. "We could go to the nearest land-based army unit. Walk in the front door with our hands in the air. Then they'll have to listen to us."

"And what happens to Raoul in the meantime?" Xris demanded.

Olefsky was immediately concerned. "Raoul? What have you done with the Peacock?"

The Bear was fond of the Adonian and of the Little One and would frequently invite them both to the castle. Raoul's

burning goal in life was to instill a sense of fashion consciousness in the Olefskys and, although the Adonian found
the task daunting, he bravely and resolutely refused to shrink
from the challenge. He was constantly carrying over various
ensembles, spending fatiguing hours endeavoring to convince Olefsky that smelly deer hide—while practical—was
not suitable for formal dinner invitations to the Glitter Palace. All of which the Olefsky family found highly diverting
and hung the new clothes up on the walls as curiosities.

"Where is the Peacock?" Olefsky peered around.

"Someone snatched him. Beat up the Little One. We don't
know why. We don't think it has anything to do with . . . this
other."

The Bear glanced at the Little One, who was clinging to
Rowan's uniform jacket. Olefsky noticed, for the first time,
the bloodstained bandage. He growled, frowned, paced about
thoughtfully, trampling a small end table.

Xris took out a twist, tapped it on his knee. "I won't abandon a member of my team. I signed contracts with all of you
and I'll keep my end of the agreement. I'll go after Raoul
myself if I have to."

Jamil was defensive. "Damn it, Xris, I didn't mean we
should abandon him! You know I'm with you. I was just
being—"

"I know." Xris interrupted, softened his tone. "I understand. You were just being logical. I'm sorry, guys. I'm
tired. We're all tired. I got you into this. What Jamil says
does make sense. Go with him, take his advice. He'll know
how to handle it. You'll probably get reduced sentences."

Harry said "No!" loudly and glared at Jamil.

Jamil looked grim and uncomfortable and muttered something to the effect that it was a sound idea and they should
consider it.

Quong, his eyes closed, was apparently approaching this
as he might have approached the solution to a mathematical
equation, even to the point of absently working calculations
with slight movements of his fingertips.

Tycho yelled something unintelligible; he'd grown so
flustered he'd accidentally switched off his translator.

Jamil and Harry both loudly told him to turn it on.

"Bear," Xris said quietly, talking beneath the confusion,
"I know Dion, remember? Hell, I helped put him on the
throne! I swear to you on . . . on what's left of me"—he held

out his flesh-and-blood arm—"that we're not fomenting a revolution. We're not intending to overthrow the king or assassinate him or anyone. May this arm be cut off if I'm lying."

"Yes," the Bear said, "go on."

Xris drew in a deep breath, let it out slowly. "Give me these seventy-two hours to find Raoul and do what I can to straighten out this mess. By the end of that time, no matter what happens, I'll turn myself in."

"You are in great danger, my friend," Olefsky observed. "Not only is the Royal Navy after you, every law officer and bounty hunter in the galaxy will be out to capture you, bring you in—dead or alive."

Xris said nothing, had nothing to say to the obvious.

Olefsky stared at him, ruminated. Suddenly the Bear leaned forward, smote Xris on the back, a blow that jarred every rivet in the cyborg's body.

"I trust you. I believe you. You have seventy-two hours. What's more, if you need a spaceplane other than that yellow monstrosity in which you landed"—the Bear grinned— "you may borrow one of mine."

"Thank you, Bear," Xris said, offering to shake on it. "You won't regret this."

"I do not think I will." Bear heaved a sigh. Then, clasping firm hold of Xris's good hand, Olefsky added solemnly, "The good God help you if you are lying, laddie. In that instance, I myself will be the one who takes this arm."

The Bear squeezed his bulk back through the door. Alerting his two sons to his presence with a playful blow on the back of each shaggy head, he thudded down the stairs, strode off into the woods. His lumbering sons and the dog crashed along behind.

The Bear's final threat had been emphasized by a crushing grip. Xris could still feel the ache. He had his seventy-two hours. Just what the hell he was going to do with them was currently open to question.

He turned to Rowan. "Yes? What have you got? Did you find Raoul?"

She nodded, gently placed her hand on the Little One's small shoulder.

"He gave you the clue. A research vessel, registered to a university. The name is *Canis Major Research I.*"

The Little One made some sort of guttural, almost feral

sound, and nodded so vigorously that the fedora toppled off, revealing the bandaged face. Moving with remarkable swiftness, the empath retrieved his hat, clapped it back on his head.

"And how the hell did you figure it out?" Xris asked.

Rowan grinned. She was actually enjoying herself.

"When the Little One hugged the dog, it occurred to me that what he was trying to tell us had something to do with dogs. What could it be, except the name of the ship?

"Once I knew that, I went into the files of the local spaceport on Auriga, downloaded the names of vessels that had requested landing permission during that particular time period—"

"Wait a minute. You just waltzed in?"

"Well, maybe it wasn't quite that easy." Rowan looked modest. "I'm dead, so far as computer access is concerned. All my passwords have been wiped clean. I can't even log on to my own personal computer in my apartment. But people are always leaving back doors open. It was fairly simple, actually, given what I know. Anyhow, once I had the names, I did a search through the list. Nothing with the word *dog* turned up. But I was certain it had to be there.

"So was he." She gestured to the Little One. "He was practically glued to me. I knew I was on the right track. So I tried *dog* in other languages, merged that list with the list of ship names and there was the match—*Canis Major.* I asked the Little One if that was the name and he indicated yes. I asked him if his friend Raoul was on that ship and he nodded yes again."

The Little One was still saying yes. Whenever anybody looked at him sideways he would nod and pound his two small fists together.

Xris glanced at Quong for confirmation. "How reliable is this, Doc? How would a Tongan know the word *Canis* had anything at all to do with dogs? Unless, of course, Raoul is teaching his little buddy dead languages in his spare time."

"It is very much possible," Quong replied. "Many telepaths use mental imagery to convey their thoughts and read the thoughts of others. They do not need words. For example, Raoul hears the name *'Canis Major,'* thinks 'the dog star,' thinks of dogs, bringing up an image in his mind of a dog. The Little One brings up the image of a dog in his mind and attaches that to Olefsky's animal. Major Mohini"—

Quong bowed to Rowan—"searches for names having to do with dogs and, finding one, produces a very strong mental image of a dog in her mind, which is picked up by our small friend."

"I can track the ship, Xris," Rowan offered. "It is a Verdi-class vessel, the kind typically used for research or short hops between planets. It has no hyperspace capabilities, no weapons, no shields. A long-range spaceplane could catch it in, say, eight hours."

Xris took a drag on the twist. "A research vessel. You mean the kind colleges use to go out and chart star systems and study insect life on other planets and all that?"

"That would seem so, given the name," Rowan responded.

Xris snorted. "Then this makes no sense. What the hell are a bunch of egghead professors doing with Raoul? Writing a thesis on the correct shoes to wear with knee-high velvet pants after five?"

"Judging by what they did to the Little One, my friend, this is not a joking matter," Quong observed gravely. "The beating he took was a professional job. They intended to kill him."

"Yeah, I know. I found him, remember?" Xris considered, then made up his mind. "Very well. I'm going to pay a little visit to this *Canis Major Research I*."

"We're with you, Xris," said Jamil. He looked uncomfortable. "And, uh, about what I brought up earlier, about turning ourselves in. I didn't mean—"

"Forget it. You made sense." Xris massaged his arm. It still ached. "I know everyone's exhausted, but since we only have seventy-two hours, we need to leave right away. We can catch some sleep on the plane. Gather up your gear and let's move out."

The rest left. Xris found himself alone with Rowan. At least as alone as they could be, considering that the Little One was hanging on to Rowan's slacks like a lost child.

Xris decided the best way to go about this was quick, cool, businesslike. "You can't stay here by yourself. It wouldn't be safe. I'll take you over to Olefsky's—"

She was smiling, shaking her head. "I'm coming with you, Xris. I know you don't trust me, but—"

"I told you once," Xris interrupted coldly, "I need you

alive. Besides, it's not your problem. Raoul's my man and—"

"And he's the only way I have to prove to you I'm telling the truth." Rowan rested her hand again on the Little One's shoulder. "He can't tell you what I'm thinking and feeling. I'm not sure he understands. But his friend Raoul will. He will tell you. And you'll believe him, won't you?"

Xris believed already. He couldn't help himself. He was having to work very hard at *not* believing.

"Yes," he said. "I'll believe him." He snubbed out the twist. "Well, now I guess we go see a man about a dog."

CHAPTER
26

Therefore those who skillfully move opponents make formations that opponents are sure to follow, give what opponents are sure to take.

Sun Tzu, *The Art of War*

"Unknown spaceplane, this is *Canis Major Research I.* You are in violation of intergalactic safety regulation number 2158-B3, which requires a five-kilometer exclusion zone between—"

Harry cut in. "We're going to be in violation of a helluva lot more safety regulations unless you shut down your engines *now* and prepare for boarding."

Momentary silence, then a human voice replaced the digitized one. "This is the captain speaking. You are in flagrant violation of intergalactic law. Our vessel has no weapons."

"We do," Harry returned. "You can either shut down your engines now or we'll shut 'em down for you."

More silence. Then, "Due to modulation frequency wave interference, your last message did not come through—"

"Fire on them," ordered Xris from his place in the copilot's seat. "Don't hit anything vital. Just show them we mean business."

"You hear that, Tycho?" Harry asked over the comm.

The alien was ensconced in the Schiavona's gun turret, located in a bubble above the cockpit.

Tycho's answer was a well-aimed precision blast from the lascannon that took out a condenser coil on the ship's stern.

"You've lost the air-conditioning," Harry said cheerfully. "The next shot, you lose the air."

"It's this way, *Canis Major*," Xris added, "you have no

weapons. We do. You have no shields. We do. You're holding a friend of ours hostage on board your vessel. We intend to get him back. Shut your engines down and prepare for boarders."

The *Canis Major* had no response.

"But they've done it," Harry reported, studying his instrumentation. "They've shut down their main engines. They're dead in space. Computer, how long before they can start up again?"

"Main engine startup on a Verdi-class requires six hours to recycle."

"They won't be going anywhere soon," Harry said in satisfaction.

"We have shut down our engines," came the captain's grim-sounding voice. "We have no choice. We consider this a criminal action. We feel obliged to inform you that we have activated our automatic distress signal. All vessels in our vicinity are required by law to respond."

Xris glanced at Rowan.

"We know we don't have to worry about the Royal Navy," she said. "They're under orders *not* to respond to distress signals. But a civilian vessel could and probably would. At least, they'd come take a look."

"How long?" Xris asked.

She shrugged. "This is a busy sector. A lot of traffic. But I didn't see anything in the vicinity when I was tracking this ship, so I'd guess we have at least an hour."

"It shouldn't last that long. Not with a bunch of professors on board. Take us in for docking, Harry. Can everyone hear me?"

Xris stood up, climbed the ladder to the living quarters. The cockpit of a long-range Schiavona fighter-bomber is located below the spaceplane's main deck area, separated by a metal railing, accessible down a four-runged steel ladder. Designed for interplanetary flights—unlike its short-range counterpart, which is used mainly for ship-to-ship or ship-to-planet operations—the standard long-range Schiavona is self-sustaining. It provides adequate, if not particularly luxurious, living facilities for a two-man crew on a longer flight, short-term accommodations for a larger number of people on a brief haul.

The Schiavona on this run was extremely crowded. In addition to the extra people, they had to stow their gear on board. This included a small arsenal of weapons, Royal Naval uniforms (in case they were caught, they planned to bluff their way out), food, tools, and Quong's box of medical supplies. Xris had been forced into a slight altercation with the Little One. The cyborg caught the empath attempting to lug an overlarge suitcase on board.

"What's this?" Xris had demanded.

The Little One had opened the suitcase, proudly revealed its contents: seven silk scarves, a half-dozen frothy lace-covered blouses, ten pairs of high-heeled pumps in various shades, multicolored spandex unitards, and a flashy gold ensemble adorned with sequins and bangles.

"No," Xris had said. "Absolutely not. Raoul will have to get along without his wardrobe."

The Little One had gesticulated wildly, flinging his small hands in the air and jumping up and down.

Xris had remained adamant. The suitcase was left behind.

"You hear me, Tycho?" Xris said now over the comm to the gunner's turret.

"Loud and clear, boss."

Rowan, the Little One, Jamil, and Quong sat in small fold-down chairs bolted to the bulkheads. They gave Xris their full attention.

"Okay, this is the plan. When we dock, they'll open the airlock—"

"What if they don't?" Harry demanded from the cockpit. He liked to have every eventuality covered.

"They will, or you'll shoot something else off. I'm leaving you inside the plane."

Harry nodded complacently.

"We'll take control of the bridge. Jamil and Tycho will remain on the bridge. The Little One and I will go look for Raoul. Doc, you'll come with us, in case he needs medical attention." Xris looked at the Little One. "Raoul's alive, right?"

The Little One nodded vigorously.

"And you can find him on board that ship? Even if they've hidden him away somewhere?"

The Little One nodded again, clenched two fists and brought them together.

"All right, then—"

"What about me?" Rowan asked.

"You stay on board with Harry. I want you to monitor— What the devil is wrong with him now?"

The Little One had begun by wringing his hands and shaking his head. He ended by flinging himself onto Rowan, clutching at her and tugging at her uniform.

"I believe he wants me to go with him," Rowan said.

"Out of the question."

"I don't mind, Xris."

"Damn it, I do! Technically speaking, you're my prisoner—"

"Technically speaking," Rowan interrupted, smiling, "I'm your friend."

Xris ignored that. "—and I don't want you—"

The Little One became frenzied. He pulled on Rowan's uniform with such violence that he ripped an epaulet from her shoulder.

"He should not be exciting himself like this." Quong was on his feet, attempting to soothe his patient.

"He wants me to go!" Rowan pleaded.

"Then he can get over it." Xris was adamant.

The computer came on. "Docking in ten, nine, eight—"

"You better sit down and strap in!" Harry warned. "This is a forced docking maneuver. They're not helping us one damn bit."

The Little One refused to be pried loose from Rowan. Clinging to her, he peered at Xris from under the brim of the fedora.

"I promise I won't try to escape," Rowan said.

"At this point, it might be better if she did," Jamil muttered under his breath to Quong.

But Xris heard. "All right, then! Go on board," he snarled. "The whole fuckin' universe can go on board, for all I care."

He slid down the ladder, back into the cockpit, sat in his chair and strapped himself in. Grimly silent, he stared out the viewscreen.

The computer's mindless voice broke the uncomfortable stillness.

"Five, four, three—"

"Oh, shut up," Harry muttered, and killed the audio.

The landing was a rough one.

The hatch whirred. Xris pushed it open, pulled himself cautiously up and out. He took a good look around, but—as

Harry had reported from sensor readings—the airlock was pressurized and empty. Xris, perched on top of the spaceplane, looked down, motioned the others to join him.

Jamil came next. He slid down the Schiavona's outside ladder to the deck of the *Canis Major Research I,* aimed his beam rifle on the door to the airlock. Tycho followed, carrying his special sniper rifle. The alien joined Jamil.

There was a brief delay. Xris peered impatiently down into the hatch. The Little One was slowly climbing upward, tripping over his raincoat.

"Hurry!" Xris ordered. He was a target-shoot up here.

The Little One received a boost from behind from Quong, almost flew out of the hatch. Xris caught hold of the empath, steadied him, started him creeping across the hull over to the ladder. The doctor eased himself out next. Once on top of the Schiavona, he reached down to receive a beam rifle and his medical gear handed up to him by Rowan. She came last, moving easily and expertly. She carried a lasgun in a shoulder holster.

Xris eyed the weapon.

She caught his glance, flushed. "I can leave it—"

He shook his head, motioned her to hurry.

"We're out, Harry," he said into the comm. "Leave the hatch open and keep the engines running."

"Right, boss."

Xris climbed down, joined the others. He nodded to Jamil, who hit the controls. He and Tycho burst through the door, weapons raised, expecting resistance.

All they encountered were two extremely angry and indignant academic types in white lab coats, who fired nothing more lethal than a barrage of protests.

"What is the meaning of this? We are a research vessel! We have nothing on board—"

"Hands in the air," Jamil ordered.

"This is a piratical act. We have your spaceplane's number and—"

"He said, hands in the air." Tycho emphasized the statement with a menacing motion of his sniper rifle.

Xris took up a position where he could keep an eye on the corridor.

"I protest—"

The two, still talking, reluctantly raised their hands over their heads.

Jamil grabbed one, Tycho the other. They shoved both professors facefirst into the bulkheads. Quong patted them down expertly for weapons, reported them both clean.

One of the professors, a woman, turned her head. "I am Dr. Brisbane, leader of the research team. We have nothing on board that would be in the least valuable to you scum. We have activated a distress signal. Help will be arriving any moment now. I suggest—"

She broke off, stared in amazement at the sight of the Little One, who came barreling through the door, tugging Rowan along behind. The empath would have dragged Rowan off down the corridor if Xris hadn't stopped them.

"Take it easy," he said quietly, resting his good hand on the Little One's shoulder.

The Little One apparently understood—either Xris's words or his thoughts—for the empath calmed down, though he kept casting longing glances at the corridor. Xris studied the professors in their immaculate coats. The female doctor was tall, stern-faced, gray-haired. The other—a male—was tubby and pink-faced. Neither looked the least bit sinister, only upset and frightened and—in the woman's case—mad enough to chew off the cyborg's steel hand. She started in again, yammering about pirates.

Xris decided to continue the hard-line approach, see where it got him.

"Shut up!" His metal-edged voice cut off all further protests. He fixed his attention on the female doctor. "Listen to me, sister, and no one will get hurt. We're not pirates. We have reason to believe that you are holding a friend of ours hostage on board this vessel. His name is Raoul. He's an Adonian. Release him, turn him over to us, and we'll fly away and leave you to your books."

He expected evasions, denials, more protests. What he got instead were baffled looks, disbelief, and incomprehension. He might have been speaking Tycho's language, without benefit of the translator.

"You're accusing us—*us*—of . . . of kidnapping?" Dr. Brisbane was so angry she was spluttering.

Her tubby cohort actually giggled, then blushed red at the doctor's baleful gaze.

"Gentlemen—" the tubby one began meekly.

"Don't dignify them with that term," Brisbane snapped.

The tubby one blushed again. "We're a research vessel,

studying the effects of vented gas plasma discharge from junk-drive engines on various species, flora and fauna. We've never kidnapped anyone. I believe you've made a terrible mistake."

Xris was beginning to think so. If that was true, he was certainly on a roll. It was Rowan who'd dreamed all this up. Dog stars! If she ... If this was a trick ...

Xris clamped his teeth down on a twist.

Nothing to do now but play it out.

"Then I guess you won't mind us searching your ship," he said, watching them closely to see their reaction.

And there was the break, the crack. Not much. If he hadn't been so damned keyed up and on edge, he might have missed it—Tubby's eyes slid sideways.

Brisbane was good. She had scared but indignant down to an art form. Absolutely no reason for them to search her vessel, upset her staff. Risk contaminating the experiments, loss of months of valuable research ...

Tubby, receiving his cue, now joined in. But that's just what his sideways glance had been. He was asking for his cue.

Xris gave the team the go-ahead.

Jamil grabbed Tubby by the collar, shoved a lasgun in his back. Tycho took charge of Brisbane.

"Take us to the bridge," Jamil ordered. "We promise not to step on the flowers. And keep your hands where I can see them and your eyes straight ahead or you'll be fertilizing your 'flora and fauna.' March."

The procession moved down the corridor: Jamil and Tycho and the prisoners in front; Quong, Rowan, and the Little One right behind; Xris bringing up the rear, watching their backs. They met no one on the way. Apparently everyone else on board the vessel had been warned to keep out of sight.

They continued down the corridor leading from the airlock, until they came to an intersection. Their corridor went on ahead, another branched off to the right. Dr. Brisbane—her jaw clamped—indicated the right turn. At this, they nearly lost the Little One. He came to a dead stop, pointed frantically straight ahead.

Brisbane eyed the Little One narrowly. When she caught Xris watching her, she shifted her gaze.

"The bridge is that direction," she said coldly.

Xris nodded, gave Jamil the sign to go ahead. Rowan said something to the Little One, who trailed along reluctantly, holding on to Rowan's hand.

Apparently their progress through the ship was being monitored, because the door to the bridge was standing open. Captain and crew were waiting for them. No security guards; no one was even armed. So far, the *Canis Major Research I* was what it claimed to be—a lumbering, inoffensive research vessel, cruising studiously through space.

Xris began again to have doubts. Jamil's rigid back and set jaw and the fact that Tycho's skin had not changed color to match his surroundings indicated that they were also dubious about their mission. Rowan wore her enigmatic expression, which Xris remembered from the old days. That expression meant either she thought he was way off target, but wouldn't jeopardize the operation by saying anything, or she was on to something. Quong was impassive; but then, he was always impassive. If it hadn't been for the Little One's excitement, Xris might have muttered an apology and slunk off.

"Captain"—Xris stepped forward—"we're going to take control of the bridge. Instruct your people to stand aside and let my men do their jobs and no one will get hurt. We'll do what we came to do, then leave and let you carry on."

The captain looked at Brisbane, who said bitterly, "We have no choice. We must do as they say. They have some insane notion that we have kidnapped one of their friends. They intend to search the ship."

The team went to work, swift, efficient. If they had any doubts about Xris or their reason for being here, they did not let these doubts interfere with their jobs. At a command from the captain, the crew—three people—rose to their feet, moved away from their consoles. Tycho herded the crew, Dr. Brisbane, and her tubby companion over into a recessed bay area. Quong kept them covered. Xris stood by the door, keeping watch down the corridor. Jamil made the captain return to the pilot's chair, a gun to his head.

A red light was flashing on the console—the distress signal. Jamil motioned to it. "Shut it off," he ordered.

The captain shook his head. "I can't."

Jamil examined the control. "My guess is that he's telling the truth. Once it's activated . . ." he shrugged, "company."

Rowan could probably kill it, but it was unlikely the Little One would turn her loose.

"No help for it," Xris said. "Jamil, you keep everyone here. Tycho, take over for Quong. Doc, you're with me."

"You are wasting your time," Brisbane said, her voice loud and strident. "The only people aboard this ship are the crew and my fellow scientists."

But as she said this, her eyes shifted involuntarily to the Little One. The empath stood near the door, hopping impatiently from one foot to the other.

"If that's true, Doctor, you have nothing to worry about. If it isn't . . ." Xris motioned his group out, headed out himself.

"Okay," he said to the Little One. "Lead on."

Keeping hold of Rowan, the Little One took off down the corridor, kicking impatiently at the hem of the raincoat. Xris and Quong trudged after their small friend.

"They're all hiding something," Rowan said, over her shoulder.

"Oh, yeah? How do you know that?"

"We were expecting to see a research ship—intellectual types in white coats, nonprofessional crew, that sort of thing."

"Yes."

"And that's what we're seeing."

"I'm seeing exactly the same things I'd see if I were on a research vessel, which means that I'm not . . ."

"You know what I'm getting at," Rowan retorted.

Xris did. It was the main reason he was marching down this corridor behind an empath in a raincoat who had gotten them all here by hugging a dog.

They headed down the same corridor they'd used to reach the bridge from the airlock. But when they arrived at the intersection, the Little One turned right instead of left. He continued down another hallway, made a left-hand jog at another junction, then another left. He paused only at the intersections, and then he didn't appear confused as much as he appeared to be attempting to determine the fastest way to reach his goal.

No one and nothing interfered until they reached a section of the vessel separated from the main part by a huge, heavy blast door labeled AUTHORIZED PERSONNEL ONLY.

Odd. Xris was familiar with the Verdi-class vessel and this

door was not standard equipment. He got on the comm to Jamil.

"Rescue-two, this is Rescue-one. Can you see us?"

"Rescue-one, I've got you on the security cam."

"What's on the other side of this blast door?"

"An empty corridor. Doors leading off of it. Nothing special that I can tell; but then, the cams don't pick up the inside of the rooms, only the hallways."

"Any change in radiation levels, Rescue-two? Air quality? Pressure?"

A pause. Jamil was checking out instrument readings. "No, Rescue-one. None. Everything reads normal."

"Okay," Xris said. The Little One was glowering at him impatiently from beneath the fedora. "Open it up, Rescue-two."

The door clanked, began to revolve ponderously to one side. The Little One let go of Rowan's hand, jumped through as soon as the crack was large enough to contain his small body. He was halfway down the corridor before Xris, Rowan, and Quong managed to catch up.

Xris stared curiously at the other doors as they passed, wondering why this particular area had been made off limits and who it was off limits to. "Authorized personnel" might mean the crew only, excluding the profs, or it might mean the profs, excluding the crew. The first would tend to indicate that this area had been sealed off because it had something important to do with the running of the ship—which seemed unlikely, since there were only doors and a corridor, no high-voltage electrical equipment or thrumming machinery. The other might mean that the crew was being kept in the dark about the experiments being carried on inside.

Some of the doors were marked, but the marks were in a strange language, not the usual Standard Military. Rowan slowed her pace to stare at them. Xris nearly bumped into her.

"Aren't those weird?" she said.

Xris agreed, caught hold of Rowan's elbow, steered her on. It had not been unknown, when they were agents together, for Rowan to stop in the middle of a guns-drawn, badges-flashing raid to read a flier tacked on a wall.

The Little One made a sudden turn to the right. He was running now, dashing along at such a rapid, eager pace that he tripped himself up completely and sprawled flat on the floor. He was up again before anyone could reach him, racing madly down the corridor. He skidded to a halt in front of a door, pointing and jumping up and down.

"This is it? Raoul's in there?" Xris asked.

The Little One nodded so violently that the hat slid over his eyes.

Xris was back on the comm. "Rescue-two? Can you see us now?"

"I have you, Rescue-one. You're on Deck eight, level B-two. And you're in the clear. That corridor's empty in all directions."

"Everyone behaving themselves up there?"

"Two indignant outbursts, one request for a glass of water—denied—and one promise to see us all behind a force field, but that's been about it so far. There's a blip on the screen; someone coming to check on the distress signal. Looks like a freighter, moving pretty slowly, but it *is* moving, so don't dawdle."

"Right. You reading anything inside this room?"

"Nothing here. But like I said, I can't see."

Xris glanced again at the Little One. The fedora bobbed. "Rescue-two, we're going in."

Xris touched the controls. The door stayed shut.

"Or maybe not. Rescue-two . . ."

"I'm on it, Rescue-one. Just a sec. Okay. Ready when you are."

Xris motioned to Quong. Lasgun in hand, the Doc took one side of the door while Xris covered the other. Rowan had drawn her lasgun. With her other hand, she grasped the Little One firmly, dragged him behind her, out of the line of fire.

"Ready."

The door slid open. Quong dove low, lasgun ready. Xris dodged in after him.

They were inside what appeared to be a sick bay. Three hospital beds, separated by hanging curtains, were lined up side by side. Various monitors, computers, and other equipment, including a deactivated medicbot, cluttered the room.

An extremely startled-looking medic, seated in a swivel chair in front of a lit screen, spun around, said, "What the—" and jumped to his feet.

"Hold it," Quong told him, aiming the lasgun at the man's chest. "Right there. Don't move. Hands up."

The medic, looking bewildered, did what he was told.

Xris glanced swiftly around the room, saw no one else. No one else living, that is.

A still form, covered with a white sheet, lay on one of the beds. A hand was all that was visible, hanging limp and lifeless off the bed. The delicate fingers were decorated with gaudy rings. The nails were long, manicured, and painted mauve.

"Damn. Damn it to hell," Xris said softly.

He turned, with some idea of telling Rowan to get the Little One out of there, but he was too late. The empath broke away from her, ran past Xris, heading straight for the shrouded figure.

"Doc!" Xris called warningly. "I've got the medic covered. You go take care of ..." He left the sentence unfinished. There was probably very little left to care for ... except the Little One. And what they'd do with him, Xris couldn't imagine.

The Little One was climbing up onto the bed.

Quong lowered his weapon. With soothing words, he endeavored to stop the empath. But the doctor was too late. The Little One plucked the sheet from the body.

Raoul lay beneath it. The Adonian was dressed in a hospital gown. ("He *must* be dead!" Xris muttered to himself.) The long black hair was uncombed, disheveled. Wide, unseeing eyes stared at the ceiling.

The Little One grabbed hold of Raoul's hospital gown with both small hands and tugged.

"My friend, please!" Quong attempted to remonstrate. "He is dead. There is nothing—"

"How did this happen?" Xris demanded.

The medic started to babble. "We found him stowed away on board our ship. He was in a drugged stupor. We did what we could, but—"

"I'll bet." Xris sneered. "I also don't believe a word. Rowan, go help the Doc. Rowan ..."

She wasn't looking at him or listening to him. She was staring at the medic's computer. Rowan could have no more walked by a computer without stopping to look than poor Raoul could have walked past a cosmetics counter. She sat down in front of it.

"Stay away from that!" the medic yelled.

Rowan bent nearer, reading the screen.

"My God . . ."

She placed her lasgun on the console. Her fingers went to the keyboard.

The medic was livid.

The Little One shook Raoul's body. Quong attempted to pacify the distraught empath.

Xris turned back to his prisoner. "You've got five seconds to tell me the truth about what happened to my friend there before I start shooting holes in various parts of you—parts that won't interfere with your mouth."

"Xris . . ." Rowan said, excited. "You won't believe this! Come look—"

"Rescue-one!" Jamil was on the comm. "You've got trouble. I don't know where the hell they came from, but a whole goddamn regiment is closing in on you!"

"Seal off Deck Eight, all levels!" Xris shouted.

He made a spring for the door control and, at that moment, the medic made a spring for Rowan.

Xris had time to shout a warning to her, but that was all he could do. His main concern had to be for the door. Reaching it, he caught a glimpse of armed men racing down the corridor. Laser fire burst over his head.

Xris slammed his hand on the controls, shut the door. He spun around.

The medic had Rowan in an expert stranglehold. He held her own lasgun to her head.

CHAPTER
27

If your advance is going well, you're walking into
an ambush.

Murphy's Military Law

Xris could hear banging on the door, but that didn't last
long. He could trust Jamil to keep the door controls
locked up, make sure the door stayed shut—at least until
someone came back with a plasma cutting torch.

"Just take it easy." Xris raised his hands in the air. "We
don't intend to hurt anyone. We just want to find out what
happened to our friend there. You said you found him in—"

"Shut up!" the medic snarled.

The man was rattled; he was in charge of the situation, but
he had no idea what to do with it. He pressed the gun against
Rowan's temple, glanced nervously around as if looking for
help. His gaze went involuntarily upward.

Guessing that he wasn't searching for spiritual guidance,
Xris followed the medic's gaze and saw the security cam. He
cursed himself for not having seen it sooner. Someone had
been watching, and not from the bridge, apparently, since
Jamil couldn't see them. Which meant there was some sort
of centralized control on board the vessel that had nothing to
do with the crew.

What the hell was going on?

Rowan knew—he could tell it from the excited, eager expression on her face. She was within a finger's twitch of
having a hole burned through her skull and she was only interested in relating what she'd found out.

I know what they're after! She was telling him silently.

Her dark eyes gleamed. She cast a look at the computer and then her gaze became pleading. *But I need more time!*

He could hear her as clearly as if she'd spoken out loud. And he felt the same familiar rush of frustration and irritation that he'd had in the old days, working together. Not only did Rowan expect him to get her out of this—to get them all out of this—but she wanted him to buy her time on the computer as well! And all with a gun to her head!

The medic had decided on a course of action. He began dragging Rowan backward toward the bed, where he could get a clear view of Quong and the Little One.

"You there. You two. Move out in front of me where I can see you." The medic tightened his choking grip on Rowan, motioned with the lasgun.

Rowan had gone a shade paler; she was gasping for breath. Her eyes were enormous in her white face and their gaze never left Xris. She was slowly suffocating.

Quong lifted the Little One from the bed. The empath went limp in the doctor's grasp. Quong set the Little One gently on the floor, stood protectively near him.

"Move this way. Over by the tin man," the medic ordered, waving the lasgun. "You. Cyborg." He turned to Xris. "Shut your battery down."

"Rescue-one." Jamil was back on the comm. "I've sealed off the corridors, but they're using manual overrides to open the blast doors. It'll take them a while, but not long. You've got five in your immediate vicinity. There were seven, but two of them left, probably to get a cutting torch. What's it like at your end?"

"Hostage situation. I can't talk," Xris returned.

"Shut up!" the medic yelled. "And shut down. *You've* got five seconds before I start shooting body parts. Hers!"

Panic began to rise, to bubble up inside Xris, creep out of his pores in a cold sweat. His worst nightmare, his only nightmare, his constant, continuous nightmare was shutting down. With his battery turned off, he was helpless, the cybernetic parts of himself died, froze. Weighted down with the heavy hunks of wire and steel, he couldn't move. He could barely keep himself alive—if you wanted to call it alive. The artificial heart would continue to pump, but the blood would flow to paralyzed, unfeeling limbs.

"Five ... four ..." The medic was counting.

And behind the medic, the corpse of Raoul was slowly sitting up.

For a stunned moment, Xris wondered if his battery pack *had* shut down. His heart lurched and then reality hit him. Raoul was *not* dead. He'd never *been* dead! He'd been lying in the bed—God and the Loti only knew why—with the sheet pulled over his head!

All of this went through Xris's mind in a flash, just as he realized he'd been staring too fixedly in Raoul's direction. The medic had noticed his gaze, started to look around.

Raoul was on his hands and knees, crawling to the end of the bed. He held an injector in his hand.

"There's obviously been a mistake," Xris said loudly, and took a step forward. "Let me talk to Dr. Brisbane."

"Dr. Brisbane gave us permission to come down here," Quong added. He, too, had seen Raoul. The doctor took a step forward.

Alarmed, feeling threatened, the medic shifted the lasgun from Rowan, aimed at Xris, and fired.

Raoul leaped on the man from behind, plunged the injector into the medic's back.

The burst caught Xris in the left arm, spun him around, knocked him to the floor. His electrical system went berserk; three fingers on his weapons hand shorted out. Tiny jolts of electricity slivered through his body and then the automatic relays kicked in and closed down the damaged circuits, rerouted the power.

Xris rolled over, fighting to catch his breath, waiting for his heartbeat to stabilize. There was one thing he could still do. He raised his lasgun, which he carried always in his good hand—mainly because of situations like this. He didn't aim at the medic, who was writhing on the floor, in a tangle with Rowan. Taking careful aim, Xris shot out the security cam.

Quong was bending over the medic, who had gone suddenly limp.

"Dead," the doctor reported.

Quong turned to Rowan.

She was on her feet, waved the doctor away. "I'm all right. Go see about Xris."

"I'm okay, Doc." Xris picked himself up. He was out of breath and dizzy, but that would pass. "Some circuits fried. Nothing major." He touched the comm. "Rescue-two, this is

Rescue-one. All secure down here. What's going on outside our door?"

He didn't really need to ask. He could hear the hissing of the plasma cutting torch, see a charred spot start to form around the door controls.

"Seven men on Deck Eight, your level," Jamil reported. "They've got a torch and they're cutting their way through the door. Someone tried to shut down my view, but I was able to block the attempt. Rescue-three is on his way under my guidance. He's on Deck Six, but he's going to run into a few delays. They're still playing with the manual over-rides. I'll keep you posted."

"Are they attacking the spaceplane?"

"Harry reports all clear. They're only interested in you, my friend. Out."

Xris tuned in Tycho, picked up the sound of laser blasts. "Rescue-three, can you hear me?"

"Barely!" Tycho shouted. There was a pause, then the whine of the iridium sniper rifle. A blast. "Three down! One to go! I tell you something, boss"—the alien's tone was grim—"these guys sure as hell aren't college professors!"

No, they sure as hell weren't.

Quong was beside Xris, inspecting the damage.

"I'm okay, Doc. Nothing you can do about this now. You go cover the door. Tycho's coming down to get us out, but he may be delayed. He's facing resistance."

Quong, who could hear for himself in his own comm, nodded. Rowan could hear, too, but she was back at the computer, working feverishly. Xris limped over, stood behind her.

"What have you got?"

"I'm not sure," she murmured, her gaze on the screen, her brow furrowed. "I'm establishing a link between our plane's computer and this one. Hopefully, I can do it without them finding out—at least not right away." She looked up at him. "I need time, Xris."

"We're not going anywhere real soon," he said wryly. "How long?"

"Ten minutes?"

"Five," he modified, and hoped he meant it.

She grimaced, shook her head, and went back to work.

Xris turned to Raoul. The Little One had his arms around his friend's legs, hugging him. Raoul was patting the empath on the shoulder.

"I don't suppose it would do any good to ask you what's going on?"

Raoul's eyes were glazed, unfocused. "I am afraid not, Xris Cyborg. They did terrible things to me. They were going to kill me. That deadly drug"—the eyes sharpened, their gaze rested on the injector lying near the body—"was meant for me."

"You don't know who these people are?"

Raoul shook his head, the eyes once more vacant, vacuous. "I have no idea. They did terrible things. They made me wear this. . . ." His hands plucked at the hospital gown.

Xris was struck with sudden inspiration. "*That's* why you were lying under the sheet!"

"Of course." Raoul lifted his plucked eyebrows, astonished that Xris hadn't arrived at this conclusion earlier. "You don't imagine I could let anyone see me like this." His hands fluttered in disgust. "In this . . . thing! And with no makeup!"

The charred arc was halfway around the door controls. Rowan, her teeth clamped down on her lower lip, was concentrating on her work. It would take a bomb blast to get her to leave now.

"Rescue-one, this is Rescue-three. I'm on Deck Seven, moving your way." That was Tycho, and the next moment Jamil was on.

"Rescue-one, this is Rescue-two. They've broken through the door controls on Deck Three and there's nothing more I can do to stop them. You're going to have about twenty armed soldiers on you."

"Five more minutes," Rowan begged.

Raoul was plucking at Xris's sleeve. "I have to go back to my room, change my clothes. It's just down the hall—"

Xris caught himself about to laugh. He took a twist, thrust it in his mouth, bit down on it.

"Rescue-three, let me know when you're in position on Deck Eight."

"Coming up on you now, Rescue-one," Tycho responded. "Targets in sight."

"Right. Quong, grenade. Everyone—take cover!"

Quong took a thurmaplasma grenade from his belt, placed it in front of the door, set the timer, and ran like hell. He dove behind a steel cabinet. Raoul quit complaining about his wearing apparel, grabbed the Little One. The two of them hit the floor and scuttled underneath the bed.

Xris was on his way to finding his own cover when he noticed that Rowan hadn't moved. She was still sitting at the damn computer.

He jumped for her, took her down, chair and all, just as the door blew.

The blast knocked out the lower section of the door, plus anyone standing near it. Xris, peering through the smoke and flame, could see bodies on the deck. But there must have been someone up and moving around because the next moment he heard the whine of Tycho's gun.

"Move out, Rescue-one," Tycho called over the comm. "I've got you covered."

Quong, at a sign from Xris, made his advance. Cautiously, weapon raised, he looked out the door.

Rowan was on her knees, back at the computer.

"We're in," she reported triumphantly. She touched a key. The screen cleared, then filled with text. "And, hopefully, they won't find out for a while."

Scrambling to her feet, she wiped away a trickle of blood from a cut on her scalp. "We've got to hurry," she said to Xris impatiently. "I want to get back to the plane and log on."

Xris grunted, hauled Raoul and the Little One out from under the bed.

"My clothes are in my room, which is down the hall to your right, about six or seven doors—" Raoul began.

"Never mind your clothes. Get moving."

Raoul came to a dead stop, regarded Xris with a cold stare. "If you think that I am going out in public, wearing *this* . . ." Words failed him.

"Damn it!" said Xris through teeth clenched over the twist in his mouth. He gave Raoul a shove that sent him staggering. "There are people out there shooting at us! Now get going!"

Raoul recovered himself, drew himself up with dignity. "May I remind you, Xris Cyborg, that people are generally always shooting at us. That is no excuse for not appearing at our best."

"Hurry, Xris!" Rowan was shouting at him from the door. Quong had stepped outside, was motioning for them to come.

Xris was on the comm to Jamil. "Rescue-two, what's our status?"

"You're safe where you are for the moment, Rescue-one, but you're going to run into a major roadblock in front of the spaceplane. Sorry, Rescue-one. Nothing I could do. They were laying for us."

Laying for us. An ambush. A bunch of professors. Why? What the devil was going on?

"How many?"

"Thirty, thirty-five. Forty. Armed to the teeth."

Xris shut his eyes, tried to think. He hadn't switched off the comm and in the background he could hear the distress signal. And he remembered that, too—a freighter, coming to investigate. Just one more damn problem. A small problem, compared to the fact that there were forty or so armed and well-trained soldiers standing between his team and their only way off this mother of a ship. He could either go out and meet them and try to blast his way through or wait here until they came to get him, and try to blast his way out. Lousy odds, either way. He was going to lose some people, some damn good people. It—

The distress signal . . .

Only way off . . .

The plan was there, bursting inside his head with dazzling clarity. Elation, excitement tingled through him like a powerful narcotic. He lived for moments like this.

The problem was how to explain it. It was unlikely that their transmissions were being monitored, but Xris wasn't putting anything past this bunch.

He was on the comm to Jamil. "Rescue-two, leave your post. At my signal, we're getting out of here. But before you go, turn out the lights and lock up the house. Then follow the signs. You got that, Rescue-two?"

A pause. In the background, the distress signal. Then Jamil said quietly, "I've got it, Rescue-one. Waiting your signal."

Xris shut down the transmission, glowered at Raoul. "You coming with us or not?"

Raoul fluttered his eyelids demurely. He always knew when Xris'd had enough. "I'm coming."

The Adonian stepped daintily over the bits of burning wreckage, making futile attempts to pull his gown shut in back. At length, shrugging, he gave up. Pausing, he took a look at his reflection in the carbon-streaked metal wall.

"Oh, well." Raoul shrugged. "Fortunately, I have a nice tight ass."

"You better move your nice tight ass or it's going to get shot off," Xris said grimly. Grabbing hold of the Little One, the cyborg lifted the empath over the ruins and the bodies, plunked him down on the floor near Quong. "Keep an eye on these two. *And* Rowan," he told the Doc.

Quong nodded.

Tycho stood at the end of a corridor littered with bodies. Seven humans. All of them, Xris noted, were wearing black uniforms decorated with silver insignia. He didn't recognize either the uniforms or the insignia, but that didn't count for much. Every planet, country, city, city-state, corporation, and radical fringe group had its own paramilitary force. These guys just happened to be better than most. They'd fooled him completely.

Xris motioned for Tycho to join them.

"All clear down here," Tycho reported.

"Yeah," said Xris, spitting out the twist. "That's because there's a reception committee waiting for us at the spaceplane."

"How many?" asked Tycho.

"Too damn many. We're clearing out."

Tycho's face darkened. "Jamil's trapped on the bridge—"

"He's abandoning ship. We all are."

They stared at him.

Xris switched on the comm to Jamil. "Rescue-two—*now!*" Xris hoped Jamil had truly understood his message. *Turn out the lights and lock up the house. Then follow the signs.* If not . . .

A second's worry-packed delay, and then the lights went out. The air went off. Emergency lights flickered on, casting an eerie bluish glow over everything. A computerized voice echoed through the corridor.

"Warning! Life support has shut down. Follow the white lights and proceed to the emergency exits. Stay calm. Warning! Life support has shut down. Follow the white lights and proceed to the emergency exits. Stay calm. Warning! . . ."

Small white lights, embedded in the deck, began to flash in a distinct pattern, leading in one direction.

Quong nodded his head; he was beginning to understand. Rowan had it; she was smiling in approval. Tycho was already changing skin color to blend into the semidarkness. Raoul looked delighted. He was probably enjoying the light show.

"Move out," Xris ordered.

Following the guide lights, they headed down the corridor

at a run. Tycho took the lead; his rifle scope had infrared sights. Quong shepherded Rowan, Raoul, and the Little One. Xris brought up the rear. They met no one. All resistance, apparently, was gathered around their spaceplane.

"Rescue-five." Xris alerted Harry. "Take off. We can't reach you."

"Rescue-one, I didn't catch that. Would you repeat?"

Xris sighed, shook his head. "Rescue-five, dammit, take off! We're going out in the escape pods."

"But Xris! Spaceplanes can't recover escape pods! I—"

"Orders, Rescue-five," Xris snapped.

"Sure, Xris. I mean, Rescue-one."

It was all very easy after that. So easy, in fact, that once they reached the pods, Raoul announced that he had time to go back after his clothes. Xris, not even bothering to comment, shoved the Adonian into the escape pod.

The pods aboard a Verdi-class vessel are built to hold eight people—not comfortably, but then escape pods weren't meant to be used for extended periods of time. Since Verdi-class ships had no hyperspace capabilities and were not armed, they weren't likely to venture into the wilds of space. Traveling near the busy trade routes, a ship in trouble was likely to have help within hours. And, as Xris knew, help was already on its way.

When everyone was crammed inside the pod, perched on the hard benches, their heads and backs pressed against the curved walls (the tall Tycho was bent double), Xris sealed the pod, pressed the emergency release. The pod dropped off. Small rocket thrusters fired, taking them a safe distance from the ship before shutting down.

Bursts of fire indicated the launching of a second pod, not far from theirs—that would be Jamil. In the distance, Xris could see the Schiavona spaceplane hovering near the pods like a distraught mother hen. They had escaped neatly, easily. He wondered how long it would take the soldiers lying in ambush for the team to figure out they weren't coming. All they had to do now was sit back and wait for that freighter. And think up a plausible story.

"Harry," said Rowan into the comm, almost as soon as the pod had ejected, "put me through to the computer."

She gave detailed instructions to the computer on how to break into its counterpart aboard the *Canis Major,* how to sneak around without being noticed, what files to find, and how to begin downloading them. Then she sat and fidgeted.

"I suppose it has occurred to you, Xris, that we may be rescued, then immediately tossed into the brig." Tycho was often grumbling and irritable after a raid. "What's to keep the professors"—he jerked his long thumb toward the vessel—"from claiming that we seized their ship, terrorized them, then fled when things got too hot?"

"They won't," said Xris, chewing lazily on a twist. He began investigating the damage to his arm. "In fact, it's my guess they won't even stick around."

"But Harry said they couldn't start their engines for another six . . . I'll be damned." Quong was keeping watch out the porthole. "You were right. There they go. Full main thrusters."

"Stop them, Xris," said Rowan suddenly. In her urgency, she reached across, rested her hand on his good one. "Tell Harry to shoot them down. Now!"

"Are you crazy?" Xris stared at her. "Fire on an unarmed ship—some helpless research vessel? In full view of that freighter? Okay, the bastards weren't so helpless, but that freighter captain doesn't know that. We'd not only be tossed in the brig, we'd be thrown into the disrupter!"

"Not after they saw the evidence I'm downloading. Do it, Xris!" She was in earnest. Her grip on him tightened.

"Too late," Quong said coolly. "By the Holy Master, they had hyperspace, as well! They're gone!"

Xris pushed his way forward, peered out the porthole. No sign of the *Canis Major.* The ship had jumped into one of the nearby Lanes. He sat back down. *What* the devil was going on?

"Someone went to a lot of expense to modify that ship," Tycho observed. "Imagine, adding backup linear drive *and* hyperspace to a Verdi-class!"

"Of course they would," Rowan said irritably. "They would have to, with what they're planning."

"What *are* they planning? What have you got on them?" Xris demanded.

She looked over at him.

"Less than sixty hours from now, they're plotting to assassinate the king."

CHAPTER 28

Let fortune's bubbles rise and fall. . . .
John Greenleaf Whittier, *A Song of Harvest*

"And that," said Raoul, spreading his hands dramatically, "is my story."

He was obviously enjoying himself, enjoying his audience, enjoying being the center of attention. So much so that Xris, sucking on a twist, regarded him with suspicion.

Quong rolled up the Adonian's sleeves, made a brief examination of his arm. "He's had blood drawn. You can see the discoloration on the skin."

"It's all in the computer files, Xris," Rowan added. "Well, not all of it. We were only able to download a small segment before they made the jump. There are a lot of holes. But it adds up."

"Maybe. But to what?"

"To regicide," Rowan said. "Like I told you."

Xris shook his head.

Within an hour of their escape from *Canis Major Research I*, the team had been picked up by the freighter. The captain listened to their story—how they'd heard the distress call, stopped to help what they thought was a disabled vessel, boarded the ship, were then set upon by thugs, and barely escaped with their lives.

The captain had been dubious: not surprising, considering Tycho standing there holding a specialized iridium sniper rifle; Raoul, blushing in shame, in his hospital gown; Xris with half his left arm sizzling and popping; and Rowan bleeding from a scalp wound. To say nothing of the Little One.

There was the possibility, of course, that the captain watched the nightly news, would recognize them. But Xris wasn't overly concerned about that. Even if the captain had seen the news, freighter captains were notorious for minding their own business. They had their own problems, including delivery dates to meet.

The vessel that had sent the distress signal had disappeared; the crew wasn't around to speak for themselves. The captain asked a few questions—just enough to make his report look good—then was only too happy to transfer Xris and his team back to their spaceplane and be rid of them.

Once on board the Schiavona, Xris attempted to put together the pieces of what was turning out to be an extremely bizarre puzzle. Just what did the kidnapping of a fashion-conscious Adonian Loti have to do with the assassination of a king?

"You said Dr. Brisbane asked you questions." Rowan pursued Raoul's debriefing. "What about?"

Raoul shrugged. "My late former employer, Snaga Ohme. The time I spent with my late former employer. I must say that it brought back very painful memories."

The Adonian was lucid—or at least as lucid as Raoul could ever be, considering that no one was actually certain where he ended and his drug-induced euphoria began. Quong had given Raoul, now dressed in a flight suit, a mild sedative—to help him get over the shock of the hospital gown, which seemed to bother him more than any of the other torments he had suffered. With the exception of his true concern for the Little One.

Raoul's gaze strayed often to his friend, as if reassuring himself the empath was safe, and he occasionally patted the Little One on whatever part of the small being was handy. The Little One huddled possessively near Raoul, the one visible eye gleaming in triumph.

There was still the matter of Rowan. Here was Xris's opportunity to ask Raoul and the Little One about Rowan's veracity. He'd been looking forward to doing just that, but now that the moment had come, he put it off. This other matter was more important, he told himself. Or maybe it was because he already knew the answer.

"What specific questions did Dr. Brisbane ask you about Snaga Ohme?" Rowan persisted patiently.

Raoul fluttered his hands. "It was all so . . . dreadful and confused. That hideous gown. I was not my accustomed self, if you know what I mean." He glanced at them from the corners of his eyes.

"We get the idea," Xris said wryly.

Raoul sighed, attempted to concentrate. "I believe that the dreadful female kept asking me if Snaga Ohme had ever given me any sort of injections. If he had used me for any sort of tests or experiments."

"And did he?" Rowan sat forward, interested.

"No." Raoul looked bewildered. "Why would he? My late employer, Snaga Ohme, was a purveyor of weaponry. What had I to do with such onerous devices as bombs and tanks?"

"What indeed. . . ." Rowan murmured. "You told Dr. Brisbane this?"

"Yes."

"And . . ."

"She did not appear to believe me. It was at that point that she announced that she was going to terminate me." Raoul shuddered delicately.

"But she didn't," Xris said.

"I don't believe so." Raoul was forced to consider the matter.

"Did she give you any reason why?"

"The only thing she gave me was an extremely powerful sedative. At which point," Raoul added gravely, "I began to feel much better."

"I'll bet you did," Xris muttered. "You don't know why she kept you alive?"

"I didn't say that," Raoul returned with dignity. "You asked if she gave me a reason. No. She did not. But I heard her talking to the ugly man. The ugly man said—and I quote—'Some of the micromachines in his body have not yet exploded. He will be an excellent test subject for the device.' Unquote."

Rowan was nodding her head, looking well satisfied. She was the only one who had read the stolen computer files. This must be making some sort of sense to her. It made none to Xris.

"Come off it, Loti." Harry chortled. "The only people who have micromachines in their bloodstream are Blood Royal. You don't expect us to believe you're Blood Royal, do you?"

"Do you suppose I could be?" Raoul was blissful. "A cousin to His Majesty!"

"I think it highly unlikely," Xris responded.

Raoul gave the matter thought, shrugged. "You're probably right. Mummy and Daddy were both courtesans and it is a well known fact that the Blood Royal did not generally go in for that line of work. On the other hand—"

"Don't expect an invitation to the Starfire family reunion," Xris interrupted. "So far as we know, there's only one person left alive in the galaxy who is Blood Royal, and that's the king." He was going to add, *Look, Raoul, level with us. Why did they really snatch you?* But before he could get the words out, Quong interrupted.

"This is incredible." Quong was studying the computer printouts. "They *did* find micromachines in Raoul's bloodstream!"

Jamil snorted in disgust. "You're not telling us the poisoner over there is in line for the throne?"

"No. No. The Adonian is *not* Blood Royal. He could not be; Adonians were not considered a suitable race for genetic altering, which was how the Blood Royal became Blood Royal, how they were able to take the micromachines into their bodies and use them. Which brings up the question: How did the micromachines get into the Adonian's bloodstream? And what do his captors mean by 'exploded'?"

"That's why they kept asking him about injections," Rowan said, excited. "Snaga Ohme must have *injected* the micromachines into Raoul's blood."

"But why? And where would Ohme get them?" Quong wondered.

The Little One tugged on Raoul's sleeve, demanding his attention.

Raoul listened to that silent voice, then translated. "The Little One recalls that there was a bloodsword in the possession of our late former employer. If you remember, Snaga Ohme was not only a purveyor of weapons but a collector as well."

"That's it, then!" Quong announced. "Ohme could have removed some of the fluid containing the micromachines from the sword and injected it into Raoul."

Xris was thoughtful. "But why? As far as I know, the only Blood Royal Snaga Ohme ever had long-term dealings with was Warlord Derek Sagan. There was no love lost between those two. In fact, the Warlord once hired me to do a spy job on the weapons dealer. Derek Sagan had given Ohme the plans for the space-rotation bomb and the Warlord wanted to make damn sure Ohme wasn't trying to double-cross him. Of course, Sagan didn't tell me all that. No one knew about the bomb then. But Ohme appeared to be dealing fairly with the Warlord at that time."

"Because Ohme was plotting to murder Derek Sagan!" Rowan said. She pointed to the computer printout. "That's in this file. Ohme planned to murder Sagan by using some sort of weapon that would only kill Blood Royal. React with the micromachines in their bodies."

"Is that possible, Doc?" Xris asked.

"Certainly," Quong replied. "What was it Raoul said? 'Explode.' There are millions of micromachines in the bloodstream of the Blood Royal. If Ohme had found a way to cause them all to explode . . ."

He regarded Raoul with interest. "Ohme *must* have injected you with those micromachines! Otherwise how could these people have found them in your bloodstream? You're positive Snaga Ohme *never* gave you any type of injections?"

"Positive," said Raoul.

Quong frowned, perplexed.

Xris shook his head. "Look, this theory is all very interesting, Doc, but it *is* just a theory and—"

"Unless you count the collagen treatments," Raoul added offhandedly.

"What collagen treatments?" Quong and Rowan both spoke simultaneously.

"I took them to erase wrinkles. I was developing a few around my eyes. Very few, and they're not noticeable now, due to this new cream I'm using. It is an extract of the—"

Quong was triumphant. "Ohme *did* give him injections! He claimed they were collagen treatments for wrinkles!"

"What else did he do?" Rowan demanded.

"Nothing"—Raoul looked slightly dazed—"that I can remember."

"Damn it—" Xris was losing patience.

Rowan reached out, laid a hand on his arm, his good arm. Her touch was cool, oddly soothing.

"Perhaps Ohme had you test out a new machine at the same time," she suggested to Raoul.

"Why, yes. Now that you mention it, my late employer Snaga Ohme had just recently purchased a new tanning bed. He offered to let me try it out. He said it would assist the collagen treatments to eradicate the wrinkles."

Quong and Rowan exchanged knowing glances, nodded.

"Did the wrinkles go away?" the doctor asked.

"No." Raoul was aggrieved. "Now that I think of it, they did not. And not only did the wrinkles *not* go away, I didn't get a tan and I developed the most terrible skin condition. Huge purplish splotches—like these bruises, only worse—broke out on my face and arms. No amount of makeup would hide them. I was unfit to be seen in public. I took to my bed for a week."

"That's it," stated Quong, looking around at the team. "The collagen treatments were, in reality, micromachines being injected into Raoul's bloodstream. Then Ohme put the Loti in this 'tanning bed' that was, in reality, a device designed to blow up the micromachines. If Raoul had been injected with a significant number of micromachines, he'd be dead. All of them would have burst at once, like bubbles in champagne, causing massive hemorrhaging. Death would be rapid and extremely painful. As it was, the small number of micromachines that did explode caused only minor damage—the bruising on the arms and the face."

"Xris," said Rowan excitedly, clutching his hand, "do you realize what this means?"

He looked at her. She flushed, removed her hand from his arm.

"I see where you're headed. But you two can't be serious! This is . . . ludicrous!"

"Look at how it fits," Rowan argued. "Snaga Ohme invented this machine in order to kill Derek Sagan. But Fate intervenes. Snaga Ohme dies before he has a chance to use the machine. Then Derek Sagan dies. All the Blood Royal are dead."

"Except one," Quong added.

"One," Rowan repeated. "And while Ohme may be dead, his machine could be very much alive."

"Which means—" Quong began.

"I know!" Raoul cried, ecstatic at having figured it all out. "I know! Bubbles in the blood!" He was pleasurably horrified. "They're going to carbonate the king!"

CHAPTER
29

"Holmes!" I cried. "I seem to see dimly what you
are hinting at! We are only just in time to prevent
some subtle and horrible crime."

Sir Arthur Conan Doyle, *The Speckled Band*

"And, according to the files, they're going to go through
with the assassination in sixty hours. Less than that
now, of course. That has to be what this means." Rowan exhibited the printout, read it aloud.

" 'Synchronize chronometers to Zulu Time—now. Mission go/nogo will be transmitted in sixty-six hours. Mission
completion, barring nogo, will occur by eighty-one hours.
You have your orders.' "

Raoul nodded his head. "I heard them say that."

Xris regarded him skeptically.

"I did," Raoul protested. "I remember quite clearly. That
dreadful female was, after all, coming at me with an injector
full of poison at the time. Such an occurrence does tend to
stimulate the cerebral cortex. The message about Zulus and
nogos—whatever *they* are—came over the loudspeaker.
Then the ugly man came in and said that God was with them
and that dreadful woman asked him why and he said because ... because ..."

Raoul's lashes fluttered.

Xris, exasperated, sucked in a breath, but Raoul waved his
hand.

"No, no. Just a moment. It's coming back to me. I have
it! No one could stop them, because the Royal Navy was effectively paralyzed!"

Xris looked swiftly at Rowan. She stared fixedly at him.

"My God," she murmured.

"You can say that again! Son of a bitch!" Throwing down his twist, stepping on it, Xris stalked over to stare gloomily out the Schiavona's viewscreen at the stars.

"What the devil do we do now?" Jamil asked.

"Your guess is as good as mine," Xris said grimly. "Anyone got any bright ideas?"

Tycho, who had absentmindedly allowed himself to turn the gray color of the metal bulkheads, shook his head.

Quong might not have heard the question. He had placed his hands on his knees, was gazing at a point in the center of the deck.

Pleased with the response, though he had no idea what caused it, Raoul pattered on. "The Royal Navy. Something about the military has big problems and those dreadful people intended to take advantage of the situation."

"Did they say anything else?" Xris asked.

Raoul's brow furrowed in thought, something he never would have permitted—furrowing was bad for the complexion—but the situation appeared grave. At this point, the Little One nudged him with an elbow. They held one of their silent conversations and Raoul's brow cleared. He assisted the dewrinkling process by smoothing his skin with his hand while he talked.

"Yes, that is correct. My friend reminds me that the dreadful woman mentioned something to the effect that the number of hours stated didn't give them a great deal of time. The ugly man replied that the 'device' was completed. They merely had to transport it to the location and set it up. And then he said that my termination order was canceled. But I don't see how—"

The Little One climbed up beside his friend and shook his arm. Raoul listened to the unspoken voice. His eyes widened; his gaze went to Xris.

"Dear, dear," he said. "I'm beginning to understand. We *do* have a problem, don't we?"

"Well, *I* don't understand." Harry was bewildered. "You guys always do this to me! What's going on?"

"Just this," said Xris, turning around. "If something does happen to the king, *we're* the ones who're going to be blamed for it."

"Huh?" Harry was baffled. "Why?"

"It will look as if we kidnapped Rowan in order to disrupt

the communications of the Royal Navy in order to assassinate the king."

"Oh," said Harry. "Gotcha." The news sank in. "Wow!"

"But we're still not sure that's what they intend," Jamil
argued. "Who are these people? What is their motivation?
How did they get hold of the plans for Snaga Ohme's machine? And are they really serious about this?"

"They're serious, all right," Rowan said, studying the
computer printout. She looked at Raoul. "Did you know
someone called Bosk?"

"Oh, yes." Raoul and the Little One exchanged glances
and nods. Raoul sniffed. "We never liked Bosk, personally.
He thought far too highly of himself. Everyone knew his
hair wasn't his own. And what he did have, he bleached.
Yet, for some reason, our late employer, Snaga Ohme, took
a fancy to the man."

"Bosk was in Ohme's confidence," Rowan continued.

"His confidence, his bed, you name it." Raoul flipped his
own long hair languidly over one shoulder.

"And if anyone in that household knew Ohme's secrets, it
would be Bosk."

"Yes. Not a doubt. *He* was the one who could have used
the collagen treatments," Raoul added in an undertone to the
Little One.

"Bosk is dead, Xris," Rowan said. She handed him the
printout. "They murdered him to get the plans for the device. It's all right here."

It was: a detailed report on the murder of the wretched
Bosk, related in a completely professional, detached manner
that chilled the blood.

I shot the subject through the head, read one portion. *I
then proceeded to cut out the subject's eyeball. Holding it to
the scanner, I was thus able to obtain the necessary files.*

Yes, there was no doubt these people were serious. They'd
murdered once. And, judging by the beating they'd given the
Little One and the threats they'd made to kill Raoul, they
were prepared to murder again. Xris read through the rest of
the material. It was disjointed, incomplete, the downloading
of the files having been interrupted by the *Canis Major*'s unexpected jump to hyperspace. But he was finding enough to
make him start to believe that the young king's life was truly
in danger.

Xris had been one of the envied few invited to attend the

coronation. Dion Starfire, the embodiment of hope for a war-torn galaxy, kneeling at the foot of the archbishop, pledging himself to serve the people, to dedicate his life to that service.

And Xris remembered another time—a time tinged with smoke, hot with fire, soaked in blood. The time he'd seen Dion Starfire work a miracle.

And then there was the king's wife, the beautiful Astarte.

Xris shook his head irritably. He was spending far too much time these days tromping down memory lane.

"But who are these people?" Jamil sounded irritated. "I've asked twice now."

"The Knights of the Terra Nera," Xris read, flipping through the printout.

"Sounds pretty hokey to me," Jamil observed.

"Nothing on them," Xris said. "I wonder—"

"I can still get into the bureau's files," Rowan offered.

Xris regarded her silently. She flushed beneath his gaze.

"I needed to keep track of the Hung," she said defensively. "What they were doing. Who was in prison. Who was out."

"I take it the bureau doesn't know you're rifling through their secret files?"

She shook her head.

"Go ahead, then. See what you can dig up on these knights—if anything."

Rowan went down to the bridge. A moment later, he heard her conversing with the computer.

"I'll . . . just go along with her. See if she needs some help," Harry added, blushing.

"Damn!" Xris took out another twist. He stared at it gloomily, thrust it back into the case—the case the king had given to him. "If only I could get hold of Dixter!"

"Maybe we're worried about nothing," Jamil argued. "With the Navy on alert, expecting revolution, the Royal Guard will certainly be taking extra precautions to protect the king."

"Unfortunately, they won't be able to protect him against this type of device," Quong pointed out. "Since it must use an energy beam to explode the micromachines, the device doesn't have to *look* like a weapon. It could look as innocent as . . ." he paused, shrugged, "a microwave oven."

"That's sort of what the damn thing is," Xris said, scanning the file. "Here"—he tossed the file to Quong—"see if it makes sense to you. It reads like a lot of scientific voodoo to me."

Quong read. The more he read, the graver his expression. "It is not voodoo, Xris." He looked up. "They're talking about building a phase-modulated maser with a tungsten core guide in the ten-point-two-hundred-twenty-eight-gigahertz-band transmitter. If they have truly developed such a device, it will do exactly what Snaga Ohme intended it to do. It will kill anyone with micromachines in the bloodstream. It will kill the king."

"How? Explain in words of three syllables or less."

Quong gathered his thoughts. "I said it could look like a microwave oven. That is basically how it works. A microwave oven resonates water molecules when tuned to the correct frequency. This device—they call it a negative wave device—both transmits and pulses energy waves. These waves are designed to cause the crystal power lattice of each micromachine in the king's body to resonate. The resonation causes the lattice to become unstable, the pulsing causes the lattice to shatter. The process takes just over a minute.

"At that time, all of the micromachines in King Dion's body will explode. The explosions will perforate every vein and organ, causing the young man to bleed to death. The pain would be excruciating, a terrible way to die. No matter how quickly medical help arrived, no one could save him. Once the explosions go off, there is no way possible to repair such massive damage.

"I would say these knights are quite serious," Quong added. "They have gone to enormous expense to produce such a device. They intend to use it."

"We can send a message to the king," Jamil offered. "Warn him to cancel all his plans for the next few days. Certainly *that* would get through."

Xris almost laughed. "Do you know how many warnings like this Dion gets every day? His Majesty has a secretary who does nothing but handle death threats. Dion's never let it stop him before. Why would he do so now?"

"We have a saying, 'One who lives in fear of death has already died.' He is a wise young man," Quong remarked.

"He may be a dead young man," Rowan said, climbing up from the cockpit. Harry trailed along behind her. "I found that group. They've got quite a thick file, dating back a good long time. Here's the gist of the report.

"The organization is known as the Knights of the Terra Nera. Translation: the Knights of the Black Earth. This group dates back to the time when Earth—through overpopulation, pollution, and a few local nuclear wars—was starting to become uninhabitable. That was when humans took to the stars.

"Originally, the knights began as a group of environmentalists. They disapproved of space travel. They tried to convince people to remain on Earth, use their talents and money for improving the planet, not abandoning it. But, of course, no one listened.

"At about this time, the knights turned violent. They went from holding passive sit-ins to blowing up rocket-launching sites. But they were unable to stop progress."

"So what's their problem now?" Harry asked. "Are they still against spaceflight?"

"Hardly. Over the years, their organization changed, evolved. That's what has kept them going. According to the information the bureau was able to gather, the Knights of the Black Earth now see their mission as one to preserve mankind's heritage. All things related to Earth are held sacred. The knights' home base is on Earth." Rowan glanced at Tycho. "Anything produced on other, alien planets is considered corrupt. This goes for everything: food, customs—but especially religion.

"To most of us, Earth is a world of skeletal cities, rotting garbage, unbreathable atmosphere. But to the knights, the Terra Nera is holy ground. Only those humans who are born on Earth or who can trace their ancestry back to someone born on Earth are permitted to enter the knighthood."

Rowan looked over at Xris. "The bureau had a heck of a time finding someone who was capable of infiltrating."

"They sent someone in?"

"Yes." Rowan nodded. "The bureau takes this group very seriously. Here's what they found out. And, unfortunately, here's where our theory starts to break down. The knights were pleased when Dion Starfire became king. It seems that his ancestry can be traced back to Earth."

Xris caught on. "So the knights have no reason to kill the king."

Rowan shrugged. "Maybe he did something to make them change their mind."

"You said they were fanatics about Earth-based religions. The queen is a High Priestess of a religion that got its start on another planet. The king's been promoting that religion pretty heavily these days. Maybe that's what got them pissed off," Xris said thoughtfully.

"And maybe that is what this means." Quong referred back to the printout. " 'The king's death will serve as a warning to all nonbelievers. The galaxy will be thrown into chaos, but, since our Knight Commander is a well-known person in a highly visible position, he will arrange for one of our own to take over the government.' "

"It *is* revolution, then," said Jamil grimly. "What the Navy is afraid of happening is going to happen."

"And the Navy will figure that we're the ones making it happen," Xris said.

"And when this machine goes off and the king drops down dead, our lives won't be worth the paper they're printed on," Tycho added darkly, if somewhat obscurely.

"Does the bureau have any idea who this Knight Commander is?"

Rowan shook her head. "The infiltrator couldn't find out. Apparently no one in the knighthood knows for sure. His identity is kept a closely guarded secret, even from his own people."

"Well, what do we do now, boss?" Harry asked.

The others regarded Xris expectantly. He took a twist from its case, stared at it, not them.

"The way I see it, there's only one logical solution. I go to the nearest Naval base. I turn myself in. I tell them this was all my doing, you guys were just obeying orders. I cut a deal."

The others were silent.

Xris didn't see what they were doing; he was looking at the twist. "As for His Majesty, I'll tell them what we know—"

"That's good," Jamil growled. "Plead insanity."

Xris glanced up.

"It won't work, Xris." Rowan shook her head.

He started to argue, but Jamil waved a hand.

"I can see it now. You stroll onto a Naval base, apologize for breaking into their top-secret facility and kidnapping their number-one code expert at gunpoint. Then you tell them that it was all a mistake and you're sorry and oh, by the way, you've discovered a bunch of knights from old Earth who are planning to microwave the king."

"And they send you to the loony planet for twenty years or so," Harry added, grinning. "Not much of a plan, Xris."

"It won't save His Majesty," Quong pointed out. "You yourself said he gets threats like this every day. We're the only ones who know that this threat is real. That these people are both willing and able to put it into action."

"And it may not save you, Xris," Rowan added softly. "Especially if what you predict actually comes to pass. They'll blame you—and they'll execute you."

"I suppose you want to go after these characters yourselves," Xris said, looking around.

One by one, they all nodded.

"I will abide by the decision of the majority." Raoul yawned. Pillowing his head on the Little One's small lap, the Adonian was almost immediately asleep.

Xris suddenly realized how tired he was, bone-hurting, muscle-aching tired. The rest of the team, he guessed, were in much the same condition. They were all casting envious glances at the slumbering Raoul.

"How much time have we got?"

Rowan consulted her watch. "Fifty-eight hours. About two and a half days."

"String up the hammocks," Xris ordered. "We'll get some rest while we can. Odds are we won't be getting much later."

Jamil pulled the rolled-up hammocks out of storage, handed them to Tycho, who strung them across the living quarters. Harry went down to check on the computer. He returned to announce that they'd be coming out of hyperspace in about eight hours, near Olefsky's home planet, and did Xris want to change that?

Xris thought about it, said no. They'd have to find out the king's traveling and speaking schedule, especially where he'd be at the end of fifty-eight hours. Olefsky could do that for them.

Nodding, Harry went back to confirm the course before he went to bed. The others had already climbed into the hammocks and were soon at rest, rocking slowly back and forth with the motion of the spaceplane. Raoul remained where he was, curled up on one of the steel benches, his head on the Little One's lap. The Little One remained awake, one small hand gently stroking Raoul's shining black hair.

Xris paused, stood in front of the Little One. The empath stared up at him with that one bright gleaming eye.

"She's telling me the truth, isn't she?" Xris asked in a soft undertone. "About Armstrong, about the explosion, about everything. She's telling the truth."

The single eye closed, opened again. The fedora bobbed up and down.

"And I've put her life in jeopardy. I've blown her cover. I've killed her just as surely as if I had shot that poisoned needle into her."

The Little One made no response. The single eye flickered. Perhaps he hadn't understood a word Xris had said.

It didn't matter. Xris knew the truth now anyway.

He found his hammock by the lambent light shining from the cockpit down below, where the computer was awake and working. No one else was, except him. The silence of their sleep was thick and warm.

That wouldn't last long. Harry snored; Jamil ground his teeth. Tycho made a weird bubbling noise in his chest, like a teakettle coming to a boil, while Quong occasionally performed surgery in his sleep, talked himself through the operation. But for now, the plane was quiet.

Xris lay in his hammock a long time, staring into the silence.

CHAPTER
30

One man in a thousand, Solomon says,
Will stick more close than a brother . . .
But the Thousandth Man will stand by your side
To the gallows foot—and after!
　　　　　　　Rudyard Kipling, *Rewards and Fairies,*
　　　　　　　　　　　　"The Thousandth Man"

"Xris," said Harry, shaking him by the shoulder. "Xris. Wake up.

We got trouble."

Xris was awake immediately. "What? What's wrong?"

"We came out of hyperspace and contacted Olefsky on that special channel he gave us. He says that your house is under surveillance. Guys in suits. They're monitoring space traffic. I did a long-range scan. There's some sort of big ship around on the far side—"

"Who's got us under surveillance?" Xris tried to wake up.

"Darlene says that it's probably the bureau. Likely they got a make on us from the Navy before communications were shut down."

Xris fumbled for a twist. He eyed Harry. "Darlene?"

Harry blushed. "Major Mohini."

"Rowan."

"All right, then. Rowan. Anyway, I jumped us back outta there. We're in the Lanes again. A short hop. I didn't know what you wanted to do."

Xris didn't, either. He'd planned on communicating their information to Bear Olefsky, but that now appeared to be impossible, what with the bureau crouching in front of the hole, waiting for the mice. Besides, Xris reflected, what could I really tell Olefsky? That he'd believe? Or that would be at all helpful to the king or those guarding him?

Keep on the lookout for a bunch of radical knights wielding a deadly microwave oven?

He started to follow Harry, noticed a red light flashing on his arm. His battery was running low. Opening his leg compartment, he switched packs, put in a fresh charge. When that was done, Xris glanced at his chronometer. The assassination was scheduled to take place fifty-nine hours from when they'd left the *Canis Major*. Subtract ten hours for sleep and travel. They were down to forty-nine hours now.

Xris went forward, descended into the cockpit. He found Rowan awake, looking rumpled and bedraggled. She was sitting in the copilot's chair, staring bleakly out at the unending blackness of hyperspace. She looked depressed, unhappy. Harry looked guilty.

"So what have you two been up to?" Xris demanded.

Harry flushed again. "Nothing," he mumbled.

"Come off it, Harry. You can't lie your way out of a paper bag." A Tychoism.

"Don't blame Harry, Xris." Rowan rested her head on her hand. "I asked him to try to put me through to Dixter."

"I didn't think you'd mind." Harry was defensive.

"I had to, Xris," Rowan continued. "Don't worry. I didn't put us in any danger. The call was brief."

"How brief?"

"Very." Her mouth twisted in that lopsided, sad smile. "Oh, well." She shrugged it off. "I didn't expect anything else."

But it was eating at her. And it occurred to Xris, for the first time, that Rowan had enjoyed life at RFComSec. She had worked long and tirelessly, gained the respect, esteem, and trust of her superiors. It was what—he knew suddenly—she had lived for. That, too, was ruined. Gone, beyond reclamation.

Xris chewed on a twist, but even that noxious weed couldn't eradicate the bitter taste in his mouth. Maybe, just maybe, this was one way he could make things good for her again.

He rested his hand, his good hand, on her shoulder. The movement was awkward, clumsy. But her face was illuminated. She looked up at him.

"I'm sorry," he said softly.

Her eyes dimmed with tears. She placed her hand over his, paused a moment to clear her throat. "I'm not. I hadn't realized . . ." She stopped, swallowed, started over. "I was in prison, Xris. A comfortable cell, but it was prison. Now I'm free. I'm free."

She swiveled the chair to move herself out from beneath his touch, briskly wiped her eyes and dragged her hand across her nose. "If we can't talk to Dixter or Olefsky, we're going to have to go it alone. The first thing we need to do is find out the king's schedule of public appearances. We need to know where he's going to be in two days' time. Because that's where the assassination attempt will take place."

"Ask Raoul," Harry suggested. "He's a Royal watcher. He reads all those gossip mags. If anyone would know, he would."

That was true. Raoul knew everything there was to know about the Royal Family, plus nine-tenths of what there wasn't. Last year, Raoul and the Little One had been honored by a personal visit and commendation from Their Majesties for bravery and valor during the Ghost Legion incident. Raoul now considered himself a friend of the family and deemed it his right and duty to listen to every bit of gossip about their private lives, to know and criticize every dress in Her Majesty's wardrobe, and to comment freely (and severely) on His Majesty's taste in neckwear. The Adonian's fondest dream was to emulate the queen's ability to apply her eyeliner in a subtle, yet highly effective, manner.

Xris climbed back up the stairs to the Schiavona's living quarters. The rest of the team was awake and moving. Tycho and Jamil were both gone and, by the sounds of it, one of them was in the head, the other in the shower. Quong was in some sort of meditative state, his hands folded ceremoniously across his chest.

The Little One was rummaging around in a pack, probably searching for something to eat.

Raoul lay in a relaxed pose across the metal bench. The Loti's eyes were heavy-lidded. He was smiling at nothing, lost, blissful. It wasn't sleep he was drugged on, though where Raoul could have come across anything else was beyond Xris's understanding. Then he glanced at the Little One, at the raincoat, with those capacious pockets. . . . Stupid question.

Xris shook the Loti roughly by the shoulder.

Raoul's smile widened. His eyelids fluttered.

Xris shook him again, dragged Raoul to a sitting position. Raoul leaned back against the bulkhead, opened his eyes, looked at Xris without apparent recognition.

"Come off it, Loti," Xris snapped. "I need information. Have you been keeping up on all your gossip mags?"

Raoul's eyes blinked, semifocused. He sat up straight, looked down at the flight suit he was wearing, sighed deeply, and said in bored tones, "Of course."

"Is there any big event coming up that His Majesty is attending? Something that's being well publicized? Think about it. This is important."

Raoul concentrated. His eyes narrowed, as if he were searching inside a crowded and confused closet. At that point the Little One emerged from the pack holding two bars of chocolate. He handed one to Raoul.

"Ah, yes," the Loti said softly, and lifted his gaze to Xris. "Perfect for them. Absolutely perfect."

"Perfect for who?"

"The knights, of course. You said they were opposed to alien religions. In three days . . ."

The Little One grunted, shook his head.

"Beg pardon." Raoul corrected himself solemnly. "In two days' time, both Their Majesties will be on Ceres to celebrate their wedding anniversary and prepare for the forthcoming birth of the heir to the throne. It is rumored that the king and queen will then participate in the ritual to dedicate the unborn child to the Goddess."

"Which," Rowan added, coming to stand behind Xris, "would infuriate the Knights of the Terra Nera. The king is formally acknowledging a religion established and developed on an alien planet. Not only that, but he's giving his child—who is a descendant of Earth, so to speak—over to this alien culture."

Xris thought it over. "It sounds plausible, but remember—we only get one chance. If we guess wrong—"

"It's more than guessing. It fits with the time frame, doesn't it?" Rowan looked at Raoul, who inclined his head in assent. "The knights have the motive and they'll have the opportunity. The crowds on Ceres will be enormous, plus every reporter in the galaxy will be in attendance. They'll get the publicity they seek."

"Live coverage," said Raoul, "on all the major networks."

"Is there anything else on the king's schedule?" Xris asked. "Anything near that time?"

Raoul devoured the chocolate bar, considered, consulted the Little One by tugging on the sleeve of the raincoat. The Little One responded in the negative.

"All right, everybody," Xris called, "listen up."

Jamil emerged from the shower, stood wrapped in a towel. Tycho left the head, grumbling at Harry's inability to jump into hyperspace without making everyone on board sick as something the cat dragged in. Quong sat up carefully, hung his feet over the edge of the hammock. Harry came from below. Rowan sat down on the edge of the seat beside Raoul. The Little One ceased rummaging.

Xris explained the situation. "This is our one and only shot. If we blow it, we'll never get another. I've got the beginnings of a plan, but it's not subtle. It can't be; we don't have time. The knights, as well as everyone else in the galaxy, will see us coming."

"What if the knights figure we're on to them already and stop the countdown?" Jamil asked. "After all, we did damn near take over their ship."

"All the more reason for them to act immediately," Rowan argued. "Besides, I don't think they're on to us. Look at it from their point of view. We were after our friend. We found him and took him away. What did we see while we were there? Well-armed soldiers on board a research vessel. Okay, it might make us curious. We might figure they're pirates or something, but we're outlaws ourselves. We're not likely to go running to the authorities."

"But we raided their computer—" Jamil protested.

"I erased all my tracks. They'll never be able to tell I was ever in there," said Rowan.

Jamil looked dubiously at Xris.

The cyborg took out a twist, nodded. "If she says she did, she did."

Jamil appeared satisfied.

"Any other questions? No? Then I guess it comes down to this: Do we go for it on Ceres? It's not," Xris added grimly, "going to be easy. You saw those guys on board the *Canis Major*. They're professionals. Fanatics. They're willing to kill for their cause and to die for it, as well. To make matters worse, the whole goddamn universe is out to get *us*, not them. I think we'll be damn lucky if any of us—including the king—come out of this alive. I want you all to know that, up front. And finally— What?" he demanded.

They all looked bored.

Jamil yawned. "Cut to the important part. How much does it pay?"

"The usual."

Jamil grunted. "I don't know. Those guys are awfully good—"

"All right, double."

"Your own personal account, not the corporation's," Tycho said.

Xris shook his head. He was trying to keep from smiling. "My account."

"Before taxes," Tycho insisted.

"Before taxes," Xris agreed.

Jamil thought it over, raised a hand, thumb up.

Tycho, doing some rapid calculating, indicated he was satisfied by turning a rosy shade of pink.

Harry, confused, said, "What's before taxes?"

Raoul, his eyes closed against the boredom of discussing business, nudged the Little One, who tipped his fedora in response.

Quong removed a small pocket computer, made a notation, studied it, pursed his lips, then, returning the computer to his pocket, he crossed his arms over his chest—an indication that he accepted the deal.

Rowan stared at them, shocked, disapproving. "This is your king! And for that matter, Xris is your friend—"

Xris laid a hand on her shoulder, silenced her.

"She's been in the Navy seven years," Xris said, in apology.

The others solemnly nodded.

Patriotism, loyalty, the last full measure. Crap. For the team, it all came down to plastic credits. Or so they made it seem. They were doing this for him. But they had to make it look good—in front of strangers.

Someday, Xris thought, I'll have to explain things to her.

He glared around at the now-grinning group, pretended to be angry. "You characters drive a hard bargain. I'll have to think about it."

Jamil waved a negligent hand. "Sure, take your time. Tycho here'll draw up the contract. Oh, and, speaking of time, how much do we have?"

"Forty-eight hours."

"You said you had a plan."

"I've been thinking about it some, yes," Xris admitted, taking out a twist and lighting it.

"What's our first move?"

Xris took a drag on the twist. "We go shopping."

Raoul opened his eyes.

CHAPTER
31

I came like Water, and like Wind I go.
  Edward FitzGerald, *The Rubáiyát of Omar Khayyám*

The long-range Schiavona slid out of the Lane and into the warm glow of Rengazi, an orange-yellow star circled by ten bustling, self-important planets. Located near an intersection of several highly traveled hyperspace lanes, Rengazi had been one of the first systems reached by human explorers. The climates of the various planets had not been at all suitable to human habitation, but the humans, noted among the galaxy's races for their energy, ambition, and eagerness to make money, had either adapted to the mineral-rich planets' environments or forced the planets to adapt to them.

Consequently, Rengazi boasted the first major settlement to be established off-Earth. The fact that the settlers had all perished in a bioplague—caused by an attempt to cross Earth and native plant species, resulting in the creation of several amazingly deadly viruses—was beside the point. A statue had been erected to the intrepid humans, who looked particularly prehistoric and clunky in their bubble-shaped headgear and bulky space suits. A small matter such as lethal viruses had not kept the humans away long. Now space traffic in the area was crowded, congested. One long-range Schiavona with official Naval markings went unnoticed.

The tenth planet, Zen Rengazi, was the most distant from the sun and, consequently, the least populated. Primarily a mining planet, it was also home to a large penal institution—a fact Jamil noted with grim irony—and its most important feature, as far as the team was concerned, was a NOROF, or Navy Orbital Rebuild and Overhaul Facility.

Harry set the Schiavona's course for that destination.

"Not quite the shopping trip I had in mind," Raoul remarked, sniffing.

Xris gave the Adonian a soothing pat in passing, entered the cockpit.

"Malfunctions working?" he asked with a wry grin.

Harry gazed intently at the instrument panel; he'd shut down the computer's shocked warnings and frantic squawks of alarm.

"Yeah." Harry wiped sweat from his face. "We now have no shields. Of any sort." He gazed out at the enormous orbital platform—shining like a metal moon—emerging from the far side of the planet. "I hope to hell you're right about them not having any guns."

Xris smiled, gave Harry a soothing pat. "Relax. That'd be like arming your neighborhood garage."

"Where I grew up, the mechanics carried more'n grease in their guns," Harry muttered, gloomily watching an array of angry red lights begin to flash on the console. "Should I transmit the distress signal now?"

Xris looked around. Jamil, Rowan, Quong, Harry, and himself were in Naval uniform. Rowan wore her own, which she'd been wearing when she took this unexpected trip. The rest were outfitted from the team's extensive "wardrobe," as Raoul termed it. Impersonating Naval personnel was highly illegal, of course, and if captured, they could all be executed as spies, but since, if captured, they were all likely to be executed anyway, Xris didn't figure it much mattered. When flying a long-range Schiavona with military markings, it made sense to dress the part, and he'd ordered the uniforms brought on board against just such a contingency.

If anyone at NOROF bothered to check, they'd find out that the Schiavona was registered as belonging to Olefsky's "home guard" and that the uniforms should also be "home guard," but with communications shut down because of Operation Macbeth, NOROF wouldn't be able to check.

"At least this damn Macbeth's turned out to be good for something," Jamil had remarked irritably.

Tycho wasn't wearing a uniform—no human-issue type would fit the alien's tall, slender physique. But he had obligingly changed skin color in order to blend in. Raoul had tucked his long hair up under his hat, was dressed in uniform, sort of—if one discounted the glittering rhinestone earrings and other pieces of gaudy jewelry he'd added to "liven things up." Since the Adonian was to remain on board the plane, with orders to participate in the raid only in case of emergency, Xris hadn't wasted time in arguing. Raoul was applying his lipstick with particular care—it was the poisoned variety. Xris watched a moment, turned away. He hoped to God it wouldn't come to that.

As for the Little One's disguise, Raoul had pinned commander's bars onto the fedora—with what intent or purpose Xris had no idea and knew better than to ask. He started to pull out a twist, decided against it, stashed the case in his pocket. He might be picked up on visual and he had to look the part.

"We're ready. Begin transmission."

Harry flipped a switch, activated the distress signal. He sat back, wiped his face again.

The response was immediate.

"Navy Four Four Lima Three, this is Zen Rengazi Naval Control. Do you receive me?"

Harry opened a vid channel. "Zen Rengazi, this is Navy Lima Three. We are declaring an in-space emergency. We require landing clearance at your facility."

The female ensign whose face appeared on the screen didn't blink, didn't pause. "Navy Four Four Lima Three, you are *not* cleared for docking. Repeat: *Do not dock.* Proceed to the civilian facility at Veer Rengazi."

"Damn it, Zen Rengazi!" Harry banged his fist on the console. "Your own fuckin' censors should tell you that we can't survive a planetary landing! Our goddamn computer's malfunctioning and our goddamn shielding's down and that includes our goddamn heat shields! Ma'am," he added belatedly.

Harry's anger and frustration weren't all play-acting. His sweat was real. He'd actually shut the shields down and there was nothing more vulnerable in space than a Schiavona with no shields.

Rowan had warned them that the Naval facility wouldn't dare countermand the orders given under Operation Macbeth. Xris's contention was that the commander of one insignificant NOROF post—which, since it was unarmed, couldn't possibly be considered a threat to anyone—would be likely to make an exception in the case of a dire emergency. He waited tensely to see which of them had been right.

As usual—it was Rowan.

The ensign's face hardened; so did her voice.

"Navy Four Four Lima Three. I repeat: *Do not dock!* We are on red-alert status. We cannot allow you to dock. We can activate a tractor beam, hold you in place for the duration—"

"Cut communication," Xris ordered.

The screen went dark. Xris hoped NOROF would figure they were having power problems as well. "Back off. The last thing we need is a blasted tractor beam grabbing hold of us! What'd the sensor scan pick up? Anything we can use?"

"Hang on a minute."

While Harry was studying the scan, Xris stared out the viewscreen at NOROF—which looked exactly like a large and shining metal ball covered with spikes. Each spike was, in actuality, a docking arm. Ships arriving at the facility would maneuver to connect to the end of one of the arms. Once attached, the arm would lower the vessel to the main body of the station, if major overhaul or rebuild was required. Minor repairs could be effected while the ship was attached to the arm.

Xris counted twenty vessels of various types docked at the facility—a light load, considering that each NOROF could accommodate well over one hundred at a time. As he watched, the docking clamps on all of the arms retracted and the arms began to pull back telescopically into the station. NOROF was serious.

"Shit!" Xris swore. All he could see were frigates, and they wouldn't be of any use whatsoever. He looked at the chronometer. Twenty-four hours. It had taken them half an SMT day to find this place, another half day to reach it. This time tomorrow, unless they stopped the assassins, the young king might be dead.

"I thought you told me there were two drop ships docked here," he said over his shoulder to Rowan.

"There are, according to the parts requisitions I found," she maintained. "They specifically listed two drop ships, located at this site. One is an LST-208 and the other—"

"Got it!" Harry announced triumphantly. "Sensors are picking up two drop ships, both on the other side of the facility. One's an LST-208 and the other is a 209."

"Let's take a look."

Harry was dubious. "Are you sure, Xris? They might suspect what we're after."

"Hijacking a drop ship? Not likely. They'll figure we're hanging around sulking, trying to make them feel guilty. Take it slow. Don't make it look obvious. Oh, and go back on the comm. Whine a little."

Harry whined. The NOROF ensign was overly patient, as if dealing with a child having a temper tantrum. The Schiavona glided, apparently aimlessly, around to the far side of NOROF where they worked on the larger vessels.

And there were the two drop ships. One was obviously in dry dock. It had been lowered to the main portion of the facility. Covered with scaffolding, the drop ship looked like a bug caught in a steel web. But the other . . .

Harry, whining and sulking, once again ended communications.

"That's our ship," he announced. "The LST-209—there, on the docking arms. Sensors indicate the engines are still operational. It doesn't look like they've started any major work. My guess is that the ship's being prepped for overhaul."

"Bring it up on visual," Xris ordered.

Harry brought it up, adding magnification. The drop ship filled the screen.

"It sure is a weird-looking son of a bitch. Sort of like a grasshopper holding on to a pie plate. I've seen 'em before but I've never flown on one. You, Xris?"

Xris shook his head. "The major has, though. This was his idea. Jamil! Come take a look at this!"

Jamil came clattering down the stairs, stood behind the pilot's chair. "I served on several when I was in Special Forces. The drop ship's actually two separate units. That part you call the grasshopper"—he pointed—"is the command module. Where the cargo hold would be on a normal ship is the landing module. They cut the cargo hold out, leaving the supports and ductwork that connects the engines at the rear of the command module to the bridge. The 'legs' hold the landing module on during flight. When we orbit the planet, the landing module disconnects, drops to the planet's surface."

"The landing module has no maneuvering controls, no

way to fly itself, huh?" Harry asked, regarding the drop ship with interest.

"It has inertial nullifiers," Jamil responded, adding with a grin, "That's so you don't end up as space mush plastered on the ceiling when you land. Even so, it's pretty rough. We call the ride down the 'elevator to hell.' The landing module's intended for ground-based deployment. Like I told Xris earlier, the landing module normally houses a mission command bunker and a bay holding small armored attack vehicles. Our Special Forces unit was moving on the ground less than five minutes after touchdown. Once the mission is complete, the blast rockets under the landing module fire, lift the module into orbit. We rendezvous with the command module, reattach."

Harry was giving the drop ship the once-over. "Not much in the way of weapons. Why's that? You Army guys working in favor of gun control?"

"The command module has special intruder shields," Jamil said. "A destroyer could blow up a ship that size with one lascannon tied behind its back, to quote friend Tycho. And generally, when you're on a special mission, you don't want to alert the local bad guys to your arrival. Once in space, these shields go up, and the drop ship is—to all intents and purposes—invisible. Of course, if anyone actively goes looking for it, they'll find it. But you've got to know it's there first.

"The landing module is armed to the teeth, though. Once on the ground, you want a good firebase for operations. See over there? That's the lasgun turret and below it is the vehicle bay door. This thing is a fortress once it hits dirt."

"Sounds perfect," Tycho said, leaning over the rail, peering down into the cockpit. "Now how do you suggest we get hold of it? They won't even let us dock."

Xris took out a twist, thrust it in his mouth. They were no longer in visual contact with NOROF, and besides, he was going to give them a lot more to worry about than the fact that a Naval officer was caught smoking on duty.

"Harry, can you land the Schiavona on top of the command module?"

"Shit, I could land this thing on Tycho's head if you wanted me to."

"Maybe next time. The facility doesn't have any guns; all

we have to worry about is that damn tractor beam locking on to us."

"They have to catch us first. I can do it, Xris, but it'll be a wild ride."

"Oh, dear God!" Tycho rolled his eyes. "I hate it when he says that!"

"Strap yourselves in good," Xris warned, and gave Harry the go-ahead.

Harry permitted the computer to return, ordered it to go into combat mode but advised it to leave the shields down until further orders. The computer began rerouting and shutting off some systems, activating others. The interior lights dimmed to emergency status only; the supply of cool air was cut off, replaced by circulating air. It would soon grow moderately warm in the living quarters. Power to onboard amenities was cut. No showers, no hot food, no flushing the head. Tycho and Jamil climbed into the gun turrets. A bombardier wasn't needed; they'd opt for speed over heavy weaponry.

When each person reported ready, Harry nodded his head slowly, placed his big hands on the controls. On his face, an expression of intense concentration—which Xris had come to associate with these times—replaced the slightly foolish and occasionally goofy look Harry generally wore. Almost like an idiot savant, Harry was good at only one thing—flying. But he was supremely good at that, one of the best pilots Xris had ever known.

Harry melded with the plane in some strange way, as if it were just another body part. Weird to watch and see in action, scary to be along for the ride, but worth it at the end. Or so Xris hoped.

"I'm taking over manual control," Harry said, and even his voice sounded different—confident, deeper. "When I give the signal, computer, activate shields. Brace yourselves," he added for the benefit of everyone on board. "This is going to be one mother of a dive. *Now!*"

Shields came on. NOROF, picking this up on their sensors, wouldn't be overly concerned. They'd probably be relieved, in fact, figuring that this nuisance of a Schiavona had managed to repair itself and would now fly away and leave NOROF in peace. They were going to be in for a shock.

The Schiavona rocketed through space, traveling far too fast near a solid, massive object such as the orbital platform. The highly unpleasant sensation of negative Gs dropped the stomach down around the bowels, jumped the heart into the throat. The plane hurtled forward. The orbital platform seemed to be rushing at them. It grew and swelled at an alarming rate.

Slow down, Harry, Xris found himself ordering mentally. You've got to slow down! We'll crash! We're going to crash!

But he didn't order aloud and Harry didn't slow down. He wouldn't have heard Xris anyway. Harry was thinking, feeling, reacting, responding only to his plane.

The orbital platform was coming at them so fast that objects on it were now clearly visible, or would have been if they hadn't merged into a dizzying blur because of the dive.

The computer warned of approaching impact.

Harry flew on. Heat vectors, rising from the platform, began to buffet the plane. It bounded from side to side, lurched wildly up and down. Cries and howls echoed throughout the plane as the team members made involuntary and painful contact with certain hard objects. Xris managed to turn his head, which was plastered against the back of the chair, looked up into the living quarters. Rowan, white to the lips, was staring with wide eyes at the viewscreen, at certain death. Quong, seated beside her, had shut his eyes, his lips moving either in prayer, a mantra, cursing Harry, or maybe all three.

The computer announced imminent collision.

Xris decided that shutting his eyes was a wonderful idea. He heard a crunching sound, wondered vaguely what it was, paid it no attention. He would discover, later, that he had gripped the chair arm so hard, his cybernetic hand had crushed the metal.

Through a dry throat, with a dry tongue, he managed to croak, "Harry, stop—"

Harry had been, in actuality, slowing their rate of descent, a fact that wasn't immediately obvious—they had drawn so close to the platform that the proximity made it appear as if they were going faster. At the instant when it seemed to Xris that he could count the number of rivets in the deck plates, Harry brought the spaceplane out of the dive.

They were flying among the docking arms, weaving in and out, dodging through a forest of girders and cranes and metal scaffolding. The Schiavona flipped and rolled and sailed up and slid down and went around and over and slipped in between such tight cracks that Xris was certain he could have gone back and found that they'd left paint streaks from their hull on the platform's steel beams.

The grasshopper body of the LST loomed ahead of them. Xris again opened his mouth. Harry, with a look on his face of wondrous satisfaction, eased back on the controls. The spaceplane changed instantly from a darting demon to a delicate dancer. It floated, glided, and finally set down on top of the command module with a very slight, very gentle bump.

Xris breathed.

"I think I peed my pants," came the plaintive bleat of Tycho's translator.

CHAPTER
32

When on surrounded ground, plot. When on deadly ground, fight.

Sun Tzu, *The Art of War*

"I'll give everybody time to catch your breath and throw up, if you have to," Xris said, unstrapping himself.

He reached into the storage compartment in his steel leg. After that wild and unnerving ride, he wouldn't have been surprised to pull out his stomach. Instead, he replaced his steel hand with his weapons hand, issued orders.

"Jamil, Tycho, Doc, you're with me. Harry, program the Schiavona for a return flight and send it back to Olefsky. Rowan, help Harry on the computer. Raoul, you and the Little One sit tight and wait for further orders. Everyone got that?"

Everyone did, with the possible exception of Raoul, who had lost an earring during landing and was searching through the seat cushions for it.

Xris left his chair, headed for the airlock. The Schiavona had two airlocks, one located on the deck and one up above, in between the gun turrets. Harry had set the plane down on top of the command module and so Xris went to the lower deck airlock. He waited until he heard the magnets clamp on, then tapped the control to override the safeties. He found himself staring—not at another hatch, but at solid durasteel hull plating.

"What the—Harry, you missed the hatch!"

"There isn't one," Harry said serenely, still on an exhilarated high. "Didn't I mention that?"

"How the hell are we supposed to get on board the damn drop ship?" Xris demanded.

"Spacewalk," Harry advised.

Tycho scoffed. "We'd be target practice out there, like sitting ducks in a barrel."

"Cut through the plating," Harry suggested after a moment's profound thought.

"Great!" Xris fumed. "So we fly merrily around the galaxy in a drop ship with a goddam hole in it!"

"Calm down, Xris," Rowan said crisply. She managed a strained smile; she was still pale and shaky. "We're in an overhaul-and-rebuild facility. We'll cut through the plating, then patch it back up. Most of these ships are designed to assist in repairs. If I can get to the computer, I can—"

"All right, all right." Xris knew where that conversation could lead and he didn't have time. Resignedly, he took off his weapons hand, replaced it with his tool hand. "Someone find a cutting torch."

The plasma cutting torch melted through the metal efficiently, but far too slowly—at least as far as Xris was concerned. He'd counted on swooping in, grabbing the drop ship, blasting out before anyone quite caught on to what was happening. But it took half an hour to cut through the hull plating supports, time enough for NOROF to call in a fleet of Naval battleships.

He swore softly and fretted, until he remembered Operation Macbeth. NOROF couldn't even call home to Mother, let alone squawk for help. Still, a Naval facility was more than likely to be able to take care of itself in an emergency.

"What do you suppose they're doing in there?" Xris had to yell over the hissing of the torch. He gestured in the direction of the main NOROF building.

"Handing out the guns," Jamil answered grimly.

Xris grunted, returned to work.

The last support melted away, the hull plate fell, hit the deck below with an ear-shattering clang. Xris peered inside, could see nothing. The interior of the command module was in semidarkness, lit only by various red, blue, and green instrument lights and the faint glow of computer screens.

"That should be the bridge," said Jamil, squatting down for a look.

They kept their voices low, although after the racket the hull plate had made, whispering seemed a bit ludicrous.

"You couldn't prove it by me," Xris muttered, replacing his tool hand with his weapons hand. "Jamil, you know your way around—you go first. Set weapons on stun. We're trying to save lives, not end them."

"That include ours?" Jamil grumbled.

Carrying his beam rifle, he jumped through the hole. Xris heard a clatter and a soft curse.

"You okay?" he asked softly.

"Landed on top of a goddamn chair." Jamil groaned. "Banged hell out of my knee. I—"

A bright flash of light ended the conversation. Jamil hit the deck. The shot hit the chair.

"Marines," Jamil reported, reverting to his comm. "The door leading from our position on the drop ship's bridge to the facility's airlock is standing wide open. The Marines must be in the airlock itself. They have a clear shot at us through the door. Their weapons are *not* set on stun!"

The chair's upholstery was starting to smolder.

"Can you reach the controls to shut the door?" Xris asked.

"I can try." Jamil rose to a crouch, using the chair for cover. He made a tentative move.

A laser blast nearly took off his head.

He flattened back down. "They've got scopes, infrared."

"Damn!" Xris sat back on his heels, tried to think. "Tycho, get down there. See what you can do."

Tycho dropped lightly through the hole, carrying his favored sniper rifle. He was nothing but a blur in the shadowy darkness, yet laser fire zipped and crackled all around him. He dropped on all fours, crouched like a spider, and skittered for cover behind a navigator's platform.

"They've got them pinned down," Xris reported for the benefit of the rest of the team. "Probably jammed the door open. I'm going to have to try to shut it manually, using the emergency override. Doc, we'll need some of those sleepgas grenades—"

He was interrupted by sounds of a scuffle from down below. More laser blasts.

"Hold your fire!" Jamil shouted to the Marines, using Standard Military. "We've got a hostage! Talk to 'em, kid."

Xris heard a whimper.

"I said talk to 'em!"

"Don't . . . don't shoot!" came a frightened croak.

Xris jumped into the hole. He remembered about the chair

at the last moment, clumsily attempted to swing wide, and missed, but just barely. He ended up slamming his good elbow into the chair's back.

"Doc, watch out for that damn chair when you come down. Tycho, turn on some light. They might as well get a good look at us. Who've we got?"

Jamil, on his hands and knees, had something by the throat up against a bulkhead. Tycho crouched back to back with Jamil, rifle raised, alert and watchful. Quong dropped onto the deck, flourished the sleep-gas grenades, and ducked behind the chair. At Xris's command, Tycho scuttled sideways over to the console, found the switch, activated the lights.

The door was wide open. Beyond—the narrow tunnel of the airlock. At the opposite end, Xris counted five Marine sharpshooters. Anyone going anywhere near that door would be toast.

Keeping well clear, Xris edged his way around the bulkheads to look at their captive.

"Don't . . . don't shoot me, mister!"

It was a kid, maybe eighteen, dressed in coveralls and carrying a torque wrench in his shaking hand. He was wretched and scared to the point of passing out.

"Artificer's mate, third class," Jamil said, indicating the rank on the uniform. "Mechanic. I found him hiding underneath the navigator's platform."

The kid's eyes rolled in his head. "Don't shoot me!" The torque wrench slid from nerveless fingers, fell on the deck.

"He was probably working in here, panicked when he heard our ship land, and froze."

"I don't care if the angels dropped him down from heaven," Xris said. "It's about time something went right for a change. Come here, kid. We're going to take a walk. If everyone keeps calm"—Xris raised his voice for the benefit of the Marines—"no one'll get hurt!"

Jamil shoved the unresisting boy at Xris, who caught hold of the kid by the arm.

Weapon hand raised, his other hand—his good hand—dragging the kid along, Xris edged toward the open door. He walked into the sights of the Marines, could almost see them scowl in disappointment and frustration when the interior lights reflected off Xris's metal body parts.

"Yeah," said Xris loudly, walking as he talked, keeping

the hostage near him, "you sharpshooters might hit me and miss the kid, but what good will that do you? Very few parts of me bleed. And with your first shot, either I take out the kid here or one of my team shoots him.

"Believe it or not"—Xris was coming closer and closer to the door controls—"we're on the same side. There's been a little misunderstanding, that's all. If you can get hold of the Lord Admiral, tell Dixter that Major Mohini's no traitor. Neither are we."

The Marines were watching every move. The barrels of their beam rifles followed Xris as he went. At his side, plastered against him, the hostage was sweating and gulping, but at least he hadn't fainted.

"You're doing good, kid," Xris said to the boy, to keep him going. If the kid went limp on him, it'd all be over. "You won't get any medals for this, but with luck you'll live to tell your grandkids about it."

The controls were a lunge away. Xris braced himself for the jump. Out of the corner of his eye, he saw Jamil, Tycho, and Quong prepared to lay down covering fire.

"One last thing, kid," Xris said quietly, "tell the Lord Admiral that the king's life is in danger. Twenty-four hours from now. On Ceres. You got that?"

The kid stared at him, baffled, befuddled by fear. Xris doubted if what he'd said had made it through to the terror-crazed youngster. Not that it much mattered. NOROF wouldn't be able to contact Dixter even if they wanted to. Still, it was worth a try.

"When I shove, you hit the deck. Keep your head down," Xris advised, and, with all his strength, he heaved the boy through the door. In the same motion, the cyborg made the lunge for the door controls.

Either the boy took Xris's advice or he had sense enough to know what was going to happen. He dove for the deck, hugged metal. Laser fire burned through the air above him.

Xris's good hand yanked the emergency lever on the airlock, pulled it down. Screeching and grinding, the door began to swing shut. Xris had a final glimpse of the Marines attempting to rush it.

Quong tossed two sleep-gas grenades out the rapidly closing gap. An invention of Raoul's, the grenades looked like the real thing, but instead of exploding, they emitted a gas that would send every oxygen-breathing person on a quick trip straight to the arms of Morpheus.

The last Xris saw, the kid, still lying on the deck, was valiantly attempting to kick one of the grenades back toward Xris.

Kid's braver than he thinks. He might get a medal after all, Xris said to himself.

The door was only half a centimeter from closing. Groping for the controls to seal the door shut, Xris heard a hissing sound. He smelled a not unpleasant odor, was suddenly fuzzy and light-headed. Everything on the other side of the door had gone very quiet.

The door shut, sealed. Xris locked it, then sagged onto the deck. Quong and the others hurried to him, their faces worried, anxious. He waved them off.

"I'm all right. Just caught a whiff of Raoul's slumbertime concoction." Xris coughed, shook his head, fighting an overwhelming desire to take a nap. "Jamil, you and Tycho see if there are any more nasty surprises hiding inside the landing module. Doc, get everyone else down here and then replace that hull plate."

"I doubt if there's anyone in here," Jamil said.

Limping on his injured knee, he headed for the airlock that led from the command module to the launch module below. "This is the only access."

He hauled the airlock open. He and Tycho disappeared below.

Quong touched his comm, but at that moment Rowan appeared, swinging herself from the hole, jumping lightly to the deck below.

"Toss my equipment down," she ordered someone—probably Raoul—above.

A duffel descended with a thump, followed by Raoul.

"I've lost an earring," he announced plaintively. "I don't suppose anyone's seen it?"

Xris struggled to get back on his feet, touched the comm. "Harry, you finished up there?"

"The Schiavona's programming is complete. She'll fly back to Olefsky—"

"With *my* earring!" Raoul mourned. He stood beneath the hole, waiting to assist the Little One. "What good is one earring? I'm lopsided—"

"Start handing down the gear," Xris commanded.

"Right." Harry signed off.

Rowan was at the command module computer. Quong was searching the bridge for tools. Xris walked over to the airlock that led down into the landing module.

"Any problems?" he called.

"Nope. Looking good," Jamil reported. "It hasn't been unloaded yet. We've got one armored vehicle. Under wraps—"

"Computer reports indicate that it's in good working order," Rowan said, bringing up the files. "It's a PVC-48 Devastator, if that means anything to you. It doesn't to me."

Jamil grunted. "Yeah. Well, it could or it couldn't. I don't suppose I have time—"

Xris shook his head.

"All right. Later. We have supplies and rations for a ten-day mission. Weapons, gas masks. Makes me feel nostalgic." Jamil looked up through the airlock, grinned. "Like you said, about time something went right."

"Don't break out the champagne. We're not out of this yet," Xris advised. He was wondering why the Marines weren't continuing their attempt to retake the drop ship. It wasn't like them to give up. "Make sure everything's secure down there."

Straightening, he saw the Little One—arms outspread, legs dangling—being lowered through the hole.

"You got him?" Harry called from above.

"I'm not tall enough!" Raoul returned. He glanced around. "Xris, could you—"

The cyborg clumped over, reached up. Harry let go and the Little One fell into Xris's arms. He stood the empath on his feet. Raoul straightened the Little One's hat, which had been knocked askew on landing.

"I've lost my earring," Raoul told his friend.

The Little One shook his head.

Xris, shaking *his* head, caught and stowed the rest of the gear. He had just finished when he heard Rowan give a low whistle. In the old days, Xris had come to hate that sound.

"Trouble," said Rowan.

Xris hurried over. "What? The Marines trying to blast open the door?"

"Huh?" Rowan stared at him. "Oh, that. No." She waved her hand airily. "I managed to break into their computer, shut the door that leads to the airlock. Then I changed the codes. And because of the new safety standards that were instituted after the disaster two years ago on board *Valiant*, they'll have to—"

"Then what's the trouble?" Xris broke in impatiently.

Rowan turned to face him. "We have no fuel. In other words, we're out of gas."

CHAPTER
33

Take calculated risks. That is quite different from
being rash.

> General George Smith Patton,
> Letter to Cadet George S. Patton,
> June 6, 1944

"No fuel pod? Standard operating procedure," said
Harry. He was red in the face and puffing, having unloaded all the gear, weapons, flight suits and helmets, the
medical supplies, and what was left of the food.

"Safety measure," added Rowan. "It's the first thing they
do when a ship goes into dry dock. According to the manual,
all fuel pods are to be—"

"Fuck the manual!" Xris swore in bitter anger. "You mean
to tell me we took over this bloody ship and now we can't
go anywhere in it? And you two *knew* about this?"

"Not exactly," Harry said, shamefaced. "I mean, I did, but
I didn't, if you know what I mean."

"In all the excitement, it never occurred to me," Rowan
admitted, her cheeks burning. "Sorry, Xris. I should have
thought ahead—"

"Don't think, damn it! Do something!" Xris was shouting.
He knew he was shouting, knew he was losing it, but he
couldn't help himself.

Jamil poked his head up out of the landing module.
"What's the problem?"

Harry and Rowan looked at each other. Rowan bit her lip,
turned back to the computer. The Little One had shrunk to
almost nothing, was cowering behind Raoul.

"Excuse me, Xris." Quong was attempting to refit the hull

plate. "Could you lend me a hand with this? Your tool hand, preferably." He chuckled, looked around, grinning. "That's a joke."

Xris, grim-faced, strode over.

Quong was perched on the infamous chair, holding the hull plate in place with one hand.

"Calm down, my friend," he said in a low voice. "We are all doing the best we can under very trying circumstances."

"Yeah, Doc, I know." Xris took out a twist, stuck it in his mouth. "What do you need me to do?"

"I have shut the airlock on the Schiavona. Now we must—"

"The Schiavona!" Rowan cried.

"That's it!" Harry said excitedly.

"What's it?" Xris demanded.

They spoke simultaneously. "We can use the fuel pod from the Schiavona!"

"Will it fit?"

"Of course!" Harry sounded nonchalant, but he wiped his forehead and heaved a relieved sigh when he thought Xris wouldn't notice.

Rowan issued orders to the drop ship's computer, told it to tie in to the Schiavona's onboard computer.

"You're positive this will work." Xris had come to expect trouble. "The Schiavona's nowhere near the size of this command module—"

"Doesn't matter. All fuel pods for all ships are interchangeable," Harry explained. "They're made that way on purpose so that the Navy can rescue ships that run out of gas. It's been standard Naval policy for years."

"Safety measure," said Rowan in a solemn tone.

Xris looked over at her.

Rowan caught his eye, smiled, and winked. Then she went back to work. "I've initiated fuel pod ejection. . . ."

Xris fitted on his tool hand, climbed onto the chair, began to weld the hull plate into place.

"I thought Rowan said this blasted ship could heal itself," Xris muttered.

Quong watched the job with a critical eye. "It will. When activated, the drop ship's internal damage systems will detect any air leak in the hull. Once you have the plate welded into place, the ship will check it out for the tiniest leaks and cracks—those we couldn't even begin to see, but which can grow and split a plane apart in hyperspace. The ship will inject sealing fluid on the outside of the hull around the breach. This way we don't have to spend six days crawling over the hull with fancy equipment looking for cracks the size of one of Raoul's false eyelashes."

"*If* it works," Xris said gloomily.

"It will work, my friend," Quong said gently. "It will work. Can you take over from here? I'll go initiate the repair program."

Xris nodded, grateful for the opportunity to be left alone. He let his mind drift and odd thoughts came into it, the oddest being that Rowan was certainly pretty and that this fact irritated and bothered him. Xris didn't like to think of his friend as pretty. He didn't want to think of Rowan as womanly in any way, shape, or form. Rowan *wasn't* a woman. . . .

Any more than I'm a machine, Xris said to himself.

A heavy thud shook the vessel. Xris shut down his welder, looked over to Harry for an explanation.

"Fuel pod dropping into place."

Harry had taken his seat in the pilot's chair—right next to the chair on which Xris was standing. Rowan moved to the navigator's position, was forced to squeeze past Quong, who had to sidestep Raoul, who tripped over the Little One. Everybody was tumbling over the gear.

The bridge hadn't appeared small until now. Jamil, watching from below in the launch module, his head poking up out of the deck, had a suggestion. "All those not needed up there can ride down here. It's meant to work that way, in fact."

"We're certainly not needed," Raoul said thankfully. "And I have to redo my makeup."

Meaning he had to remove the poisoned lipstick before he accidentally poisoned himself. Retrieving his handbag, he helped the Little One to his feet. The two of them descended, with Jamil's assistance, through the airlock. Quong remained to finish his computer work, then he, too, departed.

Xris inspected the hull plate, climbed down off the chair. He took off his tool hand, stowed it away, replaced it with a hand fitted with smaller tools, designed for more delicate work—in case any of the computers went down or needed adjusting.

"We have fuel enough in the command module for the

jump to Ceres," Rowan reported, completing the calculations. "And maybe a short hop after that."

"Just get us to Ceres," Xris said. Chewing on the twist, he sat down in the copilot's chair, glanced back up at the hull plate. "I hope to hell that thing holds. Don't shake this baby around too much, will you, Harry?"

Harry gulped, glanced sideways, cleared his throat loudly.

"What now?" Xris demanded.

"NOROF's locked us out of the docking computer. I can't retract the mooring clamps."

"What *can* you do?" Xris asked resignedly. He was, he realized, almost past caring.

"Well . . ." Harry ruminated. "I can try to rip us free, using full engine power. But that hull plate might give—"

"I don't think so," Rowan reported, studying her screen. "According to the stress factor calculations—"

"Do it," said Xris. "Put on vacuum suits and helmets, just in case." He stood up, went to the airlock, peered down into the launch module. The rest of the team were settled into their seats. "I'm going to shut this, seal you guys off. This may be a bumpy ride. Hold tight."

The last he heard, Tycho was asking worriedly, "Where's the head?"

Xris shut and sealed the airlock, then began struggling into the bulky and cumbersome flight suit.

"Of course, once we get free"—Harry eyed Xris nervously—"we have to dodge that tractor beam. And then—"

Xris held up his hand. "Just answer me this." He put on his helmet. "Has anyone ever made the jump with a hole in his spaceship?"

"If they have, they haven't come back to talk about it," Harry replied.

Xris nodded, settled himself in his seat, strapped himself in. "Just checking. All right. Let 'er rip."

The commander of NOROF stood beside the operations officer. Both of them were staring intently out the gigantic observation screen.

"They're breaking free," said the commander.

"Yes, sir," Ops returned. "Sorry, sir, but those mooring clamps were never meant to hold under that kind of pressure."

"Can engineering lock the tractor beam onto them?"

"No, sir. We're faced with the same situation we had when they flew in here. That pilot is damn good. Begging your pardon, sir, but it's like trying to track a mosquito with a flashlight. We can hit the ship with the beam, but the second we're ready to lock on, he's flown out of it."

"Very well." The commander stared back out the viewscreen.

Ops shrugged, shook his head. "Maybe if we had tracking equipment as sophisticated as those on the big cruisers . . ." He shrugged again.

"Maybe." The commander agreed. He watched in silence as the hijacked drop ship successfully eluded all attempts to capture it.

"They've jettisoned their spaceplane," Ops reported. "We've got hold of it."

"Nice we can do something," the commander said acidly.

"Yes, sir," replied Ops. "Hijacked ship has made the jump, sir."

The commander could see that for himself. The drop ship had disappeared into the black void of the Lane. The commander returned to his office.

The debriefings of the Marines who had attempted to stop the hijacking were on his desk. Also the interview with the artificer third class who had been taken hostage. The commander read them, pondered them, read them again.

Odd, he thought. Damn odd.

He reflected, then he gave his computer instructions.

"Put me through to Naval Headquarters, the Lord Admiral. Use the emergency code. Bring them up on-screen."

He sat back and waited. It didn't take long. A pleasant-faced young officer appeared. "I am sorry, Commander, but due to Operation Macbeth, your access has been denied. Please refer to Section 8, paragraph—"

"I know, Lieutenant," the commander cut in crisply. "I need to leave a message. The matter is urgent, of the highest importance. I can do that much, can't I? Belay that," he added hastily, guessing by the lieutenant's frown that he was about to cut the commander off. "Tell the Lord Admiral or whoever needs to know that the men he's after—that cyborg and his commandos—were here on this facility. They hijacked a drop ship. We tried to stop them but failed. Add this, however. And this is important, Lieutenant.

"The cyborg told one of my men, quote: 'Tell the Lord

Admiral that the king's life is in danger. Twenty-four hours from now. On Ceres.' The cyborg risked his life to deliver that message. Do you want me to repeat it?"

"No, Commander, I copy. Thank you, sir."

The screen went dark. The commander sat back in his chair, stared through his own small viewscreen into the patch of black where he'd last seen the drop ship—a bright spark that had suddenly winked out. He stared at it a long time, repeated, "Damn odd," to himself. Then, heaving a sigh, he went off to console the enraged captain—former captain—of the drop ship.

CHAPTER
34

If it be now, 'tis not to come; if it be not to come,
it will be now; if it be not now, yet it will come: the
readiness is all.
William Shakespeare, *Hamlet,* Act 5, Scene 2

"His Majesty will receive you both in a few moments,
Sir John, Commander Tusca. If you would like to
walk in the Gallery while you wait, I'm certain it will not be
long. His Majesty is just finishing breakfast."

The king's confidential secretary and assistant, D'argent,
led Tusk and Dixter down a hallway that had become known
as the Gallery, for the works of contemporary art which
adorned its walls. The artwork was exhibited on a rotating
basis, all pieces personally selected by either the king or
queen. It was a rare honor for artists to have their work selected, an honor that guaranteed them fame and fortune.

Despite their worries, both men found their steps slowed,
gazes constantly shifting from one painting to another. The
two had differing tastes. Dixter was fond of abstract art, pre-
ferring to find his own messages in a painting. Tusk liked,
as he put it, "an apple that looks like an apple, not something that my kid barfed up after dinner."

All art forms were represented in the Gallery, including
sculpture, photography, tapestries, and an example of the
new and highly controversial "plant" art.

"That painting's a Youll, if I'm not mistaken," Dixter
said, pausing before a portrayal of a spectacular spaceplane
battle between a Corasian fleet and Royal Navy forces on
the frontier.

"I like that," Tusk said emphatically. "Makes you feel like you're right there."

"Doesn't it?" said Dixter dryly. He had never enjoyed spaceflight. "I prefer this."

"The Gutierrez." D'argent nodded. "Quite exquisite. A commissioned piece, actually. Presented as a gift to His Majesty by a group known as the Knights of the Terra Nera. Have you ever heard of them?"

Tusk and Dixter indicated that they had not.

"The name means Knights of the Black Earth." D'argent translated the Latin, and such was the secretary's charm and skill that he managed to impart the knowledge without sounding condescending. He seemed to imply that the other two knew the translation all along, were merely testing him. "Gutierrez is known for his planetscapes. This is a representation of Earth, along with its moon."

"Doesn't look much like it," Dixter said, eyeing the painting. "The last I saw of old Earth, it was all kind of gray and mottled."

"This is ancient Earth," D'argent explained. "When it was known as the 'Blue Jewel' of the galaxy. Actually, this painting came with rather a strange message: 'One generation passeth away, and another generation cometh: but the earth abideth for ever. The sun also rises.' That's the translation. From the Holy Bible, of course," he added offhandedly, confident that they had both recognized it. "Ecclesiastes."

Tusk nodded, said, with all seriousness, "Ecclesiastes. I think he was one of my old drill sergeants."

D'argent smiled politely.

Dixter wasn't smiling. " 'One generation passeth away.' That sounds like a threat."

"It does, doesn't it?" D'argent agreed. "We ran it through security." He gave a delicate shrug. "At least it was more original than most, I'll give them credit for that. *And* His Majesty is quite taken with the painting."

A servant appeared, opened double doors that led to an outdoor terrace. Catching sight of D'argent, the servant gave a slight nod.

D'argent acknowledged the signal. "His Majesty will see you now. This way, gentlemen, please."

The morning was beautiful, as always on Minas Tares, home planet of the galactic government. The weather was rarely inclement and when it was, even the rain fell in a gentle and picturesque manner. This day dawned bright and clear. The young king and queen were relaxing on their patio, taking advantage of the few precious moments of privacy and relaxation accorded them by their hectic schedules.

An abundance of flowers and plants gave the patio a rustic, homey look, filled the air with fragrance. The Glitter Palace housed an enormous botanical garden made up of rare and exotic plants brought from all over the galaxy. Hordes of experts and gardeners labored in it, made it a showplace. By contrast, all the plants on the patio had come from either the queen's home planet of Ceres or the desert world of Syrac Seven, which had been Dion's home. Both of them tended the plants, which ranged from roses to sagebrush and were grown in clay pots or cedar boxes—the patio was twenty-five stories off the ground. The plants appeared to be thriving in their disciplined, constrained environment, perhaps because of the care lavished on them.

This patio had come to be a favorite sanctuary for the royal couple. Very few people were permitted entry—only those considered close friends.

"We hope you don't mind the informal setting," Dion said, smiling and rising to his feet, as he always did when in Dixter's presence.

"On the contrary, I am honored," the Lord Admiral responded.

Tusk glanced around, sniffed the air. "That smell, the sage. Always reminds me of that night on Syrac Seven. The night Sagan came after you, kid. I mean—Your Majesty."

"The night you sat on my chest and slammed my head into the dirt," Dion recalled, smiling.

"Had to keep you quiet. You would have gotten us both killed. Well, maybe just one of us." Tusk shook his head. "Sagan wouldn't have killed _you_, at any rate. Not that we knew that at the time. We didn't know much of anything. Sort of like now."

Dion appeared somewhat startled at this off-the-wall remark, waited for Tusk to explain himself.

Tusk raised his eyebrows, cast a significant glance at Dixter, then walked over to investigate the sage.

Further perplexed, Dion turned to the Lord Admiral. But Dixter was talking to the queen.

"It's good to see you, my lord." Astarte was widely acknowledged to be one of the most beautiful women in the galaxy and her pregnancy had added to her beauty, not detracted. Within a month of her time to deliver the long-awaited and much anticipated heir to the throne, she looked radiant and, most important, happy—both in her pregnancy and in her marriage.

The time had been, not long ago, when that could not have been said. But that is another story and it was now in the past. She and her husband were friends, if not precisely lovers. Each held a genuine regard and respect for the other. Nourished and tended with the same care they gave their plants, love might yet take root and grow.

"How are you feeling, Your Majesty?" Dixter asked, bending down to kiss the queen's hand.

Astarte caught his hand in hers, pulled him close, tilted her face to be kissed. "Come, Sir John." She laughed. "No such constraints between us. You are the baby's godfather and that makes you *my* father, in a way."

Dixter kissed the petal-soft cheek. His face was flushed, uncomfortably warm. "I am truly honored and flattered, Your Majesty, but I really think you should reconsider that decision. I'm too old—"

"Our minds are made up," Dion interrupted. "It has all been discussed, written down, documented, officially stamped, sealed, and stowed away. Even the prime minister agrees. If something were to happen to me, sir"—the king fell back into the old way of talking, as if he were once more the kid Tusk had rescued from Warlord Sagan, Dixter once more the outlawed mercenary general—"my last moments will be easier knowing you are there."

"Thank you, son," Dixter said, a huskiness in his throat. "This is the greatest honor, the best compliment—" He stopped, coughed, and, frowning, turned away to pretend to contemplate the magnificent view from the balcony.

"Coffee, my lord?" D'argent was pouring.

Dixter shook his head.

"Coffee for you, Commander?"

"No, thanks, D'argent." Tusk, nervous and moody, had absentmindedly begun to pull leaves off the sage.

Dion and Astarte recognized the symptoms. They exchanged glances. The queen rose, rather cumbersomely, to her feet.

"I will bid you good morning, gentlemen."

"If you could stay a moment, Your Majesty." Dixter turned around. "This concerns you both, I'm afraid. Unfortunately, it has something to do with what we've just been discussing."

Astarte resumed her seat, sat with her hands resting on her swollen abdomen.

"I thought that might be the case," Dion said calmly. "You have more information about the Mohini kidnapping?"

"Not precisely." Dixter ran a hand over his chin, noticed that he'd missed a spot shaving this morning. "If anything, the situation's grown more confused."

"According to Olefsky," Dion said, "Xris told him it was all a mistake. Have you heard Xris's side of the story?"

Dixter was mildly exasperated. "Olefsky! You're not supposed to be in contact with anyone, Your Majesty."

Dion smiled ruefully. "You know the Bear. When he couldn't get through to me via the usual channels, he flew here to see me in person. 'Attempts against your life are a compliment, laddie.' " Dion imitated, as best he could, the Bear's rumbling baritone. " 'It means your enemies take you seriously. Be worried when they *don't* threaten you!' "

"And then he laughed, broke a vase, and demolished an antique book stand." Astarte sighed, shook her head.

"It is not a laughing matter, Your Majesty," Dixter said gravely. He looked over at Tusk.

"Yes, sir." Tusk sat bolt upright. "A report came in that one of our NOROFs was attacked by a group whose descriptions match those of Xris and his commandos. They hijacked a drop ship."

"Was anyone hurt?" Dion asked.

It was Dixter who answered. "No, Your Majesty. Xris is apparently going out of his way to avoid harming people—"

"Just like I said. He's on our side," Tusk added. He caught Dixter's grim gaze, looked abashed. "Sorry, sir."

"According to the report, Xris passed along this message. Here, let me read it." Dixter removed a small computer notepad from his pocket. " 'Tell the Lord Admiral that the king's life is in danger. Twenty-four hours from now. On Ceres.' That report came in eight hours ago."

Again the king and queen exchanged glances. Beyond that, neither reacted. Astarte asked, in quiet tones, for D'argent to pour her another cup of tea.

"Are you certain you won't have any coffee, my lord?" Dion inquired.

Dixter heaved a frustrated sigh. "Your Majesty—"

"I know what you're going to say, sir."

The king rose to his feet. He walked over to where the sage grew in its large clay pot and, like Tusk, plucked several of the leaves. Dion ground them between his fingers. The air was suddenly filled with the sharp, pungent odor.

"You're going to say that this is one threat I should take seriously, either because Xris is involved in it or"— Dion looked up, smiled; the Starfire blue eyes were clear and sunlit and dazzling— "or because he isn't. You don't seem to know which."

Dixter, feeling somewhat foolish, started to speak.

The king raised his hand. He was suddenly cool and imperious. He had retreated into his formal self; even his appearance altered. He was, unquestionably, the king.

"We want you to know, sir, that we take all these threats seriously. We take sensible precautions."

"I am well aware of that, Your Majesty," Dixter argued earnestly. "I'm not suggesting you cancel this trip, but you could alter your plans. Change the date, perhaps."

"Would that really help? Speaking of Lord Sagan, what was that dictum of his?" Dion reflected. " 'If a man is truly determined to kill you, he will. There is nothing you can do to stop him.' In order to be completely safe, we would be forced to move to a nullgrav-lined bunker a hundred kilometers below ground. And even then, I suppose someone could blow up the planet."

He tossed the crumpled sage leaves back into the soil, much in the manner of a man scattering flowers over a grave. Then, wiping his hands and clasping them behind his back, he turned around.

"We thank you for your trouble, my lord, Commander Tusca. But today's trip to Ceres is most important, both to Her Majesty and myself. We will not cancel it, nor can we alter arrangements that have been months in the planning and preparation. The diplomatic consequences alone would be disastrous. We will, however, pass your concerns on to the captain of the Royal Guard. Captain Cato will be in contact with your office to receive the details."

"Unfortunately, we don't have a lot of details, Your Majesty," Dixter said ruefully. "That's part of the problem. I'd feel better if I knew what we were up against. But ... we still have sixteen hours. . . ."

He motioned to Tusk. The two prepared to leave, well aware that the interview was at end.

"Keep a lookout, kid," Tusk said in an undertone, gripping Dion's arm.

"I will, Tusk," Dion said softly. "Thanks."

"God bless and keep both Your Majesties." Dixter bowed.

"He does, my lord," Dion responded. "He does."

"The king's death will appear extremely mysterious. The weapon will leave hardly any trace. Not even the most careful autopsy, performed by someone who is familiar with the unusual genetic makeup of Blood Royal, would reveal the true cause of death, since the micromachines will all be destroyed. It will look as if the hand of God has struck the king down." The Knight Officer was making his report.

"It *is* God who strikes, Knight Officer. We but work His divine will," the Knight Commander reminded his subordinate. "Once the king is dead, we will claim responsibility through divine intercession."

"Yes, Knight Commander." The Knight Officer's response was subdued; he was sensible of being reprimanded. He continued.

"As for the primary negative wave device itself, it functions well, far beyond expectations. It is easily disguised. The waves are not visible, nor are they detectable by any means. They are completely harmless to everyone but the king. He will drop down dead. The people standing around him will suffer absolutely no ill effects. The waves penetrate all shields, including laser-proof steelglass. Only divine intervention *could* save His Majesty."

"Unlikely. Still, we will take no chances. You have completed the construction of the smaller, handheld device?"

"Yes, Knight Commander. It has been made to your specifications, but . . ." The Knight Officer's voice trailed off. What he had been about to say amounted to criticism of the head of his order.

"What is it, Knight Officer? Is there a problem?"

"The unit requires a power source, Knight Commander. The device itself is disguised as you required. It looks innocent enough, but the power source—"

"All is arranged. You have your orders. Proceed."

"The mission is go, Knight Commander?"

"God is with us. The mission is go."

The Knight Commander ended communication.

The Knight Officer paused a moment, waited for the seconds to blink down. Then he was on the comm.

"Zulu time—sixteen hours. Mission is go. I repeat. Mission is go."

"We have sixteen hours, by my calculations," said Xris. "What's our status?"

The team had assembled in the launch module. The drop ship—intruder shields up—had come out of hyperspace, was now lurking about the far fringes of the Ceres system, avoiding any vessel that looked the least official. Fortunately, most space traffic traveled in from a major Lane located near Ceres itself. And if any Navy ship would happen to run across them, Operation Macbeth gave the team a perfect reason to sit tight and keep quiet.

"I've been monitoring the newsvids," Raoul reported. "According to news anchor James M. Warden, who is reporting live from the location . . . Have you ever noticed the whiteness of that man's teeth? It is said that they are all his own, down to the last bicuspid. He must use—"

"Back on track, Raoul," Xris said patiently.

The Loti rerouted himself. "Ah, yes. Where was I?"

The Little One reminded him.

"Opening ceremonies. They will take place on the steps of the Temple of the Goddess. The same place"—Raoul waved a hand at Xris—"in which we had our most stimulating, albeit terrifying, adventures. A viewing stand has been erected to accommodate the king and queen and the numerous dignitaries during the ceremony. After that, Their Majesties will retreat inside the temple for a private religious service, which will not be made public. As you know, my friend, it is extremely difficult to get inside the temple. Security has been tightened since the attempted kidnapping of the queen."

"So if the knights are going to assassinate the king, their best plan would be to strike during the opening ceremonies."

"His Majesty would be an ideal target," Rowan said thoughtfully. "Seated on a platform out in the open. His bizarre and mysterious death witnessed by millions. Yes, that would be the time *I* would kill him."

"When do the ceremonies begin?"

"High zenith two descending," Raoul replied promptly. "Ceres time."

Xris glared at him. "Put that in real time."

Raoul's eyelids fluttered. "Real time. What an extraordinary concept. When time itself is an arbitrary device, inflicted upon events by those who—Oh, very well." Sighing, he began counting on his fingers. "Ten hundred hours. Eleven hundred hours. Twelve hundred . . . I always get confused after that. Twelve hundred is high zenith. Thirteen hundred would be high zenith one descending. High zenith two descending would be—Where was I?"

"Fourteen hundred," Xris said grimly. "Jamil, double-check that. Next: locating the negative wave device. Did the computer files we stole from the knights give us any clue what it looks like or how it's going to be disguised?"

"Sorry, my friend," Quong said. He and Rowan both shook their heads. "We've been over it and over it and nothing."

"How do we locate the damn thing, then?" Jamil demanded. "Sniff it out?"

"We use this." Rowan tossed a long thin sheet of paper, which curled around Xris's arm like a flat snake.

He stared at it curiously. "Looks like my EKG the last time my battery malfunctioned."

To his astonishment, Rowan cast him a hurt and angry glance, irritably snatched the tape back.

"So what is this?" Xris asked, wondering what he'd said to upset her.

"A spectral analysis of the power source of the negative wave device," she returned, her voice cool.

"But we don't know what the power source is," Jamil protested.

"We don't need to, do we, Dr. Quong?"

The Doc smiled, nodded complacently. "I will explain. Because of the power band the device uses, it emits a bizarre wave pattern that can be picked up *if* you know what you're looking for. If not, you'd never notice it. That wave pattern is, effectively, the signature of the negative wave device. Once the knights turn it on, that signature will show up on our monitor. We set it to locate the source, and we have them."

"There will be a time lapse while they bring the machine

up to full power in order to activate the device," Rowan added. "Unfortunately, we can't be sure how long that will take, but hopefully enough to enable us to find them and stop them."

Harry, completely lost, scratched his head. "What's to keep us from blowing up some microwave pizza joint?"

"That would be one well-cooked pizza," Rowan told him, smiling. She was obviously growing fond of Harry. "No other microwave on the planet—on any planet, for that matter—would be this powerful or have quite this same configuration."

"So we drop out of the skies and go looking for a giant microwave," Tycho's translator squawked. "What then?"

Xris shrugged. "I can't say. Sorry, guys. I know you're used to having it all laid out in advance, but there are too damn many variables here."

"Including the fact that the good guys are going to be shooting at *us*, thinking *we're* the bad guys," Jamil grumbled.

Xris had no reply to that.

"Hell of a way to run an outfit." Jamil continued his bitching. "And speaking of getting shot at, I've checked out the so-called armored vehicle." He glared at Rowan. "I thought you said it was a PVC-48 Devastator."

"I did. At least, that's what the computer files indicate."

"Well, the computer made a mistake." Jamil was grim. "It's a PVC-*28*, and this must be the first one they ever built. That tank's older than I am. I trained on one! They must have been hauling it to a museum."

"Probably fixing the tank up for some special mission," Rowan suggested. "Maybe inside Corasia, behind enemy lines. The Army doesn't like sending new armored vehicles onto enemy-held planets, in case the Corasians capture the tanks and learn from the new technology."

"What's the tank's condition?" Xris asked, unperturbed. A former Army major, Jamil could have been given the very latest in technological wonders and would still have complained about it for days.

"Not bad," Jamil conceded grumpily. "If you don't count the fact that something's leaking all over the deck, probably because the tank's engine hasn't been tuned up since the fall of the monarchy twenty some-odd years ago. The engine is a solid-fuel job, they get clogged up real easy. Which is why no one's using solid-fuel engines anymore, not even the Corasians.

"The Devastator—and I use the term loosely—does have a forty-thousand-bhp engine driving the tracks and blower motors for hover operations. But the air-cushioning unit has been shot to pieces. The tracks are caked with some sort of gunk that's been left to harden and *might* come off if we took a thurmaplasma torch to it."

Jamil paused to draw breath. "Now for the good news. The tank's gun is in great shape—a seven-cm particle cannon."

"That *is* good." Xris nodded.

"Yeah. The bad news is we can't fire it. But it sure will look impressive. The power link from the gun to the engine is completely rotted away. Or maybe mice ate it. The magnetic repeller shields seem to be working, though." Jamil appeared almost disappointed. "And the armor's intact. At least anyone shooting at *us* will have a tough time penetrating our defenses."

"The tank sounds good enough for our purposes. Have Doc give you a hand with the wiring. We're going to need that gun. Now, anyone got any questions?"

Several hands went up.

Xris amended. "That I can answer."

All but one hand went down.

"Yes, Raoul?" Xris sighed.

"I am uncertain what to wear. These daytime affairs are so difficult. It is a formal occasion, but one feels such an ass wearing black-tie before moonrise. I was wondering if you thought it would be correct for me to don my—"

"Raoul"—Xris attempted several times to interrupt, finally succeeded—"this is immaterial. You didn't bring any clothes."

Raoul cast a glance from lowered eyelids at the Little One. The single eye visible beneath the fedora winked at him.

Xris recalled the altercation he and the empath had had over the suitcase. He glanced around, half expecting to see it.

"Actually, I did," Raoul murmured, cheeks flushed. "Or rather, the Little One acted in my behalf. The box you assume contains medical supplies ..."

"What?" Quong yelped. "My medical kit! You brought *clothes* instead?"

The Doc was on his feet. Yanking open the metal box—painted white with a red cross and marked MEDI-KIT—Quong stared, dumbfounded, at, among other items of apparel, a mass of red silk petticoat and a pink feather boa, which slithered out of the box like a long-incarcerated snake.

"Why do we need medical supplies? We hardly any of us ever get sick." Raoul was defensive.

"I think one of us is about to," Xris commented, grinning, and followed Jamil to check out the PVC.

An hour later, Xris came up to the bridge. He found Rowan alone, seated at the computer.

"Harry wanted to get something to eat. I told him I'd keep watch." She barely glanced at him; her voice was cool, impersonal. "How'd it go with the armored vehicle?"

Xris sat down, fished a twist out of his pocket. "It *may* hold together long enough to get the job done. Or it may blow up with all of us inside."

Having said that, he sat in silence. Rowan refused to look at him. "What's eating you?" he asked finally.

She stopped working. Her hands rested on the keyboard. Suddenly she turned, faced him. "Damn it, Xris, why—"

She stopped, swallowed.

"Why what?" he asked, perplexed.

"Oh, nothing. Never mind." She had turned away from him again, began moodily tapping at a key on the console. "You know the king personally, don't you? I remember watching you in the vids during the ceremonies. It gave me a strange feeling, seeing you like that. What's he like?"

I wonder, Xris thought, staring at Rowan, what you started to say. Aloud, he answered, "Yeah, I know King Dion. What's he like? That's hard to answer. Someone—I forget who—described him as a comet. He's ice and fire and you get burned if you get too close. But once you meet him, you can't forget him. He captures you and you get pulled along behind. I never told anyone this before," Xris added casually, watching Rowan, "but I saw him perform a miracle."

Rowan glanced up at him. "Really?"

"Cross my heart—or maybe I should say battery pack. Anyway, it was when I was working for Lady Maigrey, helping His Majesty escape from the Corasians—among others. One of Dion's friends—a man called Tusk—was with Dion. Tusk got shot up pretty bad. Belly wound, sucking chest wound. About as critical as I've seen. Anyway, I managed to rescue him, get him back on board his own spaceplane.

"His wife was there. Great gal. Name's Nola. She was a soldier. She knew how badly Tusk was hurt. I had a dose—a hefty dose—of painkiller. Enough to kill the pain in this world, ease him into the next. I was going to use it, when Dion boarded the spaceplane.

"Nola asked him to save her husband. Hell, I thought she was crazy with grief, but no. And what I saw next, I'm still not sure I believe. Dion took hold of Tusk's hands and he started talking to him, real soft, and . . . and Tusk got better."

Rowan was looking at him oddly.

"What do you mean?" she asked finally. "Tusk 'got better.' Did his wounds heal that instant?"

"No." Xris shook his head. "It wasn't a change you could see. It was more of a change you could feel. All I know is that Tusk lived when he should have died. And Dion Starfire was the man who did it. That's what he's like."

"Why are you telling me this, Xris?"

"I don't know. Maybe because I've been thinking about it a lot lately. Maybe because his wife reminded me of my wife. Maybe because I always wondered if Tusk felt the same way about being healed that I sometimes feel. That it might have been better to have died."

Rowan lowered her head. Her hand on the keyboard clenched into a tight fist.

"What is it you're *not* telling me?" Xris asked.

"Not now, Xris," she murmured. "Not now."

He hung around for a while, but Rowan didn't say anything more. She went back to the computer, went back inside her machine. Finally he left, climbed back down into the launch module to see if he could help Quong and Jamil fix the PVC.

Either that or help Raoul decide between the red silk or the gold outfit with the sequins.

Twelve hours to go.

CHAPTER
35

So a skillful military operation should be like a swift
snake that counters with its tail when someone
strikes at the head, counters with its head
when someone strikes at its tail, and counters
with both head and tail when someone strikes at
its middle.

Sun Tzu, *The Art of War*

The drop ship, intruder shields up, entered into orbit
around Ceres, slid silently and invisibly into place amidst
the space traffic. They were thankful for the shields. Numerous Royal Naval vessels were in the vicinity and, though
Operation Macbeth was still in effect, the sight of a special
force ship dropping by—"No pun intended," Quong had
chortled—the king's ceremony might have been enough to
make a destroyer's captain seriously consider disobeying orders and opening up communications—or the big guns.

"We're over the drop site," Harry reported, studying his
instruments. "Right on target. We should land about a kilometer from the temple. That should let us pick up the signal
from the negative wave device, find it, destroy it."

"I'm entering the signature in the launch module's computers," Rowan added, heading below. "I'm going down to
make final transfer now."

"Good. Very good."

All was going well. About time, too.

Xris took a final glance at the other ships of the Royal
Fleet silently maintaining their positions. All of them watching, wary, mistrustful. But none of them was actively looking for him.

"Operation Macbeth's been a pain up to now," he remarked to the rest of the team, who had gathered in the launch module below. "It's about time it worked *for* us for a change."

"Don't say such a thing, my friend!" Quong remonstrated, looking grave. "You will jinx us."

"Doc, you're a scientist. You know there's no such thing as a jinx." Jamil winked, grinned at the others. This was a long-standing joke.

Quong shook his head. "I know that it is not wise to flaunt good fortune. It is said that the gods never like to see mortal man too happy. It gives him delusions of godhood and so they are always tempted to strike him down. *Hubris,* the Greeks called it."

"Hubris. I smoked some of that once," Raoul remarked.

Jamil laughed loudly. Quong frowned, offended. Xris opened his mouth, prepared to say something to avert a quarrel.

Harry, above on the bridge of the command module, said it for him. "Oh, shit!"

Xris scrambled awkwardly back up the ladder. "What? What's the matter?"

Harry pointed at a flashing red light on his console as he might have pointed at a poisonous snake. "Someone out there's spotted us."

"That's not possible. We've got the damn intruder shields up. How did they find us?"

"They must be scanning the area, probably on account of the king being here. I thought I heard something ping against—"

"Rowan, get up here!" Xris called down below.

"They found us! Maybe Doc's got a point about that jinx," Tycho observed.

"Balls!" Jamil sounded angry. "The only jinx we have on board is the Doc talking about jinxes!"

Rowan pulled herself up the ladder onto the deck. "What's wrong?"

The commlink spoke in answer.

"Navy Lima Sierra Tango Two Zero Niner. This is Ceres Military District Command, relayed through the dreadnought *Jeanne d'Arc.* Operation Macbeth is ended. I say again: Operation Macbeth is ended. Stand-down code is Rubicon Three Five Hadrian Niner Alpha Two. Prepare to issue your stand-down code in two Standard Military minutes. I say again: Prepare to issue your stand-down code in two Standard Military minutes. *Jeanne d'Arc* out."

"What's our stand-down code?" Xris looked at Rowan.

She bit her lip. "Beats me."

He glared at her. "Hell, you probably wrote the damn thing."

"I probably did." She was unperturbed. "But each ship has its own code. It's given to every captain along with his sealed orders."

"Would he enter it into the computer?"

Rowan shrugged. She was already seated at the keyboard. "Captains aren't supposed to. Some do, of course. The sealed orders are required to be kept in a vault in the captain's quarters. But," she added, as Xris was already headed in that direction, "he would have undoubtedly taken them with him when he left the ship to be overhauled."

Of course. That was only logical. Still, they might get lucky. The captain might be either forgetful or an idiot.

Entering the tiny, cramped room that was the captain's quarters, Xris was already mentally preparing the plastic explosives, only to find the vault standing wide open. Half-heartedly, he peered inside.

He hit the comm. "What the devil am I looking for?"

"Is it there?" Rowan sounded amazed.

"No, I don't think so." He searched for a scrap of paper, anything. "But tell me anyway."

"Well, it would be a series of digits and numbers, arranged in what would appear a random pattern. They're not, of course. The way it works is that the command vessel of this fleet gets its own stand-down from the admiralty, then they work through each ship in the fleet. They issue a single cipher and each individual ship completes that cipher with one that is uniquely its own."

"Huh?"

That was Harry, but Xris could have echoed his pilot. The cyborg stuck his hand inside the vault, groped about in the shadows.

"As an example"—Rowan was in lecture mode—"as commander, the code word I would issue to every ship in the fleet might be 'Raoul.' The correct response for one ship is 'Loti.' For another it would be 'Adonian.' For a third, 'the Little One.' Naturally, it's far more complex than that."

"Naturally," Xris muttered on his way back to the bridge.

No need to ask what would happen when they couldn't return the code. "We'll be ordered to shut down our engines. The tractor beam will lock on to us, drag us ignominiously onto that dreadnought. Any attempt to flee and we'll be blown out of the stars. And fleeing isn't going to save the king."

Of course—the thought came to him—being taken prisoner *would* give us a chance to talk to someone, warn them about the danger. . . .

Once we are tractored on board. Xris went over it all in his mind. Once the commander makes certain our ship is secure, isn't going to try to escape. Once the guards have boarded and made us all prisoners. Once we have given our names and voice prints and hand prints. Once the sergeant turns our request over to the lieutenant, who might or might not see fit to mention it to the captain, who would have to get it approved through channels . . .

"Fuck it!"

Xris arrived back on the bridge. "How much time . . ." He paused. "What are you doing? Have you found it?"

"I didn't look." Rowan was wearing that smug, self-satisfied smile that always sent a tingle up Xris's spine. She was on to something. "The codes are all in my files back at RFComSec."

"They would have shut those down—"

"The front door," she answered, her hands busy on the keyboard, her eyes scanning each screen as it flashed past. "They shut the front door. Not the back. There!" She glowed with pleasure and triumph. "I'm in! Now . . . ship's name." She was talking to herself as she entered the information. "Registration number. Come on. Come on."

Lines of type flashed past in a blur. Suddenly the scrolling stopped. A white bar began to flash.

"This is it!" Rowan hit a key, laughed, jubilant. "You have it on your computer now, Harry! Give them *that* when they ask for it!"

She was inside the machine. Xris recalled the old days. Why hadn't he ever noticed? Dalin Rowan had never come alive except when he was hooked up to that machine.

A lot alike. Xris flexed his mechanical hand. A lot alike . . .

"Dear God!" Rowan was on her feet and moving away from the computer as if it were a bomb, ready to explode. "Oh, dear God!"

"They accepted our stand-down code," Harry announced.

Xris was at Rowan's side. "*Now* what?"

"A trap." She was white to the lips. "It was a trap. They've put the worm on me."

The worm. A computer trace that had latched on to Rowan's transmission and would race like a heat-seeking cybermissile through the convoluted paths of cyberspace until it found her.

"Shut it down!" Xris urged.

Rowan appeared to be in shock. She stared at the computer as if it had physically assaulted her. A blow from a trusted friend, a lover . . .

"Shut the damn thing down!" Xris repeated, shaking her.

Rowan blinked, sprang suddenly back to the computer. Feverishly, she issued verbal commands. When that didn't work, she struck keys. At length, she struck the keyboard.

"Harry, cut the juice!" Xris commanded.

Harry spread his large hands, helpless. "I can't, Xris."

"We'd lose everything," Rowan said in a shaking voice. "Engines. Life-support. Everything. I used the central computer. I didn't think— There." She fell silent.

Nothing happened onscreen that Xris could see; he'd had wild visions of a blinding flare of glaring white light. But apparently Rowan could read the signs.

"They have me."

Only minutes, perhaps, before the word went out. Glancing at the viewscreen, Xris saw the destroyer suddenly begin to come about. It *might* be coincidence. . . .

"Rowan, get down below. Harry, set the controls to release the launch module. Now! Let's go."

Rowan cast Xris a look—an apology, pleading, he didn't know. He didn't have time to care. Taking her gently but firmly by the arm, he guided her down into the launch module.

"Launch release set," Harry reported.

"You're next. Down the hatch."

Harry climbed down. Xris was up above, his hand on the airlock controls, set to seal off the launch module from the command module. Harry was halfway down when a thought struck him. Xris had been wondering how long it would take the big man to figure things out.

"Uh, Xris." Harry halted in mid-descent, peered back up. "If *I* go . . . and *you* go . . . who's left to pilot the command module, bring us all back up?"

"No one," Xris said grimly.

Harry shook his head, slowly assimilating. "But that will mean—"

"Damn it, I know what it will mean! Get your ass down there!"

Xris took one last look through the viewscreen. The dreadnought was most definitely headed in their direction. A red light was flashing on the console. Xris didn't wait to hear what they had to say. It could all be perfectly innocent.

"Yeah. And I'm going to model nude for the cover of *Celestial Bodies*." Xris chomped down on a twist, bit it clean in two. Part of it fell into the launch module below.

He shut the hatch, sealed it, slid down the ladder to land on the deck with a thud.

"Time?"

"Six and a half hours. We're off schedule by thirty minutes," Doc pronounced worriedly.

"Can't be helped."

Everyone was at his post except Rowan, who sat huddled in a corner, staring bleakly at nothing.

Xris headed forward, to where Jamil sat at the controls of the launch module. He passed Rowan, but said nothing. He had no comfort to offer, knew it wouldn't be welcome even if he did. Let her alone for now. She'd be back to normal once they landed on the planet's surface, once they began to track the negative wave device.

Jamil was at the helm, Harry alongside. Screens filled the wall, but there were no windows anywhere. All the seats were high-backed, with multiple straps to hold the Special Forces teams in place during the descent.

"Jeez." Harry looked at the crude and simple controls, and was shocked. "You call this flying?"

"No," Jamil said shortly. "We call it dropping. Don't worry. It'll get us there in one piece and that's all it was meant to do."

"Ready, Xris?" Harry glanced over his shoulder. He looked and sounded reluctant.

Xris didn't blame the big man. Once the launch module let go, they would be hurtling down to the planet's surface with no defenses and only minimal guidance systems to get them there.

The "Elevator Ride from Hell," Jamil had called it.

And there would be no going back.

CHAPTER
36

The Great White Mountain Man said, "The reason
deception is valued in military operations is not
just for deceiving enemies, but, to begin with,
for deceiving one's own troops, to get them to
follow unknowingly."

Commentary on Sun Tzu's *The Art of War*

The Temple of the Goddess on the planet Ceres was an
enormous edifice. Built on the steppes of a mountain held
sacred to the people of Ceres, the temple dominated the
landscape, as it dominated the lives of its people. The complex was enormous, housing the priests and priestesses as
well as the numerous acolytes and novices who served the
Goddess.

The inner portion of the temple was sacrosanct, could not
be entered by the uninitiated, with only a few exceptions.
Today's private religious ceremonies would be performed
within the temple confines, but the public ceremonies pre-
ceding would be held outside the temple, on a specially built
platform raised above the temple steps.

As Dion had told Dixter, months of planning and preparation had been devoted to today's ceremony. It was vitally
important not only for religious, but for political reasons as
well. The Baroness DiLuna, mother of the queen, ruler of
Ceres, and a powerful force in the galaxy, had forced this
marriage on the young king in return for helping him attain
the throne.

The young king and his queen had both been desperately
unhappy in the marriage, which had very nearly ended in a
divorce. The rift threatened the political stability of the gal-

axy, almost toppled the young king. Disaster had been averted, but at great cost. The near tragedy brought king and queen together as husband and wife. The birth of a Royal Prince was to be their reward.

This day would celebrate the anniversary of the Royal Couple's wedding and, most important, they would enter the temple together to dedicate the unborn child to the Goddess—an important ritual in Ceres. Thus, the king would officially sanction the religion of the Goddess throughout the galaxy; their child would be raised in the religious beliefs of both parents. And Baroness DiLuna would no longer threaten to take away her fleets, her armies, her systems, her shipping routes, and all the immense wealth these generated.

Press coverage of the day's events was unparalleled. So many reporters had converged on the planet that they almost outnumbered the populace of the capital city. Restrictions and regulations had been issued in regard to the ceremony itself and were being strictly enforced. Only the major nets could cover the event for vid broadcast; all others had to tie in to these.

Galactic Network News was present, with its highly sophisticated off-world beaming and image enhancement equipment. It would, as promised, make the viewer half a galaxy away feel as if he, she, or it were seated beside the king. In addition, GNN news anchor James M. Warden was the envy of every journalist from Ceres to Hell's Outpost for having landed an interview with the Royal Couple immediately prior to the opening of official ceremonies.

Back when Dion was Dion and not His Majesty, Warden had been the first journalist to actually predict that this young upstart with the intense blue eyes and red-gold mane of hair would someday become a powerful force in the galaxy. Warden's first interview with the would-be king was seen by political analysts today as being a major factor in the ascendance of Dion's star. The young king never forgot those who had helped him in his rise.

Warden and his cam crews were on the dignitaries' platform, trying to set up their equipment and getting in the way of the fevered workmen. A last-minute potential disaster had occurred—a swathe of bunting, draped above the royal thrones, had torn loose in an overnight windstorm and now appeared ready to tumble down and engulf both Their Majesties in billowing purple silk.

To Warden's mind, the workmen were interfering with his cam crews, who were positioning cams for the best angles and attempting to untangle and anchor down the masses of cable that wound, like the sacred snakes of Ceres, up, down, and around the platform's stairs and supports.

Warden guessed what must be going on in the mind of Cato, head of the Royal Guard. To him, all these people were damned nuisances at best, potential assassins at worst. No one was allowed this close to the king and queen without security clearance. Every living being on the platform or on the steps leading up to the platform or on the road leading to the steps that led to the platform was supposed to be wearing ID tags emitting impulses that permitted them entry into the electronic surveillance net surrounding the area.

Anyone entering without the tag would cause a break in the net, bring the guards down upon them with a swiftness that rivaled a jump into hyperspace. There had been, at last count, ten such incidents in a twenty-minute period. Four badges had fallen off. Three badges had malfunctioned. Two drunken college students, acting on a dare, had been caught without badges, as well as an elderly priestess, who had forgotten to wear her badge and was highly indignant at being detained and searched.

Warden was active in the proceedings, keeping a critical watch on his team, though he left the placement of cams and crews up to the producer and director. Frequently, he would indicate—with a wave of his hand, a nod of his head—a change, such as getting a shot of the priestess slapping at the hands of one of the Royal Guard. Warden's wishes were always accepted as commands; he was known to have an eye for such things.

He checked camera angles, tested sound levels, all the while keeping a sharp lookout for anyone of interest who might flutter into his web. Not that this was likely. The dignitaries would not arrive until they were scheduled, each being driven up to the base of the platform in official limojets in order of their rank and position. The king and queen would arrive just as the last of the others were being seated. It was during the interval of these few minutes that Warden would conduct his interview.

He was just conceding to his director, via commlink, that it seemed unlikely he'd have a chance to talk with anyone else, when he caught sight of the Lord of the Admiralty making an unexpected—to judge by the reaction of the Royal Guard—inspection tour.

Warden advanced to meet Dixter. The two came together in the midst of the fray, like enemy generals meeting on a hillside above a battle. They had known each other for years, had mutual respect for each other, if not mutual regard.

"Delighted to see you, my lord," Warden said, shaking hands. "Your name wasn't on the guest list."

"I happened to be in the vicinity," Dixter parried, "and thought I'd stop by."

Warden went in from another angle. "Any truth to the rumor that Operation Macbeth was put into effect in response to the discovery that rebellion was fomenting among the members of the armed forces?"

Warden obliquely motioned his assistant, a cam-wielding young man, to switch on his vidcam, get a good shot of the two of them, just in case the Lord Admiral happened to let anything slip.

Dixter smiled. "No truth to that rumor at all, Mr. Warden. We are, as we said, conducting Naval exercises."

Warden gazed intently at the Lord Admiral's face. "Do you always find Naval exercises so stressful, my lord?"

"When you detest spaceflight as much as I do, yes," Dixter returned mildly. "That's public knowledge, by the way. You won't get any mileage from seasick admiral stories."

Warden grinned amiably. "There goes my lead for tonight's broadcast. Now what about the rumors that your top code breaker has disappeared and that Naval security has been breached? Anything to that?"

"I can assure you, Mr. Warden, and the public, that galactic defenses remain strong." Dixter added politely, firmly, "And now, I'm certain you will excuse me. The other guests are arriving."

James M. Warden straightened his tie, motioned the young assistant to pan the crowd. He cast a bored glance at the first arrivals; these would be local government officials and their wives—small fish, not worthy of notice.

Warden spoke into his commlink. "Something's up. The Lord Admiral's here and he's not supposed to be. Contact your sources in the Navy and find out what the devil's going on."

It was hot standing here in the sun. Warden did not want

to be seen sweating; he walked over to stand in the shade of the purple bunting. Someone found a chair for him. His makeup artist swooped down on him, began to make minor retouches. Warden watched the continuing procession of dignitaries with bored eyes. The cameraman was filming a group of children armed with flowers to be presented to the queen.

"Cute, aren't they?" Warden said to his producer.

"Yeah." The woman didn't glance at them.

"It will make a nice opener."

"I'll see that it feeds to editing. Any idea why the Lord Admiral's here?"

"I've got someone on it."

The producer nodded and left.

The dignitaries were becoming increasingly important. The cameraman switched his cam from the children to the new arrivals. Warden nodded affably at these, occasionally waved his hand. The greetings were either returned warmly or not returned at all, depending on what he'd last reported about the individual in question.

Many people remained yet to be seated, when Warden noted heads turning, the minor officials—relegated to the back—craning their necks to see what was going on. Whispers swept through the crowd.

"The king and queen are arriving," reported an assistant.

Warden had already glimpsed the sleek limojet with its massive armor plating and steelglass windows. A private area for the interview had been set up beneath a canopy. It was provided with comfortable chairs and even a refreshment table. The Royal Guard had the canopy cordoned off, was now scanning the chilled fruit for poison. Warden could hear the faint hum presaging a break in the electronic net. Other members of the Royal Guard went prowling through the stands.

Warden strode leisurely over to meet Their Majesties. The queen was beautiful, radiant. The king was smiling, dignified, coolly aloof and detached, but not offensively so. He was what his subjects wanted in a king, someone sublime, perfect, set apart. He was all of that and more and yet he had the rare gift to be able, on occasion, to descend from his lofty throne and remind his subjects that he was mortal—as were they.

The children were being shepherded forward to deliver

their flowers. They were frightened by the commotion, overwhelmed by the prospect of being this near the king and queen. All made it, except one little boy, who dropped his flowers and burst into tears. The king knelt to the child's level, ruffled the hair on the small bent head with a gentle hand. Then, picking the flowers up from the dust, the king offered them to the queen, who accepted them with a gracious smile, a comforting word.

"That's the Blood Royal in him," Warden remarked to his cameraman.

"This will have them in tears," the cameraman predicted, his cam following the little boy, who was looking bewildered but happy, not certain what had happened, yet realizing—from the fuss the grown-ups were making—that he'd done something remarkable.

"Poor kid'll probably develop a phobia about flowers," said the producer.

The dignitaries continued to arrive. The king and queen had come early for the interview in order to be on time for the opening ceremonies. King Dion was noted for his punctuality, made it a point to always be where he was supposed to be on time, insisted on doing whatever it was he was supposed to be doing on time. This was undoubtedly due to the king's tight schedule—a minute late here could mean hours late somewhere else. And so no longer was it considered appropriate to be "fashionably late." The fashionably late often discovered that His Majesty had started without them.

King and queen were accompanied by Archbishop Fideles, whose religion was once viewed as being a rival to that of the Goddess. The archbishop had worked hard to close the gap, was doing everything possible to make the two differing faiths compatible.

Baroness DiLuna was also in attendance. This was her moment of triumph and she was just brazen enough to exhibit it. She would have some choice remarks today.

Captain Cato, who had once served the late Derek Sagan, kept near the Royal Couple, watchful eyes scanning the crowd. John Dixter was also on hand.

"That man hasn't slept in seventy-two hours," Warden said to himself.

His comm buzzed in his ear.

"What've you got?"

"Operation Macbeth has been canceled."

"Did they find that missing major? What was her name—Mohini?"

"No, sir. Or if they have, my source doesn't know about it. The Navy's changed all the codes. Everything appears to be back to normal."

"Not from where I stand," Warden said, eyeing the obviously nervous Lord Admiral. "Something's up. Keep digging."

The king's secretary, D'argent, appeared at Warden's elbow. The secretary announced that they were ready for the interview, hinted that His Majesty wasn't to be kept waiting.

Warden advanced, bowing, the cameraman following every move. The king and queen turned to greet him. Pleasantries were exchanged; offers of fruit, champagne were politely refused. Their Majesties sat down. Warden—on invitation—sat down. Cams zeroed in. Warden had opened his mouth to ask his first question when his quick eye noticed Admiral Dixter suddenly go rigid with attention. The admiral's gaze became the abstracted look of a man listening to a commlink connection.

The Lord Admiral spoke only a few words, then touched Cato's arm, said a few brief words to him. The captain's face remained impassive. He gave a sharp nod, gathered his men about him with a gesture, and walked up to the king.

"Your Majesty." Cato's tone was low, cool, urgent. "You and the queen must return to the limojet now."

Warden watched attentively. The king glanced swiftly at the Lord Admiral. Expression anxious and grim, the admiral nodded, confirmed whatever silent question the king had asked. Dion rose, gave his hand to the queen. Astarte extended her apologies calmly, managed to make this all look as if she were returning to the limojet to retrieve a forgotten lipstick.

Warden was on his feet, hastening after the king, the cameraman at his side.

The Royal Guard closed their ring of steel around the Royal Couple, hustled them back to the safety of the limojet.

"What's happening?" Warden demanded, frustrated.

A ripple of motion and a collective gasp from the crowd attracted his attention. His commlink buzzed.

"You're right, Mr. Warden. Something is up. The Navy's gone on red alert around this planet! My source doesn't know why."

"I do," said James M. Warden.

He stared in astonishment as a drop ship plummeted out of the blue, cloudless sky, thrusters firing to slow its descent.

At first Warden thought the ship was intending to land in the midst of the million or so people gathered to watch the ceremonies—in which case the carnage and death would be horrendous. He was directing his cameraman not to miss that shot, when he realized he had misjudged the entry. The drop ship was actually landing in a parking lot about one kilometer from the platform.

An assassination attempt? Armed uprising? A publicity stunt?

The king and queen were being hastily and unceremoniously bundled into the limojet. The dignitaries were bewildered, incensed, indignant, or hysterical; the Royal Guard swarmed the platform.

Warden was in contact with all his camera crews, which were positioned at various sites throughout the city. "All of you, switch over to pick up that drop ship, except you, number twelve." That was the main GNN long-range image enhancer camera. "You stay focused on the king."

Warden lifted his left hand, shoved back his suit coat and shirtsleeves, looked at his watch. He depressed a small button located on the side of the dial, saw a tiny flash of white light. He smoothed his suit coat, turned to his assistant.

"Bring your cam. I'm going to try to get close enough for an interview."

CHAPTER
37

When opponents present openings, you should
penetrate them immediately. Get to what they want
first, subtly anticipate them. Maintain discipline
and adapt to the enemy in order to determine
the outcome of the war.

Sun Tzu, *The Art of War*

"Touchdown in five, four, three—"

Two and *one* were lost in the ear-shattering, spine-jamming, metal-screeching, bone-crunching landing. The drop ship rocked precariously, during which Xris could hear the PVC, strapped down in the center of the vehicle, shake and rattle. He had sudden visions of several metric tonnes of armor-plated tank breaking loose from its moorings, hurtling through the bulkheads, and careening about the cramped confines of the launch module.

At least no one would worry about recovering the bodies. They'd just wash out the module's insides with a fire hose.

The shaking stopped. All was suddenly very silent, except for the hissing of the hydraulics attempting to level the tilting floor.

Xris gave himself a moment to recover from the shock, took time to make a few minor adjustments to his system—red lights were going off up and down the length of his arm. Then, unstrapping himself, he pushed himself out of his seat, was amazed at the effort it took.

"Everyone okay?" he asked.

He had heard of people scared speechless, but this was the first time in his life he'd ever encountered that phenomenon. No one said a word, not even a bad one. Most sat in various frozen poses, white-knuckled hands clutching the arms of the chairs, sweat beaded on their faces, eyes wide and staring. Two, however, appeared to have enjoyed the ride.

Jamil swiveled around to face them. "We've landed," he announced. His handsome face was grinning; he rubbed his hands. "God! I miss my days in the Army sometimes. I'd forgotten what a rush that was!"

Apparently Raoul agreed with him. The Loti was lying back limp in his chair. He looked up at Xris with lustrous eyes.

"Wow!" Raoul whispered dreamily.

But Xris had to help Tycho stand. The alien was in a deplorable state, shaking so badly he could barely get up out of his chair.

"Not healthy for a sharpshooter," Xris said. "Doc, can you give him something to calm him down?"

"What do you suggest?" Quong demanded coldly. "A golden-beaded handbag or a string of pearls? I have both in my medical kit."

"Ah. Right. I forgot." Xris started to take out a twist, noticed his own hand was far from steady. He went to check on Rowan.

She was up and out of her chair, tottering but walking. She was headed, naturally, for the computer. She gave Xris a wan smile.

"Now you know why I joined the Navy," she said faintly.

Quong came to assist her. He sat beside her at his own console, and they began to coordinate their search for the telltale negative wave signature.

Xris glanced at the chronometer. They had arrived earlier than planned, earlier than the appointed time—according to the knights' own countdown. But their unexpected and dramatic appearance might jolt the knights into action. Certainly Xris hoped it had jolted the Royal Guard.

"Jamil, fire up the PVC Devastator. Hopefully we won't need to use it. We can just blast the negative wave device to hell and back with the launch module's lascannon. Tycho, go up in the turret, check the cannon out. Make sure it wasn't damaged in the landing."

Tycho groaned, nodded, and—hanging on to the railing for support—dragged himself up to the gun emplacement located on top.

"Harry, anything on the screens? What's going on out there? And where did we land anyway?"

Xris had originally cursed the fact that the drop ship had no windows, only outside cams and vidscreens. He had since had reason to bless the foresight of the designer. He could only imagine what that harrowing, plummeting descent in the Elevator from Hell would have been like if they'd been forced to view the sights along the way.

Harry switched on an array of vidscreens. The cams provided three-hundred-sixty-degree coverage of the terrain outside the drop ship.

Xris looked out over what appeared to be—at first, startled glance—a veritable sea of gleaming metal.

"We've landed in a parking lot," Harry announced.

Xris recalled the sound of screeching metal, the uneven, bumpy touchdown. A few hovercar owners were going to be extremely unhappy when they returned to the pancakes that had once been their vehicles.

"Any activity?"

"Choppers circling, but not getting too close. Probably won't. We have surface-to-air missiles."

"Yeah, well, they've got air-to-surface missiles."

"I don't think they're going to be keen on using them. Look at this."

Harry adjusted a camera angle, pointed to a vidscreen. A few thousand spectators stared back, pointing and exclaiming and jostling for position in order to get a better view. They were alarmed and panicked now, but soon curiosity and the safety-in-numbers kind of euphoric courage that sweeps over a crowd would set in. The drop ship might survive a direct missile attack; it had already survived entry into the planet's atmosphere. But it might fall to a mob.

"Fire a few tracers over their heads. Well over their heads. Just enough to make them keep their distance," ordered Xris.

Tycho fired off the lascannon. Most of the people in the crowd flung themselves flat on the ground. The local police force had arrived on the scene, began doing what they could to clear people out of the area. At least, no one would be firing rockets at the drop ship anytime soon—not with the possibility of injuring untold numbers of innocent civilians.

"Can you see the king?" Xris asked.

Harry shifted camera angles.

"That must be the dignitaries' platform. There's the Royal Flag. I'll zoom in."

They had an excellent view of the backs of the Royal Guard. Xris detected what might have been a flash of red-golden hair in the midst of the ring of steel. And there was the Royal Limojet.

"Looks like the king's safe, for the time being," Xris reported to the rest of the team. "They're hustling him and the queen into the Royal Limo."

"Good!" Rowan breathed in relief. "They shouldn't have to take him far to get him out of range." She looked up at Xris, smiled shakily. "I'd say mission accompl—"

"They're not moving," Harry reported, frowning.

The king and queen were seated safely in the limo, the Royal Guard had taken their places on the outside, the crowd had been hastily cleared from the area, but the limojet wasn't going anywhere.

Xris took a look. "He's right. They're not moving."

"Maybe they're waiting to see what we do," Harry suggested.

Xris snorted. "That is *not* standard procedure. When you're guarding dignitaries and there's some type of danger, you get them the hell out of there. You don't wait around for the shooting to start."

Harry was studying his instruments. "It looks like— Yeah, I'll be damned."

"What?"

"Engine trouble. The limo won't start. They're running diagnostics on it now, but—"

"They won't find the cause," Rowan interrupted, excited. "It's the negative waves. I'm picking up the signature. The knights have turned the device on. The waves must be causing the engine to malfunction!"

"At least that limo's shielded, armor-plated. A lascannon couldn't take the king out once he's inside."

"No armor, no shields will protect him," Quong said. "The negative waves will pass through unaffected."

"Damn!" Frustrated, Xris turned back to the screen. "The knights are in range. We're too late to save the king. But maybe we can even the score."

"We are not finished yet, my friend," Quong returned. "The signature is very, very weak. The knights haven't brought the device up to full power. But Major Rowan is correct in her assessment of the negative waves damaging the limo. As you can see here by the spectrum analysis, the microwaves—weak as they are—have been able to cause interference with the power coupling lattice of the limojet's engines."

Xris didn't bother to look. He wouldn't know a spectrum analysis if it smacked him in the face. "Good. That gives us a chance. Get a fix on the damn device and Tycho'll take it out with the lascannon."

Rowan stared intently at her screen, made some rapid calculations, chewed on her lip. "My fix on the position is—"

Whatever she said next was lost in a thundering, thumping blast. The engines of the PVC-28 Devastator fired, backfired, misfired, and finally—after a strangled cough—rumbled contentedly. A cloud of black, choking smoke filled the vehicle bay and began to seep into the rest of the drop ship. Raoul, who was inexplicably changing his clothes, bleated in indignation and waved a frantic hand.

"This gunk is ruining my outfit!" he wailed.

The tank's engines cycled over from deafening roar to a head-splitting hum that caused Xris to hastily shut down his augmented hearing. Even so, the irritating whine made him grit his teeth.

"Here are the coordinates!" Rowan shouted at him. "I've fed them into the computer! You should be able to bring it up on the screen!"

Xris went back to the screens. Harry had his large finger planted on one of them.

"There," he said, and he shook his head. "That's it. Got to be."

"You've made a mistake." Xris turned back. "Rowan, re-enter your data."

"No mistake, Xris," Quong confirmed. "That's it."

Xris looked back, took out a twist, clamped his teeth down on it hard. The negative wave device was located right smack in the center of an enormous forty-story luxury hotel that was standing right smack on the highway leading up to the temple. The hotel, the area around the hotel, the highway leading to and from the hotel were jammed with people.

"Third-floor balcony," Harry said.

A blast from the lascannon would blow up the device . . . The front of the hotel . . .

And about five or six hundred men, women, and children, who would never know what hit them.

"Tycho, get down here!" Xris said, frustrated. "Harry, goddam it, I need a closer look!"

Harry was already ordering the computer to zoom in on the coordinates.

"Holy shit!" he said reverently and in disbelief. He turned around, his eyes wide. "Xris, that *can't* be right! That's . . . that's the GNN nightly news!"

Yet the numbers Rowan had brought up were flashing complacently beneath the picture, assuring him that this was, indeed, the location of the negative wave device.

A mobile unit of Galactic Network News.

"Doc, get over here. There's all sorts of equipment stuck out there on that third-floor balcony. You have any idea which of those things might be the device? If any?"

Quong took a close look. Harry obligingly shifted camera angles, bringing each machine into close proximity. Xris, conscious of a wave of gardenia perfume roiling over him, sensed the presence of Raoul loitering nearby. The Loti glittered in gold, from head to toe.

"I am now suitably dressed for the occasion," Raoul announced happily.

Xris grunted.

Quong squinted, pursed his lips. He calmly placed his finger on the screen. "That's it."

Simultaneously Raoul gasped, pointed a painted fingernail at the screen. "Her! That's her!"

"Son of a bitch!" Xris murmured. "Our friend from *Canis Major,* Dr. Brisbane. Quite a coincidence, her being here. And you say that's the device, Doc? The machine to her right? It looks like an ordinary vid antenna. A bit longer, maybe. How do you know that's it?"

Quong gave a rapid-fire explanation. "Such pieces of equipment are known as image enhancers. They are used to transmit and receive high-band radio waves. They act like radar, work with the vidcam and a computer to enhance the picture of the object, make it look clear and sharp, even on the outer fringes of the galaxy. Now, as you will note, there are ten image enhancers on that balcony. Nine of the enhancers are pointed at us, as they should be. *We* are the big news at the moment. But look—look at this one! It is pointed at the limojet." Quong straightened. "At the king."

Xris was unconvinced. "Yeah, so? They'd be likely to keep one on the king, wouldn't they?"

"Of course! That is why this device is such excellent cover for them. But look at this, my friend—shielding! Why would a news crew put shielding around an image enhancer? I tell you, Xris," Quong said stubbornly, "*that* is the device."

"And that's the woman with no mouth!" Raoul's painted nails were digging painfully into Xris's good arm. "The female who was going to kill me!"

Galactic Network News—a front for the Knights of Terra Nera? It didn't make sense on the surface. And yet, in a way, in the subconscious depths of Xris's mind, it was beginning to.

"How long have we got before the device is fully operational?"

"Fifteen, maybe twenty minutes," Rowan answered.

Xris considered. "We can't blow it up from here, not without blowing up half of Ceres as well. We're going to have to go inside the hotel to take them out. Harry, you and Tycho join Jamil in the PVC. Tycho, bring your sniper rifle. Quong, you and Rowan—"

"Just a minute." Rowan stopped him. "We *might* be able to interrupt the device's signals by sending out radio waves on the same band—according to my calculations. . . . Dr. Quong, what do you think?"

Quong studied the screen. "A possibility. We don't know the right modulation, so we couldn't shut the device down completely, but we might be able to force them to boost more power, which would take time."

Xris shook his head. "Out of the question. Marines will storm this drop ship in a matter of minutes. You stay here and you won't be boosting anything."

"But you'll need longer than fifteen minutes to reach the device," Rowan argued. "Look at this, Doctor."

They huddled over the computer, talking excitedly. Xris didn't understand a word, but he realized that in order to get them to leave, he'd have to physically assault both of them. Besides, if they *could* jam it, buy him more time . . .

He rested his hand on Rowan's shoulder, touched the Doc on the arm. "All right. You stay. But listen to me. When the Marines show up, you surrender. That's an order. No heroics."

"That was always my plan," Quong said gravely, not taking his eyes from the screen.

Rowan looked up at Xris. She was smiling, but her eyes were shadowed. "Don't worry about us. You take care of yourself. And the others."

"Sure thing," he said easily, then added, more somberly, "Once again, I'm sorry about all this."

"I'm not," she answered. For a brief instant, her hand rested on his good hand. Then she turned back to the computer.

Xris straightened. Raoul, a vision in gold sequins and bangles, fluttered excitedly around him.

"What about me, Xris Cyborg? Do I get to surrender to the Marines, too?"

"I know that's always been a fantasy of yours, but not this time." Xris took hold of the Adonian by a bracelet-covered, bejeweled arm, headed in the direction of the rumbling PVC. "Grab your purse. You and the Little One are coming with me."

CHAPTER
38

Thus, at first you are like a maiden, so the enemy opens his door. . . .

Sun Tzu, *The Art of War*

"What the devil is the delay, Captain?" The Lord Admiral angrily confronted Cato. "Get His Majesty the hell out of here!"

Cato saluted, looked grim. "We're trying, my lord. The limojet is experiencing engine difficulty. It might be a faulty fuel line."

"Faulty fuel line, my ass!" Dixter swore. "Has that engine ever been known to fail?"

"No, my lord."

"Damn odd it should fail now, don't you think, Captain?"

"I understand your meaning, Admiral. We're doing all we can."

"Transfer the king to another vehicle. Use my car. Call in the hovercraft."

"I've done that, my lord." Cato was carefully patient. "But in those instances, the king and queen would have to leave the limojet. At least inside there, they're safe." The captain looked over at the drop ship. "The limojet's shields could withstand a hit even from those lascannons."

Dixter stared at the drop ship, then cast a swift look around. It was all chaos: milling, panicked crowds; sweating police attempting to contain the mob; confused, bewildered dignitaries; and infuriated Baroness DiLuna; shoving, determined media. The Royal Guard provided an island of calm. Drawn up in a cordon surrounding the Royal Limo, the guardsmen and women were protecting the already well-protected vehicle with their own bodies. And there was the mysterious, potentially deadly drop ship squatting squarely in the middle of a hotel parking lot.

Naval hovercraft converged on the scene; the sky was dotted with them, the air filled with their buzzing whine. But they only circled the drop ship.

"Why haven't they fired on it, my lord?" Cato carried the battle into the enemy camp, so to speak.

Dixter, realizing this, offered a brief apology. "Sorry, Captain. You know your job. And—unfortunately, at times like this—I know mine. That drop ship is designed to withstand enemy attack from the ground or the air. The shielding is damn near impenetrable. You can drop bombs on it all day long and *maybe* put a dent in the damn thing.

"Oh, sure," he added, in response to Cato's frown, "we could destroy it with a few plasma missiles, which would also fuse together in one gigantic metal lump every single civilian vehic in that parking lot. Not to mention the civilians themselves."

"Yes, my lord." Cato rubbed his smooth-shaven chin.

"Besides"—Dixter spoke softly, almost to himself—"I'm not certain we should do anything to that drop ship."

"Sir?" Cato was clearly appalled.

"Just a hunch, Captain. Just a hunch. And of course we'll do something." Dixter was soothing. "Just as soon as we figure out what."

"Good God, my lord! Look!"

One side of the drop ship opened wide. A hulking machine—large and massive and mottled gray-green in color—lurched out. The thing was belching great quantities of black smoke. People in the vicinity began shrieking in terror.

"Analyze that gas," Cato ordered over the comm. "Could be poisoned," he added for Dixter's benefit.

The Lord Admiral said nothing, just shook his head.

The answer came back sounding slightly puzzled. "Chemical analysis reads . . . exhaust fumes, Captain."

"I'll be damned. That's an old PVC-28 Devastator," Dixter said, squinting into the sunlight.

"And it's headed this way, my lord. Civilian casualties or no, we've got to—"

"No, it's not." Dixter pointed. "It's turned. It's heading for the . . . hotel?"

Both men watched, bemused, as the PVC crunched and mangled its way over the vehics in the parking lot, firing bursts of tracer fire to clear people from its path. It smashed through a retaining wall, rolled down a culvert, disappeared for several long moments—when it must have come to a halt. Then it surged up the other side and trundled on, continuing its relentless drive toward the Ceres Towers.

Dixter was on the comm. "Commander, alert the local police to immediately evacuate that hotel and seal off the surrounding area."

"Damnedest thing I ever saw," Cato remarked. "At least the king and queen appear to be safe enough."

"Captain," said the Lord Admiral grimly, his gaze fixed intently on the PVC, "I have a hunch about this, too. Do whatever it takes to get that damn limo going!"

The PVC clanked and thundered its way down the side of the culvert. Xris rode in the gun turret; Jamil steered from down below. Harry and Quong, Raoul and the Little One were jammed shoulder to shoulder in the middle. The insides smelled oddly of gardenia and burning oil. When the Devastator reached the culvert's bottom, Xris ordered Jamil to stop.

"Rowan!" Xris was forced to shout into the comm over the rumbling of the engine. "Has the king been evacuated yet?"

"No, Xris!" she returned. "They're keeping him inside the limojet."

It made sense. Under any other circumstances, the shielded, specially designed limo would be the safest possible place. Unfortunately, ironically, it was likely to become the safest possible steel-lined coffin.

"Any luck jamming the negative wave device?"

"We confused them for a few seconds, but they were able to outmaneuver us. The knights know we're on to them now. You better hurry, Xris."

Sliding down out of the turret, the cyborg almost landed in Raoul's lap. The Loti had a handkerchief pressed over his nose and mouth with one hand, the other held fast to the hem of his golden cape, attempting to keep it out of the grease on the floor.

Xris stood practically on top of the Adonian, shouted to be heard.

"Try to reach the Royal Guard! Tell them that they *have* to get the king out of the limojet! The knights are using the limo as their target. The king would be safer in the crowd than he is in that damn car! You got that?"

Raoul nodded, cautiously removed the handkerchief, and shrieked, "Do you have any ideas on how I'm supposed to get close enough to tell anyone anything?"

Xris shook his head, reached for the controls that opened the hatch. "No, but you'll figure something out! You always do."

"I do, don't I?" Raoul remarked calmly.

Clasping hold of the Little One's hand, the Adonian stepped over Harry, fell over Quong, and headed for the open hatch. A trickle of muddy water ran through the culvert. Raoul gazed at it, looked back at Xris reproachfully.

Xris shrugged. "It's only water. You won't melt."

Sighing, Raoul took off his shoes, gathered his cape around him, and jumped. The Little One flung himself out afterward. They were almost immediately lost in the smoke from the PVC's exhaust.

At least they'll be out of view of the hovercraft circling overhead, Xris reflected. He ducked back inside the PVC.

"Let's go!" Xris shouted to Jamil, and the lumbering vehicle lurched forward, began rolling up the side of the culvert. "Full throttle! Don't stop for anything now!"

Coughing, choking, hanging on to his shoes with one hand, the Little One with the other, and trying to keep his golden cape from dragging in the mud, Raoul trudged up the side of the culvert. His spirits were as low as it was possible for the spirits of an Adonian Loti to get, which put them somewhere in the vicinity of the golden sash that encircled his slim waist.

Reaching a concrete wall—put there to keep children and other members of the populace from tumbling into the drainage ditch—Raoul paused to watch the Devastator slam right through that same wall, go crunching over the wreckage.

Raoul sighed. "They have all the fun."

He gazed at the concrete wall. He would have to climb over it—no jolly smashing through it—and he sighed again.

He only hoped he didn't rip a seam.

Raoul placed his shoes—low-heeled, since he was going into action—carefully on the wall. Reaching down to his friend, he lifted the Little One and swung him up onto the top of the wall, which was about level with Raoul's shoulders.

Noting the dirt on the top, Raoul sighed a third time. Really! Xris expected the impossible!

"I trust I will be fully compensated," he remarked, then put his hands on the wall and, closing his eyes to the grime, pulled himself up.

He climbed over, lowered himself to the ground, and was almost immediately elbowed, kneed, and rudely mauled by the crowd. Some people were trying to escape, others were clambering to get a better view, while still others were fighting simply to keep from getting crushed or trampled.

Raoul, who had been about to lift the Little One down, now thought better of it. He climbed hastily back up onto the wall, gazed at the mob in disgust.

"I've never seen anything quite like this," he remarked to the Little One. "With the possible exception of the night our late former employer, Snaga Ohme, was murdered and Lord Sagan spread the false report that the space-rotation bomb was about to detonate. But even that didn't compare to this because we had only a few hundred panic-stricken people stampeding about the mansion, while here . . ."

He couldn't go on. Words were simply not adequate.

At that moment, the pressure of the mob eased. The hole punched into the side of the concrete wall by the PVC had opened up an alternative route—at least so most people appeared to believe, for they were streaming through the opening and running down into the culvert with no very clear idea of where they were going or why.

"Bizarre," said Raoul. "And just think of it. Most of these people are probably sober."

The Little One nodded gloomily, tugged on his friend's sleeve, and pointed.

The Royal Limojet could not be seen, surrounded as it was by the Royal Guard. But Raoul knew what his friend meant.

"Ah, yes. The king."

Raoul contemplated the sea of humanity roiling between them and His Majesty and, for the first time in his life, the Adonian was subject to a feeling of helplessness.

"There is simply no way, my friend," he said to the Little One. "We are doomed to failure."

This feeling made him uncomfortable. Raoul hated feeling uncomfortable. He wondered if he'd brought along anything to alleviate the stress. Opening his handbag, he began searching for relief. Several sheaves of stiff, folded paper, tucked into the side of the purse, hampered his rummaging. He took the papers out, glanced at them—vaguely curious to see what they were—and started to toss them away.

And then he had an idea.

He clutched at the papers, held them fast, as if they were the most precious objects to come into his possession in a month: new diamond earrings, perhaps, or a jar of thigh cream.

"This is it!" Raoul breathed softly.

The Little One, reading his thoughts, clapped his hands and began to jump up and down—a perilous move on top of the wall. Raoul was quick to calm his friend's joy.

"We have to find a policeman," Raoul said, and was immediately cheered and delighted by the oddity. Generally policemen were out trying to find Raoul, not the other way around.

The Little One, standing on the wall, tapped his friend on the head, drew Raoul's attention to several small hovering vehicles known as chariots because they purportedly resembled the chariots of ancient times—minus the horses and the wheels. Designed for police use, the chariot was nothing more than a round section of metal floor plating surrounded by a steel railing and equipped with anti-grav plates and blast jets. When activated, the chariot rose into the air, carrying the police in rapid—albeit breezy—transit above the congested sidewalks of the city.

Police chariots were zipping around overhead, endeavoring to funnel the crowd out and away from the immediate vicinity of the hotel.

Raoul put his golden shoes on, stood on top of the concrete wall, and began waving his hands, crying shrilly.

"Help! Help me! Help! Police! Help!"

The Adonian was a dazzling spectacle in his glittering doublet and golden hose and breeches. His golden cape caught the wind, billowed around him. Jewels and sequins glittered in bright sunlight. He might have been another sun, fallen to the ground.

Just when it seemed to the harried police that they were finally getting the situation under control and the mob was starting to disperse, they noticed a crowd beginning to form around a flamboyantly dressed Adonian screaming for help on a concrete wall.

The police moved in quickly.

"Get down from there!" one policeman demanded, bringing his chariot level with Raoul. "Move along or you'll find yourself in jail!"

Raoul shoved the sheaf of papers at the startled cop.

"I'm the Ambassador from Adonia!" Raoul gasped breathlessly. "My aide and I were supposed to be among the dignitaries attending the king, but we became separated from the group when the revolt started."

"There's no revolt," the policeman said swiftly. Too swiftly.

Raoul nodded gravely. "My lips are sealed. But you must understand that I fear for my life and that of my aide. I demand that you take us to a place of safety. The nearest would be the temple, I presume." Raoul's painted eyelids fluttered. "I request the protection of the Royal Guard."

The policeman examined the credentials, which appeared authentic, down to the silver wax seal and the red ribbons. The crowd, drawn by the sight of the police, rather than dispersing, grew larger. At that moment, a burst from the PVC's lascannon split the air like a thunderclap. The crowd gasped, screamed, and surged toward the wall.

Raoul blanched in terror, threw his arms around the policeman, nearly strangling the man.

"Officer, please! Our lives are in your hands. If anything happens to us, you will be held personally responsible! This could well cause a breach between our two governments!"

"What the hell is going on?" A policewoman in another chariot sailed over.

"He's the Adonian ambassador, Sergeant. Wants to be taken to the Royal Guard. His credentials check out." The policeman endeavored unsuccessfully to pry Raoul loose.

"Then let them protect him, by all means. We don't need any more trouble. The Goddess knows we have enough to deal with. We've been ordered to evacuate and seal off the area surrounding the hotel."

"Yes, ma'am."

The policeman opened a gate. Raoul hopped inside, dragging the Little One with him. The chariot took off, soaring over the heads of the crowd, heading up to the very steps of the temple itself.

Raoul could see the Royal Limojet clearly now. Looking back, he could also see the PVC Devastator, blasting its way toward the hotel.

Raoul held his golden purse over his head, endeavoring to keep his hair from getting mussed in the wind.

"Thank heaven," he remarked to the Little One, "I was dressed for the occasion."

CHAPTER
39

. . . then you are like a rabbit on the loose, so the enemy cannot keep you out.

Sun Tzu, *The Art of War*

Laser fire burst around the PVC, but even the high-powered beam rifles carried by the local cops couldn't penetrate the massive tank's nullgrav steel armor. Xris kept up a steady stream of lascannon bursts that effectively cleared their path. Most of the police, seeing that their weapons had no effect, turned and ran, with the exception of one stalwart cop—either more courageous than his fellows or crazier—who leaped bodily onto the PVC as it roared across the hotel parking lot.

Once he was there, the cop clung to the glacis plate of the speeding, rocking tank, practically eyeball to eyeball with Xris in the turret. The cop brought up his handheld lasgun, aimed it directly at Xris. The blast, which would reflect off the shields, was liable to do more damage to the cop than it would to the cyborg.

Xris swiveled the lascannon around sharply, brushed off the cop as if he'd been a candidate for Olicien Pest Control services. Looking through the rearview cam, the last Xris saw of the cop, he was lying dazed on the pavement, muzzily shaking his head but otherwise unhurt.

The PVC rolled without further obstructions—at least that it couldn't climb over—up to the hotel. Fortunately, someone'd had sense enough to evacuate the area. Terrified guests were being herded out of the main entrance. A line of cops kept them moving—an easy task when the PVC roared into plain view.

"Head for that door on the building's north side!" Xris yelled to Jamil.

He piloted the PVC up to a side door marked AUTHORIZED PERSONNEL ONLY. The Devastator lumbered to a stop.

Xris bailed out of the turret, met Jamil coming from the driver's side, joined Tycho and Harry crouched in the tank's cramped interior.

"Tycho, you and Harry rush the door. Jamil guard their flank. I'll cover you all from here. Right. Got it? Go."

Xris hit the controls that opened the hatch; then he climbed back up into the turret.

Harry jumped out, his beam rifle swinging in an arc.

A man appeared, coming around the back corner of the building. Harry fired a burst in the air. The man leaped about a foot, turned, and fled.

Tycho and Jamil jumped out immediately behind Harry. Tycho ran for the door, while Harry covered him. Flattening himself against the side of the building to the door's right, Tycho motioned for Harry to join him.

Jamil kept Harry covered. Xris watched the rear.

Harry dashed over, took up a position flat against the wall to the left of the door. Jamil followed.

A 'copter flew in. Xris fired a blast from the lascannon, warning it off. A lascannon could bring down a 'copter. It veered away, but didn't go far.

Harry tried the hotel door. Locked.

Jamil attached a magnetic explosive charge. Everyone turned away, shielding themselves from the blast. The heavy steel door blew inward, hung crazily on its hinges.

Jamil motioned. Xris abandoned the turret. Thrusting a twist in his mouth, he ran a last-minute check on his weapons hand and his system status LEDs. The lights glimmered comfortingly green.

Xris dove out the hatch, broke into a run, and raced across the short distance that separated the PVC from the side of the building.

A kick from his steel leg knocked the door off its hinges. Xris burst inside, hit the floor, and rolled. His enhanced vision scanned the dark interior of the hallway for heat sources. None. He jumped to his feet.

He stood in a bleak and sterile corridor. A fire door at the end was marked FIRST FLOOR. Concrete stairs, with an iron railing, led upward. Xris adjusted his augmented hearing, listened closely. No sounds from above.

He waved. Harry and Jamil ran past him to the base of the stairs.

"Second-floor landing," Harry reported. "More stairs from there, going up at a thirty-degree angle."

Typical fire escape. Xris gave Harry the signal to continue. The big man started climbing. A blast from a beam rifle blew out a section of wall to his left, caused him to beat a hasty retreat.

"That ain't the nightly news," Harry said, brushing chips of concrete out of his hair.

Xris sucked on the twist. He hadn't doubted it. Not really. Not after seeing Dr. Brisbane. But it was nice to be certain. He waved Harry on.

The big man took a stun grenade from his field webbing pouch, tapped the arming code, and tossed the grenade up the stairs to the first-floor landing. He ducked; everyone ducked, eyes squinched tightly shut, hands over their ears.

A cracking sound split the air in the corridor. Before it had died away, Harry raced up the stairs, taking them two at a time. Jamil advanced, stood guard at the bottom.

Xris grabbed Tycho, drew him back to the doorway.

"Move around to the front of the building. Take a few potshots at the third-floor balcony. I want the knights to have to worry about a frontal assault as well as one from the rear. You probably can't get a clear shot at the negative wave device because of the shielding around it, but you can take out anyone standing nearby. Hit them with a few iridium jacket rounds. That should make 'em back off, at least till we get there. Understand?" He looked at the alien worriedly. Sometimes Tycho's translator did odd things.

Apparently this time the message got through.

"Clearest thing since sliced bread!" Tycho responded.

Xris took half a second to assimilate that one, but was reassured by the sight of the alien loping off to take up his position.

Xris turned just in time to hear Harry yell from the second-floor landing, "Number two!"

He was tossing another stun grenade, probably onto the third floor. Jamil, at the foot of the stairs, gave an alarmed shout. Xris started forward; the blast nearly knocked him off his feet.

Something had gone wrong. The grenade had exploded too close.

Laser fire blasted the staircase. Sparks cascaded over the railing. Harry came stumbling down, wobbling drunkenly, his face contorted in pain. Staggering, he missed the last step. Xris caught the big man as he fell, propped him up.

"Jamil! Cover us!"

Jamil was already dashing up the stairs, firing as he went.

"What happened?" Xris yelled at Harry. "Are you hurt?"

"What?"

Blood trickled out from both Harry's ears. The big man sucked in a pain-filled breath, leaned back against the wall.

"Stay here!" Xris yelled as loudly as he could. He took the twist out of his mouth, motioned with it to emphasize his words.

"No, thanks, Xris," Harry mumbled, looking dazedly at the twist. "I don't smoke."

"I said stay—" Xris shook his head. "Never mind."

Damn difficult to hear, when your eardrums have been shattered. He patted the big man on the chest, then raced up the stairs.

Crouched in a corner of the landing, Jamil was trading shots with an unseen enemy.

Xris aimed his weapons hand, fired a heat-seeking micromissile. It arced upward in a slow spiral. He and Jamil ducked. The explosion rocked the stairwell, filled it with acrid smoke. Xris thought he heard a scream. For the moment, the laser fire from that direction ceased.

"What happened to Harry?" Xris asked.

"He threw a stun grenade up and one of those bastards caught it, threw it right back down! In all my days in the Army," Jamil added, waiting for the beam rifle to cycle through before firing, "I've only known a few people with guts and discipline enough to try that trick, and most of them ended up minus a hand. These are the same well-trained bastards we faced on the *Canis Major.*"

He fired his beam rifle. A burst of return laser fire took out a section of the step on which he was standing. He moved.

"Well trained, well armed. They have the high ground and they know we're coming." Xris peered upward, through the smoke. "Tycho's keeping them busy out front. Harry's down for the count. I've only got two more of those slow missiles.

Can't use the fast ones in tight corners; they're liable to blow us up before they do the enemy." Xris chomped down savagely on the twist. "Any suggestions?"

"Yeah," said Jamil. "Give me a high-explosive frag grenade. I'll clean those knights out of the stairway."

Xris shook his head. He knew what Jamil had in mind. "I'll do it."

"Like hell. Half of you weighs in at a quarter ton. You can't move that fast. Besides, I'm a trained professional." Jamil grinned. "Hand it over."

Xris took the grenade from his field webbing, gave it to Jamil.

He tapped the arming button, but didn't throw it.

Xris automatically began counting, "Five, four . . ."

Jamil dashed up the stairs, grenade in one hand, firing his beam rifle with the other.

". . . three, two . . ."

Laser blasts and iridium bullets spattered around him. Right when Xris counted "one!" Jamil tossed the grenade, hunkered down.

The stairwell exploded. A scorching wave of hot plasma hit Xris. He shielded his face with his arm. The sounds of gunfire from above abruptly ceased.

Xris was up and running.

Jamil should have been, but he wasn't. Xris found the major sprawled on the shattered stairs, lying beneath the twisted wreckage of what had once been an iron railing.

Lasgun in hand, dividing his attention between the landing above and his fallen comrade, Xris lifted the red-hot iron with his metal hand, tossed it clattering down the stairwell. He rolled his friend over.

Shrapnel and splinters of iron had raked Jamil's left arm, tearing through body armor into flesh and muscle. He was burned, but not badly, mostly on the top of his head. But he was covered in blood. A quick check revealed that at least no main arteries had been severed, his pulse was strong. He groaned. His eyes flickered opened, rolled, then shut again.

A head encased in a shining black helmet appeared over the railing. Light glinted off the barrel of a needle-gun.

Xris fired his lasgun, must have hit, for he heard a cry and a foul curse. The head disappeared.

Fishing out a pressure bandage, Xris ripped it open. He slid the bandage up Jamil's arm, positioned it over the worst of the wounds, hit the activator. The bandage inflated, applying the correct amount of pressure to stop the bleeding, formed a seal over the wound.

The helmeted head was back. Xris traded his lasgun for Jamil's beam rifle, fired it, then sent up another of his slow missiles.

"Catch that, you son of a bitch!" he shouted.

The knight didn't take Xris up on his offer, but the soldier did have guts enough to fire a round before seeking cover.

Another blast. Xris was on the move, his metal leg kicking aside fragments of concrete and railing. He reached the landing between the second and third floors, finally had a clear view of what he was up against. Black-suited bodies lay in front of the fire door.

Xris started up the stairs. Two more black-suited figures appeared. He had no more doubts. These were the knights, trained soldiers and assassins. And fanatics.

Xris hunkered down, fired, missed, fired again. The best thing he could do was keep moving, keep shooting. Smoke filled the stairwell. He would be a difficult target for the knights to see, while Xris's heat-seeking vision could pick them out perfectly.

Two knights stood guarding the door, backs against the wall. Obviously they had orders to stop Xris or die in the attempt.

"Glad to oblige," Xris told them.

Lying prone on the stairs, he opened up with the beam rifle, swept it from left to right and back again. He caught one man across the midriff; his rifle flew from his hands, arced over the broken railing, went clanging down the stairs. The other knight vanished; Xris couldn't see what happened to him. Probably hit, maybe retreated.

"Waiting for me inside that damn door," Xris muttered. He spit out what remained of the sodden mass that had been the twist, picked himself up, and made a mad dash for the half-closed door.

He put his metal shoulder to it, burst the door open, beam rifle blasting as he ran.

He was in a carpeted corridor of a luxury hotel. He took cover in a nearby doorway, ceased firing long enough to take a quick look around. Doors to rooms to his left and right. Most were closed. One, about six meters down the hall, was open. The corridor looked empty.

Xris took a step forward.

A knight popped up out of nowhere, directly in front of the cyborg. Xris had no time to think. He just prayed and shot.

The blast struck the knight at point-blank range. The body literally dissolved in a charred and bloody mass at Xris's feet.

A man with good reflexes and two good legs could have avoided falling over the corpse. Xris's entire system had to readjust itself, however: neurocomputer responding to electronic impulses from the brain; mechanical side of the body trying to coordinate with the physical. He was struggling to retain his balance when a bullet struck him from behind.

The bullet lodged in metal, not in flesh, but that didn't make a whole hell of a lot of difference. The impact knocked Xris's cybernetic leg from under him; shorted out all kinds of complicated electronic circuitry.

He knew, as he fell, that he was dead. Sprawled on the floor, his electronics going wild, he had no way to defend himself. The next shot would blow apart his head or tear open his chest. . . .

He heard the shot, was startled not to feel it slam into him. Training and experience made up for the frantic microsecond of panic. He had managed to hang on to the beam rifle. Rolling to his left, he lifted his weapon, prepared to fire, stopped himself just in time.

Harry stood in the doorway, lasgun in hand. A dead knight lay on the floor in front of him.

"Thanks!" Xris shouted.

"Huh?" Harry returned. "Did you say somethin'?"

Xris pulled himself to a crouching position, began to assess the damage. LEDs flashed red. He did what he could to jury-rig himself, was making final adjustments when he heard Harry shout.

Xris looked up quickly. A black-gloved hand flicked out of the open door down the corridor. A grenade rolled toward them.

Xris couldn't move.

Harry had been firing at the hand, now shifted his aim to the grenade. His fourth volley hit it.

Both men cringed, waiting for the blast.

The grenade wobbled to a halt, sat there, blinking ominously.

Figuring he was about as operational as he was going to get, Xris stood up, tried walking. His cybernetic leg dragged, out of sync with his good leg.

"You stay here, Harry," Xris shouted, loaded two large micro-missiles into his weapons hand. "I'm going on ahead. Keep me covered!"

"I don't think so," Harry yelled. "You go ahead. I'll keep you covered."

"Fine. You do that."

Limping awkwardly down the hall, Xris halted in front of the door, fired the two missiles into the hotel room, then hugged the floor.

The explosion's back blast washed over Xris in a concussive wave. He'd forgotten to turn off his augmented hearing and for a moment was as deaf as Harry. When bits of debris quit raining down on top of him, Xris shook the rubble off him, stood up.

Smoke billowed out into the corridor. Fire alarms sounded, squawking loudly. The sprinkler systems activated.

Harry—backing down the hall, keeping his gun aimed at the fire door—looked up in astonishment as the water hit him in the face. Arriving at the door, he paused a moment, motioned inside with a jerk of his head.

"You hear anything?"

Xris listened. Flames crackled. Someone moaned. But if anyone was waiting in ambush, they were being damn quiet about it.

Xris took the lead. He and Harry burst into the room.

A black form leaped out at them; metal flashed. The knight—knife in hand—landed on Harry. The two crashed back onto a bed, rolled from there to the floor.

Xris lost sight of them. He could hear the two scuffling in the life-and-death struggle, but there was nothing he could do to help. His attention was focused on the phony image-intensifier antenna set up out on the balcony.

The bodies of two "crewmen" lay sprawled beside it. They wore GNN coveralls. Either they were knights disguised as GNN personnel or the knights had impressed these two poor bastards into working for them. It didn't matter much now. Tycho's aim was true as ever.

But though its crew was dead, the antenna was still up and running. Xris started toward it to shut it down, saw movement out of the corner of his eye.

Dr. Brisbane darted out from behind a curtain, a needle-gun aimed straight at his head.

Xris lunged sideways—or at least that's what he intended to do. His mechanical leg didn't get the message. He tottered, off balance, flailing wildly. The needle struck him in the shoulder of his good arm. His sight blurred red momentarily, the pain unbelievable. But the doctor would have been far better advised to aim for Xris's mechanical side.

As it was, his weapons hand was working perfectly. He aimed, fired.

The force of the blast blew Dr. Brisbane out the door through the balcony's railing, and over the edge.

He looked down at his arm, saw it covered in blood. His commlink squawked, demanding his attention. It had, he realized dimly, been squawking for quite a long time now.

"Xris, can you hear me? Xris, dammit! Are you all right?"

It was Rowan. She sounded frantic, worried.

"I'm okay," he said, gritting his teeth against the pain of his wounds. "I'm on the balcony with the negative wave device. Its operators are dead—"

"But the device is alive and well!" Rowan was panting, breathless, almost screaming at him. "It's almost up to full power. You've got to shut it off *now*! Xris! Now!"

Harry was still fighting. Xris could hear the two men, but he couldn't take time to help. He dragged himself to the device, stared at it. Lights were blinking; his augmented hearing was picking up an annoying whining sound. Frantically he searched, but couldn't find anything that vaguely resembled a switch.

"Turn it off!" Rowan yelled.

"How?" Xris yelled back.

A pause. He could hear her consulting with Quong. Xris ground his teeth. Hurry . . . hurry . . .

Quong sounded troubled. "The switch should be plainly visible."

"You come look for it, then!"

Pain jabbed him. Xris sucked in his breath. Hurry, damn it! . . .

Rowan was back. "My guess is that the device is being controlled from a remote unit. Which could be hidden anywhere—"

"Oh, the hell with it!"

Balancing himself on his good leg, Xris swung his mechanical leg like a club. His metal foot connected with the machine.

The device smashed against the balcony. Sparks flew. Xris fired a blast from his lasgun at the generator. It blew apart. The whining sound the antenna had been making ceased.

"That's it!" Rowan was jubilant. "You've done it!"

Xris nodded, too tired and hurting to answer.

Harry came out onto the balcony, wiping blood from his hands on the front of his shirt. He had a cut down one side of his face; one eye was starting to swell shut. He looked with satisfaction at the wreckage of the device.

"Nice job," he said.

Xris nodded again, pulled out a twist, almost dropped it from his shaking hand.

"You okay?" Harry asked worriedly.

"Yeah," Xris lied. "You?"

"No, thanks," Harry returned loudly. "I don't smoke. What's Tycho up to?"

Good question. Xris hit the comm. "Tycho? You read me?"

No response.

"Tycho?"

Not even a crackle.

A cold feeling spread from Xris's stomach up his spine, nudged aside the pain. It was, he realized suddenly, too damn quiet down on the ground. Motioning Harry to move back, Xris took a cautious look over the balcony.

What was left of Dr. Brisbane was lying on the ground. Tycho stood in the center of a ring of gun barrels, all pointed at him. He was surrounded by soldiers. Xris didn't recognize the uniforms or the insignias. It didn't matter anyway.

Pivoting on his mechanical leg, he stumped across the balcony.

"We're going to have company," he announced to Harry.

"Huh?" Harry cupped his hand over his ear.

Xris grabbed hold of the big man's arm, pulled him into the room.

"Xris!" Rowan's voice was frantic, halted Xris where he stood. "We're reading *another* signature! I repeat, *another* signature! It appeared practically the moment the main device went down. It's weaker than the first, but that doesn't matter. According to our readings, this device is located in the immediate vicinity of the king!"

Xris shook his head, sighed. These guys were good. Damn good.

"Okay, Rowan, you and Quong—"

"No good, Xris, I'm afraid," the doctor's voice chimed in, steady, calm. "We're not going anywhere. We're surrounded."

Xris heard ominous sounds, knew what was coming.

"Yeah," he said. "I know the feeling."

Heavily armed soldiers, their faces concealed behind helmets, surged into the hotel room. They wore some sort of markings on their body armor, but Xris was too dazed and exhausted to make any sense of them. The soldiers leveled beam rifles at him.

He raised his hands in the air. Somehow, he had to raise Raoul, warn him, tell him what to do.

He spoke into the comm. "Raoul—"

One of the soldiers slugged Xris in the mouth with the butt end of his rifle.

"Shut down your communications."

Harry looked to Xris for orders.

Xris shook his head, shrugged.

The soldiers clamped restrainers on Harry's wrists, fit two more around his ankles.

The captain of the troop—the one who had hit him— aimed his weapon at Xris.

"Now shut yourself down, cyborg."

No use arguing. Xris didn't bother to tell them he lacked the energy to fight anyhow.

"Take it slow," the captain warned. "Keep your hands where I can see them."

Xris reached for his battery pack, touched a button. The LED lights on his arm went out; the entire left side of his body went dead. He could no longer maintain his balance, flopped, helpless, onto a bed.

The captain regarded him with a look of pity.

Xris closed his eyes, reminded himself to slug that son-of-a-bitch captain one day. Right now, though, he had other things to do.

He focused his thoughts. Pictured in his mind a raincoat and a battered fedora. . . .

CHAPTER
40

Assassiner c'est le plus court chemin.
Assassination is the quickest way.
            Molière, *Le Sicillien*, Scene 12

"Well, my friend," said Raoul, looking up at the temple looming over him, "we are here. And now we are supposed to alert someone to His Majesty's danger and advise them that they should remove him from the vehicle."

The Little One shook his head gloomily.

"You are right, my friend. That will not be easy."

The chariot had set them down on the temple steps, away from the crush of the panicking crowd below, but not much closer to their goal. Up here, they were just two more dignitaries. And the dignitaries were actually causing more trouble than the mobs, for the dignitaries not only needed to be protected, but reassured, coddled, mollified, soothed, and/or placated. The various governors and parliamentarians and vid stars, mingled with priests and priestesses, all lunged about aimlessly, bumping into one another like ships caught in an asteroid field, never going where they were told, always ending up where they weren't wanted.

The king and queen, ensconced in the Royal Limo, surrounded by armed guards and now by a gathering contingent of media, remained as far from Raoul as any star in the firmament.

"I could attempt to speak to the Royal Guard, but I have grave doubts that they will believe me," Raoul continued. "In fact, my warning them about the danger to the king would look extremely suspicious. The real Adonian ambassador would be worried about only one thing at a time like this—saving himself."

The Little One scanned the crowd from beneath the rim of the fedora. He jabbed one small finger in the direction of the Royal Guard.

Raoul lifted a plucked eyebrow. "Ah, yes. Captain Cato. True, he would undoubtedly recognize us in connection with our erstwhile employment with our erstwhile employer, Snaga Ohme. I have the distinct feeling, however, that such recognition would result in our being immediately incarcerated."

The Little One, standing on one foot, weighed the force of this argument and was evidently inclined to agree. He crossed his small arms over his chest and shook his head.

"The king and queen know us and have reason to feel kindly toward us," Raoul continued. "But to reach Their Majesties, we have to penetrate the ranks of the Royal Guard, who do not know us and who have no reason to feel anything whatsoever about us except that we are, perhaps, better dressed than most people here. Still, we must do what we can. I—"

The Little One began hopping up and down, pointing frantically.

Raoul peered through the crowd. He grabbed the Little One's hand in excitement. "General Dixter! I mean—Lord Admiral Dixter. He knows us! And he actually *likes* us!"

Raoul pulled his handkerchief from his handbag, began to wave it in the air. "General Dixter! Yoo-hoo! I mean Lord Admiral Dixter! Xris sent us! We—"

The Little One whipped around, trod hard on Raoul's foot.

Raoul clapped his hand over his mouth, but it was too late. Dixter had heard the Adonian's shrill cry—as had everyone in the immediate vicinity. And he had heard the name Xris.

"I forgot—we are wanted men!" Raoul also forgot to lower his voice, causing several people near him to stare at him in horror and begin pointing at him.

Dixter was saying something to two of the Royal Guard, who started toward Raoul, shoving their way through the crowd, politely but firmly elbowing people out of their way.

"You're right!" Raoul gasped. "They undoubtedly think *we're* the assassins! In which case," he added gravely, "I deem it unlikely that they will honor our request to speak to the king."

The Little One pulled Raoul to one side, tugging him underneath the maze of scaffolding on which the dignitaries' platform had been built. People surged around them. Raoul tried his best to blend in with the crowd—not an easy feat, considering that he outshone the sun.

He heard his name, recognized Dixter's voice. "Don't leave! You're not in any danger!"

Raoul paused, half turned, and saw the Royal Guard drawing their lasguns.

A drawn lasgun—in Raoul's mind—constituted danger. He ducked under a piece of royal purple bunting.

The guns caught the dignitaries' attention, as well. They swirled away from the guard like leaves in a storm. The news media, catching sight of the action, immediately dashed after the Royal Guard. Even James M. Warden, news anchor for GNN, who had been in a heated discussion with Captain Cato, paused, turned to see what was going on. Warden said something to his cameraman, who lifted the vidcam, focused in on the Royal Guard and Lord Admiral Dixter.

Glancing through a dangling drape, Raoul caught a glimpse of the expression on Dixter's face—helpless, frustrated.

Raoul knew just how the man felt. "How will we ever get to the king now?" he asked his small companion.

The Little One had some idea in mind, perhaps, for he dragged Raoul out from under the opposite end of the scaffolding and plunged back into the crowd. Raoul tripped mincingly along behind his friend, keeping up a running stream of apologies.

"I beg your pardon, madam. So sorry, sir. We must get through. Urgent information. I adore your dress, my dear. Is it an original or a copy? Are you quite sure? It's a copy," he said in an undertone to the Little One.

His friend growled impatiently, pulled Raoul along so fast that he nearly stepped out of his pumps.

"Where *are* we going?" Raoul demanded.

The Little One pointed, indicated his plan. Raoul blinked, astounded at the idea. The more he considered it, the better he liked it.

"GNN! News anchor James M. Warden. His Majesty un-

doubtedly has a vid machine in the limo. We will get ourselves on camera and issue the warning that way! James M.
Warden will certainly not allow anyone to shoot us—at least
until after the interview."

The two hastened ahead.

"Mr. Warden!" Raoul called, once again waving the han-
kie. "Mr. Warden! You don't know me, but—"

James M. Warden faced them.

Raoul had the sudden impression that he'd been mistaken;
that the news anchor did indeed know them and that they
weren't at all a welcome sight. Warden's expression was
cold, dire.

The Little One halted so abruptly that Raoul tumbled over
him.

"Hostile? Why should he be hostile—"

Warden turned to Cato. "Captain, those two men over
there. I recognize them. They are members of the cyborg's
mercenary team!"

Cato looked, saw them, recognized them. The captain
shouted for his men, started forward.

Raoul was caught out in the open, nowhere to run.

This called for desperate measures. He reached into his
handbag for his lipstick. . . .

At that moment, the limo's jets fired.

Captain Cato whipped around, began issuing orders.
"Clear the area! Get His Majesty to safety!"

The Royal Guard instantly sprang to action. The ring of
steel expanded outward, firmly, determinedly pressing people out of the way. The Royal Limo started to lift off the
ground.

Raoul and the Little One thankfully mingled with the excited crowd, let the mob pick them up and sweep them away,
back to the relative safety of the scaffolding.

The Adonian heaved a sigh of relief. "Ah, nothing to
worry about now. Xris Cyborg must have disabled the device. We can— What is it?"

The Little One was leaning forward, his head cocked, as
if he were listening to a distant call.

Raoul followed his companion's line of sight. "News anchor James M. Warden appears exceedingly displeased.
Well, he's obviously just realized he's missed his chance to
interview us. Oh, that's not it? He's contacting someone.
Trying to contact someone. They're not answering. He's try-

ing to contact his news crew! The people in the hotel! You don't suppose—"

The Little One suddenly stiffened; his gaze became unfocused, abstracted. He put his hands to his head, shook it in confusion.

Raoul stared at his friend worriedly. "What—"

The Little One stomped on Raoul's foot.

Raoul took the hint, fell silent, though he mourned over the black mark on his golden pumps.

Spinning around, the Little One grabbed hold of Raoul to ensure his complete attention, and transmitted his message.

Raoul sucked in a breath. "You were talking to Xris Cyborg! We're supposed to look for a backup assassin, carrying one of the negative wave devices! Somewhere near the king! Possibly a GNN crewman. A GNN crewman? Are you sure? What else? What else did he say?"

The Little One clasped one small hand over his own wrist.

"They've been captured." Raoul sighed. "It's up to us."

He gazed around. GNN news crew were everywhere. A quick count garnered about twenty. And everyone of them seemed to be either holding or standing next to some sort of machine. And every machine, as far as Raoul could judge machinery, had the potential of being deadly.

"One of these people is going to murder the king," he murmured. "And there is nothing the Royal Guard or anyone can do to stop the assassin, because they will never see it coming. The young king will die, horribly, painfully, and no one will ever know how, why. The assassin will simply walk away."

"Get a shot of that limo!"

The voice belonged to news anchor James M. Warden, instructing his cameraman. The man shifted the vidcam to the limojet.

The engines shut off. The limo fell back to the ground, with what must have been a bone-jarring jolt for those inside.

"Now," Warden was saying. "I want a shot of the king."

"That's it! The device!" Raoul cried. "Stay here," he ordered the Little One.

Raoul pulled out his lipstick, flipped off the cap. A tiny needle flicked out of the tube. Holding the tube in his hand, careful not to touch the needle, he ran toward the cameraman.

No one, with the possible exception of Xris, would have now recognized the Loti. Raoul's gaze was concentrated, absorbed, intent on his target. He ran lightly, swiftly, his black hair streaming out behind.

He reached the cameraman, could see—in the vidcam's lens—red-golden hair. Dion was facing the camera, looking right into it. The vidcam hummed. . . .

Raoul jabbed the needle deep into the cameraman's back. The man cried out in astonishment and pain. He dropped the camera, tumbled down to the ground, and lay there—unconscious.

And then the Little One's voice sounded in Raoul's mind. *The wrong man! He's not the one! The assassin is—*

A clenched fist slammed into Raoul's jaw, spun him around. He fell on all fours, dazed and groggy from the blow.

In front of him, on the ground, lay the camera, still humming, lights still flashing.

Raoul flung his body on top of the vidcam, fumbling for the switch in a desperate attempt to shut it off. A savage kick drove into his rib cage. Bones cracked. Pain shot through him. A hand grabbed hold of him, flung him up and backward.

James Warden picked up the vidcam, aimed it at the king.

The Royal Guard were closing in—on Raoul. No one was paying the slightest attention to the news anchor.

Raoul tried to sit up, but the pain of the broken ribs was intense. It hurt too much to breathe, let alone move. He was vaguely aware of the Little One standing over him, saw the small hand emerge from the raincoat, carrying a blowgun.

The Little One put the blowgun to his lips.

Warden clapped his hand to the back of his neck, as if he'd been stung by an insect. He gave a cry of fury and outrage, fought to hold the camera steady. But the poison from the feathered dart worked swiftly. His body jerked. He staggered. Dropping the vidcam, he clutched at his throat. Then he fell to the ground, dead.

The Little One bent anxiously over his friend.

"The camera!" Raoul choked, clasping his side. The pain was horrible; he felt sick and faint. "Shut it off!"

The Little One stared in baffled consternation at the vidcam. Even if he hadn't been terrified of the mechanical thing, he had no more idea how to shut it down than Xris had of how to apply lipstick. The little Tongan, member of a primitive race, from a primitive planet, searched for and found one of mankind's very first tools. This he knew how to use.

Lifting a large rock, the Little One held it over his head, brought it down with all the force of his small body on the negative wave device. Again and again, he bashed the machine with the rock.

It worked quite as effectively as the on/off switch. The device died.

But the Royal Guard was, in the interval, thundering down on them, lasguns raised, aimed.

"I don't think they will be disposed to listen to our story," Raoul murmured. "I believe, in fact, that they are about to shoot us—"

"Raoul!" A voice called. "Over here!"

Raoul managed to weakly lift his head.

The door to the Royal Limojet stood wide open. Its engines had fired; it was ready to depart.

Lord Admiral Dixter gestured. "Quickly!"

The Little One took hold of his friend's hand, helped him to his feet.

Tottering on weak knees, Raoul stumbled toward the limo. Only a step away, he fell, unable to walk farther. The Lord Admiral caught hold of him, eased him into the vehicle, where Raoul collapsed thankfully onto one of the leather seats. The Little One clambered inside after his friend.

"Your Majesties," said Dixter gravely. "I have the honor of presenting the Ambassador from Adonia and his aide."

Lying sprawled across the seat, Raoul waved a graceful hand to the king, smiled charmingly at the queen, and fainted.

Dion looked at Raoul, looked back at Dixter.

Dixter nodded, grimaced, jerked a thumb at the crowd, the news media.

"I understand," Dion said gravely. "Thank you, my lord."

The Lord Admiral slammed shut the limo door.

"Drive on," His Majesty commanded.

CHAPTER
41

Nothing in life is so exhilarating as to be shot at
without result.
Sir Winston Spencer Churchill, *The Malakand Field
Force*

Xris woke to the touch of a soft hand on his good hand.
"Marjorie," he said dreamily, and gave the hand an af-
fectionate squeeze.

Then pain burned through the ragged edges of whatever
drug he'd been given; memory returned. He jerked his hand
away. The other hand released his.

Xris opened his eyes and stared into the widely grinning,
hairy face of Bear Olefsky.

"My friend!" said the Bear, slapping both his hands on his
knees, "by my ears and eyeballs, it is good to see you!"

But that soft hand hadn't belonged to Olefsky, who was
seated on Xris's left. Xris glanced over to his right, saw
Rowan. Her face was averted. Her cheeks were stained crim-
son. Her hands were now clasped in her lap.

Xris turned back to peer bleary-eyed at Olefsky.

"The king?" The words came out a parched croak.

"Fine, laddie, fine. The Peacock and the Small One acted
with enormous courage and much good sense."

"Are they okay?"

"The Peacock suffered two broken ribs and"—the Bear
winked—"much damage to his fancy feathers. I think that
bothered him most. But, or so I understand, Her Majesty the
Queen has been most helpful in repairs."

"The queen?" Xris was perplexed.

"A long story and one that I am certain the Peacock will

want to tell you. Suffice it to say that the assassin was killed, his heinous weapon destroyed."

"Warden, wasn't it?"

"A snake in man's skin," Olefsky said grimly. "No disparagement to the noble reptile family."

Xris nodded tiredly. "I figured as much—right before I passed out. It made sense. He had the necessary contacts in the Navy and in the government, access to the king. It made sense."

He started automatically to reach for a twist with his right hand. Pain shot through his arm, radiated from his shoulder. He sucked in a breath, grimaced.

Rowan eased his arm back down on the bed. He smiled at her.

She smiled back, tentatively, hesitantly. "We need to talk," she said softly.

"Yeah. I know. In a minute."

Xris took a look at his surroundings. There were no viewscreens, but he guessed—from the thrumming sound, the feel of vibrations through the bed—that he was on board a spaceship. He was in a large open area, probably the ship's hold, that had been hastily furnished with cots and blankets. Jamil was stretched out on one, Quong on another. Harry sat on another, tapping on his ears.

Tycho appeared, hypo in hand. "How you feeling, Xris? Doc says you're to have this shot. It'll help the pain."

"Everyone else okay?" Xris asked.

"Harry is deafer than a bread box," Tycho reported. "But he will heal. Jamil was not severely wounded. I was not injured. You want a glass of water, Xris?"

"Thanks. What's wrong with the Doc?"

"Nothing. He is taking a nap. I now intend to join him." Tycho brought the water and left for his own cot.

Olefsky rumpled his beard. "The doctor worked very hard on you and Jamil there. But you both will be well, thank the good God."

Xris nodded, chewed contentedly on the twist. A warmth spread through the good side of his body. He felt drowsy, relaxed, content. That was due to the drug. He had no reason to feel content, other than the fact that the young king was safe, the Knights of the Terra Nera thwarted. He himself was still in a hell of a lot of trouble. But that could wait.

He almost slept, then remembered something. Two things.

"Those soldiers that took us captive," Xris said, waking, looking up at Olefsky. "Yours?"

The big man grinned expansively. "Some of my troops. What the major over there would call 'Special Forces.' I call them the Wolf Brigade. I deemed it best to carry you swiftly away from there."

Xris smiled. "Or kill me if I'd betrayed you."

The Bear's expression grew grave. "Aye, laddie. That, too. It was a solemn oath I swore. And one I would have kept. But," he added, cheering up, "there was no need. For which, again, I thank the good God."

"We're your prisoners," Xris said. "Where are you taking us?"

"Wherever you want to go, friend Xris. You are not my prisoner. I have hidden you away in the hold, but that is to keep the rest of the crew from knowing anything about you. The Wolf Brigade knows, but no torture ever devised could wring such knowledge from their tongues."

Bear eyed Xris speculatively. "You are a wanted man. Serious charges: breaking into a Naval base, kidnapping Major Mohini, hijacking that drop ship. If you give yourselves up, I have it on good authority, from the Lord Admiral himself, that you and your people will receive reduced sentences. Perhaps even full pardons, due to your prevention of the assassination attempt upon the king."

"But we'd have to turn ourselves in, go on trial." Xris grimaced again, gingerly shifted his wounded arm to a more comfortable position. "A highly publicized trial." He looked over at Rowan.

"We need to talk," she repeated.

The Bear looked at the two of them, stroked his beard. "Two are company. Three is a rotten egg, as our friend the chameleon would say. I will take a walk."

He did, managing to nearly garrote himself on a hammock in the process.

Xris looked over at Rowan. "Yeah? What?"

"Don't do what you're thinking of doing for my sake, Xris," she said quietly. "I don't deserve it. You see, it was my fault."

For a moment he didn't understand what she'd said. Then it sunk in. "You're talking about the factory explosion, aren't you?" His voice hardened. "*Your* fault? According to what you told me, Armstrong was the one responsible—"

"He was. That's not what I mean. Or rather, in a way it is. Don't you see? If we'd been able to talk about . . . *me*— all that was going wrong with me, inside me—then we could have gone past that. But I couldn't talk about myself. I didn't know how to say what I had to say."

The drug must be affecting him, though he felt wide awake now. Xris shook his head. "I still don't get it."

Rowan sighed. "If I had talked to you that day before we left. Gone with you to the bar that night. If I had told you. Trusted you enough. Tried to explain." She spread her hands helplessly. "But how could I, when I really didn't understand myself? How could I, when I can't even do it now?"

She brushed a tear from her cheek with a quick jerking motion.

He knew then, realized he'd known ever since he'd first seen her, hadn't wanted to believe it. He didn't want to even now.

"So don't. Let's leave it, okay?"

"There," she returned bitterly. "You see? This is exactly what you would have done seven years ago. This is *me!*" She made a sweeping downward gesture with her hands, a gesture that included her breasts, her small waist, her hips. "Me! As I was meant to be!"

He said nothing, just shook his head again.

Reaching over, she gripped his hand, his good hand. "I didn't know back then, though I think I suspected. Or maybe I knew and I just didn't have the courage to admit it. Much less go through with it. All the signs were there. My disastrous relationships with women. How I thought I could buy love like fake diamonds. Pay enough for them and no one will ever know they're phony. No one except me.

"To make up for it, I put myself into a machine. My work was my refuge. My hiding place. In the excitement, the tension, I could forget. It was only when all that was over, when the undercover work was finished and I was alone and scared—then I understood. I looked in a mirror and I saw myself and I knew myself. And that was the day Dalin Rowan died. I wept for him, Xris. I cried for him as I cried for you and for Ito. I'd lost someone very close to me. But that's all he ever was. Someone close. And that's why it was my fault."

"And if it's your fault, then that makes it my fault, too," Xris said harshly. He pulled his hand away from hers. "Because I let you down. Because I wasn't there for you. I wasn't sensitive enough. You're saying that if we'd sat down in the bar that night and you said to me, 'Hey, Xris, old buddy, I've decided to get my wienie whacked off and grow boobs,' that this would have helped us nail Armstrong?"

He thought she'd be angry, maybe hoped she'd be angry. But she only regarded him sadly.

"You don't understand," she said in a dull, hopeless tone.

"Damn right I don't. Why don't you try to explain it?"

She was silent, wouldn't look at him. He was about to give up, go to sleep, let her sulk on her own, if that's what she wanted, when suddenly she began to talk.

"I was so hung up on myself I didn't recognize the warning signs about Armstrong. All kinds of red lights were going off in my brain, but I ignored them. I should have spotted that bastard, Xris. I should have nailed Armstrong from the beginning."

"And I shouldn't have gone into that factory when I knew in my gut it was all wrong," he said quietly. "I beat myself up with that stick every day for a year. It didn't help. It didn't bring back my leg and my arm. It didn't bring back Ito."

She was staring bleakly at him.

He looked up at her. "So where does this leave us?"

"Different from what we were. Changed." Rowan sighed. "You're right, we can't go back."

"Maybe, from what you've said, that's a good thing. Give me a twist, will you?" The mechanical taste was unusually, horribly strong.

Rowan opened his pocket, removed the case, took out a twist, and put it between Xris's lips.

"And that's why," she said steadily, "you have to turn yourself in, Xris. Clear yourself and the others."

Xris grunted. "And the moment the Hung find out who you are, where you are, you can kiss your ass good-bye."

Rowan's smile twisted, but remained. She shrugged. "I fought the Hung before. I'll fight them again. Who knows? This time I might finish them off for good."

Xris raised his voice angrily. "You'd never even live through the trial. You know it. So do I. So just shut up about it."

Rowan said nothing. She stared down at her hands, which were clasped together in her lap.

The others were awake now.

Jamil sat up stiffly, cradling his injured arm.

Harry said loudly, "I can't hear a damn thing. What're they saying?"

Quong was up, came over to attend to his patient.

"How do you feel, Xris?"

"Great. Switch me back on, will you, Doc?"

Quong frowned, but—seeing Xris's dark expression—the Doc did as he was asked.

His mechanical side working again, Xris sat up weakly on the cot, looked around. He chewed on the twist.

"Did you all hear what we're up against?"

"No, thanks!" Harry boomed. "I don't smoke."

"Doc, find a notepad, take this down, and show it to Harry. I want everyone in on this. I'll explain the situation."

When he was finished, Xris looked around at each member of the team. "I've reached my decision. I can't give myself up."

Rowan, beside him, made a small sound of protest. Xris stretched out his hand to her, his good hand.

She hesitated, then clasped his hand in hers.

Xris continued, "Not without leaving Rowan here wide open. But the rest of you can. That would be my advice, in fact. Dixter'll see to it that you're treated fairly. You might even end up being heroes."

The others exchanged glances, with the exception of Harry, who was puzzling over Quong's handwriting.

"Turn ourselves in? Is that what this scrawl says?" Harry was suddenly on his feet, indignant. "You can't do that, Xris, goddammit! You can't let them get hold of Darlene!"

"I'm not going to, Harry."

"What?"

"Doc, write down—Never mind."

"I'm not doing it, Xris," Harry continued belligerently. "I'll stay with Darlene, if you won't."

Quong was writing furiously. He shoved the notepad under Harry's nose.

Harry read, looked at Xris, blushed. "Oh, sorry, Xris. I'm with you, you know." He sat back down.

"Me, too," said Jamil gloomily. "I don't much like the idea of publicity, either."

Xris stared at him. "Why not? What have you got to lose?"

Jamil didn't immediately answer. He tugged irritably on his bandage. "Damn thing's too tight, Doc."

"Count yourself fortunate," Quong returned. "You could be wearing Raoul's petticoat. And do not loosen it! You will start the bleeding again."

Jamil scratched at the bandage, saw them all staring at him now. He gave an exasperated snort. "All right, if you must know, there's a couple of women on a couple of different planets who both think that, well, I'm married to each of them. It's all perfectly legal. Well, it's sort of legal. I do right by them both, mind you, but if one ever found out about the other . . ." He shook his head gloomily.

"I am with you also," Tycho announced. "It has occurred to me that if I am a hunted criminal, I will not have to pay income taxes."

"That's because you won't have any income," Xris said dryly. "Things are going to be tough. We'll be spending most of our time dodging bounty hunters, the bureau, military police. With that kind of action, it's going to be difficult finding work."

"Nevertheless," said Tycho, "it would not do to break up the team. One for all, and damn the torpedoes."

By now Xris was smiling. Rowan was gazing at them all in wonder. Maybe he wouldn't have to explain things to her, after all.

"You will need a doctor," Quong said stiffly. "As well as a mechanic. Besides, I want to make a thorough study of the Tongan. I will be the first human doctor to notate their physiology."

"They might even reinstate you," Jamil muttered, but he took care to keep his voice low and Quong, fortunately, did not hear.

"We'll need a computer expert," Xris said offhandedly. "A code breaker might come in handy, too."

"Are you sure, Xris?" she asked softly, so softly only his augmented hearing enabled him to hear her.

"Yeah. I'm sure."

Rowan squeezed his hand. She looked up at the others. "Thanks. All of you. I know you're really doing this for me and I . . . I—" She choked, covered her face.

Xris lay back down, shut his eyes. The drug was dragging him under.

Where do you want to go, laddie?

Olefsky's question drifted to the cyborg through a thick, pleasant mist.

Xris shook his head. It didn't matter. From now on, one place would be as good—or as bad—as another. He shut off his hearing, shut down his battery.

Rowan, seeing him drifting off to sleep, tried to gently withdraw her hand.

Xris tightened his grip, held fast to her.

To Rowan. To his old friend.

He held fast to every one of them. All seven.

His team.

One for all, and damn the torpedoes.

Read a special preview featuring
the next adventure of the exciting
Mag Force 7 mercenary team, *Robot Blues*,
by Margaret Weis and Don Perrin
coming in 1996.

> Thus it is said that one who knows the enemy and knows himself will not be endangered in a hundred engagements.
>
> Sun-tzu, *The Art of War*

Now," Tess said, flipping the blond hair back over her shoulder, "what do you want to know about Jake's? It's a bar—a dive, I suppose most people would call it. It's run by a Pandor who likes money more than he hates offworlders. The beer's cold and the whiskey's okay and the place isn't raided more often than once a quarter. The restrooms are filthy—at least the women's is. I wouldn't know about the men's. Anyone who can get off base—legitimately or otherwise—goes to Jake's. And that's about it."

"Does the Colonel know?"

"Sure he does. Like I said, the bar gets raided three or four times a year. They shut the place down. The locals write editorials. Strebbins gives us a lecture. We go thirsty for about two weeks. Then Jake's is back in business and life goes on."

"I'm surprised Strebbins puts up with it."

"You wouldn't be, if you lived here," Tess said, her tone serious. "Duty on Pandor is the pits, a real morale buster. We're confined to this base, never allowed off it, except when we've built up enough leave time to be able to fly to some more hospitable planet. I have leave coming up in a month. Got any suggestions?"

Xris said nothing. He was watching the storm, watching the lightning flash and spread in sheets over the bottoms of the clouds. He could hear thunder now, faint and far away. A few drops were starting to splatter on the windshield.

He opened the window, tossed out what remained of the smoldering twist, and closed the window again. He reached over, took hold of Tess, pulled her close. She hesitated just a moment, not to make it look good, but studying him intently. Then she slid into his arms and they got to know each other a little better.

"Now I *am* thirsty," she said, drawing away.

"We better go in before the storm breaks," he said in agreement.

She tilted her face for one more kiss, then they climbed out of the car and walked, arm in arm, to the bar.

Xris began beating himself up. He shouldn't let her get close. He shouldn't let himself get close to her. He had to keep focused. For a few moments there, he'd forgotten the job. He'd forgotten the damn robot, forgotten Jamil's mysterious disappearance, forgotten the real reason he'd left base with Tess in the first place.

She's a tool, a means to an end, nothing more, he said to himself. Unfortunately, his "self" didn't quite see it that way.

As they neared the bar, Xris reconnoitered. Jake's was nothing special. A dilapidated, rundown building made of the Pandoran stone that must be used to build everything on this planet. It was large, two-stories—the owner probably lived on top—and was located outside of town, probably not even in city limits. Windows ran the length of the front and sides, showing those outside what a good time everyone was having inside. He could see people dancing.

As he stood in the road, the bar was on his left. Straight ahead was the construction site. He could probably follow the same road to reach it. He could see the green lights of the force field surrounding the downed spaceplane easily from this distance, and calculated that it was probably about two kilometers away.

Welcome exercise, a nice jog. Too bad it was raining. He'd have to come up with some excuse to ditch Tess. It could be done, but it wouldn't be pleasant. She'd be hurt and angry, figure he was a jerk, a cad.

That's what you want, isn't it? he asked himself. Better to be hated . . .

"They're building a new shopping mall there," Tess informed him, noting his unusual interest in the construction site.

"Yeah," he said, "so I heard."

"And now it's turned into—of all things—an archaeological dig. You see that green glow? They found an ancient spaceplane—"

"Let's go get that beer, shall we?" Xris said, rudely cutting her off. He started walking toward the bar.

"Sure," Tess replied, giving him a puzzled glance. She pulled her arm away from his and he didn't make an effort to get it back.

I had my chance, he said to himself. The perfect opening. I could have pumped her for information, found out everything she knows about the crash site, the downed plane. But I don't want to get her involved more than she already is. I should never have allowed things to go this far, no matter how useful she is to me—or how much I enjoy being with her. *Especially* how much I enjoy being with her.

The rain spit and spattered, the storm was still some distance away. The thunder rumbled over the ground. They walked the rest of the way to the bar in silence. Xris opened the door, Tess walked past him into an entryway. Raincoats hung on pegs, umbrellas stood in a stand, hats lined a shelf. A newsvid machine—broken—stood in one corner, along with a bubblegum machine. It, too, appeared to be broken. Through the glass window in a second door, Xris could see the bar. It was packed with people, most of them in uniform, laughing, dancing, having a good time. He reached for the inner door. Tess blocked his way.

"Look, Xris," she said coolly, "don't think you're obligated to go through with this. We can just call it a night and drive back to the base, if that's what you want."

No, that wouldn't work at all. He still had to get that damned robot. And he didn't want the evening to end, not yet.

A couple, giggling and kissing, came out of the bar. The entryway was small, and the coats, the vid machine, and more people made it smaller. Xris and Tess were forced to back up against the coats on the wall to let the other couple pass. On his way by, the soldier stumbled into Tess. She fell against Xris.

Xris caught hold of her, steadied her. She tried to pull away, but he didn't let go. The other couple staggered out the door. It slammed shut behind them. Xris still didn't let go.

"You said you studied cyborgs," he said to Tess.

"Yes," she replied.

"The psychology as well as the physiology."

"Some, not much," she admitted. "Xris, if I said anything—"

"No, you didn't." He drew a deep breath. "You've been

great. And that's the problem. If you've studied cyborgs, you know that it's difficult for people to relate to us in any sort of romantic way. When most women hear my arm start beeping, they don't ask me if I'm suffering from a chemical imbalance. They usually just walk off."

Tess was smiling at him. She pressed closer, took hold of his hand—his "bad" hand, his phony hand.

"I'm going to leave base tomorrow," Xris continued, "and the odds are that we won't see each other again."

To his surprise, she didn't protest or argue. She was grave, thoughtful.

"I understand," she said.

And Xris had the odd feeling that she really did.

The Pandoran stout was as good as its reputation. Xris regretted he couldn't enjoy it to its fullest, but he had work to do that night and needed a clear head. He sipped slowly at his, explained—when Tess asked him if he wanted another— that the delicate chemical balance of his body didn't deal well with alcohol.

Tess's roommates spotted them; came over to get a good look at Xris, exchanged a few bantering remarks, then left to return to the dance floor.

Xris and Tess sat side by side in a high-backed wooden booth next to a window. They had to sit practically chin to chin to hear each other over the roar of the music, which was provided by a couple of soldiers on portable synthesizers. The soldiers had more enthusiasm than talent, but they knew enough to lay down a steady, thumping beat, which was all the dancers needed. Xris and Tess shouted companionably at each other, enjoying the stout and the company.

His earlier half-formed plan of ditching Tess to flirt with another woman was out. Tess would know it was an act. She wouldn't believe it for an instant. And, Xris had to admit to himself, he just wasn't the type. Women weren't exactly doing nosedives over the bar to get close to him. He had about decided that the best policy was honesty—perhaps not complete honesty, but as honest as he could be. He would simply tell her to drive back to the base without him. He wanted to be alone, to do some thinking. Maybe he wanted to be alone to rehearse his speech.

That was it. Rehearse his speech.

It was nearing midnight. Tess was standing in line at the crowded bar, waiting to place her order for two more glasses of stout. If he was going to make his move, he needed to make it soon. He stood up, started to go over to Tess, to feed her his line, when there came a crash on the door that was audible even over the raucous music.

A soldier, seated at a table near the front windows, sprang to his feet.

"Raid!" he bellowed.

Soldiers scattered in every conceivable direction. The Pandoran police smashed through the front door.

Xris looked at Tess. She turned to look over at him. There was no way he could reach her. Flailing, pushing, and shoving bodies churned between them. Xris's instinct was to fight his way to Tess's side. His second thought was more rational. *This is it, chump! This is your chance!* Still, he might have ignored the rational, gone for the instinctual, if Tess hadn't made the decision for him. She pointed urgently behind him, directing him to the windows.

"What about you?" he mouthed.

She jerked her thumb in the direction of the women's restroom and, in the same motion, turned and ran that way. Xris hesitated one more instant, and saw Tess's two roommates making a dash for the ladies room as well.

Xris lost sight of her then. A large Pandoran cop loomed in front of him, yelling something unintelligible and swinging a nightstick at Xris's head. Xris caught the nightstick in his cybernetic hand, squeezed. The nightstick crumbled into dust. The cop stared, open-mouthed, then backed away.

Xris wasted no more time. He smashed through one table, leaped onto another, aimed a kick at the glass with his steel leg. Glass exploded outward. Xris dove through headfirst. Two more soldiers were right behind him, and more were coming after them.

Xris landed heavily on one shoulder, rolled across concrete, bumped up against a curb. He picked himself up, brushed off the broken glass, and took a quick look around.

The Pandoran police, in unmarked squad cars, had the front covered. More were arriving, with lights flaring and sirens wailing. A large van—presumably used to haul away the unfortunates who got caught—was drifting ponderously down from the sky.

Tess's staff car was fenced in, fore and aft, by two Pandoran cop cars. If she managed to escape, she'd be traveling back to the base on foot.

Xris fretted over this, but reminded himself that she knew the territory. She was quite capable of taking care of herself. Still, he hazarded a few more seconds he couldn't afford, hoping to catch sight of her. That proved useless. Bodies were diving through the windows. Fights had broken out. The Pandoran police were surging through the parking lot, attempting to cordon off the back of the building. Xris didn't dare wait any longer. He ran.

His running style was clumsy, awkward. His physical side always seemed to be in competition with his mechanical side, giving him a peculiar, swing-legged, lopsided gait. But he could move fast and most of him didn't tire. The parts that did grow weary, he ignored.

He found the road leading to the construction site, discovered that it was also, unfortunately, the main route the cops were taking to reach the bar. Headlights caught him. He made a mad dash to a culvert on the other side. Someone shouted, and one car swerved to try to catch him, but he put on some speed, headed straight into the desert. The cops gave up the chase, went after easier prey.

Xris loped through the desert, slogging through the shining Pandoran sand that had now—after the rain—turned into mud. A particularly clinging, sticky mud that caked on his boots and made running difficult.

He kept to the desert until the cop cars and the lights of the bar and the sound of shouting and swearing were behind him. The city proper was off to his left. The lights of the construction site shone ahead of him. This part of the road was deserted since it, essentially, went nowhere. The pavement ended, changing into ruts left by the heavy dirt-moving equipment.

More mud, and puddles of water. Xris had to stop every half kilometer to clean the gunk off his boots. They had become so caked with the gooey gray muck, they were slowing him down.

Lightning flared. Thunder crashed. The next storm in line chose this moment to dump on him. Rain slashed down in torrents, typical of desert storms. He was soaked to the skin in seconds. This did nothing to improve his spirits, which were dark, gloomy, and thunderous as the weather.

He hoped Tess had escaped the police. He felt rotten enough about using her as it was. If she were caught in a raid, ended up in a Pandoran prison cell, she'd probably be a private in the morning. He tried to sell himself on the fact

that she would have gone to Jake's with her roommates anyway, but he wasn't buying it. If anything happened to her, it
would be his fault.

And there was tomorrow to look forward to.

He'd say good-bye to her. They'd exchange a few wise-
cracks. He'd promise to vidphone—a promise that he would
never keep. He couldn't tell her the truth. She'd assume then
that he had only been using her and she'd assume right.
When you peeled back the layers, the ugly truth was there,
like the ugly mechanics in his arm. All the flesh-foam and
plastiskin in the galaxy couldn't hide it. Far better to cut the
arm off clean, never see her again. He might spare her some
pain. She'd be left with the memory of a few laughs, a few
kisses, a pleasant evening.

At least, Xris hoped that was how Tess felt about their
time together. As to *his* feelings, he pummeled himself mentally all the way along the road. This blasted job. It had
come wrapped in brown paper, looked so plain and simple
on the outside, and when he started to cut the tape, it had
blown up in his face. For a single plastic credit, he'd call the
job off, return Sakuta's money, let the Pandorans keep the
antique robot. It was theirs, by rights.

Unfortunately, Xris couldn't do that now. He had his orders. And someone had Jamil.

He stopped running, to once again clean the mud off his
boots and—now that he was alone—to equip himself for the
job ahead.

Xris detached his flesh-foam hand, and replaced it with
his working hand. His fingers were now tools: drill, cutting
torch, screwdriver. The hand that had been ordinary had suddenly become something monstrous. Tess wouldn't be so
eager to jump into his arms if this steel hand was attached.

Sure, he could always take off that working hand, replace

it with the flesh-foam hand, replace the steel with Captain Kergonan.

But he wasn't Captain Kergonan.

This hand would always be steel, cold, without life, designed to do a job.

That was all it was good for.

All he was good for.

Xris began to run again.

The Roc Frequent Readers Club
BUY TWO ROC BOOKS AND GET
ONE SF/FANTASY NOVEL FREE!

Check the free title you wish to receive (subject to availability):